The Secret Life

of

Sofonisba Anguissola

The most famous woman you've never heard of

By

Melissa Muldoon

Matta Press · Austin, Texas

MelissaMuldoon.com

Cover Illustration, Cover Design,
Interior Design, Interior Illustrations,
Typography & Layout
by
Melissa Muldoon

MATTA

PRESS

Matta Press
2303 Ranch Road 620 S.
Suite 160 - 124
Austin, TX 78734

Cover Design by Melissa Muldoon
Interior Book Design by Melissa Muldoon

Manufactured in the United States of America

1st Edition
Muldoon, Melissa
The Secret Life of Sofonisba Anguissola

ISBN: 978-1-7351764-1-3

ISBN: 978-1-7351764-2-0 (E-Book)

Life is full of surprises.
I try to capture these precious moments
with wide eyes.

– Sofonisba Anguissola

Dedicated to my Italian muses,
who transport me to places I never thought possible.

Sofonisba Anguissola Self Portrait (circa 1554)
Featuring Signor Campi, Sofonisba's first painting instructor

Sofonisba Anguissola was the first female painter to achieve fame and respect in the sixteenth century. Due to her talent and extraordinary patronage, she was able to work without the constraints of competing against male contemporaries. Her portraits and paintings of her family advanced the values of familial life and personal history and her remarkable expertise challenged ideas about what it meant to be an artist and made it acceptable for women to devote themselves to painting. (*Image: Public domain. Pinacoteca Nazionale, Siena*)

Sofonisba Anguissola Self Portrait (circa 1624)

Painted in the last year of her life in Palermo

Throughout her lifetime, Sofonisba painted at least twelve self-portraits—perhaps more as many of her paintings were destroyed in 1734 in a fire that swept through the royal palace in Spain. Her interest in self-study and the transformation of her physical and intellectual self depicted on canvas is remarkable. Still, it would be Rembrandt in the next century who would be lauded and recognized as the first artist to do this. (*Image: Public domain. Private Collection*)

Author's Note:

The Secret Life of Sofonisba Anguissola
is a fictional piece of work, based on
historical facts. Most events, people, and places
described in the story are real although admittedly
embellished and creatively imagined.
The purpose of the story is to inform, entertain,
and inspire further investigation.

I invite you, dear reader, along with
Sir Anthony, to determine the fabrications.

*I loved her against reason,
against promise,
against peace, against hope,
against happiness, against all
discouragement that could be.*

—C. Dickens

Chapter 1
Her Eyes

*H*e had known women more beautiful than her. In his younger days, he had laid his head upon the ample bosoms of glamorous paramours and promiscuous country maidens, tracing their luscious lips with the tip of his finger. Yet, he could barely remember their names, nor could he recollect the shape or color of their eyes.

But this woman.

This one particular woman, he could neither forget nor dismiss from his mind.

For more than a decade, he had been fascinated by her. It wasn't because she moved with effortless grace or was particularly stylish. Nevertheless, the swishing of her long skirts made from sensible materials and the serviceable apron she often wore splattered by telltale markings of paint intrigued him. Her lips—the color of coral—while nicely shaped and not overly lush, were more often than not set in a demure expression; that is when she wasn't biting them with her front teeth or pressing them together in deliberation as she painted.

Often, he'd studied her intriguing mannerisms, noting the curious way she tilted her head in concentration. She would mix her paints on her circular board and then hold up her brush and look in delight at the glowing amber color. By her knowing and satisfied smile, it seemed she alone had discovered a way to mine the surface of the moon and mix its fine powders into the pigments of her palette.

Her face was pleasant—attractive even—yet there was something innocent and guileless about her that had disarmed and called out to him. She was slender in form—just a tiny slip of a woman who had no need of artifice to darken her lashes or enhance her cheeks. And her thick brown hair—quite rich in color—was never powdered or teased. She kept it sensibly pulled back, tied with a ribbon, which tended to emphasize her dark brows, that like raven wings, slashed across the white sky of her forehead.

Yes. From the start, he found her physical traits mildly inviting—nothing so special that should attract a man such as himself. He was a duke, a decorated soldier, confidant to the king. When he measured her against all the colorful preening peahens who graced the courts and the circles he was used to frequenting... he found her sturdy northern Italian stock rather plain and dowdy in comparison.

Yet this artist from a provincial Italian town possessed something he'd seen in no other woman—a remarkable pair of eyes. And they had been his undoing. When he met her intense gaze straight on, it had pierced his blurry melancholia and shattered his composure.

Unlike her other facial features, the shape of her eyes was uncommon and spectacular. They were luminous and expressive, the color of slate. But, despite being large dark tidal pools in which a man could get lost, they never hid the quick flash of wit that signaled the woman harbored a thousand unspoken questions. One instantly knew she was filled with ambition and confidence, and that her cleverness and resourcefulness extended to great depths—like a sea that had no end and no beginning.

Thinking back to the day they'd met, he remembered how those penetrating eyes had followed his every gesture. In a whisper of a moment, as he watched them travel over his form and under her wary assessment, his stiff noble posture became slightly undone. He shifted nervously, like a young soldier standing on the front lines for the first time.

As the artist regarded him politely, a desperate feeling washed over him. It seemed her astute observance of his person had turned inward, and reached deep into his very soul, uncovering its blackest and most secretive parts. Her face had become an unforgiving mirror that reflected the good and the evil inside him. At that moment, his ghostly heart was seized by an intense passion—the kind that burns and marks a man's soul forever. He wanted to fling off his wicked ways and become the kind of man worthy of such a rarefied and perceptive woman's affections.

And so had begun his obsession.

Recalling the memory of that day long ago, perspiration dampened his brow, and an old sorrow boiled up from his belly. As darkness and hopelessness overtook him, he reached for a decanter and poured himself a drink. On the table was a single candle that had burned low and was nearly gutted. When a clammy draft of sea air blew in from the veranda, making the candle flicker chaotically, he shrugged out of his black coat decorated with military insignia and tossed it recklessly aside. He stared down at his glass, then picked it up and, in one long swallow, greedily gulped down the contents.

As his body heat continued to rise, fueled by muggy island temperatures and the vast amount of alcohol he had already consumed, he set his glass down, reached up, and with his long fingers loosened his cravat. Free of the constriction that seemed to strangle him, he then began to unbutton his shirt. With the linen garment splayed open, revealing a gray mat of hair, he reached once again for the decanter but stopped when he saw the letter on the table he had just composed. He gazed at it dully, knowing someone would send it to her eventually, and she would finally learn the truth about him—the things he had done and the things he was about to do.

With a shake of his head, he walked to the terrace and observed the ships in the harbor floating on a silver sea illuminated by the full moon. He closed his eyes and repeated the last line he had written. "I have loved you more than you will ever know. But you never once looked at me that way."

In his head, a voice replied, *She was never yours to lose. Why regret what cannot be?*

Pain gripped his heart, and he raised his hands to his ears and shouted, "Enough!"

Then, picking up a violin that lay on the table, as was his nightly habit—even if she couldn't hear—he serenaded her. At first, he drew the taut bow across the instrument's strings, and a cacophony of strident chords pierced the night air. He paused, lifted his head, and peered up at the swirling stars. For him, such heavenly heights would never be attainable, and it seemed the planets above him mocked him with their ethereal beauty. He let out a heavy sigh, then, nestling the violin under his chin, as he had so often wanted to do with her, he drew the bow back. This time the music slid into an assembly of recognizable, if not sad, harmonies.

Bending slightly at the waist, rocking to and fro, he played on until the music crescendoed and wrapped itself around his body, consuming him. With his head lowered, he again gave in to the notes' richness and played out his anguish and fears, trying to forget... desperately seeking salvation.

But it was no use.

The demons that had long taunted him drifted closer, pulling him back into their cold embrace. As if by a miracle, her eyes came into focus for a brief second, swimming up through the darkness. Slowly the music died away and with a soft sigh that sounded like an ocean wave, he whispered her name one last time... *"Sofonisba."*

Genova, Italy—1624

A man is not old until regrets
take the place of dreams.

—*J. Barrymore*

Chapter 2

An Esteemed Visitor

Sofonisba squinted at the clock on the mantel, wondering what the time was and what was detaining him. She speculated he had been delayed by a flirtation with some pretty young thing, or perhaps the ship that transported him from England had encountered a storm and had yet to land in Genova.

Well, she thought, *whatever is keeping him, he'd better arrive soon.*

She picked up his letter from her lap and held it close to her face, trying to check the time of his arrival, then muttered, "Damned old eyes."

With extreme concentration, she brought the page closer and peered at it intensely. Despite her best efforts, however, the words remained blurred and indistinct. More light from the far window was needed, she decided.

Determined to rise out of her chair, the one with the red leather seat and brass hardware that Pietro—the master furniture maker—had crafted for her last winter, Sofonisba gripped the wooden arms and attempted to lift herself up. But, feeling the stiffness of her joints, she winced and sank down into the seat again. As she did, her heavy black skirts settled in a heap around her small frame.

Peering across the room again at the fuzzy clock, she muttered waspishly, "Dear Lord, I can endure my rickety bones, but rob me of my sight, really! I find that highly unforgivable."

Frustrated, she ran a finger around her neckband to adjust the stiff white ruff. She let out another annoyed sigh. It seemed tighter than usual today. She'd have to tell Cecilia not to put so much starch in her undergarments and ruffled collars.

"Come on, old girl! You are better than your old bones. Up you go, again." Exerting more effort this time, she boosted herself into a standing position. Before taking a step, she first assessed all her moving parts, ensuring she was in full command of her rig. Then with a slow, faltering gait, she made her way to the mullioned glass that overlooked the courtyard. Lifting a heavy velvet drape, she pushed it back to let in more of the afternoon sun.

Sofonisba shook out the letter, confirmed the time, then turned to face the mantel clock. She blinked several times as more light filtered into the room and the old timepiece with its ancient hands was more discernible. With a nod, she said, "Good. He's not late. It is just a quarter past the hour. It seems, for a change, I'm the early one."

She looked down and noticed the embers glowing weakly in the hearth. Lifting her skirts, careful not to stumble on the braided rug, she moved a little closer until she could feel the delicious warmth radiating out toward her. Sofonisba sighed, stretched out her hands, and rubbed them together, easing the familiar ache that came from years of holding a brush. Then gingerly, she picked up a poker and began to shakily stir the logs. Coaxed into life, after a moment, they burst into flame, illuminating the salon and chasing away the last shadows from the corners.

Satisfied, she surveyed the room again and said, "There... now I can see things better." Cecilia had done an excellent job. Things were tidied and in order. This was her private space, and she took great pride in it. She often retreated to these chambers to reflect and meet with influential guests but, most importantly, this was where she painted. The room was lined with easels and low-ornate cabinets filled with boxes of painting supplies and a large mahogany table in the center upon which were strewn tablets, powders, and brushes.

Regardless of the impressive array of painting materials, the most striking feature of the room was the collection of portraits that adorned the walls. But the canvases were not likenesses of patrons. Those all hung on the walls of her clients. Here, instead, were displayed all the paintings she had done of herself over the years, ranging from the age of fourteen to the age of eighty-seven.

Sofonisba glanced first to the left and then to the right, and followed the progressive arc of time, taking her from girlhood to maturity and finally old age. The portraits—twenty-five in all—seemed to dance around her in a swirl of memories. She admired the young, naive, idealistic girl she had been in her heyday and even more so the proud, sophisticated woman she had evolved into.

She wasn't a writer who kept diaries or a musician who communicated through song—she was a portrait artist who expressed herself through color, gifted with an unparalleled and uncanny talent for capturing a person's essence on canvas. From a very early age, her father had seen her ability and encouraged her. It seemed once she picked up a brush, she never put it down, and soon she far excelled her painting masters.

Still, her fascination with capturing her own face on canvas never grew old. She painted her likeness not because she possessed a vain streak or thought herself particularly beautiful; on the contrary, Sofonisba had often considered herself only passably attractive with perhaps a nicely shaped nose. No, what had driven her was a natural curiosity and desire to honor herself at every season of her life and record how life's experiences had changed her.

Sofonisba let her attention drift to a canvas she had just completed, its surface still glistening with fresh paint. In this painting, she saw a woman who wore a stiff white ruff and the same dress she had on now. Her hair was slicked back to reveal a broad forehead, and a filmy veil covered her sparse hair. She was seated slightly hunched over in her favorite red leather chair. In one hand she held a treasured book of sonnets and in the other, one of Anthony's letters.

After a moment of critical assessment, Sofonisba righted her stooping posture and tried to stand a little taller. With a chuckle, she thought, *Ah, well. Not bad, Sof. You are an old girl... and if God should take you tomorrow, what better way to show the world, one last time, what an accomplished, intelligent woman you are... equal to the best men in the profession!*

She shifted several steps to her left and regarded another painting hanging closer to the window. In contrast to the picture she had just completed, this painting captured the dewy-faced girl-woman she had once been. This version of herself stood supple and straight and wore a striking blue gown. Her thick russet mane was pulled up in a crown of curls, revealing the same high forehead. In this portrait, instead of the liver spots and wrinkles that blemished the woman in the recent painting, the girl's skin was firm and milky, and her mouth was set in a winsome smile.

When was this painted? Then the memory came to her. Of course, she had made this in Madrid during her time at the Spanish Court. The curious thing was that, despite the march of time, she felt more like the young woman in that painting than the old crone in the other.

As if she were peeking into a mirror, the old woman subconsciously touched a hand first to her wrinkled face and then brushed the creases around her mouth and pondered, *How could my once impossibly large eyes now be reduced to such small dark raisins? When had that change occurred?*

With her fingers, she absently toyed with a wayward lock of hair that had escaped her cap. She enjoyed the silky texture and wrapped it around her finger a few times before tucking it back into place. It was a familiar gesture that even at this late hour in her life, she had never quite broken.

Looking up at the wall again, Sofonisba was filled with satisfaction tinged with regret. Her time upon this earth was growing slim, and she wished she could recapture those heady days of youth for just one moment. What a gift it would be to have that sight again, that bright, sharp vision.

Sofonisba sighed. Then, turning back to the fireplace, she pinched the bridge of her nose and closed her papery lids. When she did, a wave of images washed over her, and she distinctly saw a graceful ship sailing toward a rising sun. A man emerged from the shadows and reached out, taking her hand and drawing her close. As they kissed, the skies turned dark and the sea began to churn.

Unexpectedly, the scene changed, and the rays of the dazzling sun exploded into tongues of fire, and a shower of sparks erupted into the air. She lay at the foot of a cross, and the flames licked angrily at her skirts. As they edged nearer, the wax figure of Christ suspended above her, melted slowly, and burned her with his dripping tears. Suddenly, there was a terrible boom, and the ceiling crashed down. Smoke and ash overwhelmed her senses. Then out of the darkness, she saw a face covered in soot and grime, smiling down at her. Brushing back her hair, he leaned down and lifted her up, up, up...

A sharp knock disrupted the old woman's thoughts, snapping her back to the present.

"Come in," she called, letting her eyes flash open.

The door swung in, and she saw Cecilia on the threshold. "Good afternoon, Signora Sofonisba." She tilted her head, indicating a tall man standing behind her. "There's a visitor here to see you."

She noted Cecilia's flushed cheeks and quickly discerned the maid was quite taken with him. Sofonisba watched as the man, no more than twenty-five years of age, swathed in an elegant cloak, stepped into the room. As he moved gracefully to her side and bowed over her hand, she thought he looked a little thinner and his beard a bit fuller than the last time they'd met.

"Signora Anguissola, it is a pleasure," he said as he rose up.

Her tired old eyes that had teared at the thoughts of past events sparkled once again at the sight of Anthony. As he removed his cape, she captured every detail of the young man's attire, from the toes of his shiny brown boots and brocade jacket to the tip of the feather plume in his hat. The young man, always a showman and usually so full of pomposity and zest, seemed a little more subdued than she last remembered him.

He appraised her, too, for several heartbeats. Then it seemed something of his old self rekindled, and he gave her a wan smile. "You are looking astoundingly well, signora. How do you do it? What is your secret for longevity?"

"Dear boy, it is no secret at all! I always leave a painting a little undone... so I must rise and face a new day and complete it!"

"Words to live by, I'm sure! You always have such good advice for me... Ever since Rubens introduced us several months ago, I've so enjoyed our correspondence."

"I dare say, my spirits have been lightened by your letters as well."

"It seems an age since we met in London... I've been counting the hours—no, the minutes—until we could be united again, and I could share the pleasure and privacy of your company."

"Sir," she said, tapping him on the arm and speaking in an admonishing tone, "be careful with your words! I will entertain no illicit propositions. I *am* a married woman, after all."

Despite her solemn words, the coquettish tilt of her head betrayed her, and Anthony, caring not a fig about decorum, burst into a peal of hearty laughter. It was a genuine sound, nothing like the delicate chuckles she'd heard him muster at court to hide his disdain at a poorly delivered joke or to mask his boredom. No, this was a deep chortle of mirth that started in his belly.

"*Cara* signora! I've only just arrived, and how you delight me!" With a hand on his heart as if she had wounded him, he said, "You have crushed my secret desire, sending me into the depths of despair. But perhaps, I'll take my chances and spirit you away with me after all."

As she took a seat in her red leather chair, she said briskly, "Even if I wanted to run away with you, which I don't, you would meet a most untimely demise at the hands of my husband. He is a most jealous man!"

Van Dyke beamed again, admiring her spirit. Taking a seat opposite her, he said, "You are indeed a grande dame, milady. I promise to be on my best behavior."

"Good then. We can all rest easier," she said tartly.

As Sofonisba settled more comfortably in her chair, Anthony stretched out his long legs and warmed himself by the fire. He glanced about the room and said, "I see I am in quite good company. I recognize the style of your portraiture, as well as the woman who is the subject."

"Ah, yes," she said with a grin. "It seems we are all here to keep you company this afternoon."

"I'm delighted, of course, and couldn't have been more pleased to receive your invitation. It came at a most favorable moment."

"Nonsense! My dear sir, the pleasure is all mine. You are always welcome in my home. I've taken an extreme interest in your work and your well-being." With a sweep of her hand, she said, "You and I share a passion for painting and portraiture."

"Your words of instruction have been useful, but your insights into other matters have helped my outlook tremendously." With a self-deprecating frown, he added, "As you know, Signora Sofonisba, since leaving Antwerp, I've not been the happiest of men. As you said... amongst the English, there was little scope for the imagination. I was drowning in an abyss of my own making and needed a change. And so, I took myself off. But the passage over from Liverpool was dismal and damp..."

"That is the downside of sea travel," she said. "But when the sun shines and the air is crisp and clean—it is a glorious way to move from one port to another. Traveling is good for the soul. I've always enjoyed the adventure of visiting new places. From your most recent letters, I gather then, you will be staying here in Italy for a while?"

"Yes, that is the current plan. England did little to restore my spirits nor help me recover from a broken heart..."

"In my experience, it is hard to recover from a love affair gone wrong, even in the sunniest of climates. Everywhere you go, you bring yourself with you. The best remedy is to focus on your work—concentrate on your painting."

"You are right, on both accounts, madame." He eyed her curiously. "But, what do you know of heartache and suffering? I thought you were a happily married woman..."

"Oh, I've had my share of sadness and sorrow," Sofonisba said with a wave of her hand. "You can't live such a long life as I have without a few stories to tell." She folded her hands primly in front of her, then asked, "Where do you plan on visiting after you leave Genova?"

"I expect I'll visit Florence and then Rome to see the ruins... I hope to make it to Pompeii... and after that, I would like to sail to Sicily. I hear it is a lovely island paradise."

"An appealing itinerary," she said. "I've lived in both Rome and Catania... a little town on Sicily's southern shores."

Anthony stroked his trim beard and regarded her thoughtfully. "You are a most intriguing woman."

With a brow raised, she said, "You'd be surprised by the things I know and the places I've been."

"So, the painter has a secret past?" said Van Dyke. "I'd like to know your stories and..." He paused and glanced up when Cecilia re-entered the room.

Sofonisba watched as the young man warmly regarded the slim young girl and noted Cecilia too was aware of his admiration by the way she self-consciously set the silver tray and teapot on the small table between them. When Anthony reached out a hand to steady one of the cups and accidentally grazed her fingers, the maid giggled, forgetting her station.

Sofonisba coughed ever so slightly and Cecilia turned toward her with a bemused expression. Then, coming to her senses as if she realized she was not comporting herself respectably, she hastily curtsied and left the room.

Pouring out the tea, Sofonisba said, "I see you are indeed a rake, sir. And here I thought your attentions were all for me."

He raised an eyebrow as he reached for a small biscuit with sugar coating. "Don't try to change the subject."

"Yes, where were we..."

"I asked if you'd share with me your stories."

"Ah, well... I'm sure any tale I had to tell would bore you to tears," she replied.

He gestured to the portraits on the far wall. "The many faces of the woman that decorate this room beg to differ. Each portrait has a hidden story that begs to be revealed."

"And how would you know?"

"Need I remind you? I am a painter too. Like you, I am an excellent judge of character—and the eyes never conceal what a person is really feeling or thinking. See that girl in the blue gown?" he asked, indicating the portrait that had captured her attention earlier.

She looked at him, interested to hear what he had to say.

"That young woman possesses such grace and extreme confidence—those are things a man can easily fall in love with. I believe that woman has something to reveal to me. After all, with a paintbrush and a rare talent, she traveled the world, painting for kings and queens..." He observed her keenly. "Signora, you have had a remarkable career. You dared to be different, and I want to know how you managed to accomplish all you did."

"Fair enough," she finally admitted. "Yes, I defied them that I did. I was never one for conventions. I never believed I needed a husband to keep me and be my master. I always thought I'd live a solitary life, never to be bothered by love."

"But love found you..."

"Yes, it did. Several times," she admitted, gazing over his shoulder at the portrait of the young woman in blue.

"Tell me about the one you've never forgotten."

She studied the man before her, then said with a gleam in her eye, "He was a handsome lad, with a head of thick black curls. The kind of man that steals a girl's heart the moment she lays eyes on him." She assessed him again, taking in his elegant coat and deerskin breeches. "Kind of like yourself, *tesoro*, though not in such a dandified manner!"

Her retort caught him by surprise, and when his shoulders started to shake, he nearly spilled tea on his jacket.

"Still," Sofonisba continued, "despite his striking good looks, he was a man of courage, one who dared to dream, took chances, and risked everything to win my heart... then broke it in two." She was quiet for a moment and then sighed. "You don't forget the first man you ever loved—especially if you lose him..."

"There, I knew it! You do have intriguing tales to tell me."

"Oh, I admit I have many," Sofonisba said with a soft laugh. "So... it is my life you wish to hear about, is it? You want to learn the secrets of Sofonisba?"

"I'm all ears, signora. Please don't hold back." He filled his cup and then, looking over the brim, said, "I want to know everything from the beginning. I'm sure it will be quite diverting."

"From the beginning... *Ehi*, you do realize how old I am? That would take more than an hour!"

"We have all afternoon... Goodness knows, I've only just arrived in Italy and have no urgent appointments. Besides, there is no place I'd rather be than in your company."

"There you go again with your flattery, sir." She looked at him askance. "Are you really sure you want to hear the ramblings of an old woman?"

"Just tell me the titillating parts..."

Sofonisba eyed him with amusement. "Messer... I am a lady!" Modestly she looked at her hands resting demurely in her lap, but when she glanced up and saw him watching her with a raised eyebrow, she let out a snort. "Well... all right, since you've traveled all this way, Anthony, I'll entertain you with a story."

She paused and leaned forward. "But to keep me amused as well, it will be far more enjoyable to play a little game with you..."

When he looked at her curiously, Sofonisba said with a chuckle, "Beware, Anthony! I caution you to pay close attention to what I am about to reveal because woven into my words of truth will be one small fabrication."

She settled back into her chair, took a sip of tea, then added, "It is up to you, dear signore, to determine fact from fiction. See if you can discover the single lie in all I am about to tell you."

Chapter 3

Princess, Serpent, and Lion

Sofonisba contemplated the flames flickering over the logs in the grate as she sifted through the jigsaw pieces of her life. There were so many bits and pieces of stories, and they fit together so intricately. How could she possibly communicate such a vast and intimate story in only a single afternoon? Then rallying to the challenge, she cleared her throat and said, "It all started with my name. When I was—"

Hearing a rustling sound, she looked over at Anthony and abruptly shut her mouth. She watched with interest and growing amusement as the younger painter opened his leather satchel and rifled through it.

"Are you paying attention?" she asked. "Stop fidgeting, young man. I'll not repeat myself."

He gave her a sheepish grin as he pulled out a thick pad of paper and a small wooden box. "I hope you don't mind, signora."

She raised an eyebrow and peered at him questioningly.

Anthony gestured around the room. "Your portraits have inspired me. I thought I'd sketch your likeness as you talk so that later I can paint your image to remember this visit."

"Mind? Of course not," she replied, sitting a little taller in her chair and reaching up to straighten the veil that had slipped slightly over her ear. "Do you require drawing utensils... a piece of pressed charcoal or a bit of graphite crayon?"

When he opened the lid of the box and indicated the vast assortment of drawing pens and pencils, she nodded, clearly impressed. Sofonisba followed his agile movements as he began making strokes, admiring his technique.

Noticing she wasn't speaking, Van Dyke looked up and waved his drawing tool in the air and said, "Please, don't mind me. I listen best when my hands are engaged. Really, I implore you to continue. Tell me about your surname—Anguissola. It is quite unusual."

"Yes, it is, isn't it?" she admitted. "As if it wasn't enough to be given the name Sofonisba when paired with Anguissola... Right from the start, I was quite an odd kind of girl—different from all the rest. But I have grown into the name and now rather quite like it. Remember, Anthony, to be irreplaceable, one must always be different."

Angling her head to catch a better glimpse of his drawing, she said, "Make sure you get my nose right. I believe it is one of my finer features."

When he held up the drawing for her to see, she smiled in approval. "That will do nicely... Now, where was I?"

"You were telling me about the origins of your last name."

"Right you are... Well, you see, the name Anguissola derives from the Latin word for serpent."

"Serpent?"

"Yes, it originated with the Byzantine general Galvano Sordo—a distant relative of mine—who helped liberate the city of Constantinople. Because he was a clever man, invading when least expected and never getting caught, he was nicknamed the slippery eel. So, when the battle was won, the people cried out: *Anuis sola fecit victoriam...*"

"Ah..." said Anthony. "In Latin—the snake who brings victory."

"Exactly," she said, pleased he knew his Latin from his Greek. "In Italian, *l'anguilla che porta la vittoria*. Anguissola, my surname, was carried on by my Italian ancestors, who were proud of their sly and intelligent traits."

"And where does the name Sofonisba come from?"

"I was named for a Carthaginian princess."

"A princess!" he said, duly impressed.

He then tilted his head askance and drew his brow together. "Be careful, Signora Sofonisba, I am keeping track of your story. Suddenly, this sounds a little far-fetched. Perhaps, right from the beginning of your tale, you start with a lie. Even though I am occupied with my drawing, I warn you I am paying attention and will hold you accountable."

"As you should, my dear young man," Sofonisba said with an appreciative look.

"Go on then," he encouraged.

"Well, from the moment my father learned I was on the way, regardless of my mother's protests, he wanted to call me Sofonisba. He was a learned man and took great pride in the fact that our family's lineage can be traced back to Byzantium and to ancient Carthage. My father often told me about Princess Sophonisba—who spelled her name with the Greek *ph* and not the Roman *f*."

"So... you claim to be descended from royalty?"

"Yes," she said matter-of-factly. "Sophonisba spelled with a *ph* was the daughter of a great Carthaginian general who led his men into battle against the Romans at Trebbia."

Anthony eyed her intently, and Sofonisba spelled with an *f* could tell the young man seated opposite her was already questioning whether from the start she was dressing up her fabrications with believable facts.

As if on cue, Anthony queried, "And this would be... how long ago? Forgive, signora, but my knowledge of the ancient Punic battles is somewhat limited."

"Excellent, sir!" Sofonisba exclaimed. "I see you are indeed paying attention—ready to catch me in the lie."

Peering into the fire, she calculated, "This would be close to the third century before our Savior's birth."

He lifted a brow as if he were more curious than ever. "And this Carthaginian princess—what was she like?"

"She is reported to have been a beauty, with long dark hair and eyes that put a spell upon a man. She was highly educated in music, literature— Why, she was even an accomplished painter. It is written, the princess was so altogether charming the mere sight of her, or even the sound of her voice, enchanted everyone—even the most indifferent."

"Sounds similar to someone I know," said Van Dyke.

"As I said before... you, sir, are a flatterer," she said in a warning tone.

"And you, madame, are proving to have quite an imagination. I'm beginning to wonder if I'll ever be successful in capturing that quick-witted spark of imagination I see on your face."

Sofonisba ignored his compliment and continued. "Because of the princess's intelligence, her father employed her as a spy to collect information he could use against the Romans. To this end, he arranged for her to wed King Masinissa, an ally to the Roman king."

"And did she become his bride?"

"Oh, good heavens, no! Sophonisba would never marry a Roman sympathizer. Besides, she loved another."

"And what was his name?"

"Syphax. He was the chieftain in western Masaesyli."

"And did this Syphax reciprocate Sophonisba's love?"

"Of course, he did! He was a wild adventurer and a brilliant swordsman. From the moment he saw Sophonisba, he was captivated by her and actively pressed for her hand in marriage."

"So, *they* were united and lived happily ever after."

Sofonisba shook her head in mock despair. "Unfortunately, their young lives were fraught with difficulties. Before they could be united, war broke out between Carthage and Rome. Syphax was sent into battle. But when the Carthaginians were defeated, he and Sophonisba were captured and fell into the hands of King Masinissa."

"That didn't bode well for the two young lovers," said Anthony.

"I'm afraid not," she admitted ruefully. "Masinissa—who still desperately loved the Carthaginian princess—wanted to make her his wife. Once again, she adamantly refused, admitting she loved another and carried his child. When the king learned this, he was heartbroken. Because she was Rome's enemy, if he released her, his people would kill her instantly. Not being able to possess her as his own or let her go free, he had no other option than request she sacrifice herself heroically—like a true princess—in honor of her people."

"What? He killed her, even though he loved her?"

"Apparently so. It seems a drastic measure, I agree... even to uphold one's reputation. The Roman king, though, wanting her to depart this world nobly, gave her a cup of poison to drink, and it was in his arms she died. After that, Masinissa, so overcome with grief, murdered Syphax and then threw himself into the sea."

"Good heavens!" said Van Dyke, "That is a tragic tale... one of love—true and unrequited—as well as heroism, honor, and death."

"My relatives were rather fascinating," she agreed.

Looking at her mischievous grin, he said dubiously, "If I am to believe you—you were named after a Carthaginian princess and your last name derives from a snake."

"Yes, precisely," she replied proudly. "I am the oldest of five children—four of whom were girls. My father, Amilcare—also named for an ancient Carthaginian ruler—had quite a talent for picking out exotic names... You see, he named my younger brother Asdrubale."

"Oh, my... I've never heard of such a name."

She laughed at his expression. "My baby brother was named after the warlord Hasdrubal Barca, the brother of Hannibal and..."

Anthony waved a hand in the air. "Let's stay focused on *your* name, Signora Sofonisba, and return to *your* story. Don't attempt to confuse me with other inconsequential familial details to throw me off track."

"All right," she said with a chuckle. "Then let me tell you how I acquired my nickname, *Sorella Leone.*"

"Sister Lion?"

"It is quite comical, actually. My little brother..."

"Asdrubale?"

She nodded. "As a small child, he was quite annoying. Unfortunately, he never grew out of it."

When Anthony looked at her questioningly, she said, "You see, after my father died, he was the only male heir in the family, so he controlled my fortunes, despite being the youngest. Once, he even tried to tell me *who* I could and couldn't marry!" She waved her hand and added, "I'll tell you about that when we get there."

"So, this little pest—your brother... He has something to do with your nickname?" asked Van Dyke, adding shading to his drawing.

"Yes, when he was very young, Asdrubale was always toddling after my sisters and me, begging to play our games—or steal our treats. We did our best to hide from him, but it never seemed to deter the little imp. I was the eldest of my siblings, and my sisters—Elena, Europa, and Minerva—used to call me *sorellone,* which means..."

"Big sister," said Anthony.

"Very good, young man. I see your Italian is improving!"

With a wicked grin, she said, "Once, I couldn't take Asdrubale whining any longer, so I wrapped a fringed shawl about my head and wiggled my fingers like sharp claws and growled fiercely at him. Oh! You should have seen his face—his eyes grew wide with fear as if a lion from the jungles was ready to pounce and eat him up. Well! Asdrubale was so terrified, he burst into tears and toddled off to find Nanny Fabia, stammering, '*Sorella Leone, Sorella Leone, Sorella Leone!*'"

"Big sister lion," said Van Dyke with a laugh.

"My mother wasn't too pleased when she learned of this, but it was worth every moment to see the look of terror on Asdrubale's face."

Anthony chuckled at the thought. "Well, at least this part of your story seems credible. From what I know of your career and character, you have the courage and the heart of a lioness."

Sofonisba scoffed. "Again with the compliments. Keep it up young man and I might just run away with you after all!"

At the sound of another soft knock, they looked up to see Cecilia again on the threshold. In her hands she held a plate of sweets, and soon the fragrant smell of lemon tarts enveloped the room. "This is the first batch—they are fresh from the oven. While they are still hot, I thought you might like to have a taste. There will be more later."

Anthony thanked her, took one of the cakes, and chewed it slowly. He watched the maid retreat, then, wiping his hands on a linen napkin, picked up his drawing pencil once more. "Continue, madame. I've yet to complete my portrait of you."

She lifted her head and tilted it slightly. "So, I gather thus far, you are convinced I am telling you only truths?"

He eyed her thoughtfully. "I'm quite in awe of your storytelling abilities… Let's just say it is too early in the game to know for sure. But, if your story is as dramatic as that of the Carthaginian princess for whom you are named—filled with love triangles, conquering generals, poison, murder, and suicide—I'm sure I will be entertained."

"You'd be surprised how many things I have in common with my beautiful ancestor," Sofonisba said with a cryptic smile. She took a bite of the lemon tart, savoring the familiar taste that made her think of sunlight and Sicily. "All right, Anthony!" she said, brushing the crumbs from her skirts. "We are about to set sail on a journey filled with curious characters, enchanting palaces, and lively anecdotes. I experienced most of what I am about to tell you personally, while other details were revealed to me later by the very players in the story—either by word of mouth or through letters. After all, it is the story of my life… and it is my intention to entertain as well as trick you."

She winked at him and said, "You keep drawing, my dear boy, and I will keep talking. Before the afternoon is done, and we have eaten all the lemon cakes, you will know the secrets of Sofonisba… Well, almost *all* of them."

Cremona to Rome—1554

The purpose of life, after all,
is to live it, to taste experience to the utmost,
to reach out eagerly and without fear
for newer and richer experiences.

— *E. Roosevelt*

Chapter 4

But Girls Don't Paint!

A clash of musical notes sounded throughout the house, followed by a loud groan. "I'll never get this piece right," the young female voice cried out in dismay.

"Elena!" said Sofonisba from the window ledge, where she was curled up reading a book. "Have you not played that piece enough for today? Give it a rest, dear sister. I can barely hear myself think."

A shriek issuing from the upstairs hallway caused both girls to sigh and roll their eyes.

"Minerva, what's happened?" called out Elena.

"Europa, the little sneak, has stolen my best petticoat."

"Did not," came a stubborn response.

"Did so, you little brat!"

"Sofonisba! Help me!"

"I'll do no such thing," came Sofonisba's reply. Calmly, she turned the page of her book, raised her voice, and said, "If you leave your dresses and ribbons lying about in a heap, you deserve to have them stolen. I'm tired of the both of you. All you've done all day is cry and moan."

"But Sofi, she—"

"Will you two stop arguing! I'm at the most interesting part of the story. They are just about to enter the city of Troy and—"

Sofonisba heard footsteps running down the hallway, followed by another screech. "Elena, surely you will take my side!"

Ignoring her sister's pleas, Elena positioned her hands on the clavichord and sighed. "My fingers are not long enough to play this piece, and the chords are too difficult." She straightened up and resolutely began playing, but when Europa screamed once more, she banged her hands down upon the keyboard in a discordant clash and cried out in exasperation, "Quiet! How am I to learn my piece if you girls keep interrupting me? Make your peace and be done with it."

Scuffling noises could be heard from the upstairs gallery, followed by the noise of ripping cotton. "Oh, look what you've done, Europa," Minerva howled. "You've ruined my best petticoat! Because of you, now none of us can wear it!"

"Enough, you two!" called Sofonisba. "You will wake the baby."

"As if Elena's playing and your mean bossy voices haven't done that already," Minerva retorted. "If you won't help me..."

"Ouch! *Ehiii*!" howled Europa. "You wicked girl!" To those below, she cried, "Minerva's gone and pulled my hair! Nearly tore it out by the roots!"

"Serves you right, Europa. Now, get out of my room."

Punctuating the statement, a door slammed shut and then, on cue, a piercing wail issued from the nursery. Sofonisba heaved a sigh of dismay and called out, "There! See what you've done, Minerva? You've gone and woken up Asdrubale! Mother will be so angry. She said to keep the peace for two minutes while she finished her errands."

"That's right!" said the raspy voice of Nanny Fabia sailing into the drawing room. "Girls! Girls! Stop your bickering this moment."

Immediately Elena and Sofonisba appeared contrite; one turned back to the keyboard, the other to her book. From the hallway, they could smell the enticing aroma of freshly baked lemon tarts.

As the toddler's cries grew louder, Nanny Fabia glanced up at the stairway and sighed. Her angular face set in a grim frown. "With all the yelling and banging of doors, it's no wonder they haven't woken the spirits from their graves."

Sofonisba smothered a laugh and turned a page. "They are all menaces. But what do you expect, Fabi? With the rain and the gloom, there is nothing to do than pester one another. If truth be told, we are all pining for a new adventure to amuse us."

Fabia only clicked her tongue. "I'd better go settle the young master down. He will continue bawling his eyes out if we let him!" She turned her keen eye on Sofonisba and added, "You, little missy... attend to your sisters. Go mend the wounded chicks' feelings!"

"I believe you have the easier task. Asdrubale will be appeased with a hug and a piece of cake but the other two... From the sound of things, they've gone and ripped Minerva's petticoat, and that is a crime that won't readily be forgiven."

The old woman chuckled as she left the room. Soon her heavy tread could be heard ascending the stairs, and shortly after that Asdrubale's cries abated. Sofonisba tossed her book aside, picked up a drawing tablet and pen, and began to sketch her sister on the opposite side of the room. As Elena plodded patiently through the musical piece, she captured the look of grim determination on her sister's face.

Sofonisba, lost in a world of her own making, only ceased drawing when she heard the other two girls clatter down the stairs. Into the room they tumbled, the incident over the petticoat already forgotten. Behind them followed Fabia, who held Asdrubale in her arms.

"There now, little man! For now, the storm has blown over," cooed Fabia, chucking him under the chin. "Who's Fabi's favorite?"

Sofonisba shook her head. "You spoil him rotten."

"Someone needs to," Fabia replied tartly. "Goodness, you all tease the little master far too much."

As the music crescendoed, Minerva covered her ears and cried, "Elena! Stop that incessant noise."

"What shall we do? Shall we play a game?" asked Europa.

"We could do some play-acting," suggested Minerva. Then, grabbing a fringed shawl from a nearby chair, she wrapped it around her head like a turban. With a hand to her brow, she intoned, "I am Pythia, the high priestess of the Temple of Apollo. I will recount for you stories of bygone men, heroes, and kings and palaces made of jade and ships of gold..." She paused for dramatic effect, and Europa clapped her hands in approval. "Minerva, you are a wonderful storyteller." Then, looking at her older sister, she said, "Don't you agree, Sofi?"

Begrudgingly, Sofonisba nodded. For as long as she could remember, she and Minerva had battled wills. Unlike Elena, who was demure and obedient, and Europa, who was sweet and gullible, Minerva was prickly and demanding. Who knew why their relationship was so contentious? Perhaps it was because they were more similar than different.

Raised under the same roof, the sisters had sat with their father reading by the light of the fire every evening. They'd begun with Aesop's Fables, and as they grew, she, along with her siblings had tackled meatier fare like Homer's Odyssey and the Iliad. Sofonisba took for granted that other families were like hers and that other fathers inspired their daughters to study the classics and read stories passed down through time.

But Amilcare was not like other fathers. Along with Sofonisba's mother, Bianca, he believed in the unorthodox notion of giving his children, despite their gender, a well-rounded education. And because of her father's immense pride in his noble Carthaginian roots—they were descendants of illustrious stock, after all—he took specific pains to teach his daughters about the past.

So, following her father's well-planned curriculum, Sofonisba, along with her sisters, read classical literature and learned the history of the great wars of Rome and Carthage as well as mathematical equations. From their mother, the brood adeptly mastered Latin and Greek and was taught musical theory and how to play the clavichord.

As time went on, Sofonisba's parents began to note with interest and encourage each of their girls' unique talents—Elena for music; Minerva for prose; and Europa for numbers. And although Sofonisba showed a great interest in the classics and history, it was her natural talent for drawing that had made her parents sit up and take notice.

When she was only six, Amilcare had been the one to hand her a pencil, encouraging her to draw. And when he'd seen her first designs and shown them to his wife, it was as if they'd been struck by lightning. Fluttering the drawing around in the air, he had exclaimed, "Sofonisba, this is simply delightful. You have a natural ability, and we must cultivate it. You, daughter, are destined for greatness! Your ancestors were tenacious and intelligent—you are just like the princess for whom you were named."

At first, it had embarrassed her to be called after the proud but tragic Carthaginian princess. Sofonisba Anguissola! It had always been such an odd mouthful to say and set her apart from girls with more conventional names. Yet, as Sofonisba grew older, she began to make a connection with her courageous ancestor and vowed she'd, too, become a shining example for future generations.

To pay tribute to their famous forebearers and other literary heroes, Sofonisba and her sisters often invented stories about them and re-enacted great battle scenes in the garden. Looking at the book of Greek mythology lying on the couch next to her, Sofonisba remembered an afternoon when they had play-acted Troy's great siege and the bad blood between King Agamemnon and the warrior Achilles.

Always the bossy one, Minerva took charge of their dramatizations, casting her sisters and outfitting them with props. That day Minerva placed an embroidery hoop on her head, pretending to be King Menelaus of Sparta. She then declared Sofonisba should take the part of Paris because she was thin as a boy... and Elena, being the pretty one, should play the role of Helen. Airily, she instructed them to drape themselves in the expensive gold material their mother had chosen to adorn the front room windows.

Later, the girls had gotten into serious trouble borrowing the expensive stuff without Bianca's permission. Of course, true to form, Minerva laid the blame at her older sister's feet, and it had been Sofonisba who had been punished and sent to bed early.

Brought back to the present by Minerva's imperious voice, Sofonisba watched her sister unwrap the shawl from her head and toss it aside. "Come now, sisters. Sofi... Elena... what shall we recite? Shall I be Petrarch's Laura? Oh, better yet, let's tell the story of how Dante met Beatrice and was charmed by her ethereal beauty."

"It is a timeless tale of unrequited love," agreed Europa.

Minerva looked pointedly over at Sofonisba and said, "You can play Dante. He had a crooked beak of a nose…"

"But my nose is quite lovely," retorted Sofonisba.

"Says you, *sorellone*!" Minerva laughed. Slowly she circled the room reciting the familiar lines, then suddenly let out a piercing cry. "*Ahiiiah!*"

Minerva whipped around and glared at Sofonisba, who had just lobbed a small leather book at her head. It flew like a missile over her shoulder, narrowly avoiding its target. When Minerva saw Sofonisba pick up another volume and take aim again, she yelped, "Don't you dare, Sofi!"

But when Sofonisba only laughed and advanced upon her, Minerva darted behind the couch. From her sheltered position, she cried out, "Stay back, Sofi! Don't come one step closer, or I'll—"

"Enough!" cried Fabia. "Girls! Stop your quarreling at once. I've looked after each and every one of you since you were in swaddling clothes, and I'm not afraid of spanking any of you despite your advanced ages. Behave, or there will be no cakes for tea."

She gave them a penetrating stare, then singled out Europa. "Here, you take your little brother's hand and keep him amused while I talk to the cook and prepare your suppers."

"Oh, Fabi, we'll be good…as long as there are sweet pastries soon," pleaded Europa. "We are all famished."

"Only if you promise to hold your tongues for more than five minutes."

At the mention of dessert, Asdrubale pulled away from Europa and began stomping around the room, chanting, "Sweets! S'durbale wants a treat to eat! Treat…treat…treat! S'durbale wants a treat to eat! Treats—"

"Asdrubale, hush! For the love of peace, all of you! Find something quieter to do." Fabia glanced around, then seeing the chessboard Europa had carried down the stairs, said, "Play a game… That should calm you down."

"Yes, let's have a match!" said Elena. Standing up from the spinet, she shook out her long red skirt and began setting up the board with

Minerva's help.

When it was ready, Elena glanced over at Sofonisba. "Shall you and Minerva go first?"

"No, no. I'm quite happy with observing you both. I'd rather draw your faces instead. Besides, Minerva isn't a worthy opponent. I have beaten her too many times. I'd take her queen in three moves."

Europa giggled but straightened her face when Minerva scowled at her. Loftily, Minerva then looked back at Sofonisba. "You, dear sister, you'd do better to keep to your pictures. You can document my victory!"

Sofonisba only smirked in response. She flipped back a page in her sketchbook and began drawing the scene. First, she concentrated on Elena's triumphant face as she skillfully thwarted Minerva's repeated attempts to win her rook.

"Careful, Minerva, it seems you are about to lose," Sofonisba said.

"The game isn't over yet," warned Minerva, narrowing her eyes.

In rapid strokes, Sofonisba caught her younger sister's perturbed expression.

When Fabia returned a quarter of an hour later with a plate of gooey cakes and fragrant lemon tarts, Asdrubale slipped off Europa's lap and waddled across the room toward the table. Before anyone could say anything, he reached out two hands and filled his fists with the still warm tarts. But, seeing Sofonisba observing him intently, Asdrubale hesitated. He watched with wide eyes as she set down her pencil and picked up the fringed silk scarf Minerva had tossed aside and draped it over her head. Then, still holding his gaze, she raised her hands and wiggled her fingers, pretending she was a lion ready to pounce, and let out a low "Grrrrrrr!"

Instantly, Asdrubale jumped back and tumbled to the floor. The other girls, caught up in the game's intrigues, didn't see Sofonisba teasing their younger brother. But Asdrubale—terrified at the sight of his older sister, who now was mouthing the words, *I'm going to eat you up*, dropped the sweets he was holding and burst into tears.

"*Sorella leone, sorella leone*, don't eat me up!" he wailed.

"There, there love," said Fabia, coming to his rescue and cleaning up the mess on the carpet. "No need to cry—no one is going to eat my little man up today!"

Fabia gave Sofonisba a stern look, wiping away Asdrubale's tears. Then she selected another fruit tart from the tray and wrapped it in a napkin. "Here, take this, love. Now, leave yer sisters in peace. Let us go play with the dog on the terrace."

The old nanny gently swatted his well-padded bottom and indicated the door. Asdrubale hesitated, eyeing the plate loaded with sweets. But when he caught sight of Sofonisba raising her claws again, he quickly toddled in the direction of the veranda where a black and white collie wagged its tail and eyed the small boy's treat, its tongue hanging out.

Sofonisba smirked, glad to have the whimpering toddler out of their midst. She returned to drawing, adding details and ornamentation to her sisters' dresses, but looked up again when she heard Minerva exclaim, "Ah-ha! Got you now!"

To Sofonisba, at first glance, it appeared Elena's queen indeed had been compromised.

Europa clapped her hands together and pleaded, "Elena, you can't let her win. She's been such a pill today."

"Be quiet, Europa!" threatened Minerva. For a moment longer, she studied the remaining pieces, and then with a triumphant grin, said, "There! See if you can work your way out of my trap."

Sofonisba quickly assessed the board, and after a moment realized it would be only a matter of moments before Elena would announce, "Checkmate!" Without saying a word, she picked up her watercolors and began adding pastel tints to her drawing, and after a few ticks of the clock, her prediction came true.

"What? How can that be?" squealed Minerva indignantly. "I had you blocked! You must have moved a piece when I wasn't looking!"

"No, she didn't," exclaimed Europa smugly. "I was watching. You just play badly, Minerva. You aren't as good as you think... and you are a sore loser!"

The two glowered at one another. Sofonisba, observing their perturb expressions, could almost hear the petticoat ripping all over again. She imagined her sisters, too, were remembering the unfortunate incident.

"You just need a little more practice, sister," said Elena finally, fingering her pawn.

"It is a game of finesse, Minerva," said Sofonisba. "You must play the game with patience and learn how to outsmart your partner." She pointed to the black queen. "Take, for example, this piece. She can be quite versatile and move in any—"

"I know how the queen moves, Sofi!" Minerva snapped. "Don't be such a know-it-all." She looked at Elena and loudly said, "I want a rematch! This time—"

"What is all the commotion?" a voice said from the doorway. "Girls, I could hear you in the hall."

In unison, the sisters turned around and burst into a bright chorus, welcoming their father home. Sofonisba was especially pleased to see him, as he had promised her a special surprise when he returned. She sprang from her chair, and her forgotten sketchbook fell with a soft thud to the floor. Guiltily, she bent to retrieve it.

As she raised back up, Sofonisba became aware of a stranger who followed her father into the salon. Her sisters, too, seeing the young man, quickly stopped their chattering.

The Anguissola family, being entitled landowners, held a position of respect and importance in Cremona, even if their fortunes were declining. They kept an elegant house in the wealthier part of town, and daytime guests were not uncommon. The girls had been taught well by their mother and immediately came to attention, pressing their skirts down with the palms of their hands. They appeared contrite and politely directed their gazes at the carpet, knowing it was rude and not their place to gawk at the newcomer.

Still, Sofonisba, beside herself with curiosity, dared to peek at the young gentleman, wondering what business he had with her father. As the stranger took in the chaotic scene in the drawing room, he chuckled despite himself.

At first she thought he was one of the Spanish courtiers that had taken up residence in the town. But, with an artist's keen eye for detail, Sofonisba realized the man was Italian. What gave him away were little things—his dress and his familiar fluid mannerisms. He stood straight and confident, and it was evident he took pride in his appearance—from the shiny buckles on his shoes to the silver buttons of his dark blue jacket. The man had a pleasant demeanor, too—not disdainful and haughty like many of the Spaniards she had seen in the city center. By his reaction to the drawing room scene, she could tell he had a sense of humor—something the foreigners didn't possess.

"So, these are your daughters, Amilcare," the man said with a hint of amusement. "They are delightful."

Signor Anguissola raised an eyebrow in silent acknowledgment and then turned back to the four girls standing before him, descending in height and age. "Well, now, don't you all seem prim and proper—and well-mannered. You almost have me fooled." To his guest he said with pride, "I must keep my wits about me, raising these young women. They are as intelligent as they are boisterous—all have exceptional minds. The tallest girl is my eldest daughter, Sofonisba. Next to her is Elena, followed by Minerva and Europa and finally…" He glanced around, then asked, "Where is Asdrubale?"

From the patio came the yap of an excited dog, followed by a high-pitched sob of a timid child. Nodding toward the large window that faced the garden, he added, "And that would be my youngest, the only boy in the family. He is still but a toddling tyke… Time will tell what his intelligence will be, but these young women do me proud."

The visitor acknowledged the girls with a slight bow, then noticing the chessboard and the scattered pawns on the table, he asked, "Do you all play?"

Being the eldest, Sofonisba responded. "Yes, the Marchioness of Mantova taught us last summer."

"Impressive," he said. "I am well acquainted with the Gonzaga family. Francesco, her husband, is a friend, and his wife is quite an accomplished lady in many things... music, art, and literature."

"The marchioness is a marvelous role model for my girls," agreed Amilcare. "Isabella is quite favorably connected. She is also a chess enthusiast and, when she visited us last, she taught the girls the new rules for queen's chess. She also let slip she frequently played with Leonardo da Vinci and had instructed him as well."

"I've not yet heard of this innovation," said the man.
"It is all the rage... The girls are clever and picked it up quickly. The queen piece used to be quite weak, moving only one spot at a time, but now she can move in all directions."

Amilcare addressed Sofonisba. "Wouldn't you agree, Sofi? It is quite entertaining, is it not?"

"By far more diverting than the old game," said Sofonisba. "The queen is now more powerful than the king, but he is still an important player. Although they are different, the new rules level the field and make the pair more equal."

With a tilt of her head in Elena's direction, Sofonisba said, "My sister is the best of us all. She really is quite clever, and in our last game, she thoroughly slew my little sister."

"It is commendable, signore," said the man, "that you take the time to educate your daughters and expose them to novel ideas." When he bestowed an approving look on them all, Minerva squirmed under his scrutiny, clearly angered by Sofonisba calling her a loser in front of their guest. She kept her mouth tightly clenched, but when the man turned back to Amilcare, she stuck out her tongue at her older sister.

Amilcare, seeing Minerva's antics, shot her a disapproving look. "My daughters are like young seedlings. They show great promise of becoming strong saplings, given the right nourishment, care, and discipline. Their mother, Bianca, and I—"

"Did I hear my name mentioned?" a familiar feminine voice said behind him.

"Ah, there you are. My dear, I was just introducing the girls to Signor Bernardino Campi."

"We are pleased you are here," said Bianca, sweeping into the room. She was dressed in a russet gown, and a bodice trimmed in embroidery held her voluptuous curves in place. Around her neck was a family heirloom—a pearl necklace with a ruby pendant. Her complexion was smooth and glowed from the walk to and from the apothecary's shop. Despite her exertion, not a hair on her head was out of place. The dark auburn hair that all her girls had inherited was slicked back off her forehead and secured by a delicate gold netted band.

Amilcare took his wife's hand and drew her to his side. "This is my wife, Bianca née Ponzone." He turned to her and added, "I was just telling Signor Campi, we are in agreement that our daughters should be brought up knowing more than how to needlepoint and keep a good house."

"All young ladies are capable of many things if they are allowed to expand their minds," agreed Bianca.

When Signor Campi acknowledged her statement with a tilt of his head, Bianca smiled at him, then turned her attention back to her girls. "Elena, my dear, won't you provide us with some music?"

Elena dutifully obeyed. She curtsied to their guest, then took her place at the clavichord and began playing a piece she knew by heart and in which she excelled. As the room filled with soft music, Bianca inclined her head toward the chessboard. "Minerva and Europa, busy yourselves with tidying up the pieces and then off you go to the schoolroom to work on your Latin exercises. I'll be up to review them later."

Finally, smiling at Sofonisba, she said, "And you, my love, come here. You are the reason Signor Campi is here today."

Sofonisba looked questioningly from her mother to the distinguished young man.

"Signor Campi is a talented painter, Sofonisba," said her father. "Your mother and I have decided you should have formal lessons. It has been decided you shall have a painting career."

The news reverberated around the room like a shockwave. Elena stopped playing and swiveled her head around. Europa, engaged in placing rooks and pawns back in a box, gasped and let the pieces clatter to the table.

Minerva, all at once jealous of her sister, stood up and stamped her foot. With hands on her hips, she said, "But Father! Girls don't paint!" Stubbornly she glared at him. "Not really. Not like men who paint. Name one girl who does."

Amilcare shook his head at Minerva and sternly reprimanded her. "That will be enough, daughter! In this household, it matters not if you are born male or female... Each of us has special gifts to be cultivated."

He motioned for Sofonisba to hand him her drawing tablet. Taking it from her, he began turning pages, letting Signor Campi admire her work. But when they came to the most recent one of the sisters playing chess, both men glanced up from the parchment page and looked at the artist.

Holding the drawing up for all to see, Amilcare said with no small amount of pride, "This is wonderful! See here, all of you. I think this contradicts your statement, Minerva. Apparently girls *do* paint! And her name is Sofonisba Anguissola! She will be the first female to make a name for herself as an artist."

"But, why is it that Sofi always gets special treatments?" asked Minerva stubbornly.

"Your father and I believe that Sofonisba has a rare kind of talent," said Bianca.

"She was born to be an artist," said Amilcare, glancing meaningfully over at Signor Campi.

"Minerva, you must be patient. You are still quite young," said Bianca. "Your abilities lie elsewhere."

"If you could draw a fine picture like this," said Amilcare, "you too would have painting lessons. You, *mia cara*, have a gift for words and verses. Your mother and I think you will make a fine poet someday."

Slightly mollified, Minerva surveyed her father for a moment and then glanced at her mother for confirmation of this fact. Then, with a defiant toss of her head, she said, "Fine! Let Sofi become a painter. I care not a fig!" She took her younger sister by the hand and said, "Come on then, Europa!" Without a backward glance, she flounced out of the room with poor little Europa in tow.

Bianca shook her head at the scene, then turned to her eldest daughter and asked, "What do you say, Sofonisba? Would you like to be an apprentice for Signor Campi?"

With the commotion over Minerva's outburst, no one had actually noticed Sofonisba's reaction yet. When she said nothing, Signor Campi glanced up from her drawings, watercolors, and sepia sketches. Observing the young girl's bright face and her expression of incredulous disbelief, he let out a ringing laugh. "Signorina! Such beautiful eyes you have. They speak volumes when you do not. I must admit, when your father approached me, I was a little dubious. But, now seeing this... meeting you... understanding what you are capable of... I, too, am a bit speechless."

Politely, he handed back her sketchbook and said with great earnestness, "I believe, given time, it is *you*, signorina, who will be teaching *me* how to paint!"

Chapter 5

The Lessons Begin

*B*ernardino Campi's studio soon became a second home to Sofonisba. Being a prominent painter in the town of Cremona, Campi lived in an elegant house set on a modest swell of a hill not far from the city center. From such a high vantage point, one could enjoy a glimpse of the medieval church tower that rose high above the other buildings, dominating the entire city and the crenulated rooflines of the Loggia dei Militi—the city's commune and seat of government.

Campi's villa featured an expansive park that was decorated with Greek urns and classical busts of Roman statesmen. In the mornings, the light filtered through the trees in a beguiling way, and as the sun journeyed across the sky, the over-arching branches sheltered the terrace and provided welcome shade from the midday heat of summer.

During lesson breaks, Sofonisba liked to follow the pebbled paths lined with colorful flowers and explore the grounds. Lost in thought, she admired the classical artifacts and the delightful array of dancing nymphs and lusty satyrs. The ancient stones inspired creativity and made her contemplate her ancestors, the early Carthaginians, and the princess for whom she had been named. She imagined how bravely they had fought against the stronger Roman forces to maintain control of the advantageous location situated on the banks of the Po River about a day's ride from Milan. Sadly, they had been defeated.

As she let her mind drift, she ruminated about the original Sophonisba spelled with a "ph." Her ancestor had been a warrior princess, talented, and intelligent—in love with one man and pursued by another. In the end, the Carthaginian woman had met a tragic fate, forced to drink poison to ensure an honorable death.

Sofonisba shook her head at the notion. In her innocence, never having encountered strife other than her siblings' squabbles, she thought it entirely insane that someone should take their life so as not to fall prey to a mortal enemy. With bravado, she thought, *For all my ancestor's clever ways, surely she could have found a more intelligent strategy to escape the king and be reunited with her true love.*

Sofonisba gazed out at the flat plains to the east, laid out like a jeweled tapestry, and imagined the first fort established there. The struggle to control Cremona and northern Italy had led to a series of bloody tribal battles. After the Carthaginians, control of the city succeeded to the Romans. After that, it had fallen to the Lombards, the Byzantines, and even the Venetians. More recently, after the battle of Agnadello, Cremona was now ruled by the Duchy of Milan controlled by yet another foreign power—Spain.

Amilcare had often told her, "Rulers come and go, but we who descend from the first inhabitants—we are survivors. The land upon which this city was built is steeped in things that endure: tradition, bravery, creativity, and integrity. Remember the courage and intelligence of the original Princess Sophonisba... Like her, and later the great Roman poet Virgil also raised here, you too will be remembered—I will make sure of that. Never forget you are descended from nobility, and someday you will be celebrated for your wisdom, talents, and virtues."

Sofonisba marveled at her father's words. His faith and belief in her abilities often left her breathless. In a time when women were barred from becoming apprentices to master artists, he had waved his hand and made it a reality. Just like the new rules for queen's chess, Amilcare was inventing new rules for her. And like the queen's piece, she too was moving with greater freedom, in new directions.

If her father could level the playing field for her and grant her a painting career, what else might the future hold? Would his prediction come true? Would she paint the portrait of a king?

At first Sofonisba had shaken her head in wonder. It seemed an unobtainable goal—especially since she had never traveled beyond the confines of Cremona. Sofonisba could only imagine what lay beyond the mountains to the north, let alone the Italian seaports to the west and the Venetian empire to the east. France and Spain were far-off kingdoms, just as inaccessible to her as Milan and Rome.

But, lately, since becoming Signor Campi's apprentice, her small world had been expanded, and her dreams seemed more obtainable. She had taken her first step into a man's world, and now that her appetite was whetted, she only longed for more adventures. She was beginning to believe, like her father, she could conquer the world.

Suddenly, a fanciful image of her painting for royalty and receiving the praises of a king flashed into her brain. Surrounded by courtiers and gaily dressed ladies-in-waiting, she saw herself curtsying to his consort. *Just imagine, me, meeting a queen,* she thought. *Goodness, what would I say...*

"Sofonisba!"

Her thoughts scattered, and guiltily she swung around.

"Yes, Signor Campi?"

"Have you finished stretching the canvases and adding the first coats of gesso?"

"Why, yes. Everything is ready, just as you instructed. In fact, I prepared not only my own but also showed Giovanni, the boy who joined us last week, how to accomplish the task. He was going about it all wrong."

"You are a quick study, indeed," Campi said. "I should have known everything would be in order and that you'd soon be teaching others the things I taught you." He peered up at the sun and then commented, "The day is getting away from us. The light is changing rapidly. Come, let us finish our lesson on perspective before we can no longer see."

He gave her a warm smile, and Sofonisba flushed slightly under his gaze. She lowered her eyes and reached for the dangling strings of her apron, which had come somewhat undone and retied them. When she looked up, she saw Signor Campi was already retreating down the path. Not wasting any more time, she hastily pulled down the sleeves she had pushed up around her elbows and followed him back into the house.

The past months, in Signor Campi's studio, had been the happiest days of her life. She lived to paint and was now spending time with a master artist who was respectfully and patiently guiding her hand. She studied and copied his work and proved an agile and able student. Advancing rapidly under his instruction, she skated through her technical drawing lessons and slipped easily into the realm of more complicated techniques. Her skill with the brush was remarkable, as was her coloring and attention to detail.

It was her routine to arrive each morning at Signor Campi's estate, accompanied by her sister Elena. For propriety's sake, Amilcare had deemed it necessary for the girls to take care of one another. Sofonisba hadn't minded. Her sister, after all, in addition to her musical abilities, had artistic talent as well. Sofonisba was also happy her father had chosen Elena to join her as she far enjoyed her company to that of Minerva's.

When the girls entered the studio, they took off their cloaks and straw bonnets decorated with satin ribbons and hung them in the foyer next to the gentlemen's leather hats and caps with feathers. After tying linen aprons around their waists, they would set to organizing their palettes, crushing small bits of minerals and rocks into finely ground colorful powders they would mix into oils to make translucent paint. Then, taking their places with the male students, they began to sketch the still life arrangements of flowers and an odd assortment of crockery and cups that Signor Campi arranged in the center of the room.

At first, they were gawked at, seeing as they were women, but after a few weeks, viewing the quality of their work, the men begrudgingly accepted them as colleagues. Soon, Sofonisba became so engrossed in composition and color she barely noticed the other painters in the room. She rarely heard their muted conversations—let alone had time to worry that she was different from the rest because of her gender and her unusual name. Here, all that mattered was her art. Her full concentration was on her lessons now, but it would be insincere to say her heart didn't beat a little faster when she heard Signor Campi's footsteps in the outer hall or heard him call out her name. The way he said it sounded musical and made her feel special.

"Buongiorno, Signorina Sofonisba Anguissola," he would call out gaily as he made his way to her side. "What have you to show me this fine day?"

She smiled in pleasure and proudly showed him her work. By now, Sofonisba was accustomed to his person, handsomely groomed hair, tailored jackets, and polished black boots. When he stood next to her, she breathed in his heady scent as he politely conducted a discourse, pointing out the passages of her painting that he admired, as well as the flaws and imperfections.

One afternoon, when he approached her, she let out a frustrated sigh and exclaimed, "I doubt if you know the effort it is to paint! The trying and trying... and trying again... and oh, the failures!"

Campi only chuckled. "Welcome to being an artist, Sofonisba! We all experience the highs and lows. Just keep working. Practice, practice, practice! Don't stop, and you will make progress."

As the months slipped by, she began to relax, finally pleased with the way she captured sunlight glinting off a silver spoon or droplets of water on delicate petals. However, as her eyes roamed around Campi's salon, she realized with displeasure that she and her sister were the only ones still painting arrangements of inanimate objects and flowers. The male students were now engrossed in painting muscular men and battle scenes.

Fuming once again, she voiced her dismay. "Painting endless scenes of books on tables, violins, and pieces of fruit is all fine and good, but I find it extremely dull. I, too, wish to paint dramatic scenes filled with rearing horses, fallen soldiers, and triumphant victors. There is a range of human emotions I wish to explore and—"

"Signorina," exclaimed Signor Campi sternly, "it is one thing to open my studio to a young woman... It is quite another thing to allow her to observe a naked human body. It is simply not allowed! Life drawing classes are reserved only to male students."

"But how am I to paint authentically if I'm not allowed to study human anatomy?" Sofonisba boldly countered. "How will I learn to capture muscles and bone structure? The other young men are given private lessons to this end. I feel that I shall fall behind if I'm not allowed the same privileges."

"I'm sorry," said Signor Campi. "It won't be tolerated."

Angered by Campi's verdict, Sofonisba took the case up with her father. But, to her chagrin, despite his lenient ways, Amilcare was unbending. So, in the end, reluctantly, Sofonisba capitulated. She had no other alternative if she wished to continue her lessons.

Still, she was not happy, and it showed on her face. For a week, she painted in a gloomy mood. Aware of her discontent, Campi finally approached her and said, "Sofonisba, do not despair. Your talents lie not in grandiose history paintings and the contorted muscles and bodies of men. But perhaps it would appease you to paint the human visage."

Instantly her spirits lifted. "That would indeed be a welcome change from the endless bouquets of lilacs I've been forced to capture on canvas."

That very day, under Campi's tutelage, Sofonisba switched from flowers to faces and focused her attention on the various shapes of noses, cheekbones, and eyes. But as Bernardino advised, she soon learned that for a portrait to be successful, it wasn't enough to only delineate the lines of a person's features and fill them with color; instead, she needed to capture the vital essence of her subject.

"Each person has a story to tell," Campi explained. "With each new subject, it is your task as the artist to see beyond a person's coloring and shapes of their features... You must look deep into your sitter's eyes and uncover the subtleties of their emotions and capture their unique personality on canvas."

He patted her arm gently and gazed a bit longer than necessary into her large brown eyes. "If you apply yourself, I believe you could be a fine portraitist, Signorina Anguissola."

Sofonisba felt a rush of warmth wash over her. Of all the things he had communicated to her previously—Signor Campi fulfilled his obligations as a mentor and painting instructor with those simple words. All of a sudden, something inside her crystallized, and she readily accepted the gift he gave her. No, she was not destined to paint glorified tributes to Apollo, the gods, and all the virtues. She would not paint rippling muscles, sinewy tendons, and dramatic battle scenes. Instead, she would focus on the internal private thoughts and yearnings of men. She would look deep into her subject's eyes and she would reveal their inner truths. This was her talent; this would be her life's work.

To this end, Sofonisba focused her concentration on the complexities of quiet human drama and captured it on her canvas. Soon, the paintings Sofonisba made of her family members and other students in Campi's studio took on a new dimension and depth.

The days melted into months until one day Bernardino, passing by her work station, stopped and exclaimed, "Signorina Anguissola... This is outstanding work indeed." He was silent a moment admiring the nearly completed portrait of one of the other apprentices, then looked back at her and nodded. "Yes, this is quite good. I'm captivated by the story you have told using your paintbrush. With grace and ease, you have expressed so much about Signor Stefano's personality... If truth be told, I find the portrait you have made to be psychologically superior to battle scenes filled with a dozen men."

Sofonisba looked at her canvas, and in that moment, she, too, knew her work was excellent. And as she glanced around the studio, although a modest girl, she felt her work was superior to others... and perhaps dare she admit it, more accomplished than her painting masters.

When the girls returned home each night throughout the long blustery fall and winter, they recounted to their father, over plates heaped with mutton and veal, what they had done and learned that day. In a light and airy voice, Elena told the family amusing anecdotes about the other apprentices. Sofonisba, on the other hand, focused her observations on her painting instructor, and when she spoke of Campi, inevitably her tone became warmer and increasingly enthusiastic.

"Signor Campi speaks highly of my abilities. He has given me such gifts... I don't believe I could have come so far without his astute advice. At times he takes my hand and directs my brush... but only when I'm really in a quandary as to how to deepen a shadow or bring highlights to a person's cheekbones." She put down her knife and fork and gushed, "He is such an inspiration... He teases me at times in private, saying that I will soon be teaching his classes."

"I dare say you will," Amilcare said.

"He is the kindest man. Really I've never met anyone like him."

As the others ate, she continued telling them how Campi had spent a full hour helping her mix and measure powders for her paints. Finally, out of breath, she stopped to take a drink and glanced at her father. Seeing him slowly chewing his bread, regarding her thoughtfully, Sofonisba carefully set down her glass. Then with a small shrug, she said off-handedly, "Oh, Father, you mustn't worry. He treats me with the greatest respect."

"Just keep your eyes on your canvas," he said. "You must focus on honing your skills. For now, you mustn't be distracted."

Sofonisba blushed and looked down at her plate.

"You are much too talented to fall in love at such a young age. I haven't spent a fortune on painting lessons for you to go off and marry Campi."

"Your father is right," said Bianca. "Think of the advantages we are providing you... You will become a great lady and be respected for your talent if you continue along this path. This is my wish for you... as it is for all my daughters."

Amilcare patted his wife's hand, then looked at Sofonisba. "Someday, when the time is right, I hope you will find someone worthy of that bright mind of yours. But for now you are meant for other things."

Sofonisba glanced from one parent to the other, realizing the sacrifices they were making for her, and resolved to make them proud. She vowed to refocus her attention on her work; still, as the winter holidays melted into spring days, and as the blossoms in Campi's garden began to bloom again, she couldn't deny the heightening of her senses when he was near. Despite Amilcare's warnings, she wondered, *Is this love?*

As the spring progressed, the world seemed more colorful and fragrant, and she became increasingly preoccupied with delicious thoughts that had nothing to do with painting techniques. She drifted along in a blissful state until a balmy evening in the middle of June. With the scent of wisteria floating through the air, Sofonisba found herself seated once again in the family's dining room. She and Elena had just returned home late from Signor Campi's studio and hastily took their seats as the cook ladled broth into their waiting bowls.

Through the open window, a breeze gently wafted in, making the candles waver ever so slightly. Picking up her spoon without preamble, Sofonisba eagerly exclaimed, "Mother, Bernardino has paid me the highest compliment! Why, just today he said—"

"Oh, shut up!" spat out Minerva, thumping down her glass and sloshing a bit of water onto the linen cloth. "Enough! Can't you find something else to speak of? It's either Signor Campi this... or Signor Campi that... For months that's all we've heard about!"

Realizing she held center stage, Minerva said in a sing-song voice, "I don't think Sofonisba really cares about painting at all..." She paused dramatically. "Look at her! Her eyes have always been as big as saucers, but now they are dreamy and larger than harvest moons. I think instead, our Sofonisba is in love!"

"Take that back, Minerva, you nasty girl," Sofonisba demanded, waving a soup spoon at her younger sister, flushing violently.

"Will not! Just listen to you going on and on. It's enough to make a placid rabbit mean." She started to giggle. "You should see your face. It's as red as a beet! If I have to sit here one more evening hearing you extol the virtues of your painting instructor one more time, while I—"

"You are just jealous that Elena and I have painting lessons and you must stay at home with Europa attending to Latin grammar. You are a sourpuss."

"Don't you dare call me names!" cried Minerva.

"Girls!" said Bianca. "We are at the table. Mind yourselves."

"Sofi has a beau!" Minerva started to chant. "His name is..."

"Minerva, hush!" said Amilcare.

He looked at all his daughters' faces, cleared his throat, and said,

"I've been thinking about this for a while, and I've just made a decision." Directing his gaze at Sofonisba, he continued. "It's time for you to finish your apprenticeship here in Cremona. You have exceeded your lessons and time with Signor Campi."

Sofonisba looked at Amilcare in distress. "What are you saying, Father? Don't mind what Minerva says..."

"I think it is time for you to quit his studio."

"No! Father... please don't punish me. I've done nothing wrong. I love to paint..."

He waved a hand, ignoring her protests. "You are descended from noble blood. You are destined for greater things. How many times have I told you this before?"

"But, but..." she said helplessly. Then, turning to Elena, she implored. "Tell him! Tell him there is nothing improper going on!"

"I know, Sofonisba," said Amilcare, dismissing her words with a small chuckle. "This is not a punishment. This is another gift I wish to give you. The gift of chance and opportunity."

Tears began to fill Sofonisba's large dark eyes and she shook her head, not understanding, fearing the worst.

He sighed when he saw her utter dismay. "Dear girl, these past months I've seen your talent flourish with Signor Campi's guidance. But you are cut out for far greater things than settling into marriage or becoming a minor painter. No, for you to continue improving your skills, you must be exposed to the world and other artists."

"But Signor Campi is—"

"Signor Campi has instructed you quite properly, but now it is time to introduce you to other masters." Amilcare pushed away his soup bowl and said, "It is time for Sofonisba to go to Rome to finish her education!"

At this unexpected announcement regarding Sofonisba's future, like before, a deafening silence descended. Everyone glanced from one to the other—all except Sofonisba, who openly gaped at her father.

As the news sank in, the family members seated around the table vociferously responded, breaking the stunned hush.

"Rome!" demanded Minerva, pursing her lips.

"Rome..." murmured Bianca, looking anxiously at her daughter.

"Rome?" whispered Sofonisba in astonishment.

"Why does she get to go to Rome, and I can't?" Minerva wailed.

"Hush, Minerva," said Bianca absently, turning to her husband and looking as if a hundred questions were brimming on the tip of her tongue.

Sofonisba glanced from her mother to her father and saw he hadn't noticed Bianca's dazed expression and also seemed not to have heard Minerva's querulous chirpings. Instead, her father's eyes were trained on her. As she continued watching him, seeing the firm resolve on his face, Sofonisba felt a lightness of being. And just like that, Cremona and her ordinary life and any thoughts of romantic entanglements receded into the farthest corner of her mind as she fully comprehended her father's intentions.

This was not the end of her painting career... This was a new beginning. She was going to Rome. A new world was opening up, giving her so much more scope for the imagination.

Suddenly anything and everything was possible.

Chapter 6

A Double Portrait

*A*milcare's plans to take his daughter to Rome hatched that warm spring night around the Anguissola supper table, surprised not only Sofonisba and the family but also Signor Campi. When she reported back to her painting instructor the next day she would be traveling to the Eternal City to further her art education, he was visibly taken aback.

"Are you not pleased?" Sofonisba asked, concerned when she saw him frown.

"Certainly, signorina. How could I not be? Your enthusiasm is positively contagious.

Together they walked down the garden path outside Campi's studio as Sofonisba gathered flowers. She turned around and held up her bouquet. "These white and yellow blooms are lovely, are they not? They will make a fine display for Elena to paint this afternoon, don't you think?"

She was about to bury her nose in the daisies but stopped when she saw a fuzzy little bumblebee crawling out of the petals. Warily, she shook them in an attempt to ward off the buzzing pest. "It seems I'm not the only one to find them delectable."

Campi nodded absentmindedly.

When Sofonisba looked at him again, she gave him a questioning look. "What is it, then?"

"I've always known our time together would conclude one day. As with all endings, I feel a bit of regret. I just never imagined your departure would be so soon..."

"I thought so also. I'd imagined remaining with you for at least another year. But my father is quite impulsive and wishes me to see more of the world and the ruins in Rome."

Campi regarded her thoughtfully. "You seem so grown up all of a sudden. I want you to know you will be missed... I will always have a soft spot in my heart—a teacher can't help but have a favorite student. You are quite talented, you know—by far the most gifted person to pick up a brush that I currently know. These past months... well... I could never have imagined growing so fond of..."

They stood together in the quiet garden, listening to the coo of a morning dove and the incessant buzz of insects. As the sun rose higher, she could feel the heat of the day increasing, and when Campi took a step closer, her heart stopped. She wondered if he would finish his thought... or make some kind of declaration.

Sofonisba held her breath. *Yes, I feel a connection to him, but if Bernardino should ask for my hand and if we married, is that what I really want? A month ago, perhaps, but now I'm going to Rome! Besides, what other common interests do we share other than painting... And if one of us should become more successful, would that ruin everything?*

With such thoughts swirling in her head, Sofonisba took a step backward and busied herself by picking more flowers. *No, whatever I feel for Bernardino must remain here in the garden. Father was right. I'm destined for other things than what can be found here in Cremona—or becoming someone's wife. It is a big world out there, and I want to explore it!*

Hesitantly, Sofonisba glanced over her shoulder, and seeing Campi's enigmatic expression, she turned to face him. "Signor Campi. I... I just want you to know..." She fumbled to a stop, took a deep breath, and began again. "With great fondness, I will remember the time I spent here as your apprentice and will always hold you in the greatest of esteem. You have given me so much. I—"

Campi sighed and placed his hand upon hers and squeezed it gently. "Say no more, Signorina Sofonisba. I understand completely. Let us keep this memory, this day, and this moment forever. We will always be friends, and you will have a special place in my heart."

She lowered her head to hide the stain of her blush. "You have taught me so much. I am what I am because of you. Without your guidance and belief in my skills, I'm not sure I'd be leaving Cremona."

"From the first day I met you, I have been impressed with your talent. I knew it wouldn't take much to tap deeper into your imagination and give you the confidence to push yourself further... and polish your skills." He laughed. "How you pestered me for weeks to be allowed to draw a nude figure."

"Yes, well, you should have let me," she admonished.

"Yet still, you have succeeded quite nicely despite that small disappointment," he said with a small chuckle. "What you create never fails to surprise me. Unlike the other apprentices, you infuse your subjects with such life; they seem to breathe. This is not something I have taught you. In fact, I believe the gift you possess is unteachable. So, tell me, where does this all come from?"

"I'm really not sure," she said after a moment of reflection. "It just comes naturally. When I concentrate, focus my attention on a person's outward demeanor, it is as if I can feel who they are—as if I can read their souls. I then lose myself in color and brush strokes, and it is in that moment when I am most absorbed in my work, it is as if someone or something..."

"Go on," he said.

Sofonisba shrugged. "You will think me silly, but it is as if a creative muse passes through me, taking control and guiding my brush, helping me transfer what I see with my eye onto a blank canvas." She looked at him in amusement. "Perhaps it is Hephaestus, the Greek god of the forge who visits and weaves his magic over me... because at the end of the day, sometimes, I am astounded by what I have done... as if it wasn't me at all but the work of a creative force I have channeled." She hesitated, suddenly feeling foolish. "Have I said too much? Do you think I'm completely mad?"

"On the contrary, you have put into words something I have felt too. I understand the sensation and have experienced the fickle wave of creativity that engulfs an artist." He paused and smiled. "But the difference between us..."

"Yes?" she asked.

"The difference between us," he said ruefully, "is that my muses tend to recede out to sea as quickly as they wash to shore. I confess I am quite envious of your gifts. You have the power to harness your creative wave and swim effortlessly in its riptide. I fear I shall always be in awe of your skill... and perhaps a little jealous."

Sofonisba shook her head at the notion. Still, she was secretly pleased by the analogy. The intensity of his speech also confirmed her suspicions that Signor Campi harbored feelings for her. Moreover, it seemed he too had pondered their compatibility and the problems that might arise if their egos might get the better of them. Mustering a smile, Sofonisba said, "Signor Campi... we will always share a passion for painting, and I assure you we will continue to be the best of friends."

Campi placed a hand on his breast and said with mock despair, "You honor me greatly, signorina, but I fear once you arrive in Rome, you will be so overcome with new adventures that I will quickly be forgotten. You will have artists and patrons buzzing around you like the bees are buzzing around those flowers of yours. I'm sure you will have to beat them away with a stick."

She blushed at the thought, but her lips tilted upward, just the same. "I won't forget you. I will write."

"A pleasant thought and something I will look forward to," Campi said as he bent down and plucked a yellow flower that grew along the pebbled path. Offering it to her, he said, "Didn't I say the first day we met that one day you would surpass your master? Well, that day has arrived. Now it is your time to shine! Show the world what I have taught you. If I am to be remembered at all, it will be because of you!"

He observed her intently. "Write to me if you must, but don't pine for home too much. Your father is absolutely correct. There is nothing more I can teach you. As I did many years ago in my youth, let the creative spirits that flow in and out of Rome be your new guides."

"Where shall I go first?" she asked, feeling a new rush of excitement.

"My advice is to visit the ruins first... Let yourself drink in the art of ancient civilizations. Learn everything you can from the great classical artists—Pacuvius, Arellius, and Iaia. Did you know Iaia was a female painter considered more talented than her male contemporaries?" When Sofonisba shook her head, he continued. "Then you must go to the Vatican, where you will see frescoes and paintings created by contemporary artists like Michelangelo and Raffaello."

Sofonisba regarded Campi affectionately. "You have given me so much to think about. My heart is heavy, and I simply can't find the words to thank you—they do no justice at all..." Smiling suddenly, she said, "Instead, I will show you and all the others my appreciation in the only way I know how."

True to her word, Sofonisba returned to Campi a fortnight before her departure with a farewell gift.

"What do you think?" she asked brightly.

When Campi directed his attention from Sofonisba's face in front of him to her canvas, he re-encountered her lovely visage. It was a charming self-portrait. But it wasn't just a simple composition featuring only one person. No, the painting was as sophisticated as she, for, in the foreground, Sofonisba had also painted Campi's likeness caught in the act of painting *her*.

It was a remarkable painting within a painting—a double portrait that united them forever. In the left-hand corner, Campi emerged from the dark shadows, his face highlighted by a beam of light. In his hand, he held a paintbrush and was putting the finishing touches on the embroidery that decorated the ruby red sleeve of her gown. The attention to detail was exquisite; the cuff around her neck was crisp and white, and the lace that peeked out from her sleeve was as delicate as if it had been spun of gossamer thread.

While Campi was handsomely rendered, it was the image of Sofonisba that completely captured the viewer's attention. The young woman was poised and beautiful, and her fresh rosy face radiated confidence.

The most fascinating detail of all, however, was the way Sofonisba had painted her left arm. If you viewed the painting closely, you could see it resting comfortably at her side. But upon second inspection, you realized she had painted her limb twice. Like a *pentimento*, where the artist's original underdrawing bleeds through to the surface, this limb was raised to touch Campi's as if it were she, instead, who had taken possession of his arm and directed his brush.

It left the viewer to question who was painting whom.

But not for long. For, as one beheld Sofonisba's wide all-seeing eyes, which seduced and mesmerized the beholder, it was clear she was the one who now controlled and guided the hand of her teacher.

She had used her wit and ingenious imagination and told the world that, just like Pygmalion, she had surpassed her creator and now was as skillful—if not more so—than her teacher and worthy of admiration based on her own merit.

When Campi saw the final results, he laughed in pleasure and said, "You are indeed a clever girl, Sofonisba—I have no doubt of your continued success."

Chapter 7

Romeward Bound

*W*hile Sofonisba had occupied herself with painting her tribute to Signor Campi, Amilcare, repaired to his study, where he remained ensconced for several weeks, sorting out the details of their journey. Entering his library late one spring evening, Sofonisba caught him deep in reverie standing over a detailed design of the roadways that crisscrossed the Italian peninsula. Cartography had always been a particular interest of her father's. As she slipped into his favorite leather chair, she saw that he was studying a map held down by stone weights carved like little whales that kept the parchment ends from curling inward. In one hand, he held a compass and in the other, an expandable five-point caliper.

When he finally noticed her, Amilcare put down his tools and picked up a candle so she could see the map better. "Take a look at this, Sofi, my girl." Pointing to a line he had drawn on the parchment, he said, "I'm plotting our course. Given good weather and reasonable roads, we should arrive in Rome in approximately three or four weeks."

"That doesn't seem so terribly long."

"Well, if we encounter storms or treacherous tracts that slow the horses, the trip could take a bit longer. But we are leaving at a good time of the year—the rains have passed and summer approaches." Directing her attention to a road south of Florence, he said, "I've had word from Signor Marcelli, who has recently returned from Rome, that this stretch is particularly bad." Rubbing his neck, then massaging his lower spine, he added, "I hope the journey goes smoothly; I don't think my back will do well if we bounce up and down for days hitting holes in the road."

Sofonisba leaned over and rested her elbows on the desk. She saw that he had circled several little towns along the course. "Are those to be our stopping points?"

"Yes. The first night we will rest outside Modena, then on to Bologna, Prato, Florence, and Arezzo—"

"And what town is this?" she asked, pointing to a mark he had drawn closest to Rome."

"That is the little town of Chiusi set in the hills in southern Tuscany near lake Trasimeno. Signor Marcelli informs me it is small but quite diverting. He says it is a good place to rest up prior to arriving at our final destination."

Sofonisba looked up at her father. "It seems you have everything well in hand. But are you sure we can afford such a venture? The trip alone seems quite expensive."

Amilcare waved his hand dismissively. "Over the years, I've been prudent with our funds earned from the Anguissola estates. While not as profitable as in the days of my father, we shall get by quite nicely. I believe it is as good a time as any to dip into the funds I've earmarked for you, Sofonisba." Kissing her on the forehead, he added, "At the moment I'd much rather spend it in pursuit of furthering your painting career than on securing a husband for you. Thanks to my foresight, you will have enough to spend at least a season, maybe two, in Rome."

Sofonisba was content to leave the logistics of their trip in the capable hands of her father, just as she was to leave the details of outfitting her wardrobe to her mother. Bianca, an imaginative pattern designer, set about creating a proper wardrobe worthy of a nobleman's daughter embarking on her first journey abroad. Sofonisba was to be a painting apprentice, but she was also a lady. So, in addition to serviceable frocks that could be worn in a painting studio, she needed a wardrobe befitting a young miss of her station entering genteel Roman society for the first time.

Her father's and mother's enthusiasm for her new adventure was thoroughly contagious for everyone in the Anguissola household— everyone except Minerva. During the final hours of preparation, it seemed Sofonisba's younger sister whined more than ever and stamped her foot frequently from perceived slights. She argued with her eldest sister over which books were hers and even removed a few when Sofonisba wasn't looking. When brought to task, Minerva only flounced out of the room in a huff, claiming it was she who should be traveling to Rome and that life was so unfair.

On the morning of her departure, in the early dawn hours, Sofonisba finally bid a tearful goodbye to her mother and embraced her siblings Elena, Europa, and Asdrubale. Curiously, Minerva was missing, refusing to participate in the tender parting scene. But, as Sofonisba stepped into the carriage, she heard a rap from the bedroom window above her. Glancing up, she saw her younger sister's face pressed to the glass. Even from below, she could see Minerva's pout.

Sofonisba raised a hand and blew her a kiss. "Don't worry, brat, I'll return."

Minerva raised the window and called down, "Don't worry, I will still be here to torment you!"

Now, sitting in the swaying vehicle as it rocked over the rutted dirt roads of northern Italy, she fondly remembered Minerva's farewell. In her heart, Sofonisba knew her sister wished her well, despite the fact she was a pest. As the vehicle pulled away, Sofonisba made up her mind; she would write special letters to Minerva to keep her informed of her adventures.

"Either she will hate me or appreciate the gesture," Sofonisba said to her father. Personally, she thought it would be the latter.

Feeling generous, she also thought, *Perhaps I'll even write one to Asdrubale... or send him a picture—after all, he is still in short pants and just beginning to learn the alphabet.*

Eagerly, Sofonisba turned her attention to the countryside through which they were passing. It was the first time she had been so far afield from Cremona. She took a deep breath and detected the aroma of horse, leather, and wet grass. Pulling back the curtain from the window, Sofonisba peeked through the wooden slats and with pleasure viewed the mists rising up from the yellow stalks of grain. As the sun grew brighter and crossed the sky, and the interior cabin grew hotter, she undid her cloak ties and removed her hat.

The initial excitement of traveling passed, and growing bored, she rested her cheek against the hard leather seat, desperately seeking a more comfortable position. She picked up a book and began reading but, eventually, her head lolled to one side and she snuggled closer to her father and fell asleep against his shoulder. The hours and days passed languidly in this manner as they slowly made their way down the Italian peninsula.

They traveled each day as far as the horses allowed them and stopped to rest a day or two in the towns that Amilcare had carefully researched and plotted on his map. Sofonisba found each new place enchanting. On the arm of her father, she strolled through the towns, taking in the sights. Every new place they landed seemed unique, and she delighted in learning more about them and their histories from her well-read father. She was especially enthralled by the towers in Bologna, the statue of David Michelangelo had carved in Florence, and the loggia Vasari had built in his hometown of Arezzo.

As they drew closer to their final destination at the end of the fourth week, Sofonisba came awake from an afternoon slumber at Amilcare's nudging. "Sofonisba! Rise up, girl. We are lodging here for the night. This is the last stop we will make before reaching Rome."

"Where are we?" she asked groggily, picking up the book resting in her lap.

"We are climbing the hill to the little town of Chiusi. Today, we have traveled a good distance, and the horses could use a rest." Amilcare stretched his arms and groaned, "Oh, my aching back!"

Sofonisba looked out the window at the sun that was dipping low in the sky, and said, "It is pretty here."

"They say there are Etruscan ruins to be found in the hills around these parts."

She gave him a questioning look, and he clarified, "Before even the Romans existed, this part of Italy was called Etruria and was ruled by a more civilized and advanced group of people. It's become all the rage in these parts—this quest to locate the remains of the past. People arrive from all over—scholars and bounty hunters—to excavate the hills searching for hidden cities and the tombs of the ancient Etruscans."

"I should like to see them," said Sofonisba.

"Yes, I would, too," said Amilcare. "The findings would be quite remarkable. Etruscans were architects, goldsmiths, and scholars—why, they were the ones who taught the illiterate Romans how to read and write! The women were influential as well; they garnered respect and were educated. They even ran businesses, held political power—some were even artists!"

Sofonisba glanced out the window in hopes of seeing men digging around in the dirt, uncovering hidden treasure. To her dismay, all she saw were rolling fields of grass and scrubby brush that lined the road. There were no men busily carving into the hill or mules loaded with unearthed treasures.

She turned to her father and said, "I don't see anything. It doesn't seem all that promising or impressive."

"I imagine not. Things are hidden from view under the ground. The Etruscans created vast mazes of tunnels and multiple burial chambers that they cut into the soft tufa stone. Like the Egyptians, they filled the tombs of their dead with everything necessary for the afterlife—urns, sarcophagi, and troves of gold and bronze jewelry—even colorful murals with images of monkeys, exotic birds, and beautiful bejeweled women reading books, painting, and feasting."

"To find a painting done by an Etruscan artist—male or female—long before there was even a Roman Emperor seems incredible!" Sofonisba marveled. "It would be like receiving a secret message from bygone days."

"Many people think like you. They too hope to uncover the past, find valuable treasures in the lost tombs... starting with the most famous one of all... the tomb of King Porsena."

"Porsena?" Sofonisba asked, intrigued. "His name has a poetic and unusual ring to it, don't you think?"

"That it does," Amilcare said. "Just like your own."

"Who was he, this mysterious Porsena?"

"From accounts dating long before the Roman historian Pliny, they say he was as rich and powerful a ruler as he was benevolent. During his time, Rome was just a backwater outpost along the Tiber River, ruled by a tribal leader. To strengthen his empire to the south and re-establish Etruscan control of the waterways, Porsena went to war with the Romans with the intent of subduing them. But, when he was victorious, instead of cruelly abusing his prisoners, he pardoned them all—even a boy who had attempted to assassinate him and a girl named Cloelia who had tried to escape his prison.

"To honor Porsena, the Etruscans built a magnificent tomb, far grander than anything they had ever constructed before. Inside, they placed all his vast wealth—pots of gold coins, jewelry, urns, and his magnificent gold crown. The thing that made this tomb most particular is this; the architects—devious and talented as they were—created a maze of corridors and passageways almost impossible to navigate to thwart potential looters. They say it was so confusing that you had to enter with a ball of string to mark your path if you were to find your way back out again!"

"So, they haven't found Porsena's tomb yet?" asked Sofonisba, checking out the window again, as if she might spot it in the distance.

"No, not yet. As I said, daughter, there are only ancient Roman reports of the legend... but many tombs are still hidden below the ground. Many men have searched far and wide, but so far Porsena's labyrinth and all the wealth inside are still buried with the remains of the old king himself."

When the carriage jerked to a stop, Amilcare said, "Ah, finally, we can alight and seek refreshment!" Climbing out before her, he turned and offered his hand. "Here, let me help you down. Watch the step— don't trip on your skirt."

Sofonisba took her father's hand and alighted from the vehicle. Standing on firm ground next to him, she took a deep breath and rolled her shoulders. It was a relief to be out of the cramped quarters where they'd been sequestered for the past couple of hours. She stood for a moment, wiggling limbs, working out the pins and needles in her legs. Then, to get her bearings, she put a hand to her temple to shield her eyes from the late afternoon sun and let her gaze wander over the low retaining wall, taking in the lovely sight of the fields far below them that changed color as they melted into the purple horizon that eventually gave way to the sea.

She then turned her attention back to the piazza and noticed a sturdy fountain at the far end and buildings modestly fashioned from rough-hewn stone. "What a charming place... the village is so quaint. Is that the inn where we will stay the night?"

Amilcare nodded, distracted momentarily by the driver, who handed him their luggage. At the rumbling of iron wheels on the pavement, Sofonisba looked back across the piazza and saw a man with a stick guiding an ox pulling a wooden cart filled with grain. She tilted her head and listened and also heard the sound of music that floated down from a window, accompanied by the clinking of tin plates and glass goblets. Sofonisba inhaled deeply, and also detected the enticing spicy smell of anchovies, pungent meats, and fried onions. Her mouth watered at the thought of the meal they would soon have.

"Come along, now, daughter," Amilcare urged. Obediently, Sofonisba picked up her cloth satchel and followed in her father's wake across the square to the inn. When they drew nearer, she could hear shouts and jeers coming from the alleyway next to the establishment.

"Stay close to me," advised Amilcare. "We are strangers in these parts. Best to be on our guard."

As he advised, she kept near to her father. But loud cheers echoing around the piazza piqued her interest once again. Intrigued, Sofonisba slowed her steps, her attention caught by a small group of men of differing heights and builds bowling on a green patch of grass between the two buildings. She had never seen anything like it and stopped to watch a chubby man in a dark coat toss a ball. She followed its rolling path down a long strip and observed the others' ensuing frantic reaction. Not quite sure what was going on, she bit her lip in concentration, trying to figure out the game's logic

So intent on observing the scene, at first Sofonisba didn't notice a slim young man who leaned against a stone wall, standing apart from the others. But as her gaze roamed over the crowd, he caught her eye. With his hat cocked to one side, he too was intently following the game. He seemed a confident sort, dressed in leather britches and a blue coat.

When the ox rumbled on by him, he looked up at the noise. Then, seeing her standing nearby looking in his direction, he pushed off the wall and stood up to his full height. With a grin, he doffed his hat and made a slight bow over an extended leg. Absurdly pleased to be noticed, Sofonisba returned the salutation with a friendly nod.

Hearing the players let out a cheer, Sofonisba glanced back at the others and noted that the portly chap had just won the match and now passed his hat around the crowd, collecting gold coins. After the men changed sides and were ready to begin a new game, she saw the man in the blue coat was the first to pick up a ball and toss it across the lawn. Sofonisba wanted to remain longer to see if the handsome stranger would win this round, but to her dismay, her father called to her from the inn's threshold. She started guiltily and hastened to his side.

Amilcare noticed her interest in the men on the field and said, "Remember I told you, according to my friend Signor Marcelli this town is known for its tournaments of chance and gaming tables. Being so close to Rome, it attracts all kinds—nobles as well as vagrants. Best to keep your wits about you and a hand upon your pocketbook."

After a brief conversation with the proprietor of the inn, Amilcare secured lodgings for the evening. He then helped Sofonisba to her room, telling her he'd return shortly and not to open her door to strangers. Glancing about, she set her valise upon a table, noting the chamber— like the others she had inhabited recently—was modest, furnished with a narrow bed, serviceable curtains at the window, and a single chair. On the wall were three hooks for her clothes.

By now used to the routine, she undid her cloak and then opened a window to shake out the dust accumulated from the day's travel. Next, she rinsed her face over a porcelain bowl, using the lukewarm water from a pitcher set on the dresser. When she dried her cheeks and forehead, she was amazed by the amount of grime a day of traveling left upon the linen towel. She took a moment to comb out her long dark hair and twist it around her head again, securing it with the little tortoise-shell pins Elena had gifted her with the night before their departure. Then, with nothing left to do, she began pacing the floor, waiting for the gentle tap and the sound of her father's voice.

When it came, she opened the door and was greeted not only by her father's smiling face but also by a burst of laughter from the common room below and the tantalizing aroma of roasted meats wafting up from the kitchen. Once again, she felt a rumbling sensation at the smell of savory fare and eagerly accepted her father's extended arm. With her hand resting lightly on his sleeve, they moved down the hall together. "How do you find your room, Father?"

"It is adequate... But the bed seems a bit hard. In the last town, it was much softer—almost too soft. But, I suppose a traveler can't be so picky. How do you find yours?"

"It's quite nice. I have no complaints..." Sofonisba paused when she saw his skeptical face. "Perhaps I'm not as particular as you. Come, let's eat. I'm famished. Do you realize, Father, up until a few weeks ago, I'd never slept away from home, nor had I supped on anyone else's food but our cook's?"

"Well, we have enjoyed some unusual meals along the way... Some better than others, I grant you. But tonight, I believe we are in for a treat. I've learned, not only is this establishment clean and reputable, the food is good as well."

"That sounds promising. I'm assuming you heard this from your friend, Signor Marcelli. But, even if he'd said they served only boiled turnips, given my state of hunger, I'd believe I'd eat them happily." They walked a few more paces down the hall, then Sofonisba whispered in a confidential tone, "You know something, Father? I really don't mind sleeping in taverns in strange little towns and tasting strange foods. I am a bit tired and, granted, we've only been on the road a month, but I believe

I like traveling—it's quite an adventure. I think it suits me."

"You are fortunate, Sofonisba. You are young, not old like me. I find it tedious." Massaging his shoulder, he continued. "I'm stiff as a board and must confess to being a creature of habit and routine. Traveling has never really agreed with me."

Sofonisba patted his arm affectionately. "Well... unlike you, I rather like the idea of being in one place one day and in a completely different one the next. Even when I am old, I think I will never tire of traveling." Hearing the popping of a wine cork, and the voices of the diners below, she added, "There are new sights, new sounds, and new people to encounter—it's all rather exciting. Plus, it is nice to be out of the company of Minerva."

Amilcare grinned. "I can't argue with that. Come... let's find a table below and talk to the innkeeper about our supper."

He released her arm and let Sofonisba proceed down the narrow staircase that led into a room strewn with straw and pleasantly lit by a fire in a massive hearth. Reunited at the foot of the stairs, they gazed around at the sturdy plank tables and three-legged stools. Overhead hung baskets of herbs, and against a far wall were stacks of wine bottles that filled the hall with an earthy, pungent smell.

From a door that led in from the kitchen, a young woman spied them and indicated for them to take a table by the far window. Sofonisba took her seat and looked through the mullioned glass and observed the last of the sun's rays dipping behind the hills that surrounded Chiusi. She turned her head when she heard a man say, "May I offer you something to drink, signori?"

Beside them was the tavern owner, holding a pitcher and two earthenware mugs.

"We will have the wine," Amilcare said. "It is decent, is it not?"

"We had a good harvest last year. The grapes were sweet," replied the robust man wearing an apron barely covering his girth. "See for yourself."

After taking a sip from his cup, Amilcare indicated his approval. Pleased, the proprietor filled the other cup and placed it in front of

Sofonisba. Directing his comments to Amilcare again, he said, "There is roast duck, rabbit, pig, and lentils. It is simple fare but seasoned with rosemary and thyme. My girl will bring you a basket of black bread after she finishes lighting the grease lamps."

He fished out two pewter spoons and two forks from his pocket and set them on the table. "I be guessing you have your own knives?"

Amilcare inclined his head and took another drink from his cup. Placing a few coins upon the table, he added, "Bring us a platter of your best grilled meats and don't be stingy. My daughter and I are hungry."

"Aye, signore." Before leaving their side, the man said in a hushed whisper, "For fine folks, like yourselves, I'll make sure to include the plumpest white bird from the dovecote. My daughter will also bring you a pitcher of water." With a jerk of his head, he indicated to the young woman across the room to hurry up and attend the refined signori who had paid in advance.

Before he could step away, Amilcare pressed another coin into the innkeeper's hand. "Count me in at the card table tonight, my good man. Make sure I have a seat."

"'Twill be my pleasure to make the arrangements," the man said, then excused himself as his daughter approached their table, bearing a large basket filled with fragrant loaves. Her hair was drawn back with a scarf, and around her waist she too wore a white apron, this one a bit more soiled than the proprietor's. As she leaned over and set it down, Sofonisba could see she toiled long hours in the kitchen, cleaning pots and chopping vegetables by the calluses on her hands. She was clearly the innkeeper's kin, having his long face, pointed nose, and small dark eyes. Although her features were not particularly refined, the girl might have been pretty, Sofonisba thought, if she allowed herself to smile.

As they waited for the rest of the meal to arrive, Amilcare struck up a conversation with a man at the next table. Absently, Sofonisba tore off a warm chunk of bread and took a bite. As she slowly chewed, she began spinning a story as to why the innkeeper's daughter had such a melancholy expression. She imagined the girl had fallen in love with a stranger—a visitor to her father's tavern. But, despite stolen kisses, he'd left the next day without saying goodbye.

Delighted by her flight of fancy, Sofonisba attentively observed the girl moving from table to table, delivering more loaves of bread and baskets of fruit. After a bit, she withdrew a small sketchbook from her pocket and began drawing the girl's forlorn eyes and downturned lips.

Absorbed in her sketching, she didn't notice a group of men seated on the far side of the room. That was until a wild burst of exclamations peppered with a few blasphemies disrupted her concentration. When Sofonisba looked up, she saw it was the same group of competitive players she had been watching earlier in the alley.

The men, she noted, had finished their suppers and now held tankards of ale in one hand and cards in another. It was apparent they had moved from the competitive matches in the gardens to gambling at the tables. Sofonisba followed the rounds of play, noting it was similar to a game she took part in with her sisters when her mother wasn't observing—a game Amilcare himself had taught them, giving them strict instructions never to betray him to Bianca.

She was about to resume drawing, but before she could, her eye caught sight of the man who had greeted her earlier. At a closer distance, Sofonisba confirmed he was quite striking. He had a well-shaped face and a strong jawline, which was only enhanced by a short black beard. Dark curls framed his face, and his eyes sparkled when his lips curved upward. Compared to the others, he didn't quite fit in. He seemed more refined, and the way he carried himself communicated a cunning intelligence lacking in the others.

With a start, she realized the luminous appraisal he had given her earlier, once again, was directed at her. Unable to stop herself, she unintentionally returned his warm greeting. Amidst the confusion, the men's cheerful jeers, and the commotion of rattling cutlery, the tavern receded into the background. It seemed to her, the only two people who existed in the room were an artist with large brown eyes and a gambler with curly dark hair.

"Sofonisba! Did you hear what I said?" asked Amilcare.

Distractedly, she looked at her father. "I'm sorry. What?"

"I just was informed that..."

Sofonisba tried to pay attention, but her gaze drifted back to the man seated across the room. Jauntily he grinned, held up his cards, and splayed them for her to see. Then, raising an eyebrow, he tapped one, as if asking permission to play it. But before he could put it down, she saw a telltale sign of another more advantageous card—the queen of hearts—tucked up his sleeve.

In fascination, she watched as he slapped down his cards and heard the roar of the losers. In a blustery display of dismay, the unfortunate players continued their good-natured cursing as the bearded young man gathered up the pile of gold coins cast into the center of the table.

As the men lifted their mugs ready to drown their misfortune in another round of drink before they began again, Sofonisba leaned forward and squinted but couldn't quite see all the winning cards. She lifted her head and caught sight of the man regarding her. But instead of appearing guilty, he only shrugged. Then his mouth slowly tilted up, and it seemed he secretly telegraphed a message, thanking her for her unwitting participation in his good fortune.

Sofonisba couldn't confirm nor deny if the man had changed out his card for the better one. Not knowing if he was a swindler or a thief, despite herself, she smiled back.

Chapter 8

The Painter and the Pirate

*A*t the end of the meal, after Amilcare finished his tankard of ale, he rose from the table and, with a stern face, wagged a finger at Sofonisba and said, "Now it's off to your room you go. I'll stay here for another hour... I have a mind to play a hand of cards with the other gents."

Sofonisba did as she was told and removed herself from the common room, solemnly swearing to her father she'd not budge from her chambers. But once in her room, seeing the light of the moon pouring through her open bedroom window, she felt a familiar urge to wander and bask in its silvery glow. Ever since she was a young girl, she couldn't help herself and often defied her parents, sneaking out of the family home and rambling around in the gardens at night, letting her imagination roam.

When she heard a low roar issuing up through the floorboards, and recognized her father's voice among the others, she thought *He will never even know I'm gone and really, what harm could there be? It is such a sleepy little town, after all. Who would be the wiser if I step out for half an hour?*

To ensure anonymity, Sofonisba picked up the shawl she'd left on the back of the chair and wrapped it around her head and shoulders. Then cautiously, she opened the door and stealthily glanced down the hall. Seeing the coast was clear, she eased out into the open and crept down the stairs, and edged past the main room. She hesitated only slightly when she saw the proprietor at the opposite end of the hall bearing a tray filled with empty bowls and plates. Before he looked up to see her poised on the threshold, she slipped out the door and into the warm night.

Once free of the inn, she let the shawl drop. Dressed in long sleeves and a modest high collar, no one would have taken her for anything but a nobleman's daughter. But not wanting to be accosted, she quickly crossed the piazza and slipped into the shadows. There she walked along the wall where she had stood earlier in the day after descending from the carriage.

Sofonisba trailed her hand along the rocky surface, which retained the warmth of the day, and breathed in the tangy aroma of jasmine and sage. The wall was a sturdy thing, craftily built and structurally sound. Sofonisba wondered who had been the first Etruscan to construct and lay the first block. Surely, he had a family, a wife and children. Had he studied under his father to become a master mason and architect? Had he passed his trade on to his sons?

Into the balmy air, as the night birds swooped in the skies above her, she said aloud the word *Etruria* drawing out all the syllables. There was something romantic and musical about the sound. Almost as if she were chanting a spell to summon the spirits of those who had once lived here.

Her head was full of romantic imaginings of a long-lost civilization, and she believed she could almost hear the voices of the ancient Etruscans. In her mind's eye, she envisioned elegantly coiffured and gold-adorned women calling to one another across the square. Joining them in the piazza were rosy-faced children playing hoops in the streets and bearded architects walking together, their heads bent, discussing the complex design of Porsena's tomb they would soon begin to build.

Focused on her thoughts, when she heard the scrape of a man's boot upon the stone path advancing toward her, she didn't give it much notice. But as the footsteps grew closer, she abruptly returned to her senses. Glancing about, she looked for a place to hide, but seeing none, she realized she was now caught in a trap of her own making. All at once, she regretted not heeding her father's warnings.

She instantly pulled up the shawl to shield her face and melted farther into the blue half-light, flattening herself against the wall, hoping to remain undetected. Sofonisba closed her eyes and, with all her being, hoped the quickly advancing man would veer off in another direction. It seemed her prayers were answered when the footsteps slowed, and a cloud shooed on by a gust of warm air—like an unleashed wraith from a grave—cloaked her in darkness.

But, to her chagrin, the feckless cloud scuttled past, and her position on the wall was fully illuminated. The masculine steps picked up again and came to a halt just a few feet away. She lifted her head tentatively, and with a fair amount of consternation, saw it was the man from the tavern, carrying a large bundle. By the way his jaw sagged, it seemed her presence on the path had caught him off guard as well.

Sofonisba sensed his agitation as they considered one another solemnly. Perhaps the cocky young man was now hesitant and leery because he hadn't intended to be caught roaming the town's environs in the middle of the night. She watched as he narrowed his eyes and looked at her closely. It didn't take more than a second before his dark eyes sparkled in the moonlight.

In a burst of recognition, he exclaimed, "Signorina! You are the last person I expected to see here tonight. Even with the veil covering your face, I'd recognize you anywhere." He removed the large sack, which was flung over his broad shoulders, and set it down on the ground. "What are you doing here?"

"I... I..." she stammered helplessly. Caught in such an unseemly position—a young woman alone in the dark—she wondered what the man must think of her.

He regained his composure and said, "It is a happy surprise for me to encounter such a lovely apparition." Then, pointing to his swarthy face, he added, "But maybe not for you! Who would want to meet this face in the dead of night? I'm sure it would give anyone a scare. They say there are thieves and dishonorable men who roam these parts in the dead of night. We aren't too far off from the coast—just imagine... I could be a Barbary pirate."

The man indicated a blade attached to his belt, which glinted in the dusky light. "I have a sack of bounty and a knife. If I were you, I'd be more than just a little afraid."

When she said nothing, the dark-haired man leaned against the wall and crossed his arms. As he intently observed her, the scarf that covered her head was caught by a soft waft of air and fell to her shoulders, revealing the ivory complexion of her face.

He raised an eyebrow. "Well, now! Aren't you a lovely sight, standing here in the gloom of night. Almost ethereal. After all is said and done, perhaps I should be the one to be afraid. They also say the walls of this town are haunted by the ghost of a dead king! Tell me... are you a meandering phantom come to take my very soul for the dark deeds I hide in my heart... or the looted goods within my satchel?"

She assessed the man; then, seeing an impish light in his eyes, she knew he was teasing her. In the time it takes for a star to shoot across the sky, her fears dissipated.

Matching his playful inflection, she replied, "Signore, I am no such thing! I can assure you I am flesh and bone. Ghost, indeed!"

Despite her bravado, with a nervous little laugh, she glanced around. Satisfied no filmy specters were floating behind her, she added, "Do you take me for a fool?"

He made a slight bow in deference to her words. "I can see that you are no man's fool, signorina. I could tell the first moment I saw you. You have the look of an intelligent woman. In fact, your eyes are so marvelous and full of promise, I believe I could lose myself in them. How could I—"

With a scoff, she interrupted him. "I'm not afraid of your talk of ghosts and the restless spirits of the dead... or that blade attached to your belt. No, on the contrary, I'm warier of your glib tongue, signore. You seem to be quite a charmer as well as a teller of tall tales. I see how you embellish your words to play upon the sentiments of an innocent female. But, beware... I'm not so gullible."

"Ah! Touché! But there is no need to fear me, signorina. I may be a gentleman with a"—he raised an eyebrow and gave a little cough—"let's call it a colorful past, but still, I am an honorable one."

"So, you are a principled thief with a gift for flattery?"

He raised his eyebrow. "What makes you think I am a thief?"

She gave him a knowing look, glanced down at the sack on the ground, and said, "Didn't you just tell me you carry loot in your bag?"

With a dismissive gesture, he said, "Just a figure of speech, signorina.

The satchel is not proof I've stolen anything. I'm a traveler on a journey..." Nudging the bag with his booted foot, he said, "Inside, you will find all the worldly possessions I own."

"So... if I were to peek inside, I'd see no stolen goods, porcelain teapots, or silver trays? Just gold coins you purloined from the other gamblers?" she asked coyly.

He looked at her in mock offense. "Signorina! Why would you ever think that?"

"Earlier, when you held up your playing cards, I took stock of your hand, and I saw you had another tucked up your sleeve. In fact, I think you wanted me to see you were a charlatan."

"Ah... well, that was our little secret, no? But to be fair... I only help my fate when absolutely necessary." He tapped his head with his finger and added, "I already have the skills, finesse, and patience to win any game, but if necessary I help lady luck along." When she tilted her head dubiously, he quickly added, "Let's just say the card up my sleeve was there only as a last resort. But tonight that wasn't necessary."

Indicating the satchel again, he added, "No, inside my bag you will find a clean shirt and the winnings from tonight's game won fair and square. I confess I haven't won such a grand sum of money in such a long time. So perhaps it is you, after all, who brings good fortune to me." He glanced down at the valley. "Or maybe my good luck is actually due to a ghost," he said in a mysterious tone. "This place is filled with the spirits of rich and benevolent rulers."

"There you go again, speaking of phantoms..." Leaning over, she said in a conspiratorial whisper, "But I have to agree with you there. The ghosts are amongst us tonight. I confess, I too was just conjuring up the image of Porsena!"

"Porsena, indeed!" The man eyed her keenly, clearly impressed. "How does a foreigner to these parts know anything about him?" When she didn't reply, he asked, "Where are you from, signorina? What are you doing here in the deep of night, wandering about the city of the Etruscans? Are you running away from something... or someone? Oh, be still my heart... Dare I hope you have broken someone's heart and are running away..."

"No, on the contrary," she said lightly, "I'm running toward something."

"And what might that be?"

"I'm just starting out on my journey to see the world. I'm a painter from Cremona on her way to Rome to study."

The man whistled softly. "Signorina, you are full of surprises!"

She tilted her head playfully. "I surprise myself sometimes. But ever since I was a little girl, all I ever wanted to do was paint. Oh, to a gambler such as yourself, it may sound quite tame and inconsequential. But I believe my brush and talent will transport me to far-off places... Maybe I'll paint for kings and noblemen."

Like him, she surveyed the valley below, then exclaimed, *"Santo Cielo!* I think I would have made a wonderful Etruscan woman. Did you know they were painters too? In my opinion, the Etruscans were far more broad-minded than our society today. I think if only..." Seeing him eyeing her intently, she stuttered to a stop. Then, securing a loose strand of hair that blew about her face in the soft breeze, she added, "Forgive me if what I say bores you... I tend to ramble on."

"On the contrary, when you talk, your passion shines through and illuminates your face. Beatrice has nothing to teach you! I believe the man who falls in love with you, signorina, will have his hands full."

"Oh, but I don't wish to marry," she exclaimed. "Well, at least not for a long, long time. At the moment, that would ruin all my plans."

"Interesting," he replied. "A girl with schemes that do not involve matrimony. Does your father not wish to marry you off to a rich suitor? How old are you? A ripe marriageable age, I should imagine."

"I am old enough," she said evasively. "How old are you?"

"I am twenty."

She studied his face for a moment. "Hmmm... that makes me older than you. I should have thought you to be the older one. You have the look of someone who knows exactly what he wants and where he is going—you speak with such bravado and assurance."

The man shrugged. "Age is inconsequential. I'm an old soul, probably older than you in many ways. I imagine you've lived a sheltered life."

"Perhaps," she said, thinking about her sisters who for years had been her only companions and the hours she had spent with her nose in a book. "But now I hope to change that. So for the moment, becoming a bride is the furthest thing from my father's or my mind."

"Truly, you are a most unusual girl. And how will you accomplish this—become a woman of the world, I mean—without becoming a bride?"

"As I said, I am on my way to Rome—"

"Yes, you did mention that earlier. And what are your plans after you arrive?"

"I'm going there to further my painting studies, make connections, and—"

"It isn't an activity that most women would desire," he interjected. "Being a painter, I mean."

"I am not *most* women."

"So I am quickly discovering," he said.

"It is not that I believe other women cannot learn things," said Sofonisba seriously. "I have met many intelligent females. It is just an unfortunate fact most women are not encouraged to do so. They are taught from the cradle not to pursue their own interests but rather think only of marriage and acquiring a husband. I have been fortunate to have parents who think otherwise."

"What about a family?" he inquired. "Do you not wish to have a husband and children?"

"Babes at my breast to distract me and a husband who would control my fortunes and decide when and whether I should be allowed to paint? Not at the moment, thank you! I'll be content to be a wonderful aunt to my sisters' children. I'm sure they will have a great many between the lot of them. No, I shall never want for familial connections."

The man relaxed against the stone wall, clearly enjoying their debate.

"And what will you do for companionship? Do you not fear growing old with no one to love?"

She glanced away, recalling what she had left in Cremona, and remained silent.

"Signorina?"

"Yes," she said, returning her gaze to his.

"Compliments to you. I think it takes great bravery... and confidence to strike out and live an independent life. Remember, signorina... those who reach for the stars have the most extraordinary experiences."

"I couldn't agree more," she said.

Sofonisba observed the man thoughtfully assessing her. By the look in his eyes, he made her feel like she had the lithest of figures and prettiest of features. But more than that, he hadn't been put off by her adventuresome spirit or her unbridled curiosity. Listening to his words of praise, she realized he applauded her vision and her courage.

She tilted her head. "And what about you?"

"What about me?"

"You seem a dashing, handsome sort. Why haven't you been drawn into some lady's arms by now, seduced by her charms?"

He raised an eyebrow, then laughed. "I'm coming to learn you say the most unusual things. You keep me on my toes, wondering what will fall out of that lovely mouth of yours."

"You are dodging the question."

He smiled at her directness, then shrugged. "There have been a few..."

"A few? How many are a few?"

"Oh, well now..." He gave her a sheepish look. "Having just met you, they all seem to pale in comparison. Simpering fools, all of them, lacking intelligence, pride, and ambition."

She raised a skeptical eyebrow. "Surely some woman has captured your heart."

"Well, when I was sixteen..."

"Yes," she urged.

He hesitated a moment more. "I'm not sure if it is in my best interest to talk of previous dalliances... seeing as we have just met."

When she only smirked, he smiled and said, "Her name was Chiara Nardella. She was a local girl from Rome."

"From Rome! She must have been quite sophisticated."

He shook his head a little sorrowfully and she laughed. "Ah, so she had other charms that enticed you."

"We spent a summer together. Her mother made the best bread soup... and..."

"And?"

"Let's just say she turned my head for a season until I really fell madly in love."

"Ah! So you couldn't outrun Cupid and his arrow... It pierced that gambling heart of yours, *ehi*! And what was *her* name?"

"Circe," he said with a wink.

"Circe? Do you mean Odysseus's Circe?" she asked enthralled.

"Yes, Circe, the sea goddess."

"Now, you certainly have caught my attention... Go on."

"You see, Chiara wasn't too happy that I was poor as Job's skinny red rooster. So, to earn money, I took a job on a frigate bound for the East African coast... and that is where I lost my heart to the sea."

"Ah, so it was the sea nymph who finally enchanted you!"

"Yes," he agreed. "When she sings and casts her net, one cannot but heed the call and become entangled in her golden chains." He turned to look at her. "But now, if you were to press me, I'd have to admit Circe's charms are starting to fade as I stand here with a girl whose eyes are big and bright, wishing to flaunt convention. I believe I could lose myself in those eyes and..."

"And..." she whispered.

They looked at one another for a moment and slowly he said, "And that you could unlock the secrets of my soul if you tried."

Sofonisba tilted her head and let out a snort. "Signore, you, sir, were born a flatterer. We have only just met... How could you know that!"

"As I said, I am an old soul and an astute judge of character... And listening to you talk here on this moonlit path... You, signorina, are starting to make me think you too sing a siren's call."

She laughed and then peered up at the stars. At first, when she had seen the man approaching her in the dark just an hour before, she had been afraid. But now it seemed they were good friends who had known one another for years. Contentedly, they leaned against the wall side by side. All around them, an orchestra of nocturnal insects played, occasionally interrupted by a hooting owl calling to its mate in the nearby wood.

A warm breeze picked up, and it seemed the ghost of Porsena was indeed drawing them closer. Caught in the magic, she let her thoughts drift back to mysterious burial sites and imagined a procession of Etruscans snaking its way up the mountain's steep incline, baring the body of Porsena. Weeping women held torches, and their stoic husbands carried chests filled with precious objects, gold, and jewels. At the summit, the point closest to God, they entered the tomb, navigating the maze to the king's final resting place with the priests intoning prayers.

Sighing softly, imagining the scene, Sofonisba said to the man, "Wouldn't it be wonderful to find Porsena's labyrinth?"

"*Sì*, that it would," came his whispered reply.

She turned to face him squarely. "What do you believe? Is this all just a magnificent legend? Or do you actually think it will be found?"

"It is entirely possible," he replied. "They say beneath our feet are miles of catacombs filled with the tombs of princes and kings, and inside they hold untold secrets and riches beyond our wildest dreams." He shrugged noncommittally. "But... Porsena and his gold still remain a well-kept mystery. I've personally scouted the ravines and valleys from here to Orvieto, hoping I might be so lucky to discover the secrets of a king..."

"So, not only are you a gambler... you are a treasure hunter, too!" she exclaimed. "And what would you do should you find the pot of gold?"

"With Porsena's coins, I'd purchase a fine ship, acquire a brave crew, and be the captain of my own destiny."

"And where would you go?"

"Ever since my maiden voyage, I've longed to find adventure and sail into foreign ports and see things I've never seen before. I'd go to places where spices perfume the air and monkeys climb in trees. I want to hear people speak in other tongues who live their lives differently from mine."

He gazed out over the dark horizon and said, "There is nothing more liberating and exhilarating than living life on the sea."

"I am beginning to understand this feeling," Sofonisba agreed. "I've just begun my travels, but already I too desire to sail to the point of no return, to the golden line where the sun touches water to venture to places I've never been before."

"*Esatto*," he responded. "I never watch a ship sailing out of a harbor and down a channel, or look up at a gull soaring over a sandbar, without wishing I was on board. It is my fondest desire to fly as they do into the heart of the storm."

Sofonisba was pleased with his answer. She thought he'd make an excellent sea captain, and in her mind's eye, she could see him standing proudly on the deck of a ship as the vessel rocked to and fro from the rolling waves beneath him.

"Circe indeed has cast her spell upon you..." she murmured.

"Yes, she has. It is my greatest desire to sail off to find her." He gave her a roguish wink. "That and become a rich, rich man."

Eyeing the bag lying at his feet, she said slyly, "Perhaps it is really a pirate's life you yearn for after all." When she saw his mischievous grin, she added, "And when you return from Circe's arms, do you also desire to have a maiden in every port of call... find another willing Chiara? Is this what brings you out in the middle of the night? If that be the case, I believe the innkeeper's daughter might just fancy you!"

He smirked. "Signorina, such an imagination! If your paintings are half as colorful as your remarks, you will become an outstanding and memorable artist. Then again," he said, "maybe I am best suited, as you say, to be a corsair and live a life of danger. I'll wear a turban and grow a longer beard and take my riches wherever I can. I'll sail away and be the terror of the seven seas. They will call me The Black Corsair and—"

"Yes, with those swarthy dark looks, you could pass for one!"

"A life of danger and adventure it will be then," he said with a swagger.

"I'll paint your portrait, Signor Black Corsair, and you can hang it in your galley for all to see what a fierce and mighty pirate you are."

"And will you join me one day on my fine ship and sail with me to far-off Zanzibar?"

She looked at him momentarily, intrigued by the idea. Then she shook her head. "No, our worlds are about to take different turns. I'll leave you to your boats and masts, your foreign ports of call. You can make your fortune upon the sea with sacks of spices and curries, and I will make mine standing upon the solid ground with a palette and a brush."

"It seems, although we are different, we are also very similar."

"How so?" she asked. "Didn't I just say we are destined to live completely different lives—you on the sea and I on the land?"

"You did, signorina. Who knows where the sea will end and where my ship will take me, or where your brush will transport you. But we are cut from similar cloth—we both believe in setting our courses for the unknown. Let us make a pact here and now to remain true to our goals and trust in God that he will see us through the storms ahead."

"To our destinies," she agreed. "Let us follow our hearts where they lead, and may the fates be kind. Calm sailing for both of us!"

Comfortable in the knowledge they were two strangers who would never meet again, a pleasant quiet fell over them. After a moment, he began to sing a song under his breath.

You are like the sea, Sweet Love
You are always there for me
You lie before me like a land of dreams
so various, so beautiful, so new.
Like the ocean that engulfs my senses
you've never made promises,
but you've always kept them.
And like the gently rocking waves
your arms are a perfect place

to which I'd return and stay forever.
Restore, restore my heart again
with your fair and lovely eyes.

She was enchanted by the song and the night, and by the man beside her. But her reverie was broken by the sound of her name piercing the night air. "Sofonisba! Where are you, daughter? Come back to the inn at once."

With wide eyes, she glanced around. "It's my father. He can't find me here with you."

"So, your name is Sofonisba!" the man said. "Once again... a most atypical girl with a most surprising name!"

"Yes. I'm Sofonisba descended from a Carthaginian princess," she responded proudly.

"Why am I not surprised! I dare say your name suits you," he said. "I believe you will live up to it and be quite famous one day."

Once again, Amilcare's voice floated out to them from the piazza. "Signorina Anguissola! Answer me, daughter!"

Urgently, she implored the man beside her, "Promise me you will say nothing. It must be as if we never met."

"Aye, Sofonisba, my princess. I pledge my word to you... I will be a loyal subject and not tell a soul of our meeting here tonight. Your honor and your secrets are safe with me."

She turned to go but stopped at the light touch of his hand on her sleeve. "We may never meet again, signorina, but it seems we had an appointment with destiny here this evening." Touching the pocket of his vest, he added, "I will always carry a pleasant thought of you right here, next to my heart."

Even if he had a golden tongue and spun a fine thread of compliments, Sofonisba believed she, too, would never forget this meeting.

"With great respect, Signorina Anguissola, may I kiss your hand?"

She eyed him earnestly. His song, and the romantic notion of finding Porsena's gold, were filling her head again—or was it something she saw once again in his eyes? Boldly, she raised her hand and he gently and courteously kissed it.

Sofonisba heard Amilcare's voice growing closer. "Really, I must go. My father..."

She attempted to pull back her hand, but before she could, he turned her palm up and pressed a metal disk into it. Then, wrapping her fingers around it, he said, "Take this with you on your journey. It will bring you good luck. Think of me and the pledge we made tonight—to follow our hearts and ambitions. Remember... we dreamers live very long lives."

"And why is that?" she asked.

"Because we have no time for death... We are too busy weaving new plans and desiring too many things. So, even though we take great risks, it is easy to side-step the grim reaper, requesting he kindly come back later as we are currently too busy to follow him into his lair."

"All right, Signor Black Corsair. I promise I'll continue dreaming. As Homer says in the Iliad: Dreams are sent by the gods—they are the doorway to truth. I will listen to them and keep moving forward—"

"Good girl," he said, shaking his head in admiration. "If only I was as well read as you. Now, go! If you keep looking at me like that, with those marvelous eyes, I fear you will steal my heart—perhaps you already have. I'll follow your career with interest, Signorina Anguissola—and hope someday to meet you again."

He leaned down and whispered into her ear, "And like the gently rocking waves, your arms are a perfect place to which I'd return and stay forever..."

Lost in his eyes, she swayed toward him, then hearing footsteps crunching on the gravel walkway, she looked over his shoulder and saw her father rounding the corner. She slipped the medallion into her pocket then hastily brushed past the man. Anxiously, she glanced over her shoulder but saw her pirate had disappeared. By the way, a low-hanging juniper branch swung crazily, and hearing the whispering sound of the tall grasses on the other side of the wall, she knew he had made his escape.

Sofonisba picked up her skirts and hurried down the trail until she met Amilcare. The worry on his face melted into relief, and she immediately apologized, promising she'd never do such a thing again. Her father peered at her skeptically. Then, taking her protectively by the arm, he shepherded her back to the inn, chastising her all the way.

In the safe confines of her room, Sofonisba crossed to the open window. The lopsided moon hung low in the sky, barely kissing the horizon. Far down the hill, a mist was rising and she shivered. The night seemed an emptier place than it had a few hours before. It had taken only a stolen moment in the company of a stranger to stir her senses and make her feel alive. She wondered if she would meet Signor...

With a start, she realized, *I don't even know the man's name!*

Sofonisba set the candle on the ledge and fished out the souvenir the young man had pressed into her palm. It was an ancient token, abnormally shaped and worn. She ran her thumb over the surface and felt the raised indentations. Curious, she held the piece closer to the taper and saw it was a gold coin, and in the center was the profile of a man. Around his head were inscribed the words: *Rex Porsena.*

Where did the gold piece come from?

She leaned over the edge of the window frame and scrutinized the dark hillside. It was an intriguing and delicious thought to imagine the mysterious stranger had lied about finding the famous labyrinth and that he was indeed a tomb raider!

What did she know about him, really, except he was a cunning gambler and a flatterer who sang a romantic song? But she also knew, like her, he craved adventure and wanted to shake off the cloak of conventionality. They were alike in many ways. If he had absconded with a sack of pilfered gold, she wished him well and hoped with Porsena's riches he'd buy a hundred vessels and sail off on a fantastic quest—just as she was about to do.

For whatever reason, there on the moonlit wall with Porsena's valley stretching out below them—the past and the present, mystery and magic—a painter and a pirate had been brought together.

Into the night, she whispered, "Whoever you are Signor Black Corsair... Until we meet again."

Chapter 9

Hidden Treasures

*A*lthough they had parted ways, swearing a pact to follow their individual paths, when Sofonisba entered the dining room the next morning to break the fast, she couldn't help but look around expectantly, hoping to catch a glimpse of her mysterious pirate. She knew she should be relieved when she didn't see him; it was for the best.

Still, when Sofonisba heard a burst of masculine voices that issued from the far corner of the common room, she lifted her head swiftly, hoping to catch sight of a man with unruly hair holding up his cards for her approval.

But there was no sign of the gentleman.

When the innkeeper's daughter set before them bowls of porridge, Sofonisba listlessly swallowed the tepid contents and drank the tankard of honey mead without tasting it. Amilcare, too, seemed abnormally taciturn this morning and didn't spoon up his breakfast with his usual zealous enjoyment. With a grimace, he pushed his dish aside, then placed a hand upon his temple and massaged it gently.

"Are you quite all right, Father?" Sofonisba asked.

Amilcare glanced up, rolled his shoulders, and placed a hand to the lower part of his spine. "I confess to be feeling the effects of travel. I think it would be good to remain here a day or two more to rest up."

When the innkeeper's daughter passed their table, he motioned for her to bring them a restorative tisane. Sofonisba looked at him and shook her head in amusement. She suspected her father's real motives for remaining in town had nothing to do with his back pains. Instead, it had more to do with having imbibed a bit too much strong alcohol after a long night of playing cards. She also believed, having won a few rounds and pocketed a purse of gold coins, Amilcare wanted to have another go of it later that night.

After breakfast, her father, still looking a bit peaked, excused himself and retired to his room. Left to her own devices, with nothing better to do, Sofonisba accepted the invitation of the innkeeper's daughter to walk the trails that zigzagged down the hills, retracing the steps of the Etruscans. Away from the tavern, the girl's disposition turned sunnier, and when she grew more light-hearted, Sofonisba confirmed she was indeed quite pretty.

She discovered the girl's name was Clarice, and as Sofonisba had surmised, the girl had suffered a tragic love story, having been jilted by the baker's son, who threw her over for the seamstress's daughter. Every now and then, Sofonisba interjected a sympathetic comment in the girl's ongoing discourse. It seemed to her no love was too great or too small to cause pain or distress—be you Helen of Troy or a poor serving wench.

As the two girls wandered through the grassy fields, inspired by thoughts of finding Etruscan treasure, Sofonisba scoured the ground, hoping to see lost coins of a previous empire glistening in the sun. But, several hours later, she despaired of finding anything other than shards of pottery. But who could tell if they were artifacts or simply broken crockery thrown out by the innkeeper's wife?

That was until Clarice led her to a crop of trees farther down in the valley. As they rested by a small stream, the toe of her shoe encountered something hard sticking out of the earth. Taking a stick, Sofonisba dug a little deeper until she uncovered a small piece of tarnished metal. With a cry of delight, she picked it up, brushed off the dirt, and saw that she held in her hand a small bronze boat with animals that lined the rim. At the prow was an elongated figure of a man.

When she showed it to Clarice, the girl said off-handedly, "Those old things? They have no value—they are just pieces of rubbish you find all over the place."

But to Sofonisba, who knew better, it was precious beyond comparison. It was proof an ancient civilization had existed, and somewhere in these hills, more treasures lay waiting to be discovered. But aside from its historical value, it also reminded her of the man she had met the night before. Back in her room, she wrapped her Etruscan sea captain in a lace handkerchief and tucked it safely into her luggage.

A few days later, Sofonisba found herself seated in the carriage next to her father. He seemed in high spirits after having rested his back and adding more coins to his purse. She imagined it was difficult to bid adieu to the possibility of increasing his earnings further. Still, once they set off, with his winnings safely stowed under his seat, Amilcare's lively chatter resumed, and his thoughts realigned to their current mission.

"By evening, we will enter the gates of Rome and find our lodgings in the city's center. I spoke to Cardinal Damiani, and he was most helpful in securing a place just a few steps away from the Pantheon... It is a marvelous temple the Romans built to pay tribute to their gods. I visited it once... Listen, I must tell you about the time..."

As they descended the rutted road that led from the town to the plains below, bouncing up and down in the rickety transport, Sofonisba idly listened to her father's descriptions of fountains and aqueducts and a young man's antics in the Eternal City. She smiled at the right places in his story, but as he continued talking, her thoughts began to drift.

When the wheels hit a particularly rough spot in the road, she was shaken so violently her teeth rattled. Sofonisba glanced over at her father to see if he was all right and saw that he had removed his jacket and now seemed less verbose due to the rising heat inside the carriage. After a spell, the highway evened out, and she relaxed and settled back against the seat. She gazed out at the sun-dappled fields of grain and up at the hawks that soared on the drafts of air high in the sky. In the distance, she could make out a group of peasants clustered about in the shade of a tree, finding relief from the high heat of the day.

Hearing a low-rumbling snore, Sofonisba looked back at her father and saw him slumped in the corner with his hat pulled over his face. From the noise he was making, she could tell he would be out for quite a while, sleeping off the effects of yet another long night with a tankard of ale in one hand and cards in another. She waited a moment more then, with her eyes still pinned on his figure, she surreptitiously reached into her pocket and pulled out the coin the young stranger had given her.

Despite a small bit of misgiving, Sofonisba hadn't mentioned anything about her secret tryst to her father; it seemed too personal a moment to share with someone else. Also, she didn't want to further complicate matters by having to explain to whom she had been in conversation with for more than an hour. Besides, she didn't even know the man's name. How would it appear to her father?

In the light of day, it seemed their meeting had never happened, and she wondered if she had dreamt the whole thing. Perhaps the man hadn't really existed at all. Instead, he had been a spirit of an Etruscan sailor sent by Porsena to enchant and beguile her. But touching the coin and turning it over between her fingers reminded her that the encounter had happened.

She replaced the coin inside her pocket, picked up her sketchbook, and began filling the page with images of an ambitious young man standing on the deck of a ship. Sometimes she focused on the shape of his lips, sometimes just his eyes with a lock of hair brushing his temple. But the version she liked the best was of the man wearing a jewel-encrusted crown, holding up a gold coin. By the teasing expression on his face, it wasn't entirely clear if he was offering or taking the medallion. She thought her drawing was quite amusing... Was he a benefactor or was he a thief?

She couldn't explain her feelings or why the man continued to fill her thoughts. He was still a bit of an enigma. Strange how she could feel this way when just a short while ago she had harbored such warm regards for Signor Campi. With a sigh, Sofonisba turned over the page to begin a new sketch but stopped when she heard her father exclaim, "Look! There! We are approaching the northern gates of the city."

Amilcare was now sitting upright. Excitedly he brushed back some of his hair that stuck up on end, all the while, his attention riveted on the horizon. Curious, Sofonisba pushed back the drape that covered the window. In the distance, she could see the outline of a multitude of domes and bell towers. It was a busy, impressive spectacle, and as they drew nearer, the traffic on the road increased, and their progress slowed.

Keenly she observed the frenetic scene full of energy, color, and noise. There were proud men on horseback in colorful military garb, weary pilgrims walking on foot in tattered rags, farmers in leather britches sitting on top of wagons loaded with vegetables and cages of squawking chickens, and others with barrels and bags of grain.

As they passed through the massive Porta Pia gate into the city, Sofonisba noted Rome's outer wall, unlike the one in Chiusi, was constructed of slickly pieced together stones. Still, as in the small hill town she had just departed, the mere sight of it was enough to conjure thoughts of previous generations. When the carriage crossed through Piazza del Popolo and ventured down a wide boulevard, everywhere she looked, old mingled with new. Third-century crumbling cornices and dilapidated Corinthian columns competed with the refined symmetry of well-placed, newly built arches and loggias by modern master architects like Bramante and Sangallo.

With so much to take in, the hubbub only heightened Sofonisba's exhilaration, and her heart hammered in her chest. This was Michelangelo's Rome! To breathe the air where such innovation and new ideas were coming to life once again was a heady experience to the young girl from Cremona. She closed her sketchbook and resolved to put aside daydreams of pirates and moonlit talks for safekeeping deep within her heart like hidden treasure. As she had promised the stranger, she turned her thoughts once again to her future.

"Soon, my dear girl," said her father, "you will be walking in the steps of Michelangelo and Raffaello. We will visit Saint Peter's Basilica and the Vatican Palace, where you will see their work." He patted Sofonisba's hand and added, "In no time at all, I will find you a new teacher and you will begin your brilliant career."

Chapter 10

The Source of Inspiration

*T*rue to his word, after making inquiries in prominent circles, Amilcare secured an apprenticeship for Sofonisba with the Master Painter Pierentino Mannino. The elderly artist's eyesight was not what it once was, and he needed assistance with mixing his paints and fulfilling some minor commissions. At first, Mannino had been skeptical about taking on Sofonisba as his pupil, but he quickly warmed to the idea when Amilcare sweetened the proposition by increasing what he was willing to pay to ensure Sofonisba's apprenticeship.

When she had objected, her father reassured her. "Listen, my dear, how many times do I have to repeat myself? This is the best investment I'll ever make... and much better than paying a dowry!"

Filled with new energy to hold up her end of the bargain, Sofonisba found herself in the capable, if not uninspired, hands of her new Roman tutor. She diligently applied herself and learned as much as she could in her new painting master's studio, along with the other young male apprentices who believed themselves to be the next Titian or Bronzino. As before in the studio of Signor Campi, it took a few weeks, but gradually she earned the other gentlemen painters' respect. Once they witnessed firsthand what she was capable of producing, however, they doffed their feathered caps and granted her a wide berth.

She was pleased to garner acclaim amongst her peers and rise in their estimation. If not from the nearly blind Mannino himself, she picked up new techniques and more modern styles by observing her peers. Still, Sofonisba's real education began as soon as she left Pierentino's apartments in the artist quarters along the Tiber a short distance from the Vatican apartments and Sant'Angelo. Given the location of Mannino's home, and despite its proximity to the pope's quarters and St. Peter's Basilica, it was still unsafe for educated and comely females to be allowed to wander freely. So, in her father's company, she ventured out to visit the ruins and temples—the forum and the pantheon.

As Sofonisba strolled about on Amilcare's arm, she noted with interest the old stones that held marvelous pagan tales. But she was also aware of the frenetic activity that had taken over the city. Rome was alive with construction, and rapidly the disintegrating Roman buildings were being stripped and disassembled to create new facades and churches. Artists, such as herself, arrived daily from all parts of Italy to learn from the ancients and be taught by contemporary masters. They came to study, and they stayed, hired by the pope to glorify the Holy Spirit. They painted frescos, and stuccoed walls with legions of colorful angels and saintly Madonnas, and each new work was a delight to behold.

But despite the artistic frenzy, as fascinating as it was, Sofonisba, being a portrait artist, found her true inspiration in the faces of Rome's people. Everywhere she turned, it seemed she met a visage that had a particular history. From high foreheads to lush, full lips, blue and smokey dark eyes—the features and expressions of those she encountered captured her imagination. So vast and varied were the Romans—after all, they were a collection of various races. Some were direct descendants of Porsena's people, and others could trace their lineage to the Sabines. Still, others had floated into the city from exotic places in Africa and Macedonia, and others had been introduced when the Huns and the Goths invaded and sacked the city.

There was no better place to observe the varied emotions, body language, and facial features than in Rome's open-air markets. As the mistress of their Roman household, it was Sofonisba's duty to shop for Antonella, their cook, and bring back ingredients for their evening meal. Each morning as the sun peeked over St. Peter's Basilica, which was currently under construction, she walked in her father's company to the Campo de' Fiori. There they meandered through the crowded stalls picking out vegetables, grains, and meats. Often she'd hold up a ripe plum, and Amilcare would incline his head in approval, and she would add it to her basket. But, more often than not, her father's attention was distracted by a passing neighbor, leaving Sofonisba to her own devices.

She didn't mind when this happened and was content to continue on through the flower stalls, where she inhaled the aroma of autumn blooms. She often stopped in the pretense of smelling a blossom only to note with interest the old women and their age-worn faces sitting on top of overturned crates and gossiping. The creases on their faces and the profoundly etched valleys around their lips made Sofonisba believe the women had experienced many seasons of joys and sorrows.

"Sofonisba! Wait up. Don't be wandering off on your own!"

At the sound of her name, she replied to her father, "The hour is growing late, and I must be getting on to Signor Mannino. If you are entirely finished with your chattering, follow me to the next street where the fishmongers are."

Good-naturedly, Amilcare complied, taking the more cumbersome packages from her hands. Keeping pace, they crossed the piazza. Wrinkling her nose as they approached the far end, Sofonisba could already detect the pungent odors of squids, anchovies, and salted *baccala* that filled the baskets of the fishermen. Entering the stalls, protected by the warm sun by an overhead canvas, she stepped carefully as the pavement was unusually wet and slick from the frequent dousing of the fish with buckets of water. The din of voices coming from the men hawking their wares echoed in the narrow alleyway, creating a confusing ruckus.

She eased her way through the crowd but stopped at the sight of a man who held up eels for his customer's inspection. She smiled and thought, *If the man only knew I am named after that creature.*

Absently she shook her head, rejecting the slithery specimen and pointing instead to a basket filled with large red prawns. She knew her father had a liking for them, and when Amilcare saw the lot, he immediately set about bartering with the man.

Sofonisba left her father to his negotiations and peered across the aisle where she noticed a small pudgy boy holding on to a woman's skirts.

When the toddler grew bored listening to his mother haggle with the fisherman over the price of cod and sardines, he turned and shyly looked at her. The sight of him reminded Sofonisba of Asdrubale, and without thinking, she made a face at him as she would have done if it had actually been her brother. Immediately the young tyke hid his face again in his mother's skirts.

Annoyed by her young son tugging on her dress, the mother impatiently reached around and grabbed the child's hand and pulled him in front of her, admonishing him not to touch anything. There, his little peepers came face to face with a table full of wiggling crayfish. The boy glanced up at his mother, but seeing she was paying him no heed, returned his attention to the tiny, seemingly innocuous waving claws.

Thinking this would make a very amusing picture to send to her little brother, Sofonisba set down her basket of vegetables and herbs and drew out her sketchbook and crayon. With deft strokes, she captured the boy's enraptured face. Then, to her delight and the boy's mother's horror, before anyone could stop him, the little man's plump hand ventured an inch too far, and one of the crabs grabbed hold of his finger.

"Woooooaahhh!"

The sound of the boy's howl escalated around them. The mother, seeing her son's puckered face, jerked him toward her, attempting to loosen the crayfish's stinging pincers. But once attached, the crustacean stubbornly refused to let go. Quickly, the burly fisherman sprang into action and worked to extricate the little sea creature from his finger. Despite the child's pain, Sofonisba thought it a comical scene and rapidly executed a series of drawings detailing the myriad of expressions—ranging from surprise to shock and disbelief to finally tear-stained remorse.

Once free of his little tormentor, the boy continued to cry, now because of his mother's harsh admonitions to be more careful and not touch things he shouldn't. But when his wails continued drawing curious looks from the crowd, the embarrassed mother picked up her child and spirited him away.

"What's going on?" asked Amilcare.

"Poor lad's curiosity got the better of him," Sofonisba said with a chuckle. Holding up her sketchbook, she showed her father her drawings.

Then it was his turn to show off his well-bargained bounty. "Just look at these succulent little fellows... And I got an excellent price," he said proudly.

"So, tonight we dine on fish *pasticcio* made with saffron, almonds, and marjoram," she stated.

"Yes," he said with enthusiasm. "My belly is already anticipating a fine meal."

As the sun arched higher in the sky, Sofonisba looked down the street in the direction of Saint Peter's Basilica. It was impressive to see the massive scaffolding temporarily constructed to support Michelangelo's half-finished dome. It was immense, despite its unfinished state, and the white stone ribs that reached toward the heavens gleamed against the bright blue sky.

Amilcare followed his daughter's gaze and put his arm around her. "Someday, Sofonisba, your work too will reach such heights. Have no doubt." He looked again at her drawing and added, "Everything starts with a simple sketch. You must first have the idea—a spark of intention—before it can grow and blossom into a marvelous painting... or a dome that adorns a cathedral!"

Chapter 11

An Uncommon Talent

*W*hile Sofonisba unfurled her artistic wings in her new environment, continuing her art education on the streets of Rome and in the studio, Amilcare worked tirelessly behind the scenes on behalf of his daughter.

Yes, she had talent, but unless it was noticed, their efforts and this trip to Rome would be in vain. To ensure a positive result, he took it upon himself to act as her *portavoce*—spokesman—to make sure the most prominent salons and elite artistic studios run by artists of merit knew her name.

To this end, Amilcare spent his days in select circles, singing Sofonisba's praises. He passed his evenings in front of the fire, with a pen in his hand, writing letters of introduction to prominent citizens and promising patrons. In the most cordial of terms, he described his daughter's gifts and even included a few of her drawings.

Among the individuals he sought out was Rome's oldest artist in residence—Michelangelo. At seventy-nine, the Florentine artist—who dazzled Lorenzo de' Medici with his statue of David and impressed Pope Julius with his ceiling paintings that adorned the Sistine Chapel—was still considered the most talented contemporary artist.

When she learned this, Sofonisba cried out in dismay, "Oh, Father, why would such a man take any interest in me at all?"

"Why, I should think he would be a fortunate man indeed to meet you and see what you have accomplished in such a short time. Michelangelo, too, was considered a genius at a young age. Did you know he was only four years older than you when he first arrived here in Rome?"

"Yes, but he is far too lofty now to pay any attention to me..."

"Hush now. Michelangelo may not be as spry as he once was... In fact, the word around town is he's a crusty, cantankerous old know-it-all... but he is a genius! So what if he is extremely picky about the materials he uses? The man has a discerning eye and has earned the right to be critical of others' talents. At his age, it is no wonder he has little patience for his work crew and colleagues, let alone the pope for whom he works."

"See," she said. "My point exactly! If he were to respond and extend an invitation, I wouldn't know how to conduct myself around such a fearsome man. And what was the story Signor Burolla told you the other day?"

Amilcare looked at her perplexed, then after a moment, he said, "Oh! You mean the story about Pietro Torrigiano? The architect who is helping build the dome over Saint Peters?"

"Yes! Didn't you tell me that Michelangelo hauled back and punched Torrigiano in the nose, angered by something he said?"

"I did... but..."

"Oh, Father, again, you've proven my point." Sofonisba shook her head in amusement. "Well, regarding Torrigiano... from what I've learned of him, I'm sure he said something foolish and Michelangelo's reaction was justified. My sympathies lie with him. I, too, at times, have been tempted to box my siblings' ears for their foolish ways. If I were a man and had to put up with idiotic people and unreasonable demands, why I'd..."

"Ah, it is a good thing you are a lady raised by Bianca," Amilcare said with a laugh.

She leaned over and draped her arms around him, giving him a hug. Glimpsing the letter he was composing, she read a paragraph or two, then shook her head. "I fear you are just wasting your time. Michelangelo suffers no fools. Besides, I've heard he is a private man and prefers to keep his own company."

"Yes, well... there is some truth to that," agreed Amilcare. "In all his years, it never occurred to him to slow down, take the time to marry, or have children..."

"Artists need space to create, and there is much to be said for solitude. It would be a miracle to—"

"But just think, Sofonisba," Amilcare interrupted her impatiently. "Despite being a difficult man, Michelangelo is a legend, to be sure... To capture the attention and the eye of il Maestro—that would indeed be a coupe."

She looked at her father sympathetically. "Yes, it would be wonderful to meet him, I confess. But good luck breaking through the throngs of admirers who wish the same thing."

"Sycophants, all of them! They don't hold a candle to you!"

Sofonisba moved to stand by the fireplace and splayed out her supple long fingers, warming them over the embers. "I appreciate all you are doing for me, but really, Father, I think you'd have a better chance of dining with the pope or flying to the moon than receiving a response from Michelangelo!"

"We shall see about that," said Amilcare. Undaunted by her pessimistic words, he picked up his quill and continued writing.

Still, breaking through the mélange of aspiring artists that would request an audience was proving to be more difficult than even Amilcare had anticipated. As the days and months passed, and his correspondence and letters of introduction were ignored, he refused to admit defeat. Instead, he continued his campaign, hoping to receive a positive response.

Although Amilcare hadn't succeeded in capturing the maestro's attention, his hard work was not all in vain. His inquiries were well received in other quarters, and he and Sofonisba were invited to society soirees and attended private gatherings. During one such encounter at the Marquess Baldassare Castiglione's dinner party, Amilcare met Niccolaio dei Genovesi, an advisor to the pope. After an animated conversation, in which Amilcare once again extolled the virtues of his daughter, the cardinal extended to the Anguissolas the kindest invitation to privately tour Saint Peters.

On the appointed day, Amilcare and Sofonisba presented themselves on the steps of the basilica, where they were to meet their host. They waited outside for a few minutes but, not seeing the cardinal, they walked inside where they admired the inlaid floors, frescoed walls, and stupendously ample interior space. After a half-hour passed, and still their host hadn't appeared, Amilcare began to grow concerned that perhaps something was amiss. Just as he was about to seek assistance, he heard someone call out, "Signor Anguissola! There you are. Forgive my delay."

Amilcare glanced over and saw a small man approaching them. He was dressed in a red cassock with buttons down the front, and around his shoulders was an elbow-length shoulder cape. Tied around the man's waist was a white lace apron and topping off his cardinal's attire, he wore a *galero*—the broad-brimmed hat typical of the man's elevated station amongst the clergy.

The cardinal came to a stop before them and reached out his hand to Amilcare. Sofonisba watched as her father dutifully bent his head and kissed the priest's thick gold ring. Rising up, Amilcare exclaimed, "We are at your mercy, Your Holiness. Knowing how busy you are, we are appreciative you could accommodate us today."

The old priest smiled and then glanced over at Sofonisba and regarded her kindly. "So, this is your daughter. By the way your father sings your praises, my dear... one would think you were an angel descended from heaven, so gifted you are with a paintbrush."

Sofonisba curtsied politely. "My father is a most exuberant man." Gesturing around her, she added, "It is an extreme honor to enter this church and walk these hallowed halls. I confess I'm quite overwhelmed."

Cardinal dei Genovesi seemed appreciative of her remarks. "Well, we do enjoy some remarkable surroundings... It helps to remind us of the beauty that exists here on earth as well as what awaits us in heaven." He tilted his head, then added, "So... today is your fortunate day, young lady."

When she looked at him curiously, he said, "The pope is not in residence... So, besides the basilica and the public salons, I can sneak you into his quarters now under construction to see the Raphael Rooms on the second floor of the Vatican Palace. In the Stanza della Segnatura— the pope's private library—you can see Raphael's painting The School of

Athens, which symbolizes the marriage between—"

Before he could go on, Sofonisba excitedly finished his sentence. "Art, philosophy, and science. Yes, it has been described to me before. I hear it is quite marvelous."

"Well," said the cardinal, chuckling and indicating the way, "come along then."

Together the threesome wended their way through the corridors of the Vatican. They stopped now and again to admire works of art by Giotto, Perugino, and Correggio. Following in the wake of the priest, Amilcare and Sofonisba soon entered the rooms that comprised the papal apartments. All around them, workers and apprentices were standing on various levels of scaffolding, painting frescos and carving stucco cornices. Careful not to bump into the many workers that swarmed the outer rooms, they passed into the pope's library and stood in front of Raphael's painting, which took up an entire wall.

"I understand from your father, signorina," said the cardinal, "you are a portrait artist." Lifting his hand, he indicated the composition before them, in which a large group of men in a classic portico discussed and debated amongst themselves. "Raphael is a master of portraiture. He has even included his friends' images in this work to represent all the greatest minds that we still respect today." With interest, he continued. "I wonder if you can make out all the identities of the wise men you see before you?"

Rising to the challenge, Sofonisba took a step closer. "I shall certainly do my best... Let me see." At a closer vantage point, she admired the figures draped in jewel-toned fabrics—the colors were exquisite. After a moment, indicating a small cluster of philosophers in the middle, she said, "Look at these men here. By their tools, one holding a compass and the other an inkwell, I believe these two must be Pythagoras and Aristotle, and the other scholar has to be Plato." She turned her head. "And over to the left—those two men must be Euclid and Socrates."

"Very good, signorina. That is Socrates, indeed. They say that Raphael used an ancient portrait bust of the philosopher as his guide."

"And who is the figure in the front?" she asked, pointing to a heavyset man who appeared to be brooding.

"That is Heraclitus, a self-taught pioneer of wisdom. He was a melancholy sort and did not enjoy the company of others, so Raphael used Michelangelo's image." In a whisper, he added, "It is well known all over town that those two never got along! It was one of Raphael's numerous little jokes he played upon Michelangelo!"

Sofonisba smiled and focused her attention again on the mural. Feeling a light touch on her arm, she looked at the cardinal. "Before you leave, my dear, would you like to see Michelangelo's crowning jewel?"

"The Sistine Chapel, you mean?" asked Sofonisba. "Is it possible?"

"It is up to my discretion who I allow in to see the chapel. And you, signorina, have charmed me with your wide-eyed youthful enthusiasm. Believe me, it is a breath of fresh air. Come, follow me."

He led them through another corridor and back down a narrow flight of stairs until they came to a heavy wooden door. He turned the latch, swung it open, and stepped back. Politely, he indicated she should precede them.

As the two men spoke on the threshold, Sofonisba did as instructed and ventured ahead into the chapel. In awe, she immediately tilted her head back and gazed upward, then directed her attention to the far end of the room. Slowly she moved to the center and turned about in a slow circle. It seemed everywhere her eyes strayed—from the wall that depicted scenes of the Last Judgement to the center ceiling panel where God infused Adam with life—she encountered a monumental figure grander than the next. It was almost too much for her to take in, and she felt a little heady with wonder.

Sofonisba sat down on one of the many stone benches that lined the chapel and craned her neck to better see the Old Testament's sibyls' faces. She admired the bulk of their figures and the many creative ways they were positioned. Some were shown from behind, others from the front, and still others twisted their spines and glanced over their shoulders. Each pose was unique, as were each of their expressions.

After a few minutes, Amilcare approached his daughter and said softly, "Sofonisba. It is time to go. Monsignor dei Genovesi wishes to show me the map room."

"Might I be able to stay a little longer?" she implored. "I know you are fascinated by maps, but truthfully they hold no interest for me... but these portraits... I would like to sketch them so I can remember them later."

"*Non preoccuparti, signorina*," said the cardinal. "I will show your father the maps and then we will circle around to collect you. Take a few more moments. You are safe in this room, in God's presence, and he is pleased you are here."

As their steps faded into the next room, Sofonisba turned her attention back to the ceiling. Wasting no time, she drew out her drawing board and several pieces of paper from her satchel and began to sketch rapidly. When she had completed one design, she threw it down upon the ground and started another. Soon a small pile of parchment sheets began to collect around her feet.

So intent on her work, she wasn't aware that another person had entered the room. It was only when a shadow fell across her page that she swiveled her head and encountered the grizzled face of a man who looked to be in his eightieth year.

He regarded her curiously and then asked gruffly, "And what might you be up to, signorina, here in this chapel all alone?"

"I... I..." she began lamely. "Monsignor dei Genovesi let me in. It was he who gave me permission to remain on my own."

"Well, stop gaping at me! Surely you've seen old men like me before." He nodded at her tablet. "What are you doing there?"

"I'm drawing."

"I can see *that!*" he intoned in an irritated voice. "*What* are you drawing?"

Hesitantly, she pointed upward. "I'm drawing the figures in the ceiling panels."

He didn't look up but said nonetheless, "*Ah, sì. Sono incredibili, vero*—they are quite remarkable, are they not?"

He observed her and the pile of drawings accumulating on the marble floor, then asked, "And who might you be? And why do you feel compelled to draw the sibyls?"

"I'm an artist in training," she said. "At the moment, I'm an apprentice to Signor Mannino. Before that, I studied with Signor Campi in Cremona."

"Cremona!" he exclaimed forcefully. "You've come a long way, haven't you?" He regarded her intently then looked at her drawing. "*Hmmm, interessante...* May I?"

"*Certo*—of course," Sofonisba said, offering it to him.

He studied her sketch, then raised an eyebrow, looked back at her, and said, "I see you've taken a special interest in the Delphic sibyl."

"Yes, she predates the Trojan wars and the Priestess Pythia, the oracle of Apollo. My sister Minerva used to play act..." Her voice trailed off when he only grunted acknowledgement, and she realized he wasn't really listening.

He is an odd sort, she thought, shifting nervously on the hard stone bench. *He certainly speaks directly and isn't one to mince words.* As Sofonisba continued to assess him, she had to crane her neck to look up at him. She noted with interest the man definitely wasn't a dandy as his clothes were a bit dirty and disheveled. Yet, despite his awkwardness and massive size, she was impressed by how gracefully he held her drawing.

As if he felt her eyes upon him, the man turned his full attention upon her and said, "You say you are studying with Mannino, that old fool?"

"At the moment, yes," she replied politely. "I've been here in Rome for several months..."

"This is quite good, signorina," he said finally. "But you need to add a bit more shadow to give the figures more volume."

"I haven't had much experience studying the human form. *They* won't let me. I have to study faces and keep to portrait painting."

"It is a pity that we artists have to submit to the will of all the *theys* out there."

"Are you an artist, too?"

He shrugged. "I am many things, a poet, a painter, but I prefer to be called a sculptor." Indicating his own leather portfolio he carried at his side, he added, "Although these days I go by architect."

"Architect?"

"Many renovations are going on here these days."

"Yes, I noticed," she replied.

There was something about him that intrigued her, and before he could turn away, hoping to hold his attention a little longer, she quickly added, "I have other drawings. Would you like to see some of them?" She paused, hoping she hadn't overstepped the bounds of propriety. "That is, if you don't mind. I'd very much like for you to tell me what I could do to improve. I am here in Rome to learn."

It seemed he was about to refuse, but suddenly he changed his mind. "I could use a rest," he said. Slowly he settled himself down upon the marble bench next to her, then added, "I'm so tired, I can barely get my old bones in or out of bed. I'm an ancient old man and hear death knocking on my door every day."

Not knowing what to say to that, she remained still, commiserating with him in silence. Then, reaching into her bag, she withdrew several loose pages and offered them to him. With a heavy sigh, he began to sort through them rapidly, then just as quickly he glanced up and said, "Signorina, I see some talent here. I've seen the work of many artists, so believe me when I say... you, signorina, have a gift. Not many have your natural ability for design."

"That pleases me immensely," she said, flushing with pride.

"What is your name, signorina?"

"Sofonisba Anguissola," she said.

"Anguissola," he muttered under his breath, shaking his head as if trying to remember where he'd heard the name before. Then, after a moment, he said slowly, "Ah... Anguissola! A most unusual name, is it not? Your father's name is Amilcare Anguissola. Is that right? You are his eldest daughter?"

"It is, messer. And I am," she said, not understanding why this old man should know her or her father.

Holding up one of her drawings, he said, "You capture emotion quite readily—take, for instance, this laughing girl's image. Her expression is quite convincing and natural, and the girl is quite pretty."

"That is my sister Elena," she supplied.

"It is neither here nor there who the girl is, or if she has a fair face," he said a tad dismissively. "It is one thing to convey an expression of mirth and good spirits. But..."

"But?"

"The artist's true goal is to blend physical realism with an intensity so profound that it speaks to the human condition."

"And how do I do that? I thought I was..."

"Signorina, I really don't waste my time critiquing the works of others, or telling them how to go about making art," he said. "When I see something done poorly... well... my response is to start my own project. I let my frustration drive me to creating something better."

Although she had just met the man, Sofonisba couldn't help but be a little vexed. It was apparent he wasn't in the mood to help her.

When she said nothing, the old man peered at her from under his bushy eyebrows and sighed. "Signorina, what have you not understood?"

"I believe you have left me with a great many questions. I..."

"It really is quite simple. Just draw, signorina! *Basta così! È semplice,*" he said, waving her drawings in front of her face. "Draw, draw, draw! Don't squander precious minutes! You are off to a good beginning... but see up there?"

He pointed to the ceiling with the sheaf of her drawings he still held in his hand. As he wildly gesticulated, they fluttered with his movements, as if like her they too trembled at his words. "Each of the sybils is different. Every finger, every toe, every twist of the spine—every emotion—deserves your attention. Only by relentless study of the human condition and every conceivable human emotion will you unleash all the possibilities."

The old man eyed her sternly. "But remember this, signorina, anyone can capture an image on paper. The true artist, however, channels what he observes and moves beyond that. He opens his mind and learns to paint with his brains and not with his hands. He sees with his heart and not with his eyes. In so doing, he creates a rare kind of beauty that speaks to the soul and transports us to new realms."

He looked at Sofonisba's drawing of the cheerful girl again and said, "A more difficult assignment would have been to convey a crying child. To successfully capture the emotion of grief and how it subtly changes the visage—that is the ability of a true master." He looked at her for a moment, clearly pleased with himself, then added, "Does that clarify things for you?"

When she said nothing, he snorted and thrust her drawings back at her. As he did, one of them slipped to the floor. With great effort, the old man reached down to retrieve it. He held the page out to her and then stopped. Clasping the sheet between his massive fingers, he considered the design with increasing interest.

Sofonisba angled a glance at the design that had caught his attention and saw it was one of her more recent sketches—that of the little boy in the market who had been bitten by the crayfish. As she reviewed her picture from over his shoulder, memories of the day—the child's cries and his mother's admonitions—came flooding back.

The man beside her also seemed to hear the blustery commotion her drawing evoked, for as he examined the boy's expression, despite himself, he let out a guffaw and turned his approving gaze upon her. "Damned if I can't hear that little tyke bawling because he's been pinched by an ornery old crab! That's rich. Look at that face all puckered up in pain—serves him right for putting his hands where they don't belong."

He shook his head in disbelief. "Signorina Anguissola... this is precisely what I've been talking about! In this drawing, you have captured an emotion so rich and full of the human condition. Yes, I see great promise here."

He began tapping his knee with one finger, and then after what seemed an eternity, he finally said, "I never expected to meet you here today or be so moved by such a simple rendering." He looked at Sofonisba as if really seeing her for the first time. "This is not a common thing for me to suggest… or something I often do… but I think you'd benefit from my guidance. That is, if you are in agreement."

In a tone dripping with disdain, he said, "You are far too talented to remain in the hands of Mannino, that doddering dullard. I have a score to settle with that old imbecile. He is nothing but a deranged…" Seeing her confused expression, he spluttered to a stop as if realizing he was in the presence of genteel company.

"Signore, that is very kind," Sofonisba said in a bemused tone, smiling inwardly at his pomposity. "I'm flattered. Really, I am. But who are you? Might I know your name?"

"Signorina Anguissola! You are standing in my chapel!" He eased his bulk off the bench and said, "I am Michelangelo."

"But…" Speechless, Sofonisba followed his movements as he ambled across the chapel.

Before stepping over the threshold to disappear from view, he turned and eyed her severely, wagged a finger at her, and said, "Be at my home in Macel de' Corvi tomorrow morning. We begin at nine. Don't be late."

Chapter 12

The Secret of Everything

"*B*last Vignola!" Michelangelo said, banging his fist on the desk.

Sofonisba, seated at a table by the window in Michelangelo's study, jumped at the sound. She had been his pupil for more than two years, visiting him several times a month, and by now, was accustomed to his angry outbursts—but this cry of dismay startled her, causing her drawing tool to slide across her page, leaving an angry smear.

She looked across the room and saw Michelangelo absently rolling the quill between his fingers as he examined the letter he was writing. "Is something amiss, maestro? You seem a bit more agitated than usual today. Surely it can't be all that bad."

When he heard her voice, Michelangelo looked up and blinked as if trying to bring her into focus. He shook his head, then sighed. "Ah, if only I had your fresh countenance and curious eyes... and optimism!" Gesturing to the letter, he scowled. "I'm too old for all this nonsense... Political games and egos that need to be continually assuaged are draining me of what remains of my energy!"

Sofonisba stood and walked to his side. "Who are you writing to?"

"Vasari. I have no wish to show my face at the Vatican today and prefer to stay here with you and write to my dear old friend Giorgio. He asked to be kept informed of Vignola's lunatic ideas."

She peeked over at the letter on the table and asked, "May I?"

"Of course, you already know the story anyway and my complaints with the man."

Sofonisba smiled. It was true. Since her arrival this morning, it seemed to be the only thing on Michelangelo's mind. Without mincing words, he had recounted the whole story and his quarrel with Vignola, his much younger colleague, who was also nephew to the pope. Michelangelo sat back and crossed his arms over his chest, and with a tilt of his head, encouraged her to peruse the letter he was composing. Accepting the invitation, she leaned over and read: *Messer Giorgio, amico caro mio... Things are progressing slowly here in Rome. I grow wearier by the day. I've gone and quarreled again with Vignola. Because of his pigheadedness, there has been another lengthy delay. The pope caught wind of this and is furious. I fear I will not live to see the completion of this confounded dome. Be prepared, my friend, for there is talk that you will be called upon to carry out the work that I cannot.*

When Sofonisba concluded reading, she said, "I'm sure Messer Vasari will be quite sympathetic."

"He is well-versed in my complaints... all the useless quarrels... the whims and vagaries of the Vatican officials that try my very soul!" In a comical voice, he said, "Do this, Michelangelo, do that! No, we need this chapel painted before you continue with that tomb!" He looked at Sofonisba and added, "And now this wretched dome! Long ago, they all approved the plan. They claimed it to be another masterpiece..."

He pounded his fist upon the desk again, but this time with less force, and said, "If they would merely concede to my original idea and not find a reason to contradict me, this dome would have been finished years ago!"

Kindly, Sofonisba replied, "It will be finished one day... and it will be a marvel—and a brilliant addition to the city's skyline."

The old artist uncrossed his arms and regarded her thoughtfully. "I've been working on this *cupola*, it seems like forever—even before you became my student. And yet, you listen to me go and on about this or that. By now, have you not tired of my complaints?"

Sofonisba responded with a shrug. She walked over to pour him a tisane from the steaming kettle the servant had placed on the sideboard only moments before. Over her shoulder, she said, "If you ask me, your grievances are just. Here, this will make you feel better."

"Ah, Signorina Anguissola. You always know the right thing to say... and how to muzzle my grumblings. You are far too patient... and more intelligent than some of the noblemen I know—ahem, namely Vignola—who claims to be scholar and an intellectual. Now come, what do you have to show me today?"

"Are you quite through with your letter?"

"For now," he said, pushing the parchment aside.

Sofonisba returned to the table and began sorting through the stack of drawings she had worked on in the studio of her new painting instructor Bernardo Gatti, whom Michelangelo had recommended to Amilcare over Mannino. Gatti had been a pupil of Correggio, and she had been delighted to make the transition to his studio. Still, the moments she spent in Michelangelo's company and the advice he gave her she treasured. And despite his fits of temper and cantankerous nature, he was less rough and more approachable with her.

"Confound this! It is so damned hot!" Michelangelo grumbled.

Sofonisba chuckled and shook her head at the sight of his irritated face. "How many times have I told you to blow on the drink to cool it..."

Michelangelo set the cup down with a little bang, then looked at her from under bushy eyebrows. "I'm an old man... I forget!" He rose from his chair and came to stand by her. "How go things with Gatti?" Before she could respond, he asked, "Did you finish the sketch of David?"

Sofonisba nodded and pulled out the picture she had copied from Michelangelo's original design concepts. It had been her fondest desire to study the human body, and finally, under Michelangelo's tutelage, she had been granted her wish. Previously, when she had told Amilcare that she was studying male anatomy under Michelangelo's guidance, her father hadn't minded. As long as it was purely academic, and she wasn't looking at actual nude bodies, he was willing to make an exception. In fact, he had even taken upon himself to write several letters to Michelangelo, thanking him for the opportunities the artist had granted his daughter.

Usually, Amilcare's letters were quite effusive in his compliments to il Maestro, but in his most recent letter, which Sofonisba had delivered to Michelangelo that morning, it contained the regretful news that their time in Rome was coming to an end. Her mother had taken ill, and she and Amilcare had decided to return to Cremona.

When Sofonisba had watched Michelangelo read the letter, the old man had relapsed into silence. Now, standing by his side discussing the drawing she had made of the David, she wondered if perhaps, other than his laments with Vignola if the contents of her father's letter had contributed to his foul mood this morning.

Sofonisba's thoughts scattered when she heard Michelangelo say, "This is excellent, signorina." Holding up the design, he continued. "Your work over the past months has matured immensely."

He turned to look at her and shook his head tiredly. "I must admit, it saddens me to no end to say goodbye, Signorina Sofonisba. That day in the chapel, my instincts were correct. I don't regret for a moment taking you under my wing. You have proven to be a rapid study, and your work is superlative in quality and grace."

"It will be with great difficulty to leave you," Sofonisba said sadly.

"Yes, the years are turning far too quickly... like spinning mill wheels. I grow wearier by the hour, and my days upon this earth are dwindling."

Sofonisba, accustomed to his laments, picked up his pen and handed it to him. "Then it is best you finish your letter, maestro," she said in a stern voice as if she were the teacher and he the pupil.

He scowled and then took the quill from her outstretched hand. "And you, signorina, should get back to work... In half an hour's time, you need to return home to your father."

She did as he bid and settled herself again at her drafting table. They worked in silence for another half hour. When Sofonisba heard Michelangelo put down his pen and the scrape of his chair as he pushed away from the desk, she looked expectantly. "So, you have finished your thoughts to Vasari?"

"Yes."

Sofonisba stood up and readied her things, placing drawing tools into her satchel. Over her shoulder, she said, "And you are pleased with your letter?"

"Before you leave, would you like to hear what I have written? The last bit... well, it pertains to you."

"You have written about me?"

Holding the parchment in front of his face, he cleared his throat and read aloud the closing remarks to his illustrious colleague.

"Giorgio dear friend...I've written to you before of my dear Signorina Sofonisba, the daughter of Amilcare Anguissola. For fear of sounding repetitive, I must yet again write to you of her achievements! She has labored at the difficulties of design with considerable study and better grace than any other woman of our time. She has succeeded in drawing, coloring, and copying from nature and making excellent copies of works by other hands—mine primarily—but has also executed by herself some very choice and beautiful works of painting. From the very beginning, as you know, I was especially captivated by that drawing she did of a weeping boy caused by a crayfish biting his finger."

Michelangelo glanced over at his young protégé and crinkled his face in amusement, then continued reading aloud. *"That was two years ago! I've never seen a more graceful design, or one more true to nature by another. And Sofonisba only continues to impress me."*

Concluding his letter, Michelangelo read, *"Giorgio, Sofonisba will be passing your way, on her way home to Cremona. I'd like you to meet her and see for yourself how talented this young woman is. After you do, I'm sure you too will see she deserves a passage in your book. Con affetto. Miché."*

The artist sat for a moment, not moving. Then finally, he looked at Sofonisba. "Have you nothing to say..."

"Your words astound me," she said at last. "Thank you from the bottom of my heart—it will be an honor to meet your friend Vasari."

"I mean every word that I wrote... You are gifted, and I believe Vasari is in for a treat." He was quiet of moment then added a bit mournfully, "Life will undoubtedly lose a bit of flavor without your visits."

She stepped to his side and leaned down to kiss his leathery cheek. "I hope to be as fortunate as you and live a long full life..."

"Ah! La vecchiaia... ci sono vantaggi e svantaggi—old age comes with advantages and disadvantages," Michelangelo said with a snort. "Someone

so young cannot possibly fathom what it means to be as ancient as the hills. If you live as long as I have, your body will begin to fail you, and your mind may start to play tricks."

He watched as she put on her cloak and hat. "But remember this, Signorina Anguissola, a life lived well comes with great rewards too. Being born once is not enough..." When she tilted her head, he clarified. "What I mean is that a long life gives you many opportunities to be born repeatedly—to make mistakes and still have opportunities to start anew. You must promise me you will never stop learning or improving—never stop reinventing yourself. Most importantly, never back down from a challenge, even if it floods your heart with doubts and fear."

Michelangelo gazed at her wistfully, then pointing his pen at her, he said, "The danger lies in not setting your aim too high and falling short but setting your aim too low and achieving the mark. Never measure the height of a mountain until you reach the top, for it is only then you will see how low it was."

"You have never allowed yourself to do that, maestro," she said respectfully. "But, then, it has always come so effortlessly to you."

He snorted again. "If people knew how hard I worked to get my mastery, it wouldn't seem so wonderful!"

When he beckoned her closer, she readily approached his side.

"Remember this, Sofonisba. All of us must leave the earth—it all ends the same way. But the thing that matters most is how we live. That is what distinguishes each of us from the rest. Choose to live by choice, not by chance. Be motivated, not manipulated—excel but don't compete."

He took her hand and squeezed it gently. Then, in a conspiratorial whisper, he asked, "*Cara mia, volete sapere il segreto di tutto*—do you want to know the secret of everything?" When she nodded, he said, "*Ascolta la voce interiore!* Listen to your inner voice, not the random opinions of others. Keep away from people who try to belittle your ambitions. Small people always do that, but the really great ones make you feel that you, too, can become great."

Leaning over, Sofonisba kissed the old artist on his cheek and said, "Just as you have done for me. *Mille grazie, maestro.*"

Cremona to Milano—1557

*Sofonisba of Cremona has not only succeeded
in drawing, colouring, and copying from
nature, but has executed some very choice
and beautiful works of painting.*

– Giorgio Vasari, Lives of the Artists (1568)

Chapter 13

Rumors

*T*he warm summer sun streamed through the large glass windows in the front parlor of the Anguissola home. The room would have been intolerably hot were it not for a cooling breeze that lifted the linen drapes and ruffled the curls around Sofonisba's forehead. As she fanned her face with a piece of parchment, she lightly wound a long strand of hair around her finger, enjoying the silky texture.

She passed by a table where a young woman was seated, leaned down, and said, "Your work shows great improvement, Signorina Barissi. Remember to establish a vanishing point." Sofonisba took the pencil from the young girl dressed in yellow silk, whose face was also shiny with perspiration, and made a few quick diagonal lines and said, "Set your ruler like this... now create at least three or four guides that lead you to a spot on the horizon." She returned the drawing tool to her student and said, "Now, please try again."

Sofonisba turned her attention next to another of her five female students. With her head bent close to the young woman's, as Michelangelo had done with her, she offered a few pointers on how to define form with light and shadow. Then peering over at the mantel clock, she said, "Signorine, that is all for the day. I will see you again next Thursday. We will work on expressions and character sketches and begin making portraits. My sister Europa will be modeling for you."

When the last of the young women departed, Sofonisba was content to resume her own work in progress—a portrait the old count of Montefiori had commissioned of his new young bride, Alessandra, that was to hang in their reception hall. The painting was shaping up nicely, and Sofonisba was now concentrating on the rich details of the Contessa's intricate lace collar and the jeweled necklace that graced her slim neck.

Several years had slipped by since Sofonisba had returned home, the first six months having been passed attending Bianca, who had greeted them with a wan smile from her bed. But, with the restoration of her mother's health, Sofonisba's parents refocused their attention on furthering their daughters' interests. Bianca had written to Isabella de Estes, and after the Marquessa's favorable reply, it was decided to send Minerva off to Mantova to live with the Gonzaga family to further her education. Elena and Europa were introduced into polite society, allowing the girls to perform musical duets at local gatherings among Cremona's nobles. Sofonisba's two younger sisters quickly became the talk of the town not only for their elegant manners but also for their witty and agile minds.

Sofonisba, on the other hand, was happy to remain at home to focus on her painting. After his other daughters had been attended to, Amilcare was only more than happy to resume his favorite project—that of advancing his eldest daughter's career as a portraitist. And when he circulated the news that Sofonisba had studied with the great Michelangelo, it caused quite a buzz amongst the local nobility and only heightened her notoriety. A word dropped at Duchess of Ghezzi's soiree and another at Count Piccini's salon, and soon his daughter's portraits were much sought after, and she quickly established an impressive clientele. As her reputation grew, he encouraged her to open a painting salon in one of the house's sunnier rooms, where she could instruct other young women of noble birth how to paint.

After assuming her new responsibilities as an instructor, as well as a portrait painter in her own right, Sofonisba had hoped to resume a professional relationship with Bernardino Campi. But he was no longer living in Cremona. Amilcare had tasked Bernardino with accompanying Minerva to the Gonzaga estate, and there he had remained to decorate their palazzo that was being renovated. Knowing Signor Campi's familiarity with the Gonzaga family, and realizing what a vital commission it was, Sofonisba was happy for him and resigned herself to carrying on their friendship via letters.

Perhaps, in the end, it was a better way to continue conducting their relationship. After receiving several of his lengthy missives during her sabbatical in Rome, so effusive were his words, Sofonisba didn't have to read between the lines to understand the depths of his feelings. She had hesitated at first, not knowing how to respond. Then, picking up a pen, clearly and concisely, she spoke of ordinary things, refraining from waxing on in romantic, poetic tones.

Now back in Cremona, having grown in confidence and with a much broader world view—Sofonisba was even more convinced she could never fully reciprocate Bernardino's sentiments. Fondly, she tied his letters with a blue satin ribbon and tucked them away in a special box, which she kept next to those of Michelangelo's and the little Etruscan sea captain standing on a ship she had found in Chiusi.

In her short life, she had earned the admiration of important artists such as Michelangelo, Vasari, Gatti and Signor Campi... as well as that of a man whose name she would never know. Each in his own way had encouraged and inspired her, and she was a better painter and a more well-rounded individual because of them.

But, if she were honest, the mysterious young man she'd met in an Etruscan village on her way to Rome intrigued and haunted her thoughts the most. In the quietest of moments, his face often appeared before her, and when it did, she remembered the song he had sung and the secret pact they had made. She would take out the Etruscan coin and remember how they'd agreed to dream big, meet the future head-on, and follow their hearts and ambitions. Just knowing he was out there in the world, sailing the high seas and following his own unique path, made her happy. She imagined he, too, would be proud to know she had earned the esteem of Michelangelo and become one of Cremona's most prominent portrait painters.

As she cleaned her brushes with a soft flannel cloth dipped in turpentine, a smile played across her lips. Then, with a shake of her head, she banished thoughts of her secret admirer and looked back at the painted features of Alessandra Montefiori she had adroitly captured on canvas. The blond-haired woman, who was younger than herself, had married the very rich but notably older Count Montefiori. During their painting sessions, Sofonisba had learned a great deal about the young contessa.

It seemed her profession as a portrait artist also served as a confessor. After long hours in close proximity, an air of intimacy often developed between painter and subject. More often than not, her clients told her things in privacy, things they would normally reveal only to a clergyman. What was left unsaid Sofonisba readily surmised by their body language and the expressions on their faces. But, just as a priest would never divulge such confidences, Sofonisba, too, would never reveal their secrets.

Upon close inspection, if an observer guessed by the way Sofonisba painted the contessa's lush lips or the wan expression in her eyes, she carried a torch for a man, not her husband—Sofonisba would neither deny nor confirm such a scandalous notion. Instead, she let her brush do the talking and allowed the viewer to draw his own conclusions.

Sofonisba mixed a little more cobalt blue into her palette to vary the hue and focused her attention on the sapphire pendant nestled into Alessandra Montefiori's ample bosom. She worked for a few minutes, then needed more paint and opened the small container of azurite powder. With her palette knife, she deftly began combining it with a small amount of oil. Once satisfied with the color and the consistency, she resumed adding glistening highlights to the multi-faceted gemstone.

She was so intent on her work, she didn't bother turning around when she heard the door open and the footsteps of her father, nor when he called out her name. In frustration, Amilcare tried again, "Sofonisba! Look at me, child! You will never guess what I hold in my hand."

"If it is a jug of cider, leave it on the table. I'm parched."

"Daughter! It has finally happened."

"What has happened? Has Minerva gotten engaged?" With her paintbrush suspended mid-air, she said with a laugh, "Poor man who asks for *her* hand."

With a dismissive gesture, ignoring her quip, Amilcare waved in front of her face a sheet stamped with an impressive gold seal. "I've received a letter from the Duke of Alba. Can you believe it? The Duke of Alba!"

"It seems an impressive title," Sofonisba agreed absently, returning her attention to her painting.

"Why, daughter!" Amilcare spluttered. "That is an understatement. He is Fernando Alvarez de Toledo from one of the oldest and most distinguished noble families of Spain."

"And what does the duke want with us?" she asked. "If it is a painting, he will have to wait. I already have several standing orders."

"Listen to me carefully," continued Amilcare patiently. "This letter could have great import for your future. The duke has written requesting a meeting. Yes, he wishes to have his portrait painted. And of course he will take precedence over all others!"

Amilcare began restlessly pacing the room. "He is the most talked about man of our day and age... a man who wields a tremendous amount of influence. He served under Emperor Charles and now has even subdued the pope in Rome!"

Sofonisba, agitated by her father's movements, all at once saw the implications of what he was saying and slowly put down her brush.

Noting he had her undivided attention, Amilcare took a deep, calming breath and began again. "When Charles died, Alba became the chief military advisor to his son King Philip of Spain. For several years Alba commanded the Spanish forces here in Italy. Philip then made him governor of Milan, and it is there he lives at the moment, continuing to keep watch over the French and Italian fronts. To honor him and the men in his service, the king has recently commissioned a series of portraits."

He beamed at Sofonisba. "And now you, daughter, are being considered to carry out this lofty work. Of course other notable painters are being interviewed—you are just one of many."

Amilcare placed his hands on his hips and said, "Now, what do you think about that? See how I take care of my daughter? People abroad— foreigners even—are starting to talk about your talents, and important men like Alba—even the King of Spain—are now seeking you out!"

Her father's excitement was contagious, and as the prospect of such a critical commission sank in, Sofonisba was flooded by a wave of emotion that made her positively giddy. She wiped her palms on her apron and looked at him expectantly. "When and where am I to meet him? And who else is he talking to?"

"It's all here," he said, indicating Alba's letter. As Sofonisba scanned the contents, Amilcare continued talking. "We are to receive him at the end of the week. After having spent some time in Rome, he is returning to Milan via Cremona."

"So, soon! There is not much time to prepare." Sofonisba gaped at him in consternation.

When she said nothing more, Amilcare comforted her. "Do not worry, daughter. He is a very fastidious man—exact and demanding—but you are worthy of the task." He placed his arm around her shoulder and said, "The duke doesn't make these requests lightly, and if he is pleased with your work, and with you... well, as I said before, this could be an auspicious step!" Then, after a reassuring pat on the cheek and a quick kiss on the forehead, he turned on his heel and left the room.

Sofonisba stood with her lips slightly parted, listening to the jaunty tune he whistled as he returned to his study. Despite her father's reassurances, to say she was intimidated was an understatement. Was she ready?

She let her gaze drift to the open window, and she stood absolutely still, watching the rustling leaves from the trees beyond in the garden. Then a warm breeze blew into the room, and she heard a familiar voice with a Cremonese accent whisper into her ear: *If I am to be remembered as a painter, it is because of you.* And then another crusty voice chimed in: *The danger for most of us lies in not setting our aim too high and falling short but in setting our goal too low and achieving our mark.*

The words of Campi and il Maestro heartened her, but those of a beguiling young adventurer encouraged her the most: *Remember, signorina, those who reach for the stars have the most extraordinary experiences.*

Buoyed by these thoughts, Sofonisba resumed painting the Contessa

Montefiori's portrait, reminding herself it was best to focus on the clients she currently worked for and please them first and foremost. It was a wise move, as the following day it boosted her confidence further when she welcomed the contessa back into her studio and heard Alessandra exclaim, "Signorina Sofonisba, you have made me so beautiful!"

The blond-haired woman swung around, her eyes sparkling. "Do I really resemble that marvelous woman in the painting? My eyes are so soulful and beguiling... and the Montefiori jewels are exquisitely rendered. The count will be quite pleased. When can it be delivered?"

"The painting must cure a few more days," Sofonisba replied. "With your permission, might I show this to an important gentleman who is also interested in commissioning a portrait?"

"By all means, *cara*. I've also passed your name to Messer Baldessari." Fanning herself, the young contessa admitted with a brilliant blush, "The man is my husband's cousin, and he is quite a charmer—why if I weren't married, I should be tempted..." She hesitated and didn't continue. Instead, she pulled on her lace gloves and busied herself with her purse.

Sofonisba could only imagine what thoughts the young contessa was entertaining but wisely said nothing. She thanked Alessandra for the reference and bid her a good day.

Left alone again, Sofonisba applied the last coat of varnish to the painting, noticing how the translucent layer made the jewels around the Contessa's neck glisten even more. She then cleaned up her painting salon, and with nothing left to do, she wandered into the garden. Deep in thought, she walked amongst the purple cyclamen plants, pondering her upcoming audience with the Duke of Alba.

Having read his letter and learning of his impressive credentials, she knew he was an influential and respected man—a military general sent to Milan to keep peace and the French at bay. But she also wondered on a personal level how he would comport himself. Would he prove to be a jovial man, or would her worst assumptions be realized that he was someone dry and without humor—a rigid unbending sort of man? She imagined being an aide to the king—he'd be more like the latter than the former.

Sofonisba sighed, sat down in the shade of a quince tree, and inhaled the fresh scent emanating from the beds of asters and daisies. On the garden table next to her was a pile of old sketchbooks that she had brought back from Rome. She planned on showing her young students character sketches she had done to encourage them to make their own. She picked up one tablet and turned the pages but stopped when she came to the face of the dark-haired man she had met three years ago in an ancient Etruscan village.

As she traced the line of his jaw with a long slender finger, her eyes glowed with fond memories of that night so long ago. She looked out over the beds of flowers, lost in thought, and wondered, *Has he indeed absconded with Porsena's gold and purchased a vessel... or has he stowed away on a pirate ship and is now making his fortunes stealing from others?*

Her thoughts scattered like leaves tossed about by a gust of autumn wind when she was addressed by Fabia. Sofonisba glanced up and saw the housekeeper approaching in the company of a younger maid who held a silver tray with glasses.

"Would you like some refreshments to calm your nerves? I think it would do you some good," said Fabia in her usual cheery voice. With a hand on her lower back, she let out a little groan, then settled into a chair next to Sofonisba. "Today I'm feeling my age!"

Fabia indicated the tray held by the servant and said, "The almond tarts are still warm... Cook just prepared them. I know what a sweet tooth you have, so I made sure to save some before Asdrubale snatched up the lot." She then waved her hand to the young servant and said, "Bibiana, dear girl, pour the signorina a glass of cider."

The picture of propriety, the rosy-cheeked girl with hair slicked back under a lace cap, obeyed Fabia's order and set down the tray on the garden table. Careful not to spill, she poured out the sweet apple wine and handed it to the young mistress.

Gratefully, Sofonisba accepted the glass and took a sip. "Thank you... Bibiana, is it?"

"Yes, miss," she said, bobbing in a small curtsy.

Over time, Sofonisba had noticed several new faces had joined the Anguissola household staff. Since returning from her sabbatical in Rome, things at home had changed in subtle ways from when she had been a girl. The house that had always seemed so grand and immense now seemed smaller. And the people in it too were different. Her mother, always round and luminous, was now thin, and her animated sparkle diminished. Her sisters were no longer children, but young ladies and Elena had recently become betrothed. Even Asdrubale, the baby of the family, was sprouting up, taller than she, and now wore long pants.

Sofonisba looked over at her old nanny, whom she had known her whole life, and thought she too looked more fragile and frail. "Fabi, you work too hard taking care of us... You need more help."

"*Carissima*..." said Fabia as she coughed dryly into her handkerchief, "Bibiana is here just for that purpose—to help me with chores and ease my burdens. Mistress Bianca hired her to help me with the washing and turning out of the beds. She comes once a week to lend a hand."

"And where are you from, Bibiana?" Sofonisba asked politely.

"I come from Crema," she said. "It is just a short distance from—"

When Fabia began coughing again, the young girl patted her gently on the back and offered her a glass of cider too. She glanced over at Sofonisba and said, "Fabia was telling me the Duke of Alba is soon to visit... and you are to paint his picture.

"Yes, that is correct... That is, if I meet with his approval," said Sofonisba.

"He is a very handsome man," the girl replied, setting the crystal pitcher down.

Looking over the rim of her glass, Sofonisba said in surprise, "You have seen him then?"

"Why, yes, my sister Anna Maria works in his household in Milan. Sometimes I travel there to visit her. The Ducal Palace is quite a place. There are many servants from the local villages that work there."

Sitting up in her chair, Sofonisba asked, "What can you tell me of the duke? What is he like?"

"I've only seen him from a distance," admitted the young girl. "He is a most dignified and fearsome man! He is rather tall and old..."

"Everyone is old seen from your point of view," said Fabia in a huff.

"Why do you say he is fearsome?" asked Sofonisba with a nervous laugh. "That doesn't bode well, or help to calm my nerves."

Bibiana shook her head. "I don't know, really. It is the way he stares at you. He seems cruel at times. He walks a bit stiffly as if he had been injured in the past—"

Fabia said with a snort, "Maybe it is because he is Spanish. All Spaniards are cold and severe... and have poles stuck up—"

Sofonisba said sternly, "Now, Fabi! Don't go and generalize people just because they are foreigners."

Fabia shook her head. "No need to get up on your high horse, young miss... I'm just pointing out that it's hard to trust the lot of them Spanish. They took control of things... and now here we are!"

Bibiana appeared fearful, as if she thought Sofonisba would admonish her too. Contritely, she bent her head.

"That's all right, Bibiana," said Sofonisba. "What else can you tell me so I can form a better picture of the man?"

"That is all, signorina," said Bibiana, folding her hands primly in front of her.

Sofonisba looked over at Fabia and raised an eyebrow.

Taking her cue, Fabia said to the girl, "It's all right, dearie. You are among friends... Tell the mistress. If you have something more to say, let's hear it."

Bibiana relaxed slightly and glanced from one woman to the other. "I'm not one to spread rumors, mind you, but I have heard a few things... things Anna Maria has told me they speak about amongst the servants." When Fabia gestured for her to go on, Bibiana said, "Well... he's profoundly religious and attends mass with rigid regularity. He keeps a rosary by his bedside and reads from the Bible every night."

"So he is a pious man," said Sofonisba contemplatively.

"Yes," said Bibiana, "but..."

"But what?"

Her face blanched white and Bibiana reluctantly stammered, "The Duke of Alba, from the time he was very young, has spent his life on the battlefield. There is talk amongst the groomsmen who talk to the girls on the kitchen staff that he is also a heartless man and has a dark and evil soul. According to Anna Maria, who is very close to the cook, in times of war he shows no mercy. He kills and cruelly tortures his prisoners—spears them through the heart despite their attempts to surrender... even cuts off their arms and legs—even cuts out their tongues..."

The maid's words hung in the air, then Sofonisba scoffed and said, "Oh, Bibiana! Surely that can't be true."

When the young servant girl remained silent, Sofonisba looked quizzically at Fabia to see what she thought of this nonsense.

But the old servant only shrugged and took a sip of her drink, then said, "It may well be gossip, *tesoro*, but I've lived long enough to know in every rumor spread amongst the serving staff, there is a grain of truth. Wherever there's evil, the devil prevails!"

Sofonisba looked at her and shook her head. Turning her attention back to Bibiana, she asked, "What about the duke's kin? He comes from a respectable noble family, does he not? What of his mother and father?"

"*Oh, sì, signorina. Ovviamente*," Bibiana said. "The Duke of Alba was born into a very old and illustrious family. He makes a great show of that... He is the sole heir to the family's fortune and keeps a fine household—yet still he is a bit frugal. His mother died in the plague and his father in battle. He has no siblings."

"Who raised him then, after his mother died?"

"The old Duke of Alba—his paternal grandfather—took the young'n under his wing." She paused, then added, "Anna Maria told me once the old man laid a heavy hand to him, sparing him no mercy for the slightest wrongdoing."

"How could she know that?"

"By the scars on his back. The steward who attends the duke told the—"

"Is this more idle talk of servants who like to defame their betters?" Sofonisba asked, waving her hand dismissively. "Surely there must be some happiness in his life? Is he married?"

"Yes, he had a wife at one time. He was married to his cousin Maria Enriquez de Toledo y Guzman."

"*Was* married? Does that mean his wife is now dead too?"

Bibiana bobbed her head and twisted her hands nervously.

"What is it?" asked Sofonisba. "What more could befall this poor man?"

"They say the duke's wife—"

"What do they say?" inquired the old nurse, leaning forward.

"Anna Maria told me the duke's wife died under mysterious circumstances." With a mournful sigh, Bibiana continued. "Bless the woman's soul! Maria Enriquez has been dead going on twenty years. They say she was beautiful... a good-natured girl who loved to dance and play at the gaming tables. Apparently, the duke pursued her relentlessly. From the moment he saw her, he desired her... no matter she had a host of suitors lining up at her door and the fact her father had promised her to another. But after they wed, Maria Enriquez didn't venture out much anymore or follow her old pursuits. It is said the duke forbade it. Instead, she remained in her chambers."

The young maid hesitated, then added in a conspiratorial whisper, "They say she often took to her bed with blood on her lip and swollen dark eyes. She also suffered several miscarriages... then fell into decline."

Sofonisba sat in stunned silence. After a moment, she finally said, "So, the duke has no heirs. No family at all?"

Bibiana shook her head. "No, that's not the case. As men often do when their wives can't bear them children, the duke took a mistress and fathered a son by the miller's daughter. He cast aside the young peasant girl, but the boy he called Fernando de Toledo he took possession of, allowing him to carry on the Alba title. It seems he was quite happy to have finally fathered a son."

"Just like a man!" said Fabia indignantly.

"But poor Maria Enrique," Bibiana whispered. "Some say she was so distraught by the news, she took to drink. Falling into decline, she poisoned herself one evening, consuming a large dose of *belladonna*. She died at the age of twenty-two."

"*Oh, Santo Cielo!*" exclaimed Fabia. "Nightshade is a potent poison that can bring an ox down... but I've known vain women who use it to improve their complexions."

"Or ease a woman's monthly pains," suggested Sofonisba. "It could have been an accident."

"Perhaps," said Bibiana. "But Anna Maria told me the duke's wife didn't take the poison of her own accord—"

"What?"

"*Si!* They say the Duke of Alba was so enraged by the fact Maria Enrique took a lover to punish him for his dalliance with the miller's daughter... They say it was he who poisoned her."

"Bibiana! Such a story! And you believe these ludicrous tales?"

"As Lord as my witness, it's what everyone whispers about in the corridors! I'm so sorry... but it's what you asked me to tell you," Bibiana said in an aggrieved tone. Wiping her hands on her apron, she added, "Bless the lady's soul. No one but the duke and God himself will ever know how she died or what turned such a happy woman into a recluse and one who favored her drink."

"And Alba has never remarried?" asked Sofonisba.

"Not to this day. After twenty years, he has yet to look upon another woman with love. They claim he blames his wife, his mistress—even his mother—for all the misfortunes in his life."

"Or perhaps," said Sofonisba softly, "he is so heartbroken over the death of his beautiful young wife Maria Enriquez he can't bear to marry again."

Chapter 14

Alba is Awakened

Sofonisba wasn't sure it had been such a good idea to speak with Fabia and Bibiana about the Duke of Alba. She had hoped the intimate chat would calm her nerves and boost her confidence; sadly, it had done neither. Despite Bibiana's initial reluctance to overstep her bounds, the servant girl had proven to be quite a font of information. But, instead of gaining more insight into the duke's character, the rumors, speculations, and opinions had only served to muddy the waters.

She had always believed herself to be an open-minded person who wasn't swayed by servant gossip. She prided herself on making up her own mind and forming her own opinions. But, notwithstanding her best intentions, a seed had been planted; Sofonisba couldn't help but wonder about the duke's troubled childhood, unhappy marriage, and brutality on the battlefield.

Regardless of the Spanish nobleman's polite interest in her work, she was just one of the many talented artists being considered to carry out the royal portrait commissions. And if she believed the tall tales the servants dished out—if he were indeed a cynic and misanthrope—she was a woman, so what hopes did she really have of pleasing him? Surely Alba would immediately discount her as a dilettante female artist who dabbled in paint for fun. Before they had even met, she believed her chances had been sabotaged.

On the day of the anticipated meeting, chased by such thoughts, she rose from her bed feeling unsettled and agitated. Still, she dressed with care, putting on her best taffeta blue gown embroidered around the bodice that also featured a high white lace collar. As she waited to be called to the drawing room, she took stock of her appearance in the mirror. Tilting her head to the left and then to the right, she reached up and pinched her cheeks to give them more color. She straightened her skirts and stepped into her blue satin slippers.

Then, hearing a commotion in the courtyard at the front of the family palazzo, she deftly slicked back a wayward curl and secured it firmly. She moved to the window, pulled back the drape and peeked furtively at the scene unfolding below. A carriage with men in livery had come to a standstill, and as the horses impatiently stamped their hooves, the door of the elegant conveyance opened and out stepped a tall man.

When Sofonisba spied their illustrious guest for the first time, he all but took her breath away. Indeed, he lived up to Bibiana's description—Fernando Álvarez de Toledo, Duke of Alba, was not in any sense of the word a man like any other.

His narrow but muscular frame towered above everyone else and, by the way he barked orders at the servants, it seemed even in peacetime he enjoyed flaunting his militaristic authority. From behind the curtain, she continued observing him, thinking his features were well-proportioned and would have been entirely pleasing if they hadn't been marked by the lines of his stern, downturned lips. His hair was cut short, as was his trim beard and mustache. Most striking of all was his prominent nose, which heralded his ancestry, proclaiming him to be of rich and noble bloodlines. It resembled those of Roman Caesars, belonging to men who were made of steely inclinations and who harbored formidable designs of power.

Sofonisba noted with amusement how Amilcare arrived with alacrity to greet the duke. Perking up her ears, she caught bits and pieces of his blustery speech through the slightly raised window. Her father was at his peak performance, trying his best to make a good impression. She couldn't help but blush in embarrassment as her elder with even greater bravado gestured to the front entrance, inviting Alba into their home.

Amilcare followed in his wake, but before entering the house he glanced up at Sofonisba's window and caught his daughter's eye. With a lift of an eyebrow and an inclination of his head, he indicated he couldn't be more pleased. Then, with a wave of his hand, he motioned for her to join them.

With more than a little trepidation, Sofonisba descended the stairs and headed to the morning room, where she knew they would be waiting. In the hallway, she met her mother, and together they moved to the salon's entrance. Sofonisba hung back just a bit and let Bianca enter before her.

The two men, engaged in polite conversation, turned toward the door upon hearing the light tread of the female Anguissolas.

"Ah! Here they are! My wife and daughter," cried Amilcare, wiping a film of perspiration from his brow. It was evident to Sofonisba, despite his giddiness, the strain of entertaining such a critical guest and providing stimulating remarks was already taking its toll.

From the doorway, Sofonisba observed her mother walk confidently into the room and give the duke a bright smile. For the occasion, Bianca had chosen her finest gown embroidered in silver thread. At her neck was a ruff of lace. Large luminous pearls dripped from her ears and from around her neck.

Sofonisba watched as Alba, under hooded lids, greeted the older woman with a stiff bow. "It is delightful to meet you, Signora Anguissola."

"The pleasure is ours," Bianca replied, respectfully raising her hand to be kissed. "You are a most welcome visitor in our home."

"It is more than just a social visit, madame. I'm sure your husband has informed you I'm tasked by Philip, the King of Spain, to find a portrait artist in the region of Lombardy. The king wishes to have paintings made of the Spanish cabinet members who report to me in Milan. It is a business proposition for which I am here. If impressed, I'll be obliged to consider your daughter for the commissions... I confess, however, I've almost set my sights on another. It will be difficult to match his skills."

"But of course," said Amilcare in place of his wife. "Sofonisba studied in Rome under the great Michelangelo, and he sings her praises."

"So I've been told. I'm curious to see what a young woman such as she can do. I won't take up much of your time... I've instructed my man to depart within the quarter hour."

Discreetly, Amilcare wiped a linen handkerchief across his lips, then nodded vigorously at Sofonisba, who remained near the threshold, encouraging her to join them. Obediently, she complied, and when she reached her father's side, with a hand on her back, he pushed her forward a few more steps. Brightly he said, "This is she. This is my daughter Sofonisba. Daughter, this is the Duke of Alba."

The Spanish noble turned his full attention upon the young woman that barely reached his shoulder. Respectfully he said, "At last we meet, signorina."

With her head bowed, Sofonisba gave a little curtsey. Then rising up, she took in his full appearance. The duke had seemed an impressive figure from her window, but now standing with only two feet between them, she was fully confronted by his formidable presence. He was dressed in a black cloak, black vest, and black hose, with only a crisp white ruff at his neck to give some welcome relief to his severe attire. As her eyes moved upward, she saw the firm set of his lips and the jagged scar, now long healed, that gave him a menacing air.

And then she looked into his somber face. At first she saw the haughty sense of entitlement, just as she had expected. But after a moment, deep in the depths of those dark pools, she discerned something else. As she continued regarding him, it seemed he responded to her frank, wide-eyed inspection and against his will a curtain lifted, revealing more than he'd intended. It caught her by surprise, and in that instant she believed it startled him too.

It was the duke who first averted his eyes. Tugging at his stiff collar, he cleared his throat, then turned to Bianca and politely answered her inquiries about his trip from Rome.

Sofonisba watched him for a moment, wondering what she had seen and what had caused him to be the first to lower his gaze and turn away. Despite the claims he was a callous and ruthless soldier, she sensed he was a man who had suffered deeply. Instead of thinking less of him, his faltering retreat dispelled any qualms Sofonisba might have had about him. Suddenly, she realized she didn't fear the man at all. On the contrary, she almost felt sorry for him.

And then the duke looked back at her and she saw, once again, he wore a mask of disdain and arrogance. Whatever she had glimpsed before was safeguarded, and in his eyes she now saw only hardness and a glint of steel. No matter. The man's personal life was not for her to pry into; she would do well to remember that from now on—whatever the outcome of this meeting.

"Sofonisba," said Amilcare, interrupting her thoughts. "It seems we owe Andrea Amati our gratitude. Duke Alba was telling me in the courtyard that he is here in Cremona today specifically to pay him a visit."

"Signor Amati, the luthier?" Sofonisba asked.

The duke turned toward her and regarded her coolly. "Yes, it just so happens Amati's studio is located just across town. Seeing as I was here on other business today, it is the only reason I agreed to organize this meeting."

An uncomfortable silence fell upon them. To ease the tensions, Amilcare wiped his brow and inquired politely, "You play the violin, messer?"

"I find it a tolerable pastime," Alba replied. "I commissioned a new instrument from Maestro Amati several months ago. I have an appointment with him in a few minutes to acquire it. He is a true artist who crafts his violins from more than seventy different pieces of wood."

"I've heard they are quite acoustically unique," said Amilcare jovially. "They say he only makes his violins from trees on which nightingales sing."

Alba looked at him and raised an eyebrow. "Yes, well, his reputation does precede him as does that of your daughter. Conveniently, Amati lives in Cremona too. I can kill two birds with one stone."

Amilcare laughed politely at the duke's witticism, but Sofonisba didn't respond in kind. She didn't appreciate being considered a cursory task to be dealt with quickly. Hesitantly, she glanced at her mother and saw her shake her head imperceptibly.

Reminded of her station and the lofty position of their guest, she bit her lip and listened as her father continued extolling her praises. "As you can see, Duke," Amilcare said, gesturing to Sofonisba's portraits of the family that hung on the walls around them, "my daughter is a skilled and prolific portraitist."

"But you must see her most recent painting," agreed Bianca. "The Contessa of Montefiori was simply ecstatic with the results."

"That is what I am here for," the duke replied patiently. "May I have a moment to review your daughter's work?"

"Certainly, messer. We are your servants and at your disposal," encouraged Amilcare.

With a polite inclination of his head, the duke moved slowly around the room. He paused before each portrait and regarded it thoughtfully. He continued his slow appraisal of Sofonisba's work but stopped when he came to the contessa's picture still sitting on the easel.

As the clock on the mantel loudly ticked, he stroked his hand through his beard and no one said a word. For a busy man, it seemed he was now in no hurry to make a rapid departure. Sofonisba studied the duke's rigid form, then glanced over at her mother and father, telegraphing silent messages as they waited to learn the Spanish governor's assessment.

The duke's reticence and arrogant nature did little to inspire her confidence, and like her parents, Sofonisba also waited in a heightened state of anticipation. Realizing she was holding her breath, she slowly exhaled and fiddled with the belt of her skirt. She watched him curiously, her heart thumping a staccato beat.

With only the scraps of servant gossip to inform her, she had no way of knowing that things rarely surprised the duke—or that he'd be struck dumb by the talents *and* the expressive eyes of a girl half his age in this provincial nobleman's household. She also wouldn't have guessed, as Alba slowly paced the room, his heart too had begun hammering in his chest, and all thoughts of his duties to the King of Spain, his previous engagement with Amati the violin maker—even the appointment with Mademoiselle Durand to enjoy her pleasures later that evening—had fled his mind.

Instead, Sofonisba, along with her parents, was treated to a view of the duke's broad back, who seemed oblivious of the anxiety he was causing her family. Finally, when the tension became too great, Amilcare coughed nervously into his handkerchief, which appeared to bring Alba to his senses. Slowly the duke swiveled around, looked at Amilcare, and with his features perfectly set said in an even tone, "Signore, it seems what they say about your daughter's talent is true."

Amilcare let out a contented sigh, and his face radiated pleasure. "My daughter has a gift, no?"

Alba nodded thoughtfully. "Your daughter's work is exquisite, Signor Anguissola. Very finely executed. Such beauty can lift a man's spirits and elevate him to divine heights."

"It is with great pleasure to hear you say such things, messer," said Amilcare.

"There is something pure-hearted, rare, and intelligent about how she captures a person's expression as if she looks into their very soul. With a lightness of brush, she reveals things that make you want to lose yourself in her colors and shadows." The duke turned back to regard the contessa's image, and without actually touching the canvas, he raised his hand and reverently traced her cheek. "The way she paints the flush of the woman's skin and the expression on her face... And her eyes... They are exquisite." He cleared his throat and added quickly, "The Contessa Montefiori's pearls seem almost as real as the ones you wear, Signora Anguissola."

"Messer, you do us great honor with your words," replied Bianca sweetly.

He shook his head in disbelief. "To think a woman, a mere female, could possess this much talent. It's rather unconventional! It is astonishing to me she paints so well, if not better, than some men I know."

Heat rose to Sofonisba's cheeks. The man was bestowing compliments upon her parents but hadn't deigned to address her directly.

I'm standing right here! she fumed. *Yes, a woman can paint as well as a man. I am the artist—and although a mere woman in your eyes—I can discuss the merits of my own work with a noble man such as yourself!*

Once again, she felt rebuked and trivialized. This time, Sofonisba couldn't hold her tongue. The man was insufferable! But just as she was about to express her feelings, she caught sight of her mother and quickly shut her mouth.

As clear as day, she heard her mother say, *Small-minded men may think women are the weaker sex, but you and I know differently. We are strong. We are born to create, not to destroy. Women are not war-like. We do not tear down and defeat. Instead, we carry children, nurture love, and foster peace. It is in our nature to bring solace and create beautiful things from nothing... Just like Elena with her music, Minerva with her poems, and you, Sofonisba, with your paintings. From nothing, you create something that will endure long after you are gone...*

Sofonisba gave her mother a wan smile, then turned to glance at Amilcare and saw him looking at her proudly. She realized this was his moment too, and she certainly wasn't going to disappoint him by upsetting such an illustrious visitor. So, instead, Sofonisba lifted her head a notch higher and swallowed the words she longed to say.

Unaware an outburst had just been avoided, Alba, with great composure, finally turned to address Sofonisba directly. He tilted his head, as if acknowledging her to be the victor, and said, "I must confess I've been enlightened today. I had my doubts, but I have been swayed. The other candidates I've been considering are not worthy of holding a candle to your work... If you are in agreement, I'd very much like to have a portrait done by your hand, signorina."

Sofonisba looked over at her father and was surprised he hadn't popped all the buttons off his jacket. Despite the excitement that also was bubbling up inside her, she managed to maintain her decorum. With a polite nod, as he had done, she accepted his invitation. "It would be my pleasure to paint your portrait, messer. I will do my best to capture a true likeness that will please you."

The duke regarded her intently, then said, "I believe you will indeed. I look forward to it. And if it is a success, you will be granted the commission to paint all the men in my cabinet." Then, turning to Amilcare, he said, "The portraits must be painted in my residence in Milan. If you agree, Signor Anguissola, I will ride onto the Ducal Palace but leave a small retinue here so your daughter may join me at the end of the week. Signorina Anguissola will remain in my care until the painting is completed. Certainly she is welcome to bring anyone from your household to act as her chaperone."

Amilcare nodded delightedly at the duke. "But of course! We accept your generous offer. If you would like to stay with us for supper this evening, we would be overjoyed to entertain you."

Without a backward glance in her direction, the two men walked across the room, discussing the commission's details and Sofonisba's forthcoming trip to Milan.

Chapter 15

For God and King

Shortly after the Duke of Alba departed the Anguissola household, there was much rejoicing, followed closely by heated debates about who should accompany Sofonisba to Milan. At first, Amilcare had briefly considered accompanying his daughter as he had done before in Rome. But Asdrubale, now almost ten, was proving to be quite a handful. His son, not as bright as his older sisters, needed more guidance with his lessons. If the boy was going to amount to something, Amilcare felt he needed to personally attend to the boy's education.

And then, of course, he was most concerned about Bianca. Despite resuming her household responsibilities, his wife still looked a bit pale and complained of tiredness. Often she preferred to rest until noon, letting Fabia make decisions for the evening meal in her stead. Amilcare feared her illness had returned and that she would not fare well without him.

Had Minerva been in residence, she would have vociferously begged to be the one to accompany Sofonisba. But, now that she was ensconced in the Ducal Palace in Mantova, Amilcare decided upon Elena. Given that his second eldest daughter was now engaged to a young Milanese count whose family had ties to court, it seemed she was the logical choice. Elena would not only be closer to Massimiliano's family, but the Viscount of Bramante would be at hand should the Anguissola sisters require assistance.

By Friday, after rapid preparation, the two sisters sat side by side comfortably in the duke's well-appointed mahogany coach. It was a luxurious affair, emblazoned with Alba's coat of arms. Running her hand over the velvet seat and fingering the silk tassels that dangled from the window, Sofonisba whispered to Elena, "Is this a dream? If it is, please don't wake me! Have you ever seen such finery?"

"I feel as if I'd died and gone to heaven," admitted Elena. "Not even Massimiliano's transport is as fine as this!"

As uncontrollable sounds of silvery glee pealed from the box upon which the groomsmen were seated, Sofonisba wondered if the men that sat atop the carriage were exchanging concerned looks. Not really caring, she shrugged and continued to enjoy the drive.

The trip to Milan was relatively brief compared to the one Sofonisba had taken to Rome a few years earlier. The sisters had bid farewell to their family in the morning, passed by Piacenza at noon, and reached their destination by mid-afternoon. Alighting from the carriage, they were warmly received by the duke's serving staff. Sofonisba was immediately informed by the residence's majordomo that Alba was tied up on official state business and would be so for the rest of the evening. This news hadn't disappointed her; she could wait until the morning to have her first audience with the master of the house.

Once the sisters had been fed an excellent meal, they bathed in ample copper tubs to remove the dust of their travels. Then donning night dresses embroidered with lilies by their mother, the two girls snuggled together in the big feather bed in the duke's guest chamber.

Before blowing out the candle and flopping back onto the soft cushions, Sofonisba sighed. "Elena pinch me! I still can't believe this is real!"

The only response she got was a pillow plopped on her face. Sitting up, Sofonisba retaliated by grabbing her sister and tickling her. Together they collapsed back into the soft sheets, valiantly trying to muffle their gales of laughter. When a chambermaid knocked and entered the room, bringing them a fresh pitcher of water, she smiled at the girls' playful antics.

"*Ehi*, there young misses! It does my heart good to hear laughter in this big ol' gloomy house again! Should you all be needing anything... anything a'tall, just call for me."

As the young girl in the lace cap bid them goodnight, Sofonisba imagined that just as the groomsmen good-naturedly accepted the girls' light-hearted spirits, so had the chambermaid.

The following morning, dressed in a dark blue dress with a scooped-out neckline, Sofonisba let herself be led by the same young maid down a long hall in the direction of the room the duke had designated as her painting studio. From the drawing room, Sofonisba could hear the sound of a spinet and knew her sister Elena had made herself at home. As she walked behind the servant, she glanced curiously at the paintings that lined the walls. It seemed the duke was partial to battle scenes, horses, and darkly religious Madonnas and saints.

She slowed her steps to admire the large canvases, noting the drama and passion with which the artist had imbued them. *Impressive*, she thought, making a mental note to return later to study the paintings some more. About to move on, her attention was caught by a young man's portrait, about her age. The likeness to the duke was remarkable, down to his dark eyes and the sweep of his aquiline nose.

"Is that Alba's son?" Sofonisba asked the girl.

"Yes, it is Fernando de Toledo. He's quite handsome, don't you think?"

"Is he in residence here, too?" Sofonisba asked nonchalantly.

"No, he is a general in the cavalry division that protects and polices Rome. Since I've been here, he's only visited once."

Sofonisba listened politely, somewhat relieved by the maid's answer. The portrait had conjured up the stories Bibiana had told her previously—how the duke had an affair with the miller's daughter after his own marriage had soured.

The maid, noticing her hesitation, urged, "Come, signorina! This way. The duke will be along shortly. He is a very punctual man."

Squaring her shoulders, Sofonisba followed the girl up a short flight of stairs to the next gallery. There they paused in front of a door with brass sconces on either side. The maid pushed it open, and then with a tilt of her head indicated Sofonisba should enter before her.

Sofonisba stepped into the bright salon, so unlike other parts of the house, and was well-satisfied by the looks of things. Alba had diligently noted everything Amilcare had advised him to acquire for his daughter's painting needs. The room was open and airy, and the expansive window looked out upon a well-kept garden. A large easel stood in the center of the room, and canvases were stacked in a far corner. On a table near the window, in a neat arrangement, were brushes of every size. She saw her case of paints, oils, and minerals, too, had been unpacked and were waiting for her inspection.

Sofonisba picked up a folded smock that lay on the table and tied it around her waist, then set about measuring and stretching her canvas. With a small hammer, she tacked the material over a large frame. Satisfied with her work, she turned her attention to mixing a gesso wash to spread over the linen to prime the surface.

She glanced at the clock and noted the appointed time of their meeting was now an hour past due. Picking up her sketchbook, she flipped it to a new page and waited for her subject to grace her with his presence. Occasionally, when she heard footsteps in the hall, she looked up from her sketching, but when they passed by, she let out her breath and wondered what was keeping her illustrious subject. It appeared matters far more urgent than a painter from Cremona occupied his thoughts this morning.

The click of the door, shortly toward midday, startled and broke her reverie. "Excuse my delay," Alba said, giving her a gracious if not curt nod. "Affairs of the state have kept me occupied since dawn."

Peering around the room, he asked, "Do you have everything you need, signorina?"

"Yes, and more," she replied as she stood up a little awkwardly to greet him. She moved to the table upon which lay her drawing tools. "I should think you had acquired enough for ten artists."

The duke turned away when he saw her confused expression and began to pace the room restlessly, then stopped by the table that held her supplies. "I hope your journey was pleasant. Did you enjoy the carriage

I left for you? Are your accommodations to your liking? If you think another salon would be better suited to your painting, you need only to ask. This palace is quite large…"

He looked up, and under his intense gaze, she stammered, "Ah, you… you have been very kind, Duke. With its southern exposure, this room is a perfect place to paint… and my sister and I are quite comfortable."

"I heard your sister… Elena, isn't it… playing the spinet earlier. She is remarkably good."

"Elena excels in music. She told me your instrument is the finest she's ever seen."

He merely nodded. To Sofonisba, he seemed larger than life—his presence filled the room, making her uncomfortable. *This is ridiculous. I have nothing to fear,* she thought. *I am here at his request. I must focus on the task at hand.*

Sofonisba took a deep breath, and to regain her composure, she turned her attention to rearranging things on the table. But instead of putting things in order, her shaking fingers knocked a box of brushes off the edge.

"Mi scusi!" she exclaimed, berating herself under her breath. Clumsily, she bent down to clean up the mess. To assist her, Alba reached down and collected painting utensils that had rolled under the table.

Sofonisba rose up, proudly lifting her head a notch higher. When she glanced over at Alba, she saw he too was standing tall again, idly caressing the palm of his hand with one of her brushes. Flustered, she realized his gaze had wandered from her eyes to the front of her apron that was now slightly askew.

He cleared his throat and averted his gaze to the scene outside the window. Self-consciously, Sofonisba placed a hand on her chest, and with a soft gasp realized when she had bent over, her tight corset had pushed her breasts up high, to the point where they threatened to spill over the edge of her bodice. Her cheeks flamed red, and she felt beads of moisture dampen her brow. With Alba's back to her, she yanked up her dress and righted her apron to cover her more modestly. When she was sure her person was in order, she turned back to him but saw his gaze was now fixed on a point outside the window.

Curiously, Sofonisba stood on tiptoes and peered over his shoulder, trying to see what held his interest. At first, she could only see the dense outcropping of woods at the edge of the garden. But as her eyes focused, she saw a small fawn amble through the shadows cast by the trees. In his wake, a pair of deer gently nudged the wobbly fellow along.

It was a serene and tranquil sight, so she was surprised when the duke turned around to see his face darkened by a surly scowl.

"Is something amiss?" she asked, thinking it was she who had displeased him. She hadn't even begun his portrait and believed she might be dispatched home the day after her arrival.

Alba contemplated her for a moment. "No, no. It has been a difficult morning... It is I who is a bit distracted."

Sofonisba relaxed and said, "Did you see the fawn in the garden? It was a tender sight."

Alba shrugged and turned back to the window. "I confess I did not. If truth be told, I'm more accustomed to battlefields than charming meadow scenes... I have little time to waste contemplating the deer that infest my gardens. I'll have the groundsman trap them."

Slightly taken aback, Sofonisba boldly countered, "Oh, but you can't! They are a family."

He turned to look at her. "Signorina, I fear you are too soft! They are pests who eat away at the shrubbery. Just like the other pests that infiltrate my life..."

"Pests?" Sofonisba asked in a confused tone.

"Yes, annoying scourges that need to be put down for the betterment of all!" Alba raised an eyebrow. They come in many varieties—Venetian, Florentine, French... Protestants."

Sofonisba nodded but remained quiet. She knew the duke was a powerful man, charged with maintaining peace in the region. Since the French defeat at Pavia and the Imperial armies of Charles V took over Lombardy, he had been on one mission after another, leading men into war to ensure Spanish rule in Italy. Of course, such banal pastoral woodland scenes would hold little interest to him.

When the pause became too uncomfortable, however, in an attempt to find common ground and placate the man, Sofonisba mustered a cordial tone and said, "I have heard of your many victories. My father told me it was you who waged war against the Papal Army of Paul IV, an ally of the French."

"Your father is correct. Fortunately, it wasn't necessary to attack Rome directly. I'm quite good at achieving the results I seek—making people comply with my demands using force—but I am best known for my cunning and masterful stratagems."

"Stratagems?"

"I won't bore you with the details. Let's just say I compelled the pope to accept peace, making it a most lucrative offer. Once he did... well, the dominoes fell. The French capitulated and Spanish domination here was consolidated." He smiled thinly at her and continued. "And here we are today. It is precisely for these reasons Philip wishes to honor those who serve him on his war council with portraits painted by you. I trust you will be more than worthy of the task at hand. If things go well, perhaps you will remain and continue your work here. There are many other friends whom I could introduce you to."

Sofonisba looked at him in surprise; she thought she was there on a trial basis. But from the appearance of things, and by the wealth of painting supplies stocked about the room—enough to paint a legion of men—it seemed he had already made up his mind to award her the remaining commissions.

Alba regarded her intently, and once again Sofonisba was confused by his enigmatic expression. Feeling a lock of hair on her cheek, she reached up and quickly slicked it back again. In a concerned tone, she asked, "Messer, is everything all right? Do you require—"

"I'm quite fine..." he replied curtly, averting his eyes again. Walking to the easel in the center of the room, he said, "I see you are ready to begin. Again, apologies for the delay. I'm usually quite punctual."

"I am here to serve you, signore. If you are ready to start, I'd like to first make a few preliminary sketches. Please take a seat."

"But of course," replied Alba. "I am at your disposal... That is, until the king demands my attention."

With a drawing crayon in her hand, Sofonisba walked over and stood before him, studying his face from several angles. Finally, she asked, "Could you lift your head a little higher and to the left, signore?"

He did as she indicated, but after pondering the pose she shook her head. "I think it will be better in the other direction. At that angle, the light will cast the side of the other cheek in shadow."

"So the scar won't show?" he asked.

"I just thought..."

"But signorina," he said evenly, "it is a mark of honor. I am a soldier, and I wear it proudly."

"As you wish, messer, I will defer to your better judgment," she said, playing with the bristles of her brush. Then, noting Alba's glance was trained on her slender hands, she quickly set it down.

Sofonisba walked back to her easel and began drawing. As she did, a quiet fell over them, and in the distance they could hear Elena's music sneaking into the room from under the door, swirling around them. As she worked out various scenarios and expressions for the portrait, Alba diligently followed her instructions to tilt his head, reposition his arms, and swivel his shoulders.

After a moment, she asked, "Tell me, Duke, shall I paint you in full battle armor?"

"Of course, signorina. That is what distinguishes me in King Philip's eyes... and the eyes of the world." He glanced over at her and added, "I noted your gift to bring the contessa's jewels to life. I expect you to do the same for my battle regalia. In itself, it is a work of art crafted by gifted goldsmiths and artisans in Castile. It is my most prized possession."

As he talked, she noticed his posture begin to soften ever so slightly.

She took it as a good sign, and she too began to relax. Not to antagonize him with inane words and blundering gestures, she held her tongue to maintain decorum. It was just as well, as she had run out of things to say. As her mind became engrossed in capturing the incline of the duke's noble head and the set of his proud shoulders, unconsciously she began to hum softly to the song Elena was playing.

"You are singing, signorina," the duke said after a moment.

Immediately, Sofonisba flushed and looked up, believing she had displeased him again. "I'm sorry. I didn't mean to be rude. Sometimes I become so lost in my work, I forget my place. I..."

"No need to apologize. I enjoy music... You have a lovely voice. Do you play an instrument like your sister?"

Sofonisba let out a small chuckle. "I fear not, messer. I've tried on occasion, but I play the spinet very poorly. My rhythm is terrible, and I'm forever massacring the chords. I have no time to practice like Elena. I'd much rather paint than make music."

Her frank admission made the duke regard her curiously. "We all have our passions, and I admire your dedication to your art." A lull descended upon them again but was broken when he suddenly said, "This evening, I will play my violin for you."

She looked at him in surprise. "The one you ordered from Signor Amati in Cremona?"

"Yes," he said. "It is a remarkable instrument." He shook his head, then added, "I must admit, Cremona was quite a revelation. I hadn't expected to meet two such highly artistic individuals there."

Sofonisba was a bit taken aback by his awkward compliment, but still politely replied, "I should enjoy listening to you. Perhaps we can convince Elena to join in." Hoping to keep the pleasant discourse alive, she asked, "When did you learn to play?"

"When I was a boy. My grandfather insisted. And now it is my only real solace."

Sofonisba was astonished at this declaration. Only moments before, the man had reined in his emotions, dismissing charming woodland creatures and idyllic scenes as poppycock and nonsense... and now here he was revealing a more sympathetic side.

Heartened by the news it had been his grandfather to instill a passion for music, Sofonisba believed it contradicted the previous rumors she had heard. Wanting to further dispel the myths about the man, she said, "Your grandfather sounds like an enlightened man... one who appreciated the arts. Tell me about him."

Alba shot her a sideways glance as if to judge her interest, then in measured words said, "My grandfather, Fadrique Álvarez de Toledo, was an exceptional man. I was born in the Province of Ávila in the Castle of Alba Tormes, my family's home. Unfortunately, my parents died when I was quite young. My father, like me, was a soldier, and he never returned from battle."

A cloud passed over his face, and he studied the ground, lost in thought. But when he heard Sofonisba issue a little cough, he righted his head and resumed the prescribed pose.

To ease the tension that descended upon them again, she said, "Your grandfather sounds like a man of honor."

Alba looked over at her and pursed his lips. "Fadrique Álvarez was a man of steel... He raised me to believe in God and gave me a mission. He made me the soldier I am today, teaching me to be a warrior, like my father before me. I accompanied him into battle when I was only six."

"Six!" she exclaimed. "But how could a child..."

He swiveled his head to look at her. "I've always been an ambitious man, and it started when I was a mere boy. My grandfather taught me how to be a man. I owe him much—my title, my career, my education. He did what was necessary to ensure I was worthy of the Alba title." With pride, he continued. "Fadrique was a stern, formidable gentleman. He disciplined me, yes... but after he died I was ready to assume the title of Alba. Shortly after that, at fourteen, I rode into battle on my own and then again at seventeen under the guidance of Inigo Fernande Velasco.

Because I served him so successfully, I was appointed governor of Fuenterrabia, and later I became the High Steward to Charles the King of Spain. Shortly after that, I married."

"Did you return to the Alba Estate with your wife..." Sofonisba began but stopped when she saw the scowl return to the duke's face.

Alba regarded her under hooded eyes, then said in a cool tone, "Yes, of course. My wife and I were married only a few years... She died unexpectedly." Off-handedly he supplied, "She was often unwell, always begging me to stay with her and not ride off to war. We often disagreed... It was a long, long time ago."

He gazed straight ahead again and didn't see her troubled expression. As Sofonisba pondered the duke's story, she couldn't help but feel compassion for the man. As a young boy, he had never known the caress of a loving mother to ease his childhood dreads. Instead, he had grown up at the hands of an elderly man who had shaped his destiny as a soldier before he had barely set one foot from the cradle. Despite the gratitude he bestowed upon his grandfather, by the shadowy expression that had crossed his face before it set into a stern mask, she began to believe there was some truth to Bibiana's gossip. She thought it was very likely the old man had beaten the poor lad into submission, forcing him to accept God's path and the career as a soldier.

And then, after finding love so early in life, Alba had lost his wife suddenly. She opened her mouth to ask another question but, by his tight-lipped expression, Sofonisba realized Alba would brook no more inquiries about his personal life. Contritely, she refocused her attention on her sketching and was relieved a few minutes later to hear a light rap upon the door.

Alba gave her an apologetic look. "I'm afraid we are to suffer many intrusions throughout these working sessions." He raised his voice and commanded the intruder to enter.

When the door opened, Sofonisba saw one of Alba's attachés on the threshold holding a letter. After breaking the seal and scanning the message, Alba, with a brief apology, dismissed himself for the day and hurried out of the room, claiming he needed to respond to a pressing matter.

Alone again, Sofonisba glanced down at the preliminary sketches she had made. With the tip of her pencil, she emphasized the classic line of the duke's nose. Then, picking up a charcoal, she began to fill out his beard and the ruff around his neck. She was starting to make some progress, but the man was full of intriguing contradictions—it was going to be a challenge to capture him on canvas.

After a week had passed and following a few more preliminary sketching sessions, the real work on Alba's portrait began. The days slipped together seamlessly, and as they spent more time in one another's company—painting and playing music—Alba's demeanor toward her softened. In her presence, his posture was less stoic, and his icy tones became more pleasant. And, although still wary, she too realized, with increased familiarity, she was learning to appreciate his company.

Sometimes the hours they spent in the painting salon were passed in silence; other times, Sofonisba coaxed a story from him. As the portrait progressed, she realized she admired the man—he had been a decorated soldier for a reason. As she listened to his stories, she learned he had trained King Philip, teaching him the practical lessons of warfare. Side by side, they fought the Italian wars, decisively defeating the French forces under the Dauphin of France's command.

It was no wonder the pope, after admitting defeat too, had turned around and anointed the duke for his bravery. Shortly after peace was restored, Alba was granted the highest honor the papacy had to offer—the Golden Rose and blessed sword to recognize his singular efforts to champion Catholicism.

In his presence, as Sofonisba worked, sometimes she recited lines of poetry and other times lines from Homer she knew from memory. Alba, in turn, regaled her with stories of his past exploits. The battle tales, at least the ones he confided, were replete with heroism and glory, and she found them quite thrilling. Like the stories her father read to her at night, Alba spoke of white stallions and garrisons of brave men—appropriate and acceptable fare for someone who worshiped Greek warriors and Carthaginian heroes.

Once, however, standing before her in his full suit armor, his hand holding his sword, the mask of discretion slipped. It surprised her to hear him admit, "War is a terrible bloody business."

He stared at the far wall, as if in a trance, saying more to himself than to her, "I've done brutal things... killed men face to face with my sword... and with my bare hands. I've seen men's intestines spill from..."

He fell silent, slouched slightly, and let his blade fall to his side as if suddenly the weight of holding it was too much to bear. When he didn't continue, Sofonisba could only imagine he was reliving moments on the battlefield that were burned into his memory. Like tragic mythological tales in which the gods mercilessly punished humans or horrific anecdotes from the Bible in which ruthless leaders killed innocent babes, the duke was responsible for brutal slaughters.

Alba frowned, and she could tell he regretted his previous words. The moment of remorse quickly passed, and despite the awful weight of his armor and the colorful medals of valor pinned to his chest, he adjusted his shoulders and stood a few inches taller.

Proudly, he said, "I am a soldier, signorina. What I have done, and I will do again, is in the name of my king and country and my God, the almighty Savior. I am the defender of the Catholic religion and will fight to overcome the heretics, the Protestants... and any single person—including their children—who would defy us."

It was an astonishing revelation but one expected of a soldier, and she believed he would go to great lengths to protect the realm and fight for what he knew to be right and good. *But still... is this really how a man of God conducts himself... murdering innocent children in cold blood... destroying others simply because they do not see eye to eye with you?* Sofonisba felt chilled, and a niggling worry entered in her heart. *He is a fearsome warrior, yes, but these things would torture a man's soul long after a battle had been won.*

At a loss for words, Sofonisba continued painting, adding a darker color along the duke's jawline to further delineate the jagged external scar that marked his face. But now she wondered about the internal lesions that couldn't be seen by the naked eye.

She looked up and covertly studied him, observing how the light and shadows played over his face and wondered, *At night when you lie in bed, do these visions of killing resurface, causing your heart to race and your breath to shorten? Do you hear the wailing of women and innocent babes still ringing in your ears?*

It seemed he sensed her questioning eyes upon him, and steadily Alba glanced in her direction. As before, at the time of their first meeting, he captured her full attention. Now, however, she believed she understood the conflicting emotions that resided deep within him. Yet this time there was something more reflected in his eyes... It reminded her of the way Bernardino Campi had looked at her.

The breath caught in her throat as Sofonisba realized what Alba's eyes communicated, and this time it was she who looked away first, confused by what she saw.

Chapter 16

The Duke's Dream

*O*nce again, he could hear the sweet strains of violin music. It soothed his tired mind and drifted around him, embracing him and providing solace. Slowly he opened his eyes, and the music took shape, changing colors from serene blue to purple. He let himself fall back into it, allowing the melody to buoy him up as he floated on its gentle waves.

He wasn't sure how long he drifted, but after a while the current picked up and began to swirl around him. Weakly he tried to fight the force that threatened to pull him under. He gulped in great breaths of air and tried to stay afloat, but it was a losing battle. Calling out for help, he reached out a hand toward a bright light, believing it was his salvation.

It was then he saw her. She was dressed in a soft diaphanous gown that floated around her slim body. A light from behind illuminated her, and he could clearly see her supple form through the thin material. He watched in bemusement as the woman languidly beckoned him with her outstretched hand. She mouthed words, but the violin music grew louder, and he strained his ears, trying desperately to hear her.

When she saw he didn't understand, the girl gave him a provocative look and moved slowly toward the bed. She stood over him, and it seemed she radiated light. She placed a knee upon the mattress, then bent over and kissed him. At the touch of her lips, he groaned in pleasure. He reached up to pull her to him, but just when she was within his embrace, she melted away, and once again he was back in the murky current. All about him was the jettisoned debris of bottles, planks of wood, dead men's bodies, and bloody heads of horses.

The music, now strident, made him cover his ears. As he touched his hands to his face, he felt the wide-open gash on his cheek that gushed blood into the dark water. Horrified, he propelled himself forward. Just as he was about to break away, a creature from the abyss grabbed his legs and pulled him under. He tried to break free, but the harder he fought, the creature held him tighter in its vise-like hold, dragging him down into the quagmire of dismembered limbs. Just as the dank water that smelled of death filled his nostrils, he shuddered violently and came fully awake.

Alba stared at the ceiling, his breathing ragged and uneven. To control his pounding heart, he lay utterly still, trying to regain control of his thoughts. Despite his best efforts, when he closed his lids, the grotesque images he had conjured in his nightmare continued to race through his mind like whirling dervishes.

The duke listened to the beating clock and the sigh of the embers on the grate. As the minutes ticked past, sanity was finally restored. Flinging off the bed covers, Alba rose and paced the room. As he walked, the floorboards creaked under the weight of him. Although his breathing had returned to normal, a vein in his forehead pulsed violently.

Hastily he poured himself a drink from the decanter on the sideboard and downed the glass in a single swallow. He stood by the window, rolling the glass across his temple as if he could iron out the turmoil in his brain. As the drink began to calm his nerves and the night air revived him, he focused on the pleasant images that had started the dream—the girl with the large saucer-shaped eyes—eyes in which a man could lose himself forever. It was only in his dreams she came and offered herself to him.

He shook his head, walked to his desk, and picked up a letter. It was a royal summons, and, for the first time in his life, he reviewed it with dismay, wanting to ignore it. He read it over and frowned. His king was calling him home to Spain. Within the month, he would leave Italy and resume his duties at Philip's royal court in Madrid. He poured himself another glass of liquor, stared into the fire burning low on the hearth, and contemplated his future and where his true allegiances now lay.

Since Spain and France had declared a truce, signing the Peace of Cateau-Cambrésis, which had ended the open wars and hostilities between the two countries, his militarized peacekeeping mission on the

Italian peninsula was no longer needed. As part of the truce and terms of the treaty Alba brokered, Philip, King of Spain, was required to marry the daughter of the French king—Elisabeth of Valois. She was the eldest daughter of Henry II and Catherine de' Medici—one of their more attractive daughters—and because of her mother, Elisabeth could trace her lineage to the Italian aristocracy and Lorenzo de' Medici.

The duke knew full well how beautiful and witty Philip's young bride was, for it had been he who had stood in for him in the church in Notre Dame in Paris to perform the proxy wedding. It was just one of his many mundane duties to ensure the union between France and Spain was secured and cemented. Alba almost pitied the seventeen-year-old French princess. She was a pawn in an intricate game played between masterful kings.

Once the negotiations had been arranged, Alba had been bored and annoyed to stand in for Philip and suffer through the posturings of the French nobility during the marriage ceremony. It was all he could do not to yawn and roll his eyes at the silly demands of the French king and queen. But when the duke first caught a glimpse of their trembling and pale daughter, he'd been amused by her nervous, breathy spasms she attempted to cover behind a lace handkerchief. But, in the light that filtered through the church's stained-glass windows, as he watched the French princess throughout the ceremony, he'd suddenly remembered the sanctity of marriage.

Later at the celebratory feast, when he'd spoken to Elisabeth for the first time, he had been charmed further by her lilting French accent and iris blue eyes. Once or twice, she had even made his tightly clenched mouth soften as she recounted lively anecdotes of the courtiers and swains who had attended her farewell feast in France.

"Just look at Lord Geoffrey over there! Dressed in his finest purple and orange britches, complete with a cock's tail in his cap. I couldn't tell him from the stuffed birds that decorate my father's hunting lodge if my life depended on it."

Alba had smiled wryly at her witty observations and had to

admit, despite her extreme youth and tendency to hiccup at the most inopportune times, he had taken a liking to Elisabeth. She possessed a sharp and intelligent mind, and he was further surprised to learn she fancied herself to be a portrait artist and wished to continue perfecting her painting abilities.

Shaking off thoughts of Spain's king and queen, Alba swirled the contents of his glass around and looked down at the amber liquid. He was tired of answering to the royal's beck and call, tired of catering to their every whim. He wished to think instead of matters that were becoming increasingly dear to his heart, things that eased his mind and gave him solace in the middle of the night.

He raised the glass to his lips and took a long swallow. As the brandy slid down his throat and the familiar burning sensation engulfed him, his thoughts drifted to Sofonisba, and he heard her velvet Italianate voice and saw her dark, handsome eyes. Alba closed his eyes and thought, *I can't bear to return home to Spain and leave her behind...*

He set his glass down, then picked up his cloak and wrapped it around his narrow frame. Lighting a candle, he left his private rooms and walked down the drafty hall to the main gallery below the sleeping chambers. There he stood in front of the portrait that Sofonisba had finished almost eleven months before.

Alba lifted the candle higher and studied the man in the painting dispassionately, as if they were not one and the same. The impressive general before him, posed in a beautiful breastplate of Toledo steel— embellished with gold and cloisonné inlays—seemed authoritative and commanding. Across his chest, he proudly wore a crucifix and the red sash indicating he was a knight of the Order of the Golden Fleece. By his noble stance and arrogant tilt of the head, no one viewing this portrait would ever question his authority, ability to lead men into war, or allegiance to God.

It was a remarkable likeness, and Sofonisba had done an excellent job depicting him as a valiant hero. Yet, if you looked closely, Alba realized the artist had also captured his humanity. There had been many victories to his credit, but if you observed the face of the man in the portrait carefully, you could see the lines of sadness in the downturned mouth, which spoke of the price he had paid to secure them.

In real life, the duke clenched his jaw, and a vein began pulsating at his temple. In consternation, once again, he realized one couldn't hide anything from Sofonisba's all-seeing eyes.

Of course, as he had known it would be, the portrait was an overnight sensation. Once it was made public, invitations and requests began to flow in, and in a short time, Sofonisba became the toast of Milan. To accommodate all the new commissions, the duke graciously extended his invitation for Sofonisba and her sister to remain as guests in his house. The canvases he had purposefully purchased in advance were being put to good use.

As her most ardent patron, the duke worked tirelessly to promote her. He allowed her to continue painting in the lower salon just off the garden and gave her access and the free use of the rest of his home. As the weeks and months progressed, she became integral to his life. Now he couldn't imagine life without her. Everywhere he turned, there were signs of her—from the flowers she collected and arranged in bouquets in the hall to the soft humming that drifted from her studio. At night, as the violet evening shadows descended after sunset, he played his violin and watched her under hooded lids as she gazed dreamily out the window.

But, mostly, there was laughter and lightness once again in his life.

It thrilled him to hear her step in the hall, and when they met by accident in the gardens when she strolled the paths with her sister, he bowed politely, maintaining his dignified air. Not once did he say or do anything that might give her reason to worry or cause alarm. As far as she was concerned, he was as old as her father and would always be considered a patron and protector—no more, no less... and that was where it ended.

But now, standing in front of his portrait, gazing into his own eyes, he saw the truth. He loved her. It was an impossible thought, but he did.

He shook his head at the absurd notion. He was a soldier, not a suitable husband for any woman. What made the situation even more complicated was that never once since her arrival had he seen a similar glimmer of what he felt for her reflected back at him. And, if he were to speak his feelings and actually touched her—if she knew the things he had done—it wouldn't just be his age that would offend her, making her flinch and turn away.

A thought of Maria Enrique suddenly surfaced before him, clouding his vision. He saw her lying on his bed, blood on her lip and a swollen eye. He shuddered and quickly buried the picture as soon as it had surfaced. As if to snatch the image away, he raised a hand and passed it in front of his face to dispel the haunting images.

No! It was out of the question. He could never speak to her of love or decent things. He had vowed he'd never touch another woman again. He'd made his pledge to God to atone for his previous sins. And if he broke his promise now, he'd only burn Sofonisba with his impurities. She would be defiled by his demons, and she would soon learn to hate him.

Alba shuddered again. He couldn't bear the thought of Sofonisba despising him, yet he couldn't bear the thought of not being near her.

In the dark, he retraced his steps down the long corridor back to his room. Picking up the letter he'd left on the table, he reread it, ripped it up, and flung away the scraps. Damn the orders that called him back to Madrid! It was all such an impossible situation, made more absurd because he was acting like a young man in love.

He stared at the paper scattered on the floor, his mind racing again, thinking of Sofonisba settled in her bed, sleeping peacefully. What was he to do?

As the moonlight flooded the room, Alba forced himself to think logically. By the time a half hour passed, and he had consumed the entire brandy decanter, an idea began to take shape in his head. Philip's new bride surely had room in her court for one more? The new queen, who was passionate about painting, would gladly welcome another lady-in-waiting, who could tutor her in the fine art of portrait-making. Sofonisba would be a perfect choice. Both young women, as foreigners in a new land, would have much in common.

The duke looked up, thinking of Sofonisba's reaction when he revealed to her his plan. Fearing she would outright reject any proposal of marriage, this was one proposition he knew she would readily accept.

"To venture on and see the world... to travel to Spain... It would be a dream come true!" He could already hear her reply. *"But to teach a queen to paint... that is beyond anything even I could have hoped for. Thank you, Duke... How can I refuse?"*

Alba congratulated himself, thinking he had just masterminded a brilliant stratagem, almost as clever at the one he had used against the pope. Together he would travel with Sofonisba home to Spain; it was just the beginning of a plan that would keep her close to him for a very long time—forever if he played his hand correctly.

He turned back to his desk and began a letter to Philip, detailing his new idea—using flattering speech and convincing arguments. When it was finished, he reread it to the very last line. Satisfied, he signed it with a flourish.

Then, picking up his violin, he drew the bow across the strings and began playing a haunting melody. As the last chord vibrated and melted away into the night, he thought, *I will continue to love and protect you from those who would harm you, Sofonisba.*

With the violin still nestled under his neck, he admitted under his breath, *But of all those you will need protecting from the most, my love... it would be me.*

Madrid
Spanish Court—1560

All the world's a stage, and all the men and women merely players: they have their exits and their entrances; and one man in his time plays many parts, his acts being seven ages.

— W. Shakespeare

Chapter 17

Players on a Stage

*T*rue to form, when Alba invited Sofonisba to accompany him to the Spanish court, she was delighted and a bit overwhelmed at the prospect of becoming court painter to a king and painting instructor to his queen. But deep down she knew she was skilled and capable of assuming the prestigious assignment. Due to her hard work and the connections she had made through Alba—her most generous patron—a marvelous opportunity had presented itself, and she couldn't be more pleased; the world seemed her oyster.

Sofonisba approached this new challenge with great anticipation. Any thoughts that Alba had a hidden agenda where she was regarded, or that his intentions went beyond their working relationship, were now the farthest things from her mind. The initial qualm she had felt that Alba harbored romantic feelings for her had abated over time. She believed her imagination had gotten the better of her because never once during her stay had the duke spoken out of turn or made her feel uncomfortable. Instead, he maintained a cordial and dignified relationship.

As far as she knew, the general's thoughts were occupied entirely with complicated affairs of the state. As he frequently traveled to Rome, Madrid, and France to attend conferences, broker diplomatic deals, and advise the King of Spain on domestic and foreign affairs, the time they had actually spent together in his palace in Milan had been brief. When he was in residence, he kept a polite distance between them. After Elena was married and left her side, a chaperone was always present when they'd dine together or when he played his violin for her during the early evening hours before retiring.

In her mind, Sofonisba had already made her decision to travel with the duke to Spain, but before giving him a definitive answer, she knew she should wait to obtain her father's approval. It was with a light heart and a joyous spirit she picked up her quill to write Amilcare to let him know this new twist of fate and ask his advice.

Sofonisba didn't have to wait long for his response. In the following post came Amilcare's reply heartily applauding Alba's proposal. She only faltered a moment when she learned her mother's malaise had indeed returned. But reading further, her spirits were buoyed by Amilcare's heartfelt encouragement. In his letter, he wrote: *Your mother shows signs of improvement, and surely by next spring you can return and pay her a visit. Go, daughter! This is the opportunity of a lifetime! This is what we have worked for.*

With her father's blessings, she focused her thoughts on her blossoming career and set her sights on Spain. Curious to know more about the court and the royal family, and to know all the players on the stage, Sofonisba made several inquiries of the duke's staff. At first, she only received a few perfunctory answers to her questions. Still, one evening after dinner, seated next to Alba's young aides-de-camp, she managed to strike up an enlightening conversation.

The man at first, like the others, was respectfully reticent. But after downing a glass of port, his tongue seemed to loosen. Leaning close to her ear, he said, "Did you know that when Philip was very young, his heart was stolen by his cousin, the Portuguese Infanta Maria Manuella? It was a love match, and with her he had a son—Don Carlos. Unfortunately, she died before ever holding the child in her arms. And then there were his other wives..."

"Other wives?" Sofonisba probed. "How many did he have?"

The man sat back in his chair, clearly shocked. "Did you not know Philip was married to Henry VIII's daughter Queen Mary of England?"

"I... well... I guess I must have known. Yes, I remember now hearing this news. Why is it important?"

The officer looked at her askance then offered to pour her a small glass of port before refilling his own. "Yes, signorina, it is highly important. Philip married Mary, the English king's daughter, to strengthen the alliance between Spain and England. In this day and age, when relations between our two countries are so fragile, he hoped to cement an alliance by producing an heir to place on the throne in London. It was his plan to keep Mary's Protestant sister, Elizabeth, from becoming regent. Sadly, despite Mary's reports of being with child, they turned out to be false. She duped both England and Spain."

"Ah," said Sofonisba, feeling ignorant. The world of politics was slightly out of her realm of interest, and she had never taken the time to delve into the vagaries of foreign power struggles. Still, she wasn't totally oblivious to competitive rivalries. She was used to strategic games of chess and outwitting her sisters at games of cards. But now she realized she would soon be entering a complex world where outsmarting one's opponent was something played out, not on a checkered board but in the battlefields and royal courts... And, instead of wooden pawns, the chess pieces were people.

Taking a sip of port, she asked nonchalantly because she really couldn't recall, "And...what happened to Philip's wife Mary after she lied to him?"

The man waved his hand in the air. "Oh, well... she didn't live much longer after that. When she died, the pope urged Philip to try again with her sister Elizabeth. They hoped to regain the Catholic upper hand in the region. Philip did as he was bid and attempted to persuade the fiery Protestant English queen into accepting his hand. But, as one might imagine, the redheaded tyrant refused him outright."

"It sounds... so complicated and ruthless. And now, instead of marrying an English queen, Philip has wed Elisabeth of Valois who comes from France..."

"Yes, that is correct. She is the consolation prize for securing peace between France and Spain. They call her Isabel de la Paz—"

"Because she brings peace," said Sofonisba.

"*Sì*, precisely so. It has been such a long time in coming. Our two countries have been at each other's throats and at war for so many years. It is believed Elisabeth from France will restore prosperity and hope amongst the people once again and present a united front against the Protestant threat."

Sofonisba pursed her lips at the thought of a marriage bartered for the sole intent of bringing peace to two nations. It seemed a little cold and heartless. Seeing her expression, the man said, "I assure you, signorina, you can trust Philip and Alba. It was a necessary move... one that had to be made. They are excellent strategists, and I've yet to meet finer men. They are fit to rule Spain and soon will have the upper hand in England. Mark my words."

"Have you met the new queen—Elisabeth? I'm to instruct her."

"Not yet, but rumors abound that the king's latest consort is quite lovely and vivacious. She is the daughter of Catherine de Medici."

Sofonisba digested this information, realizing Elisabeth and she shared ties to Italian nobility. Then remembering the man had mentioned Philip had a son by his first wife, she asked, "What of the prince—I forget... What did you say his name was?"

"Don Carlos. He..." The young man coughed slightly and took another drink.

When he didn't continue, Sofonisba prodded, "Yes go on."

He shrugged noncommittally and didn't reply. When Sofonisba raised her eyebrow, he hurried on to say, "Really, I don't wish to alarm..."

"Now you truly are making me feel uneasy," she said with a nervous laugh. "What makes you hold your tongue?"

Sofonisba gave him a questioning look, and after a moment he sighed and said, "Ah... well, if you must know, by many accounts Don Carlos is not quite right in the head. He suffers delusions of grandeur... He was born with a condition... I'm not sure exactly the nature of his infliction, but he came into the world with deformities—a crooked spine, one leg longer than the other, and he walks with a limp."

"Poor man."

"If I were you, I wouldn't pity him. He doesn't take kindly to that.

His irregularities exist on the outside... but inside his head as well. Always a sickly child, he lashes out to anyone who crosses him... or who he thinks laughs at him behind his back... or usurps his powers as prince."

"Would anyone really do that?" she asked.

"Well, Don Carlos intends to be king of Spain one day, but some believe because of his... um... delicate condition, he is unfit to rule. As a result, he has a particularly prickly relationship with his father, the king... as well as with the royal advisor who counsels Philip against succeeding the throne to his only male heir."

"And who might this advisor be..." Her voice trailed off when she realized by the look in the man's eyes it was none other than Alba himself who had placed himself in the middle of a contentious battle for the succession of power.

When Sofonisba's face clouded with concern, the assistant placed a hand to his chest and bowed slightly. "Please forgive me if I have said too much. But I say it only in your best interest. As you are connected to the duke and part of the assembly he takes with him to Madrid, you should be aware of the situation as you too could fall under the prince's scrutiny—and that is not always a good thing. So, I warn you, signorina, maintain a polite and respectful distance from the prince and your days at court will be *tranquilli*."

Sofonisba watched the man depart, feeling a bit distressed. But later that evening, her spirits were lifted when Alba handed her a letter written by Philip. When she read what was expected of her and what her duties would entail, she quickly forgot her worries regarding Don Carlos, imagining that she would have little to do with him. She would be Elisabeth's tutor, but she would also join the entourage who attended the queen, spending more time with the ladies than the men in residence at the palace.

For Elisabeth of France to thrive in her new environment, it seemed she required a troop of sycophants, and many of them were to accompany her from France. At first this had caused Alba great concern, as it put a strain on the royal purse. It was his duty to organize the new queen's entry into Spain, but he didn't see the need to pay for the likes of St. Etienne, the French woman's chaplain... let alone the others she requested accompany her—her physician, apothecary, goldsmith, gold-lace maker, furrier, *and* tailor Edouard Lacathe—or even Elisabeth's dancing instructor.

But Philip prevailed. From the moment the king laid eyes on the painting of the French princess offered to him during the peace talks, he was smitten. He wanted to make his new queen as happy as possible and instructed Alba to waive all the costs and accommodate every whim of his new consort. Respectfully, Alba acquiesced, arranging for hundreds of French adjutants, ladies, and lackeys to travel from Paris to Madrid in the royal marriage parade.

In return, Alba requested only one thing—that Elisabeth should take Sofonisba, the Italian painter from Cremona, under her wing. He asked that the queen protect his protégé and help her settle into the court life. For her part, Sofonisba would be the queen's friend and confidant and teach her to paint.

Still filled with many questions, on her journey from Milan to Madrid, Sofonisba plied those around her with more questions. She soon discovered Philip was a wise and learned scholar—a man of honor and good intentions. He was also exceedingly religious and considered himself to be the defender of Catholicism in Spain and on the European continent. To such end, he suffered no fools, reinstating the inquisition and putting down heretical reformers. Not only had Alba trained the king in the art of war but he had also shaped his brutal and decisive foreign policies.

From reports of the king's successes on the battlefield, Sofonisba had expected him to be a more robust and terrifying man. However, during their first encounter, after bowing low and then rising to look King Philip in the eye, what greeted her was a man of diminutive stature, with a round face and striking pale blue eyes. It wasn't that he was unattractive per se. His slight physical appearance was just not what she expected. At that moment, she feared the reports about his military prowess were false, and the king, in fact, was weak of character and unstable like his son.

But that impression was remedied after her first audience with Philip. He graced her with a warm smile and kissed her on the cheek. In a welcoming tone, he said, "It is an extreme pleasure to have you here with us, Signorina Anguissola. The duke recommends you highly. It is quite impressive you studied with Michelangelo. I have always been an ardent admirer of his work. The portraits you did last year of Alba and Messers Francioni, Barbagli..." He waved his hand in the air, indicating all the others in his counsel. "They are all magnificent! Now that you are here, I believe it is time you painted my likeness."

She was quite taken with his words of praise, but what she found most appealing were the numerous reports of his kind demeanor and the generosity he bestowed upon others. It seemed Philip comported himself as a sovereign should—his prime directive was first and foremost for the good of his people.

Sofonisba's favorable impressions of the Spanish court were further cemented when she was at last introduced to the queen herself. Shortly after her arrival, the artist received a summons written in the queen's hand on the thinnest of parchment papers, requesting the pleasure of her company in the petit salon. But the small salon had proven to be one of the most elegant rooms Sofonisba had yet seen in the Spanish palace.

As she glanced around the majestic room, Sofonisba noted the elaborately painted ceiling that featured the goddess Aurora and a carriage of cherubic angels welcoming in the dawn. As her gaze traveled downward, Sofonisba saw her own image glimmering back at her in the hundred gilded mirrors that lined the walls of her majesty's chambers. The attractive woman she saw reflected startled her at first; she seemed so calm and confident—almost an entirely different person altogether from the girl she had been in Cremona.

And when the queen entered the salon and dismissed her ladies-in-waiting to have a private tête-à-tête, the artist immediately stood at attention. In awe, Sofonisba admired the woman before her dressed in a gold robe made from embroidered brocade. Her long sleeves were lined with crimson satin and trimmed in ermine, and the girdle encircling her waist was decorated with seed pearls and gold braid cord.

At first glance, in all her refinement, the French woman seemed dignified and commanding, but the impression was softened when Elisabeth nearly tripped on the two yards of flowing satin that made up her train. Yet the queen hadn't been perturbed in the least. Instead, she giggled and then righted herself. When she looked at Sofonisba, her eyes sparkled brightly, just like the diamonds that glittered in her headdress and in the two large crosses she wore around her neck.

The queen took her seat and smiled at Sofonisba, sizing her up from head to toe. Then, with a nod, she invited her to join her on the small satin divan. She picked up a silver bowl filled with sugared dates, took a little nibble, then let out a squeal of ecstasy. "These are simply divine!" Elisabeth indicated that Sofonisba should try one too. Without further preamble, she said, "You are a great deal older than me, *mia cara,* but I believe you will make an excellent lady-in-waiting."

She snapped open her lace fan and waved it leisurely in front of her face and said, "Oh, don't be offended by my direct questions. I tend to speak my mind and say things that come into my head. I've just turned seventeen, and you are what...?"

"Thirty, Your Majesty," said Sofonisba.

"Practically ancient... and to think you've never been married!"

"No, Your Majesty," she said, smothering a smile. Despite Elisabeth's waywardness, there was something about the young queen's tone that Sofonisba found guileless and charming—almost like her sister Europa who had always been gentle and gullible.

Elisabeth poured out two small glasses of liquor, then glanced up at Sofonisba. "I can see you think I am amusing."

"No, Milady. I..."

"Oh, don't worry. It's all right," Elisabeth said as she raised the glass to her lips. After the first sip, she rolled her eyes heavenward and exclaimed, "Oh, you must taste this too! I've never had anything like it." She picked up the cut-glass decanter from a tray and eyed the ruby red contents. "The color is so pretty. The Spanish wines I've tried, so far, are excellent!"

She waved her hand, indicating Sofonisba should pick up her glass, too, and take a sip. Then she abruptly asked, "Do you aspire to marry? You have passable looks... but your eyes... they are quite extraordinary. Surely we can find you a suitable husband."

Sofonisba spluttered into her glass. As she brushed away the tiny droplets that had spilled onto her gown, without thinking she said, "If I have to choose between a husband and my paintbrushes, I choose my brushes. They last longer and are easier to clean and replace."

The queen looked at her in surprise, and Sofonisba held her breath. She hadn't meant to offend the woman, but when Elisabeth let out a trill of mirth, she relaxed visibly. "Oh, my dear! *That* is amusing. But don't you have feelings for Duke Alba?"

"What? No!" Sofonisba replied forcefully, surprised by the direction of the conversation and by her own vehement reaction.

"Well, the man seems very attached to you, signorina. You are here on his orders. You left Italy and your family... You traveled together from Milan and—"

"He is my patron and has been very kind to me," supplied Sofonisba quickly. "He has taken no untold liberties... He has always been a gentleman...."

"Yes, of course," said Elisabeth. "I ask because I have to know everything that goes on in my court. My husband has the utmost respect for him. Before you arrived, Alba wrote me the kindest letter, saying he had a wedding gift to present to me. The gift was you! He said you have a marvelous talent for portraiture and that you would be able to instruct me. Imagine my surprise!"

She set her wine glass down and said, "But I have to admit that I was quite terrified when I was first introduced to the duke. He stood in for Philip when we married in France. He was my surrogate bridegroom. But, oh my! When I first saw him standing at the altar, my breath grew short and I immediately began trembling in my silken shoes. He reminded me of a big dark raven, so stern and severe was he! Why, I had half a mind to turn around and run away."

"Alba is a terribly impressive man, is he not?" Sofonisba said, delighted again by Elisabeth's transparency.

"My goodness! The way he barked orders, where to stand... even daring to tell my mother... *my mother*, the queen of France... what she could and could not do. Well, I almost didn't go through with the ceremony. I wanted to speak my mind... tell him where he should stand and what I thought about this arranged marriage. That was until I looked at my mother's face. It was then I was reminded of my place and duty to France and my father."

"I must admit," said Sofonisba, "I thought as much the first time I encountered Alba. How I wanted to share my thoughts with him! But, in the end, I kept my composure out of obedience and respect I have for my parents."

"Such a man brings out the ire in us... two opinionated women who know their minds!" Elisabeth said with a hearty laugh. "You see, we have so much in common already." She leaned forward and confessed, "But keeping all those unexpressed thoughts inside of me... no more than fifteen minutes had passed when I started hiccupping... right there in the middle of Notre Dame in front of the priest! I always do that when I'm anxious... or can't express myself freely."

When Sofonisba's eyes sparkled at the queen's admission, Elisabeth shrugged nonchalantly. "But I must confess, over time, Alba has grown on me. Now I find him almost agreeable... despite his dark airs and moody disposition."

"He is a generous man, and his conversation can be engaging," admitted Sofonisba. "He is well-versed in poetry, music, and the stories of Homer. He also has a talent for playing the violin."

Serious again, Elisabeth eyed her shrewdly. "Alba was correct when he said you are an exceptional woman. You are living up to his glowing accounts. You also have a sense of humor—which I find particularly attractive—and I'm quite pleased we speak a common language. My mother often spoke to me in Italian. And your French... well, it is fairly passable... I'm impressed. It surprises me that you know any words at all!

What other secrets do you have?"

"My secret," admitted Sofonisba, "is that despite outward appearances, I am quite overcome and quaking with excitement and emotion to be here. Only in my wildest dreams did I ever believe I'd actually be standing in front of a queen, and she would be my pupil!"

"I value your honesty and your vulnerability, Signorina Anguissola! You have nothing to fear from me. In no time at all, you will be accustomed to our ways. I warn you, though! All royal courts have their fair share of delightful schemes, gossip, and romantic entanglements!"

Sighing happily, the queen added, "I look forward to beginning our painting lessons."

"I am happy to start when you are ready, Your Majesty," said Sofonisba.

"And I will teach you to dance! Do you like to dance?" Without waiting for an answer, she bubbled on, "Oh, I adore the minuet and the *couranto*. Before I arrived in Spain, I learned how to dance the *Passemento de España*. My instructors say I am quite light on my feet and always compliment me on my graceful movements."

Elisabeth, who was nibbling another sugared date, gave her a friendly smile. "As a lady-in-waiting, you too must learn the moves. You will be required to perform these very steps at the upcoming balls and festivities, and you must make us proud. I'm sure you will be a fast learner... You, my dear, are bound to turn many heads at court."

The queen clapped her hands together. "Well, this has been a delight! We are both foreigners and new to this place. It is good to know I have a teacher and a confidant that I can rely on."

Then, picking up a small bell, she rang it, and Sofonisba realized the interview was over. "Thank you, Your Majesty," she said, rising out of her chair, curtsying in front of her new patroness.

With a gay laugh, the queen admonished, "Please, now that we are intimate, in private you may call me Elisabeth. I have already made up my mind that we will be the best of friends."

Chapter 18

The Enfant Terrible

Sofonisba, pleased to have made such a favorable impression on Elisabeth, eagerly settled into life at the Spanish court. Despite the initial elation of being a stranger in a new land, and the queen's intimation that intrigue and plots—political and sexual—abounded at court, Sofonisba instead found it—well, rather boring. She was the court portraitist, but she was also a part of the royal entourage. And as a lady-in-waiting, she suffered long hours of doing just that... waiting.

She did her best to fit in, but the Spanish court, with its rigid rules, protocol, and restrictions, was not easy to adapt to. When she left Milan, she traded many freedoms to stand instead confined for long hours in the presence of the queen in tight garments that reduced movement and restricted her breath.

After attending the multitude of parties that occupied the royals every evening, she went to bed late. Then, rising the next morning shortly after dawn, to be present at the queen's breakfast, she donned a busk—the new-fangled bodice with stiff ribs that corseted the waist and flattened the chest to maintain a trim and rigid front. On the lower part of her body, she wore a farthingale that held out her skirts in a ridiculous circle. In Sofonisba's opinion, this latest fashion was the most outrageous of all, for when she stood at her easel, she could barely reach her canvas.

But most uncomfortable of all were the cork-soled platform shoes that squeezed her toes most obnoxiously. In the mornings, she could endure the aching of soles and blisters that formed at the back of her heels. At the end of the day, however, she toddled back to her room in the most undignified manner, where she soaked her swollen feet in a warm tub of water scented with lilac and verbena.

Sofonisba was not the only one who suffered through these uncomfortable fashions. The queen's retinue consisted of at least, if not more than, forty young women, and each and every one attempted to outdo the other. Every morning they entered Elisabeth's salon dressed in colorful silks and pastel satins and the most extravagant coiffures. Often they even wore mantillas in the Spanish fashion and draped their heads with swaths of lace, ribbons, and pearls. Sofonisba was never quite sure where the woman left off and the false hair, pancake makeup, and padded clothing began.

Even with the pressure to eclipse the other ladies, Sofonisba found it tedious and didn't enjoy the game or want to play along. Although she received a substantial allowance from the king each month, enough to buy twenty pretty dresses, she preferred instead her gowns of sky blues or deep russets embroidered with gold trim. And, instead of a teased back head of hair or an elaborate mountain of intricately rolled curls like the others flaunted, as she had always done she kept hers pulled back tightly from her face with a simple black ribbon.

In their sensational finery, as they paraded the halls and grounds of the palace, the ladies-in-waiting caused quite a flurry and drew furtive glances from their male counterparts. Sofonisba felt invisible juxtaposed against them; compared to them, she was a woodland bird among a gaggle of jewel-toned parrots. Of course, this apparent rejection of social vanity on her part seemed outrageous to the others. When she sat demurely aside instead of fluttering and preening around the new queen, the ladies— especially those who had accompanied Elisabeth from France—looked at her askance.

If her lack of interest in clothes made her an oddity, her command of the Spanish language—or lack thereof—only served to repudiate her further. She tried her best to be conversant in Spanish and French, but it was frustrating and isolating not to be able to express her thoughts quickly. But, more than that, it was extremely disheartening to observe the other women sniggering behind their fluttering fans at her thick Italian accent.

Given time, things began to even out, and when Sofonisba started instructing Elisabeth, her outlook improved and life at court took a definite turn for the better. The queen herself did much to make her feel at ease in her new surroundings, teaching her court etiquette and introducing her to the nobles. Along with Philip, she picked up the reins handed to them by Alba and extolled Sofonisba's virtuosity, thus furthering her professional painting career.

In her element, Sofonisba tutored Elisabeth on the finer points of perspective, foreshortening, and how to hold a brush. The queen was quite astute and rapidly excelled in mixing paints and applying delicate strokes onto her canvas, creating light and shadows to define inanimate objects. After several weeks of still life painting, she ably graduated to sketching portraits and capturing their expressions in layers of translucent color washes.

Secluded in the royal painting parlor, the two spent hours alone together, deep in intimate conversation. With Elisabeth, Sofonisba could communicate readily in her own language, and she was grateful to have made a new friend who shared her passion for painting.

Much impressed by Sofonisba's instruction, Elisabeth invited the other ladies-in-waiting to participate in her lessons. Many did so out of academic interest, others to curry favor with the queen. Still, when the flock of birds saw Sofonisba's talents put to work, she could tell she rose higher in their estimation. It seemed that painting was a language all its own—and in this she was quite fluent. After the group lessons began, and as Sofonisba rose in admiration with the royal couple, the others stopped dismissing her as an awkward, untalented foreigner.

During the morning sessions, when Elisabeth and her ladies were pleasantly occupied in Sofonisba's studios, they were occasionally graced by King Philip's presence, who was also often accompanied by the Duke of Alba. When the door burst open, the women inevitably glanced up in agitation, to receive a visit from the illustrious men. Then, settling down as Philip moved among them, they attempted to appear industrious and nonchalant. Philip always greeted them in good spirits, joking and praising their efforts. He especially doled out compliments to his wife.

Alba, on the other hand, was quite the opposite. Instead of mingling, he stood to one side, his arms crossed in front of him, scanning the room with a bored, taciturn look. Sofonisba eyed him with some amusement, thinking the duke seemed more a military general than ever, intent on surveying a battlefield. But here, at court amongst its colorful company, he appeared a bit out of place.

Still, since returning to Spain, Alba seemed more content to be back on familiar ground, and Sofonisba saw him more frequently than she had in Milan. Often their paths crossed as she walked about the palace. She was also often paired with Alba at court dinners or musical events that involved dancing. Elisabeth, she soon learned, was quite fond of parties and extravagant entertainments. Alba, on the other hand, despised circling around in front of the others in time to frivolous music.

By now, other than just a patron, Sofonisba considered the duke an important ally. Being new to the court, since he was already so well known to her, she favored his company and gravitated to him. But, despite her admiration, she found his company a little sparse. He didn't laugh or joke like the other courtiers were prone to do, nor did he ask her to dance. But she really didn't mind the lack of his enthusiasm for court frivolities. It was actually a relief they could maintain a serene and peaceful friendship.

No, these days it wasn't Alba who caused her concern and upset her life with romantic inclinations, but rather Don Carlos, the king's son.

From the first moment she entered the king's salon on Alba's arm, and they had been introduced, she felt the prince's eyes rove over her person, after which he gave her a salacious grin.

"So… this is your Italian painter, Alba," he said. "Well, well, well… she is quite pretty, I give you that." Don Carlos grinned suggestively, then asked, "So, Signorina, how do you find life at court?"

"It is unlike anything I expected…"

"Yes, well, the Spanish court is like no other in Europe. Here we take time to enjoy the finer things in life. We indulge in a multitude of pleasures. Perhaps I could show you around..."

"That won't be necessary," interrupted Alba.

Don Carlos's eyes slid from admiring Sofonisba's slender shape to the face of the duke. "Ah, spoken like a jealous suitor. Am I stepping on hallowed ground here? Are you claiming this tempting morsel for your own amusement, Alba?"

"I warn you..."

"Warn me! Who are you to issue me commands?" said the prince snidely.

When the two men locked eyes and glared at one another, Sofonisba looked at the ground, mortified and confused by the prince's words.

After a moment, Don Carlos glanced back at her and laughed. "You seem a penitent little Italian mouse, signorina. Are you hiding something behind the puritanical mask you wear? They say where there is smoke there's fire, and Alba is definitely fuming—"

Alba cut him off. "Enough! Show respect for the young lady."

Again, Don Carlos looked at Alba and sniggered. "I do believe I've finally struck a nerve and managed to squeeze a human emotion from your cold frozen heart, Duke." Not waiting for a response, he swiveled his head toward Sofonisba and said, "And what do you say, signorina? I'm sure there are delectable treasures hidden under all the yards and yards of lace and—"

"Messer, I fear you have not been informed of my position here," she said politely, if not a bit frostily. "I have come here to tutor the queen... and at the moment, I am painting a portrait of your father."

"Ah, yes, you are the artist. Anguissola, isn't it? My father extols your virtues, and the queen can't seem to say anything these days without mentioning you, signorina. It appears you have made quite an impression on this court. If truth be told, I am positively envious of your talents. Just look at how you've delighted everyone from king to clerk."

He glanced slyly at Alba and continued. "I'd like a chance to be charmed too—"

"Signore! How dare you..." Sofonisba began in a rush, but stopped speaking when she felt the light touch of Alba's hand on her arm.

Don Carlos narrowed his eyes and considered her a moment. "So... my little Italian mouse, do you think you are higher and mightier than the Enfant—the future king of Spain?"

"That will be all!" exclaimed Alba.

Don Carlos coldly scrutinized the duke, then slid his eyes back to Sofonisba. "Perhaps I too will have my portrait painted by you, artist." With a raised eyebrow, he added, "But... you must make my portrait bigger and more impressive than King Philip's. After all, I will soon take my father's place." To Alba, he said, "Isn't that so, Duke? Then you will take orders from me. How will you like that?"

Sofonisba didn't know what to say, but there was no need as Alba hastily excused them. "I see Philip and Elisabeth are waiting for us to join them. We wish you a pleasant evening... and politely take our leave."

"Fly then if you must," Don Carlos said indifferently. "But remember, artist, my request. You will be the first to paint the image of the future king of Spain."

Without further word, the duke bowed and indicated for Sofonisba to precede him into the banquet room. As they walked away, he said in a voice meant only for her ears, "Please excuse the prince. He is known for his vagaries of speech. He is our resident, Enfant Terrible."

"Enfant Terrible? What does that mean exactly?" she asked, looking over her shoulder at the king's son who was now engaged in a lively conversation with a handsome young woman. By the looks of things, their encounter, just moments ago, was already forgotten.

"It is an expression we use to refer to a child who is terrifyingly candid in saying embarrassing things to his parents or others... Someone who is unorthodox or acts unconventionally."

"I see," said Sofonisba, but she didn't really. That was until the entire company sat down to dinner.

Positioned in a place of honor near the king and queen, Sofonisba had a firsthand glimpse of the prince's eccentricities. She watched as he swaggered into the room, his limp quite evident, and took his seat across from her. As before, he smiled at her insolently then messily licked his lips. Unable to control her reaction, she instantly frowned. When she did, his grin turned sour. He arrogantly raked her with his eyes, then turned his attention to the woman next to him.

Sofonisba observed in distaste as Don Carlos draped an arm around the girl's shoulders and rubbed himself against her. When the woman dressed in white spurned his advances, it took but a moment for the enfant to knock over a glass of red wine that consequently spilled inconveniently into her lap, staining her lovely gown. With a cry of dismay, the woman rose and hastily left the room. Instead of showing surprise or remorse, Don Carlos only glowered at the company of concerned faces that turned toward him and continued stabbing his meat with a knife, chewing his food sloppily.

The scene at dinner was trifling—a minor disturbance—but more troubling was what Sofonisba witnessed later that night. While walking to her room through the rooftop garden, she heard cries issuing from the stables in the courtyard below. Immediately concerned, she looked down and saw Don Carlos. Even from her position, Sofonisba could see his red and puckered face, flushed in rage, as he berated a young steward. Then in a quixotic gesture, the prince picked up a bucket of slops and threw its contents over the head of the hired hand.

"It was horrible to watch the muck and filth cascade down the poor boy's face," Sofonisba said, relating the story to Elisabeth the next day. "In the end, all Don Carlos did was laugh."

Elisabeth let out a long sigh. "I just don't know what gets into him. I feel so sorry for the prince."

Sofonisba raised a questioning eyebrow, wondering how Elisabeth had such patience for the man and his mean-spirited and disagreeable actions.

The queen, seeing her disapproval, set down her painting brush. "Oh, my dear, you can't begin to imagine how difficult it has been for Don Carlos. His mother died giving birth to him, and throughout his fretful life he has suffered miserably. It's always been one malady after the other. Sickness, fevers, headaches..."

Elisabeth looked at her from over her easel and said, "Despite his... well... his rather unappealing demeanor, I'm sensitive to his needs. Perhaps because I miss my own dear brothers, he is like a misfit sibling to me... or a little lovesick puppy. He's always bringing me trinkets and little cakes and candies. Did you know he also writes me sonnets? Oh, the poems are only passable. He wasn't a very good student, and his Latin is filled with errors—it really is deplorable! He once confided in me he was too distracted to sit still and learn. And when he moved about, his tutors beat him with a rod... on his father's orders. Personally, I can't believe Philip would be so cruel!"

"Is that why the prince has such disdain for his father? Because he was treated harshly as a boy?"

"Yes, but more than that, he wishes Philip to include him in the military planning sessions. He'd like to sit on the council of advisors. If he is to be king one day, he wants to be treated as such."

"Why won't the king oblige him?"

"It's this terrible mean streak of his that always gets him in trouble." She shrugged. "I've yet to see it. Don Carlos is an absolute lamb with me... But with others, when his anger is provoked, it is quite troubling, as the incident with the stable boy you just mentioned." In a confidential tone, she added, "I believe it has something to do with his head wound."

"Head wound?"

"Yes, I was told after my arrival that Don Carlos suffered a terrible blow to the skull. It's a sad little tale to hear the servants tell it..."

"When did this happen?"

"About three years ago. It seems Don Carlos fell madly in love with the gardener's daughter. Apparently, she was quite pretty. One evening, he snuck out at dusk to meet her. But, as he descended a narrow staircase seldom used and in need of repair, he lost his footing and fell headfirst onto the stone pavement. There was blood everywhere..."

"How dreadful!"

"Yes, very! The prince was attended to by the court physicians. They bandaged the wound but it bled profusely. The doctors tried all kinds of remedies. Finally, they drilled into his skull to relieve the pressure."

"I fear the cure is worse than the injury," said Sofonisba. "Surely, the pain was unbearable and would drive anyone insane."

"Oh, the doctors do that all the time," Elisabeth said. "They seem to know what they are doing."

"From the sound of things, it did little to mend his disposition..."

Elisabeth shrugged. "Well, it helped to some degree, but still he suffers excruciating pain and fits of rage. When the bandages came off, and he was on his feet again and was a bit more lucid, he claimed the girl refused his kisses. He said it was she who had pushed him. Don Carlos called for her to be beaten, but when no one heeded his demands, he began throwing chairs and knocking over tables."

"What happened to the gardener's daughter?"

"Alba made sure she was taken care of."

"Alba? But wasn't he in Italy?"

She waved a hand dismissively. "The man frequently traveled back to the court to advise his king on many things... but primarily when something unpleasant arose that had to do with Don Carlos."

"And what did Alba do?"

"He removed the poor girl from harm by finding new employment for her father. They disappeared from the palace shortly after that. When Don Carlos learned of this, he swore he would take his revenge on the duke for interfering with his affairs."

"Did the prince follow through on his threats?"

"Oh, Don Carlos is all blather and temper tantrums. The duke knows that... and after all, tables can be righted and chairs fixed again."

Sofonisba looked at her, not entirely convinced.

Elisabeth untied her painting apron and took a turn around the room. When she reached the window, she stood and looked out over the lawn. After a moment, she glanced over her shoulder and said, "Did you know, I was supposed to marry Don Carlos? Of course, it might have made a bit more sense. After all, we are precisely the same age."

"And why didn't you?"

"My father, hearing reports of Don Carlos's temper and delusions... and of course of his deformity, had misgivings about betrothing me to him. And then Elizabeth of England threw Philip over and he became available. To my father, the king of France, marrying me to the king of Spain was more desirable and the more beneficial solution."

"How did Don Carlos react to that?"

"Not well. It gave him one more reason to hate Philip... and Alba."

"Why Alba?"

"Remember the story I told you before? It was the duke who brokered the peace treaty and orchestrated the nuptial agreement with my father."

After her conversation with Elisabeth, Sofonisba took great care to avoid the Enfant Terrible. It seemed she had already irked him, and she didn't want to bring further attention to her person. And the more she learned about the enfant's erratic behavior, the more distressed she became. Little bits and pieces of his odd antics flitted from mouth to mouth, and one day, while walking in the royal gardens, a particularly strange story reached her ears. Hearing a whispered conversation between two women on the other side of the hedge, she kept very still—melting into the shadows—and eavesdropped.

"Oh, Margherita," a woman's voice said, "I have such a terrible thing to tell you about Don Carlos. I heard it the other day from the young blond boy who assists the princess's first dresser."

"You mean little Diego who is the apprentice to Pedro Manuel, the royal tailor and bootmaker?"

"Yes! He is the one. What a sweet child he is."

"What did the boy tell you?"

"Well, my dear... according to Diego, it seems the king forbade the prince to wear those new-fangled boots Pedro Manuel fashioned for Don Carlos."

"The ones roomy enough to conceal a pair of pistols?"

"Yes, precisely. It is the latest fashion among the young cavaliers. But the king didn't think it wise that Don Carlos should hide a weapon in such a manner, so he ordered the bootmaker to make another pair."

"A new pair of boots... That seems harmless enough."

"You would think! But when the refashioned boots were presented to the prince, he flew into a rage and struck Pedro Manuel in the face and reviled him in the most pejorative terms."

"The poor, poor man," exclaimed the other.

"Yes, but that is not all. Don Carlos had the boots shredded and boiled, then ordered Pedro Manuel to swallow the fragments of leather. When the bootmaker refused, the prince threatened to take the man's life if he didn't do as he was ordered!"

"I can't believe this. And did the shoemaker really eat the boots?"

"What else could he do? Pedro coughed most of it down, and all the while the prince just giggled and howled as the old man—he's over seventy—nearly gagged to death."

"Terrible. Just terrible," the woman said in a horrified voice.

"In the end, after being tortured so, Pedro finally acquiesced and agreed to make those boots that conceal weapons."

"Does the king know this?"

"Well, I really don't know. But if..."

As the women's voices trailed off, Sofonisba turned away, much dismayed by this latest report concerning the prince. It seemed Don Carlos took pleasure in bullying and brutalizing the weak. She heard it from the mouths of others, and she saw it with her own eyes in the gloomy stare he gave her when they met by accident in a deserted corridor.

Now Sofonisba tended to agree wholeheartedly with Elisabeth's father—King Henry II of France. Not marrying his nubile young daughter to Don Carlos had been a wise move. Philip's son—heir to the Spanish throne—was clearly disturbed and unstable.

Chapter 19

The Queen's Confidant

*W*ith each passing hour, news of Don Carlos's exploits and troubling behavior circulated through the court, and each new incident seemed worse than the week before. Still, little was done to restrain the prince. Aside from weakly administered admonishments or orders to lock him in his room, it wasn't long before the prince was released and left to his own pranks and devices again.

By now, Sofonisba understood that life at the Spanish court could be capricious, and the royals were in a league of their own. They oozed privilege and quirkiness. All along, she had witnessed the duke's arrogant demeanor and now the prince's troubling behavior. Even Elisabeth, her new friend and confidant—who seemed light-hearted and frivolous— harbored exaggerated worries in her breast.

Sofonisba first learned of the queen's preoccupations one evening when Elisabeth called her to her private apartments to practice their dancing steps. After a strenuous half hour of movement, Elisabeth sank into her chair and waved her fan to cool her face. Breathily she said, "You perform the steps astonishingly well, my dear. I believe you fit into palace life quite beautifully. Are you content here at the Spanish court?"

When Sofonisba nodded, Elisabeth continued. "I too am most content with my fate; each day I grow fonder of my husband. He speaks a little French and a bit of Italian, and I a little Spanish. We both read and write Latin... but together we are learning a new language that requires no translation."

When Sofonisba looked at her questioningly, the queen's eyes lit up and she said, "*Amore! Cara mia!* We are learning the language of love!"

Settling back on her velvet chair, Elisabeth said, "Oh, you should have been at my real wedding—such a fabulous day. After a long and treacherous journey, I arrived at the palace hall in Toledo. That is where I first met Philip, and we became intimate." Elisabeth whispered in a confidential tone, "My husband is quite talented."

By her flushed face, Sofonisba couldn't determine if the woman's glow was caused by the dance's exertion or from the thoughts of Philip's lovemaking.

"Have I shocked you, my dear? One day soon, you too will know the embrace of a man..." Gazing contentedly up at the ceiling, Elisabeth let out a soft sigh. Then, glancing back at Sofonisba, she said, "So far, married life is proving to be quite lovely. And to think, before I met my dear Philip, I was terrified of him. I was a princess who loved to dance, was gay and light-hearted. He, on the other hand, was a formidable man—a mighty ruler. When my mother told me I was to marry him... how I dreaded leaving my beloved France."

"And what changed your mind?"

"Alba, of course. He organized the nuptials, the ceremony... even my transportation from France to Spain. It was a marvelous procession of coaches, caravans, and men on horseback that went on for miles and miles. And then on the morning of my arrival here at the palace, Madrid's streets were canopied with velvet garlands and verdant arches entwined with cupids, love-knots, and lilies. Marching in front of me were eight battalions of richly dressed infantry and cavalry whose saddles were adorned in the Moorish fashion. Behind them, maidens walked, strewing flowers in front of our caravan. It was such a lovely sight to see all the people in costume singing, followed by dignitaries of every order imaginable. Then, at the very end, the Holy Office of the Inquisition followed, mounted on horses carrying black banners."

"It must have been a wonderful procession," said Sofonisba. "A delightful tribute to your Grace's goodwill to be treated so. It seems the Spaniards have accepted you wholeheartedly."

Elisabeth hesitated, then responded slowly, "Yes, it would seem so."

"What is it, milady? Does something trouble you?"

She gave Sofonisba a rueful look. "Soon, I will be eighteen... and I worry as my marriage progresses, my husband will lose interest and..."

"What do you mean—"

"Oh, dear girl! Now that our honeymoon is over, I'm afraid Philip will resume his affairs with his comely paramours. He has a reputation, you know." Elisabeth began fanning herself vigorously and let out a small wail. "Oh, life is unbearable when you are riddled with doubts and fears regarding whether your husband is true of heart."

She stopped fanning her face and leaned forward and pierced Sofonisba with her pale blue eyes. "You are an intelligent, sensible sort, my dear friend. What do you think?"

"Truthfully," Sofonisba responded, "it is my belief you have nothing to worry about. I've heard nothing in the halls or from the other courtiers to confirm that suspicion."

"Hmmm..." was all Elisabeth said. But by the way she narrowed her eyes and looked at Sofonisba, she wondered what thoughts were brewing in the queen's head.

After a moment, Elisabeth reached out and took Sofonisba's hand. "You and I have become close... and I value your opinion above all others. I know you will always be forthright with me."

"Of course," said Sofonisba, pleased the queen held her in such high esteem.

Elisabeth squeezed her hand lightly, pleased with her answer. "And because we have become such great confidants... from time to time, should I ask you to keep an eye out for me..."

"An eye out... What do you mean?"

"You know, spy for me."

"Spy for you!"

Hearing her tone, the queen chuckled, then sat back in her chair and said, "Oh, don't look so alarmed. It wouldn't be anything terribly dangerous, mind you. Just keep your ears open... and should you hear anything, anything at all, report back to me."

"Me!" exclaimed Sofonisba. "But why me? My talents lie in painting, not in prying into the affairs of others!"

"Oh, let's not call it that! No, let's call it keeping well informed."

"I wouldn't know how..."

Elisabeth waved her hand dismissively. "If I can teach my provincial debutante elegant court manners and the intricate moves of a contradance, can't I also turn her into a clever informant? You don't have to do anything you aren't doing now."

"But..."

"You are the court painter. It is the perfect cover. All you need to do is paint... and listen. I wouldn't ask anything more of you. No harm will befall you. You will act only upon my orders."

Sofonisba looked at her skeptically and Elisabeth laughed. "You are the perfect choice. Because your accent is terrible, the Spaniards think you can't understand them... and as a result of this, they will gossip more freely in your presence." She hurried on to say, "I feel I can count on you because you are associated with Alba. The duke is a fiercely loyal man, and my husband trusts him implicitly. Philip expounds upon his virtues day and night! They both are god-fearing, deeply religious men who don't tolerate court nonsense."

"But, milady, I assure you I'd be no use to you... I have no skills! Why would it even be necessary?"

Elisabeth bit her lip. "Well, as I've told you before, I worry that my husband has a roving eye. To ease my mind, I wish to know how my husband conducts himself when he is not with me. I need to know if he is true or..."

"Surely he would never do anything to upset or betray you... He took a vow of marriage..." When Elisabeth raised an eyebrow, Sofonisba closed her mouth.

"Oh, *piccola mia*," she continued in a chiding tone, "you are so much older than me, but you are also so naive. What do you really know of the ways of men... or, for that matter, women who deceive one another or use their feminine wiles to sleep with the king?"

With a harsh laugh, Elisabeth continued. "And do you not realize all around us there are those who wish to defame Philip or me? Though there were welcome cries and garlands of flowers upon my arrival, there are still those who lurk in the shadows ready to undermine the Spanish crown. This court is the center of international power. A well-timed whisper in the king's ear could make or break all of our fortunes. There are those who would gain the upper hand and are thriving in our midst—I must keep ahead of things, especially to know if there are plots against us."

Sofonisba regarded Elisabeth's now serious face. As young, carefree, and flighty as she gave one to believe—with her dancing, giggles, and posturings—the queen was intelligent, quite shrewd, and a realist. Elisabeth's request seemed simple enough, and she owed the woman so much. Perhaps in this small way Sofonisba could repay her for her many kindnesses.

"All right," Sofonisba conceded. "If your majesty believes I can be of service, I am happy to apply myself. But what if..."

"Yes," Elisabeth encouraged.

"What if what I learn brings displeasure... especially regarding your husband?"

Elisabeth was silent for a moment. "It is a risk I am ready to take. It is better to know the truth than live a lie. At least in this way I will be armed and ready to do battle with someone who would steal my husband's heart away. I would do the same for you. I will always look out for you at all costs."

"But how do I go about collecting information?"

"That, my dear, is the easy part," Elisabeth said. "All you need to do is be receptive and listen. My mother, Lady Catherine, is quite clever in her endeavors to procure information. She enlists over a hundred beautiful ladies-in-waiting—she calls them her Flying Squadron—and sends them into the beds of courtiers to keep tabs on court intrigues and who is betraying whom." When Sofonisba blushed, Elisabeth added, "Goodness, *mia cara*, much is revealed between the silky sheets of lovers. My mother has even sent busty wenches into the beds of her own sons— my brothers! Can you imagine that?"

Sofonisba frowned slightly. Noting this, Elisabeth patted her arm and said in a reassuring tone, "*Oh, tesoro, non preoccuparti*—don't worry! As my lady-in-waiting, you will not be required to perform such bedroom duties."

"But how am I..."

Elisabeth smiled. "You are my painting mistress, no? You will have access to confidences where others do not, and Philip is soon to have a second portrait painted, dressed in his royal robes. Isn't that so?"

"Yes," Sofonisba agreed. "We are to begin at the end of the week."

"When you are working on his portrait and any others, all you need do is use your time advantageously. Get to know your sitters and their secrets—who is sleeping with whom, who likes the company of men, what expensive gowns have been purchased by my ladies—you know, the usual court trifles. Then report to me. Can you do that?"

"Of course, if that is what you request. But really, what will be accomplished by communicating such odd bits and pieces of nonsense?"

"Nothing is too big or too small. Remember, *mia cara*, knowledge is power. Even the tiniest detail can be used to our advantage."

With a trill of silvery laughter, she added, "It is best to keep your enemies close and your loved ones even closer. To that end, keep tabs on Don Carlos as well. This morning I saw one of the chambermaids with a bruised and swollen eye..."

"Angelina?"

"I wouldn't know her name," said the queen. "What do you know about this event? Was Don Carlos responsible?"

Sofonisba had heard the story from her maid and knew the prince had berated the girl for arriving late with his bath water. He had called her a bloody cow and threatened to have her whipped. But the commotion alerted Alba, who, once again, came to a servant's defense.

As Sofonisba filled her in on the details, Elisabeth's face became solemn. "See, you are already very good at acquiring useful information." With a sigh, she added, "The prince's behavior is growing quite troubling by the day. Should you hear of anything else..."

Elisabeth's voice trailed off when the door opened and the very one they were speaking of strode in. Don Carlos was dressed in a magnificent doublet and fur-trimmed jerkin, and his legs were covered in stockings joined at the crotch with an embellished codpiece. He swaggered awkwardly into the room, but despite his limp, his footsteps barely made a sound on the marble floor as his feet were encased in slippers made of the softest kid-leather.

Sofonisba couldn't help but think his footwear must have been the work of the unfortunate shoemaker, and she shook her head slightly. When the prince looked at her and saw the look of pity she knew she hadn't concealed, a shadow crossed his face. He glared at her then turned his full attention upon Elisabeth. "Excuse the intrusion but I couldn't stay away another minute!"

At the light rap on the open door, all three turned to see Alba on the threshold. In contrast to the smug grin and dandified attire of Don Carlos, the duke wore his usual solemn expression. Dressed in a dark vest, black stockings, and midnight blue pants, he appeared an oversized sullen crow.

With a scowl, Don Carlos said to him, "Are you interfering in my affairs again, Alba? Are you following me? It feels these days you are my constant companion." Then, in a commanding tone, he said, "Wait by the door, sir. I wish to speak to the queen first."

Alba politely tilted his head in Elisabeth's direction and remained where he was, doing as the prince bid. Satisfied the duke had been humbled, Don Carlos took a few steps closer to Elisabeth and said, "Milady, you are quite beautiful this evening. May I kiss the queen?"

When Elisabeth raised her cheek, he bent down and touched his lips to her fair skin. Then, rising up, he acknowledged Sofonisba with a stiff little bow. Then, in a voice dripping with sarcasm, he said, "What an unexpected sight to see you here this evening, Signorina Anguissola— here in the queen's chambers yet again!"

"Oh, Don Carlos, stop!" said Elisabeth. "Sofonisba has every right to be here. She and I were just practicing our dancing steps."

"Is that so?" said the prince. "I thought Italian church mice turned in at an earlier hour. Hopefully Alba's poppet can find her way back to his room in the dark." He added with a wicked grin, "Go... run now... and try not to get pounced on by the cats lurking about in the shadows at night."

Not waiting for or expecting a response, he turned his attention back to Elisabeth. As he continued a private, whispered discourse, Sofonisba eyed Don Carlos warily. She had just been summarily dismissed, insulted, and trivialized—even threatened. She marveled at his deplorable manners.

As he leaned closer to Elisabeth, Don Carlos languidly glanced over his shoulder at Sofonisba. He gave her an arrogant, self-satisfied grin as if to say, *See, you can't possibly compete with me—I am her favorite... You will never succeed here.*

There was no rhyme or reason to his paranoia, but it seemed the traumas he suffered in childhood went far too deep and were not the kind of ailments one could patch up with a physician's cure or bandage. Over time the wound may have healed on the outside, and after years of practice he had learned to dress elegantly to hide his crooked spine, and his limp at times was barely noticeable.

Still, the cruel intent in his eyes was far too evident, and she could very well imagine him torturing some poor little field mouse just as he might a lady-in-waiting to the queen. She knew the prince's ire, when raised, was relentless, and she began to fear for her person—even her life.

With her heart pounding in her chest, Sofonisba bid a good evening to Elisabeth, curtsied, then turned to go. Keeping her eyes directed at the floor, her mind a blur with anxious thoughts, she moved quickly but stopped abruptly when a pair of shiny black boots came into view. Hastily she glanced up to see Alba still standing on the threshold, staring at Don Carlos's back.

When Alba looked at her, she saw her own fear mirrored in his eyes and realized he had just arrived at the same conclusion.

Chapter 20

The Perfect Spy

Sofonisba's distrust of the prince only continued to escalate, and as it did, so did her concerns for her personal safety. As a precaution, she took great pains to familiarize herself with his usual patterns to avoid unwanted contact. As a further precaution, she learned the palace's layout by heart—the main corridors that gave way to the larger salons and the secret passageways that led between floors—in case she needed to make a hasty escape. Once she was attuned to their existence, it wasn't difficult to notice the hidden doors and panels that, when pushed just so, gave way to the touch, allowing for easy escape—or a clandestine rendezvous.

Following Elisabeth's instructions, she also began secreting away odd bits of conversation and unusual observations, most of which pertained to Don Carlos, to communicate back to the queen. One of the happier messages she related to Elisabeth brought an instant smile to the woman's face. After gleaning information from a footman, who had spoken to the head parlor maid, Sofonisba had reported to the queen that the king was so enchanted with his new bride he vowed to give up infidelities forever. She also confirmed the king's affections were permanently directed at his new wife, after spending several hours in the company of Philip painting his latest portrait.

"The man talks about you, milady, like a besotted groom, as if he were in love for the very first time."

When Elisabeth heard this, she jumped out of her chair and hugged her friend. "So, my dear Philip is loyal to me after all. See! You are quite good at this. What a perfect spy you are! I couldn't ask for more welcome news."

Sofonisba was happy to corroborate Philip's good character not only for the queen but also for herself. She was pleased her first assignment hadn't tarnished the man's reputation or caused Elisabeth pain.

It did, indeed, seem she had a knack for learning the secrets of the palace and its inhabitants. And as Elisabeth had said, she really didn't have to work too hard at it. There was no need to skulk about dark corners or hide about in the bushes as often gossip flowed right up and over her easel. All she had to do was extend or accept a request to paint a portrait, and by its completion, she had accumulated a vast amount of trivial information.

Throughout the week, the likes of the Count of Castilla, the Duke of Osuna, and Marquess of Santillana passed through her studio doors, where they remained for hours as she painted their likenesses. As she worked, it was an easy task to engage them in light conversation. However discreet these courtiers might have thought themselves to be, never mentioning names or specific locations, little did they know nothing went unnoticed by Sofonisba.

Later, as she acted out her roles as lady-in-waiting to the queen, and she observed those same nobles, she was soon privy to the objects of their affections and who was having an illicit affair.

One night at dinner, by the blushes of the Marquessa Diana Maria Coloma, it was easy to deduce she was the Viscount of Altamira's latest paramour, despite being a bride of only a month. Turning to the lady's husband Emmanuele Coloma, Sofonisba could see his attentions too had wandered from their marital bed. The marquis hadn't breathed her name, but Sofonisba could see by the way his eyes roamed over the jewel-bedecked bodice of Annabella Margarite of the Castilian House of Ivrea she was his new lover.

The queen was receptive to anything her artist passed along to her. But, to Sofonisba, it all seemed a bit absurd. She really didn't consider herself a spy but rather a keen observer of human follies. Still, she was happy she could serve the queen and be of some use. As Elisabeth said, one never knew if something banal might actually be something more lethal. Knowledge was power, and in the end, no one was really getting hurt from her shared confidences.

As the weeks passed, eventually it was Elisabeth who turned the tables and shared a secret with Sofonisba. "I am with child," the queen told her, barely containing her excitement. "No one must know until I start showing. I do not wish to have an evil curse befall me by spreading the news too soon."

After several months, however, well into her final trimester, the expectant mother's joy turned to sorrow and ended in grief when she lost twin girls. The queen fell into a stupor of despair and requested that only Sofonisba visit her. Together they passed long afternoons reading and drawing as Elisabeth lay in bed despondent. By the early spring, with Sofonisba's support, Elisabeth's spirits improved, and she was able to reappear in court and resume her duties.

But during the time Elisabeth had lain ill, as their friendship had deepened, it had also further fueled Don Carlos's resentment. When he knocked upon Elisabeth's door—bringing her sweet morsels, cordial wines, and sonnets—it displeased him immensely to discover Sofonisba at her bedside, holding her hand. And when she exited the queen's chambers, tasked with bringing her patient a restorative tisane, she often found Don Carlos in the hall, pacing about and angrily fuming, wondering why he was not allowed in.

So it was to her extreme amazement when one afternoon, as Sofonisba closed the door to the queen's apartments, he sidled up to her and said, "Artist, are you ready to fulfill my request and paint my portrait now?"

Sofonisba viewed him warily, not entirely sure of his motives, but could not disagree. It was all she could do to speak the words, "It would be my honor."

The next day Don Carlos arrived in her studio dressed in velvet and satin, and slung around his shoulders was an ermine-trimmed cape. He looked the part of a dashing cavalier. Walking on eggshells, knowing his capricious habits and mercurial shifts of temperament, she politely indicated he should take a seat.

As she set about determining the best arrangement and angle to paint him, she was aware of his baleful eyes upon her. He said very little; so absorbed in her drawing, she jumped and nearly dropped her brush when he finally blurted out, "Artist, do you think me mad?"

Sofonisba's fingers gripped her brush more firmly, and she hesitantly looked over and encountered his dark scowl but said nothing.

"Surely you have an opinion? Everyone here thinks I am crazy... including my father. And Alba, he thinks I'm insane and should be locked up... And now, by your silence, I gather you are of that opinion too."

Abruptly he stood up, knocking over his chair. "Come now! I've seen how you watch people, how you listen to their conversations... I know you report to the queen."

Swiftly he moved toward her and, as he did, his cape floated around him in a swirl of bright colors. "But the strange thing," he said softly, "as her health improves, and the warmth returns to her cheeks, I can't help but notice Elisabeth's feelings towards me are cooling." He took another step closer to Sofonisba and said in a menacing tone, "I'm beginning to wonder..."

"Wonder what?"

"I wonder what it could be that you are telling her. What stories you could be contriving to turn her against me."

"Why would I invent things? Elisabeth and I are friends. I only tell her the truth..."

"You lie. Don't snivel at me and try to appear innocent," he snarled. "I can tell when someone is being duplicitous." He paced the room like a caged animal and then spat out, "Do you tell her the ridiculous tittle-tattle invented by feeble minds... that I set houses on fire for fun?"

Sofonisba, who knew these were not rumors but terrible truths, stared down at her drawing, not knowing what to say. The other day she had learned that the prince, so enraged by a joke told by a man in a tavern, had lit his house on fire with his family sleeping inside. He had done this unthinkable act just after performing another—that of blinding the man's horses stabled in his barn.

"Well, speak up, *artist*!" he said. "Do you deny it?"

Carefully, Sofonisba chose her words. "Elisabeth wishes to be informed of all the activities at court... She learns things from many sources. I..."

"You are a troublemaker, that is what you are. Elisabeth is the only one who cares for me. And now, because of you, she thinks me a monster! And I *blame you* for turning her against me! I will—"

Before he could finish his thought, the door sprang open, and on the threshold stood Alba. Assessing the room and the people in it, he said in a harsh tone, "Is everything all right?"

Sofonisba nodded, grateful to see him, and with her eyes she implored the duke to act cautiously. Alba observed her apprehension. Then, addressing Don Carlos, he said, "I believe you are done for the day. Elisabeth requests the company of her tutor and..."

"Ah, Duke, so now you are the queen's errand boy? Running like a besotted fool to the aid of your little artist? I don't know what you see in the woman. She is..."

"Enough!" commanded Alba. "Stop with your disagreeable ways."

Don Carlos only glared at the man, not intimidated in the slightest. But, after a moment, he relented. He adjusted his mantle and took a step closer to Sofonisba. "We will continue the painting, and our conversation, another day." Then, leaning closer to her ear, he hissed, "Consider this a warning, artist. You are not to meddle in my affairs any longer. Be assured I will be spying on you as you do me. Wherever you go... whatever you do... I'll be watching you."

To emphasize his point, he upended her table, upsetting brushes and drawing tools, sending them crashing to the ground. Swiftly, Alba crossed the room to stop Don Carlos. However, despite the prince's lame foot, he brushed roughly past the taller man and was out the door before he could be apprehended.

Alba shook his head wearily and let him go, coming instead to Sofonisba's aid. He helped to right the table, and as he had done so long ago back in Milan the first day she had come to him, he helped her pick up drawing tools that lay scattered on the floor. When things were in order again, Alba apologized profusely for Don Carlos's behavior and attempted to assuage her anxieties. "While I am near, signorina, you will have nothing to worry about. Believe me, you are safe here."

Sofonisba wanted to believe him and tried to convince herself there was no reason to be alarmed. Surely Don Carlos wouldn't take action against her, especially with the duke on her side. But later that night, when she awoke in her bed trembling, it seemed her greatest dread was realized, and Don Carlos's threats were, indeed, real.

In a dream, a large black crow visited her, swooping around the room before coming to perch at the end of her bed. As the swirling shadows shifted, the bird only seemed to grow larger. She could see its menacing dark form silhouetted by the embers burning low in the grate. Slowly the curtain around her bed lifted, and the bulk rising up over her shape-shifted into a terrifying beast. She could see its tortured eyes, and she heard it whisper her name. She shrank away from the claw that reached out to caress her face. The thought of being touched by the creature filled her with dread, and she cried out but could make no sound. In a panic, she flailed her arms and thrashed her legs until her nightdress wrapped around her, binding her tightly.

It was the click of a door that brought her to her senses.

Dazed, she assessed the room, her heart pounding rapidly. When Sofonisba realized no one was there, she relaxed, willing the nightmare's last traces to slip away and dissolve. With the bed drapes pulled back, she could see the silvery moon rising in the night sky through the open window. In the distance, emanating from the hallway, she detected the faint music of a violin. It swirled around her, and she recognized the tune. It was one that Alba often played.

Sofonisba lay back against the pillows, closed her heavy lids, and listened. When the music stopped, her eyes flashed open and she sat up, her heart racing again.

She could see the moon.

But how was that possible? She had securely closed the brocade bed drapes before falling asleep.

Now the bed curtains were open.

It hadn't been a dream at all, she thought frantically. Someone had been in her room. Someone had been watching her.

In her confused state, terrified again, she wondered if it had been Don Carlos. But as the music resumed, wrapping her in its melancholy notes, she had a strange premonition—perhaps it had been someone else.

Chapter 21

Bird in a Gilded Cage

As the fall passed into winter and winter into spring, and the notoriety of being a member of the Spanish court began to wear thin due to the prince's antics, Sofonisba realized just how much she missed her family and sisters. Life had seemed so much simpler back in Cremona, and she read the letters she received from home with a heartsick nostalgia. Her father's notes were full of encouragement and the recent young adult antics of Asdrubale. The ones she received from Elena detailed her sister's new responsibilities as wife to Massimiliano and even intimated her hopes that soon she would be with child.

But as Sofonisba folded each letter and placed it in her special box for safekeeping, the one that held the little bronze Etruscan sailor, she couldn't help but worry. Each note she received from home bore news of her mother's decline. Although they didn't say so in words, she knew instinctively what they failed to communicate. Reading between the lines, she worried Bianca might not be with them when autumn leaves fell again.

The preoccupation she felt for the welfare of her kin began to overwhelm her. To find relief when she wasn't required to serve the queen, she took to wandering the palatial estate and its extensive gardens. She particularly liked the elaborate garden maze situated just off the ballroom terrace. It reminded her of that far-off night when she and her sea captain had talked of Porsena's labyrinth. Soon she became quite adept at deciphering its mysteries and often wandered into the maze alone. It was a relatively simple puzzle to solve, and there was no fear of getting lost or needing a twine ball to find one's way out again like Porsena's.

However, soon there was cause for cheer when she learned that

Elisabeth was with child again. As before, Philip went about with a lighter step, knowing he would have a new heir. To celebrate their happy news, the king decided to throw a party. It was to be a magnificent affair, and no expense would be spared. He even extended invitations to diplomats and merchants in France, England, and Italy—after all, it wouldn't hurt to assuage a few political tensions at the same time.

Because of his ties to Rome, Philip was pressured continuously by the pope to deal with the red-haired mess in England. Elizabeth was a staunch Protestant, and he was a dyed-in-the-wool Catholic—and they had never seen eye to eye; she aligned with the Church of England and he with the Vatican. But, since his sister-in-law had become queen, she was proving to be an even bigger thorn in his side. So, it came as no surprise to anyone, least of all Elizabeth, that the Spanish king should back the claims of her cousin Mary Queen of Scots—another stalwart Catholic— who set her sights upon the English throne.

It also wasn't surprising the pope had tasked Philip with tamping down Protestantism in the Netherlands in an attempt to gain control over a region so close to English shores.

As tempers flared and the stakes grew higher, with increased rapidity, encoded messages and encrypted codices slipped back and forth across the English Channel as the two monarchs tried to outdo the other, playing a strategic game of chess. And, for the right sum, greedy courtiers joined in and turned against one another—in a deadly clashing of stratagems and wit. Still, should one be caught in the act, it meant being thrown into a dungeon to rot. And if a man—or a woman—should hazard to enter into the realm of counter reconnaissance, cuckolding both sides, they were accused of treason, died a painful death, and their heads often ended up on top of a pike decorating a bridge.

Such a deadly game of international intelligence gathering made Sofonisba's practices of gleaning information through murmured words or eavesdropped conversations seem like silly child's play.

It was amid these religious and political intrigues, when suspicions and mistrust amongst the court members were at its highest tide, that

Sofonisba received a much-feared letter from Elena. It contained the unwelcome but not unforeseen news of her mother's death. Just as Elisabeth's spry step returned, her poor mother's faulty gait failed her. She sank into her bed and died quietly at the end of April with Amilcare, Asdrubale, Elena, and Europa by her side.

As she read the letter, Sofonisba's tears dripped down her face. It grieved her to be so far away when her family needed her most. She wanted to return home to Cremona and pleaded her case to Alba, hoping he would accommodate her in her family's time of grief. But, much to her surprise, he turned her down flatly, forbidding her to travel.

"You simply cannot leave the court at this time," he said, using a forceful tone to which she was not accustomed.

"But messer, surely..."

He eyed her severely and shook his head. "I'll hear no more, signorina. There is nothing you can do now. Your duties lie here, to the king and this court. Spain is your home now—your benefactors live here, and so do you. This is where you will remain."

His insistence seemed overbearing and dictatorial—heartless even—and she immediately resented the man because of it. Sofonisba knew the duke was preoccupied with international unrest and that was why he spoke so firmly; still, she thought it extremely cruel to deny her the chance to attend her mother's funeral. Darkly she thought, *Because you lost your mother so long ago, you have no memory of the pain nor empathy. You are but a shell of a man, devoid of love and feeling.*

And then Sofonisba received a letter from Vasari informing her that their friend Michelangelo had passed away from a brief illness just shy of his eighty-ninth birthday. He had been alone in his home in Macel de' Corvi in Rome. It broke her heart to know one of her guiding lights was no longer with her.

As Sofonisba mourned the loss of her mother and that of il Maestro, she slipped into a decline, even lost interest in painting. Previously, she had meticulously kept out of the path of Don Carlos, and now due to her falling out with Alba, she did everything she could to avoid him too. Irrationally, she blamed him for compounding her sorrows. Not able to control her anger, when they did meet she clamped her mouth shut and passed by without a kind word or smile. When they did speak, she responded coolly, with the intent of pushing him away. After they exchanged words, she watched him stride off dispiritedly in the opposite direction. She knew it caused him pain but she couldn't help the way she felt.

To Sofonisba, who had been at the Spanish court for almost five years, felt like a bird in a gilded cage—she had some freedoms but couldn't fly away. Morosely she reread letters from home and waited for a ripple of solace that would change her monotonous existence.

But the days passed more slowly than ever, and she longed for the adventures of her youth when she had traveled to Rome with her father. She wanted to feel alive again, to be filled with wonder and exhilaration... and have a conversation with someone who knew her intimately and opened her mind to new possibilities. Dare she admit it? She longed to be cherished and adored by someone she found warm, witty, and desirable.

She gazed into the distance, remembering a fascinating young man with curling hair and a far-off look. That had been a magical evening—a stolen moment—yet she recalled every word of their secret conversation.

With a touch of regret, she recalled her girlish claims of wanting no husband and no man to interfere with her independent life. What had she said? *I don't wish to marry. I have no desire to belong to anyone or share my life chained to a husband. That would ruin all my plans.*

Sofonisba looked around the splendidly decorated salon and down at her tight-fitted gown. She wiggled her toes in shoes that pinched her feet and wondered, *Is this really how I wish to continue spending my days— living a solitary life in this Spanish tomb far from my native land?*

But, despite her claims she was unloved or not valued, Sofonisba failed to take into account Elisabeth—she, in fact, was still her greatest ally. And once the queen returned to court life—filled with felicitous news—noting Sofonisba's melancholy mood, she wanted her to be happy too. Resolving to effect a change, the queen requested her painting lessons be resumed and in no uncertain terms reinstated herself into Sofonisba's painting salon.

In preparation, Sofonisba opened the drapes to let in the light and pulled the dust cloths from tables that covered her supplies. As she did, it seemed a tendril of joy unfurled within her at the thought of returning to her life's work. As the two worked side by side, their camaraderie returned, easing the pain and resentment that Sofonisba had been harboring deep inside.

Hoping to rekindle further the spark that had once shone in her artist's eyes, Elisabeth, speaking in Italian, cooed, "*Mia cara! La vita è troppo breve per essere triste!* Yes! It is spring, and summer is soon upon us. I believe life is too brief for sadness. A party will restore our happiness, make us forget about our worries, and allow our spirits to sing again."

She raised her brush, pointed it at Sofonisba, and said, "Come now, *mia cara*. You must stop being sad... and stop being angry with the duke. He seeks to protect you. My husband agrees. These are not times to be traveling abroad—there are far too many dangers beyond the palace gates. He is right to keep you here close to us." Softly, she added, "He cares for you in his own way... If you ask me, he is afraid he will lose you if you return to Cremona." She shrugged her shoulders. "Perhaps he thinks you won't return to us and he will never see you again."

Sofonisba, who had opened her mouth to speak, closed it abruptly. Elisabeth seeing her stubborn expression, only smiled. Then giving her a quick hug, she said, "*Mia cara, fido di me*—trust me... the ball will be good for you. How I love to dance and dress up in a new gown. It is good for the soul to be frivolous every now and then."

She smiled. "Besides, I know how you love to dance—you can't deny that you do... You are too well-versed in the moves not to participate. Why, I remember at Prince de La Roche's ball several years ago, you were the first female to dance and among the last to leave the salon. Philip was very charmed by your grace and self-confidence. He honored you with a very deep bow after you partnered with him that evening—after that, your position at this court was undeniably established!"

Elisabeth smoothed a hand over her stomach, which now showed a healthy bump. "Did you know for this event I am having Edouard make me something new out of the pink moire silk my mother sent me from France that will hide my growing and rotund figure? As much as I adore the thought of holding this babe in my arms, I dislike feeling like a clumsy elephant."

Finished with painting for the day, the queen put down her brush and rose awkwardly from her chair. Stretching her back, she toddled to the door. Before departing, she called over her shoulder, "I know you are not so inclined as the others to wear the most current fashions, so I have taken the liberty of having a new dress made for you too. I want you to wear it to the party. I've instructed Edouard to leave it in your room." When Sofonisba started to object, Elisabeth held up a hand to silence her. "You must never disobey a command of the queen."

Curious about what she would find, Sofonisba returned to her chambers and eyed the large package swathed in white linen, which now hung from a hook in her armoire. Slowly she pulled off the sheer covering and murmured her approval. Fluffing out the heavy full skirt, she thought the gown the most beautiful creation she had ever seen. It was made of turquoise-blue watered silk and was trimmed in gold embroidery, and the contrasting sleeves seemed to have been spun from gold.

Then she caught sight of a silver box sitting on her dressing table. When she opened it, she discovered a note from Elisabeth and a strand of pearls from which dangled a large sapphire. At the bottom of the box was a headpiece made of silk flowers with seed pearls sewn into their centers. Instantly, she recognized the work of Suor Marianna, who created the most beautiful decorations for the ladies of the court to wear in their hair.

Sofonisba picked up Elisabeth's note and read. *For once, I want you to do something new with your hair. It is much too severe for my liking. To that end, I've had Sister Marianna make a headpiece to match the dress, and I've instructed Madame Dubois to dream up a flattering coiffure élégante.*

Perhaps Elisabeth was right after all. Life was too brief for sadness.

Dancing, a pretty dress, and a new hairstyle were just the right tonic she needed to liven her mood.

So Sofonisba accepted the gift and a few days later, standing in front of the large mirror in her room, she silently thanked Elisabeth. The dress suited her perfectly and flowed gracefully about her form, billowing out in the current fashion. Her dark brown hair, now loosely swept up into a crown of curls held in place with the silk flowers, softened her face in the most beguiling manner.

She smiled at her reflection. Viewing herself in the magnificent gown, it was quite a transformation from the typical dark shifts and paint-splattered aprons she usually donned. Pivoting left and then right to see herself better, she thought she looked quite passable.

For a fleeting moment, she wished her mother could see her. "You would never believe your eyes, Mamma. Look at me! No tell-tale smears of paint on my hands or on my nose. Your wayward daughter who spilled jam on the table, argued with her sisters, and made faces at Asdrubale... When she wants to be, Sofonisba can be quite elegant... and respectable."

Chapter 22

Captain of the Sofonisba

*L*ater that evening, when Sofonisba entered the ballroom illuminated by flickering candles in sconces that reflected light into the gilded mirrors, she felt pleased with her appearance and believed she blended in with the other beautifully dressed ladies. She inhaled deeply, enjoying the scent of the warm summer air that wafted in through the large open terrace doors. As the music flowed through the salon, played on lutes, and a spinet from a small ensemble, she swayed to the captivating rhythm. After making a tour of the large elegant salon, she stopped for a moment to watch the magician's antics and the acrobats who tumbled upon a dais at the end of the room, performing somersaults and intriguing contortions.

It was a lively scene, and with each passing moment, her spirits were buoyed, and she had the uncanny feeling something out of the ordinary was about to happen. Hiding a smile behind her fan, she thought she kept a low profile, letting the others dance and preen about her, but her entrance had not gone unnoticed by Don Carlos. Dressed in a fuchsia coat and yellow britches and holding a glass of spirits in his hand, he made his way across the room to stand by her side.

Warily she glanced at him. Then, politely, she said, "Good evening, prince. Are you enjoying—"

He cut her off and said in a tone that indicated she was nothing more than dung on the bottom of his boots, "I see you for once have dressed appropriately."

Stunned into silence, Sofonisba just nodded and continued watching the swirl of colors as the pretty ladies danced with the gentlemen. She wished to be back in her rooms with every fiber of her being, but propriety begged her to stay by the enfant's side until he had released her. Hesitantly she regarded him, worried what he might say next or if he might cause a scene before the entire assembly.

Don Carlos gave her a sideways look. "Do I make you nervous, artist?" He gave a little chortle and looked back at the ballroom. "You needn't be. Despite your finery, I have no intention of asking you to dance. You see, my dance card is quite filled this evening with more tempting morsels. But I'm sure there are other men here who'd give their eye teeth to partner with a conniving-little-queen-loving spy such as yourself." He glanced up. "Ah...and look at this. Right on cue, here is Alba coming to the defense of his little mouse."

The prince gave her a stiff bow and then walked off in Elisabeth's direction, a beatific smile spread across his face. He turned back to look at her, and by the way he narrowed his eyes, Sofonisba had a distinct impression that instead of slapping her with insolent words, he could have just as easily used the back of his hand.

"Are you quite all right?" Alba asked, following her gaze that was still trained on Don Carlos.

"Yes, of course," she said briskly.

He stood rigidly at her side, keeping a respectable distance, but when the silence between them became too prolonged, he said, "It is a lovely affair. Philip and Elisabeth have outdone themselves. The musicians are exceptional this evening. I know how much you enjoy practicing your dance steps... With such musical accompaniment, I'm sure you will enjoy yourself immensely tonight. Why I'm almost inspired to dance myself."

Sofonisba glanced at him in a distracted manner, surprised to hear such pleasantries issue from the Duke's mouth. She studied him for a moment and had to admit that tonight, the Duke looked impressive dressed in black military attire. His dark coat was a bit stark but was livened by the red and gold sash he wore across his chest, which was adorned with a vast assortment of well-shined medals. His beard was neatly trimmed, as it always was, but this evening she could see his hair was groomed with scented oils. Yes, he cut a fine figure, and despite his astonishing admission that he felt like dancing, he seemed a bit too stiff and out of place amongst the lavishly and colorfully dressed partygoers.

"I've never known you to dance, Duke," she finally said with a small laugh. "But should you fancy to, the room is filled with quite an assortment of young ladies to chose from."

As the music ended, Sofonisba looked back at the ballroom floor and watched as new couples took their places. She noticed the contessa Maria Alverez García was partnered with the handsome Edoardo Fernández. She wondered what Maria's husband would think of this turn of events. As she searched through the crowd to see if the countess's husband was watching, she didn't notice the duke had moved a few paces closer.

But when she felt Alba's breath upon her shoulder, she flinched ever so slightly and glanced back at him quickly. The duke didn't seem to notice her reaction and leaned down further and said, "You look particularly well this evening. Dressed in blue... Well, the color becomes you. The flowers, too, are a lovely touch. They encircle your head like a halo..."

When he saw her bemused expression, he coughed, then continued. "I only meant to suggest the transformation suits you."

"Why, Duke, such compliments... I don't know what to say." Sofonisba tilted her head slightly to the left and eyed him cautiously. His comportment this evening seemed very strange.

He nodded as if he regretted his choice of words. But after a moment, he began again. "I... I wondered..."

"Yes," she asked hesitantly, worried now that out of all the women in the room, he would ask her to dance with him. She couldn't imagine anything more awkward than to be held in his arms or have his hands caress her back. Granted, her corsets prevented intimate contact, but the contradance's intricate steps would keep them side-by-side for at least a half an hour.

Before Alba could formally announce his intentions, a voice from behind Sofonisba spoke up. "Signorina Anguissola. Might I have the pleasure of the next dance?"

Sofonisba paused. She knew that voice. It was rich and deep and made her think of far-off places. Feeling the warm presence of the stranger engulf her senses, she slowly turned around. When their eyes met, she was not disappointed. Despite the passage of years, she recognized him immediately, and a smile spread across her face. Unlike the last time they'd met, he wasn't dressed in dirty britches and didn't carry a satchel but instead wore an elegant brocade jerkin embroidered in gold on top and wore black leggings on the bottom. The ballroom and the music disappeared, and she was instantly transported back to a moonlit wall in a small Etruscan town outside of Rome and only heard the call of night birds and felt the magic of Porsena enveloping them.

Although he hadn't spoken another word, she could tell by his expressive eyes that he approved of her sapphire gown. By the comical tilt of his eyebrow and the slight gesture he made with both hands, indicating the elaborate scene around them, she also knew he was quite impressed to find her here in the heart of the Spanish court.

When the musicians played the opening strains of a new dance, over the cacophony of conversation and dulcet chords, she whispered, "So, it is you!"

"Yes, it is me," he agreed, smiling down at her. "We meet again."

Without saying another word, he extended his hand, and she accepted it, and in unison, they stepped out onto the dance floor. Oblivious to the crowd, they stood toe to toe, breathing in each other's scent—his of the salty sea and hers of lilies of the valley. But, as the other couples began to move around them, Sofonisba shook her head and came to her senses. She looked around to see if anyone was watching them, and out of the corner of her eye, she saw Alba still standing a few steps away. A frown had darkened his face, and he wore a puzzled expression, or was it something else... Was it resentment?

But, at the gentle tug of her partner's hand, she quickly forgot about the duke. Everything faded away, as together, they dipped and swayed in time to the music, making their way around the room in a large circle with the other couples. When the last chord died away, he bowed, and she curtsied, but they didn't part company. Instead, they stood regarding one another intently until Sofonisba finally laughed and said, "I'm surprised to see you... and here of all places."

"Is it a happy surprise?"

"Why yes!" she said, shaking her head in disbelief. "I fear I've conjured a ghost from my distant past. If I close my eyes, you will disappear."

"Despite the talk of Etruscan phantoms that night, I can assure you I'm very much flesh and blood," he said in amusement, reiterating the very comment she once said on a moonlit path in Chiusi.

"I've often wondered what became of you... where your ship transported you..."

"As I have wondered about you."

They studied one another, like two long-lost friends, seeking signs of recognition. And then, like before, the connection they had forged the night they had first met was once again rekindled.

"So..." he said with admiration, "you have become the court painter to the Spanish king!"

"Yes," she said. "Just as I promised you... I remained true to my goals."

"When I heard the news that you were here and what you had accomplished, it didn't surprise me at all." He took a step back and regarded her appreciatively. "You know, you are quite lovely in that gown, and the flowers in your hair... so different from the last time I saw you. But despite the finery, I'd recognize you anywhere—even amongst all these French and Spaniards! You have a unique charm that is hard to forget."

"Oh, come now! I see you are still very much a flatterer," Sofonisba admonished. Still, she eyed him with delight. Finally here was someone who made her smile again, someone from her past who made her think of traveling and adventure. This man, with his infectious grin, made her heart pound. It was a welcome change to feel the mirth bubble inside her again.

"But it is true. Sofonisba, you take my breath away with your beauty and your talents. I've seen the portraits hanging in the king's gallery. What an honor it is to know such a gifted artist."

"And what of you? Are you a respectable sea captain, or did you become a marauding pirate?" she teased.

"I, madame, am the owner of a magnificent vessel. Before you stands Captain Orazio Lomellino," he said with dignity.

"Ahh... so, finally, I know your name! You learned mine from my father, who bellowed it out into the night air—"

"As any distraught papa ought to do searching for his lost chick!"

She smiled at the memory. "Yes. But I've always regretted not discovering yours. It is a mystery that has haunted me all these years."

"I never told you it that night..."

"Did you think I would betray you, tell everyone you were a thief and a cheat?"

He seemed slightly offended. "I believed you would never do that."

"What made you think that, Orazio Lomellino?"

"Your eyes! I knew I could trust you because of what I saw deep inside of you—your beautiful soul."

She glanced over at a group of women who were watching them with overt interest. Even at this distance, Sofonisba could hear the gaggle of women chirping and squawking, repeating frivolous phrases. When her companion turned to look in their direction and nodded politely, they burst into laughter and bobbed their heads coquettishly at him.

"I see you are still quite capable of turning heads and lavishing praise quite beautifully. But perhaps it is better used on the other ladies of the court... You will melt their hearts with such buttery fripperies."

He raised his arms in supplication. "Don't my words have any effect on you? They are meant quite sincerely." When she didn't respond, he countered, "Or perhaps you are jealous?"

"Jealous? Oh, no," she said lightly, feeling the heady sensation of a woman who had just captivated the most handsome man's attention in the room. For he was as she remembered him, swarthy and deeply tanned. His face had character and his smile was compelling, and it seemed he was always on the verge of telling an amusing joke.

"You shouldn't be," said Orazio. "Jealous, I mean."

With a nod in the direction of the other ladies-in-waiting, he said,

"Sofonisba, by far, you eclipse all of them. You are fair of skin, and your form is lovely, but it is your intelligence that renders you beautiful. I told you once, Beatrice has nothing to teach you."

She raised an eyebrow. "You always had such pretty words on the tip of your tongue... just like the ancient Greek Hedylogos—the winged love god of flattery."

"Ah!" he said, smiling at her. "It's all coming back to me now! I do remember how well-read and inquisitive you are."

"And, as I recall, you are quite the adventurer. Dealing cards, playing tricks, and with your quick wit outsmarting other men of their gold."

"Milady, you wound me! I told you one day I would buy a ship, set sail for foreign ports, and discover far-off places." Gesturing to a tall man standing against the opposite wall, dressed in silks and a turban, he added, "See that man over there? He is one of my crew."

"The Arab?"

"His name is Khidr Aruj, and I trust him with my life. I've seen my share of harrowing events, storms, and narrow escapes... and now I am a rich man because of it."

"Your man looks more like a Barbary corsair. Are you and Khidr Aruj really pirates who now trick men of their ships and their gold? Or are you actually a spy currying favors for whoever pays the highest price?"

"What do you know of spies?" he asked, raising an eyebrow.

"I've been at the Spanish court for several years now. One cannot escape court intrigues and plots...."

"So, the girl I met so long ago is now a grown-up woman who has the queen's ear. Perhaps it is you who is a spy, Sofonisba," he said.

"If I was, would I admit it?" she said with a playful shake of her head. "So, tell me, what business really brings you here?"

"I'm a merchant. I sail to the East Indies, to Venice, and back to Naples and Genova. I received a royal invitation from the king to attend tonight's affair."

"Impressive," she said. "And what is your ship called? It better be a good one for such an illustrious captain as yourself who commands such a fierce lot of men!"

He regarded her intently, then said, "She is called *The Sofonisba*."

"You named your ship after me?"

"I couldn't think of a finer name. I called her after a proud and determined woman I met once in the middle of an unforgettable, star-filled night. Someone whom I've never gotten out of my mind."

She flushed, and suddenly the room seemed stuffy and overheated. Perhaps it was because her gown was cinched too tight, or maybe it was the glass of sweet wine she had drunk earlier... When a ripple of laughter pierced the air Sofonisba glanced over again at the women tittering behind their fans, and said, "Come, it appears we are becoming a topic of discussion. Let's take a stroll and continue this discussion in the garden."

Orazio scanned the ballroom too. "I believe you are right," he said, taking her arm and tucking it in his. "Let's remove ourselves from prying fools so that we might know each other better."

With a nod, he signaled to his friend—the man he called Khidr Aruj—that he could take his leave of the party as well.

"Whatever shall we talk about?" she asked in a teasing tone, as they walked toward the large doors that led out to the garden.

"Why, of portraits and painting..." he said.

"And pirates and pots of gold," she concluded with a laugh.

Reaching the threshold, Orazio tilted his head, indicating she should proceed him, and soon they found themselves on the polished stone terrace surrounded by urns of flowers and statues of cupid. Sofonisba lifted her face to the warm summer breeze and listened to a night bird calling in the distance. It seemed the magic of the long-forgotten Etruscan king was weaving his spell upon them once again.

She glanced at him, suddenly shy, and asked, "Would you like to walk the paths? The Spanish gardeners are no match for the Etruscans architects who built the fabled labyrinth. Still... it is a passable diversion." Sofonisba peered over her shoulder, back at the ballroom, and continued. "Deep in the maze, we are free of gossip and inquisitive glances. But there is no need to worry. There is no fear of getting lost or never returning."

"Pity, that," he said with a grin. Then with a tilt of his head, he added,

"Please, lead the way."

Together they descended the stairs, but when they started down the pebbled path, one of Sofonisba's slippers slipped on the rocks. Before she could stumble, the man beside her deftly caught her arm and steadied her. They stood so close she could feel his warm breath upon her face and in the dim light, she observed him and once again and was not disappointed. She had evoked his image countless times, seeing him standing on his ship's deck, but the real man was no match for the memory. In person, he was far more vital and vibrant.

"So, you remember that evening?" she said at last. "Do you recall our conversation?"

"I remember everything you told me that night, Sofonisba."

"I still have the coin you gave me."

"I can't tell you how much that delights me."

Eyeing her elaborate gown, he added, "It seems you have sealed your reputation as an important artist—living an independent life, receiving a fine income, fancy clothes, and all the jewels you could ever want. Isn't that what you always desired?"

She shrugged in agreement. "Yes, I suppose it is so."

They were silent a moment, then pointing to the sky he asked, "Do you see that bright light in the sky? That is the planet Venus. See how she is resting so close to the moon?"

"It would appear they are kissing!"

He smiled. "Quite so... It is a rare occasion that the moon aligns so closely with Venus... practically caressing one another. They come together as if they could not bear to be separated any longer—but only for a few nights—before continuing on their separate journeys."

"How do you know this?" she asked.

"I'm a ship's captain. I chart my courses by the paths of the stars. They are as familiar to me as the back of my hand." He gazed back up at the sky and said, "But I hope to change that..."

She shook her head and said, "You may well be a fine captain who sails and tames uncharted seas, but how can you possibly change the course of the moons and the planets?"

"But what if I could?" he persisted. "What would happen if the moon and Venus decided one day to stay together—to remain by each other's side? What if their attraction was so great they could never be pulled apart again?"

"You are starting to talk in riddles," she answered lightly.

"I believe my meaning is clear. Remember, I asked you once if you feared growing old with no one to love? You replied, a man would only ruin your plans and hold you back. Well... I hope to change that." When she said nothing, he continued. "After all these years, I still think of you when I am alone with the stars and the sea."

Sofonisba listened cautiously to his words, but something in them responded to her own loneliness of late. For hadn't she also, in the late-night hours, thought of him—longing for his witty banter.

"What are you thinking?" Orazio asked her gently. "Have I alarmed you? Does what I say surprise you?'"

She shook her head. "No, I was just..."

"I have a confession to make," Orazio said, interrupting her. "I knew you were here, and that is why I have come. I wanted to meet you again. I can't explain it... I wanted to find out if what I felt in my heart was real."

"You came to the Spanish court just to see me?"

"You've always been with me, Sofonisba... on the edge of my dreams." He took her hand and gave it a light squeeze. "Do you remember back in Chiusi, I asked you to sail away with me that night?"

"I remember..."

"And would you, Sofonisba? If I asked you again?"

She met his unflinching gaze. "Be careful what you ask. This time I might not turn you down. I've been at court far too long not to have learned the ways of men and women..."

"Ah... the ways of men and women..." he said. "You have no idea how intriguing those words sound coming from your lips. I told you once before, it is you who is the thief... you who stole my heart that night."

"I also remember..."

"Yes," he whispered.

"You asked me if you could kiss my hand."

"And would you let me do that again?"

"What, kiss my hand? Perhaps. But I think it is time to stop kissing hands. Maybe it is time to..."

Before she could finish, he leaned down and touched his lips to hers, and she tasted him for the first time. The sensation of his skin against hers was the touch she had imagined since the first day they had met.

He raised his head and met her gaze. "Is that what you meant?"

"Much nicer than kissing the back of my hand," she admitted.

He rested his head against her forehead and laughed, but she could see he was trying to control his breathing. Then with soft strokes, he caressed her cheek with his thumb, and she knew he was waiting for a sign from her to continue.

As before, after only minutes of meeting, she felt herself being drawn closer to this man; it was an undeniable force she knew she couldn't resist. They shared a connection—they were ambitious and independent—two adventurers cut from the same cloth. And all this time they both had shared a secret—each had been dreaming of the other. She warmed at the thought Orazio had never stopped thinking of her... He had even named his ship after her.

Standing in his light embrace, Sofonisba knew this felt right and she was not afraid. So, with an imperceptible nod, she encouraged Orazio and slowly leaned into him. Without hesitation, her ship captain drew her closer to his chest, and Sofonisba marveled at the sensation and the scent of him. He seemed a part of her; it was as if they were two puzzle pieces joined together like this a thousand times before.

Lost in a sea of new emotions, there on the threshold of the garden maze—in the purple evening shadows as the chirping crickets crescendoed—Sofonisba sighed contentedly. As the pressure and fervor of their kisses became stronger, the heat between them rose. And when Orazio's hands caressed her bodice, she did not push them away. Instead, she helped him undue ribbons and brocade, allowing him access to her soft, warm flesh.

As the girl with the large brown eyes and the man with the golden smile surrendered to one another in the queen's garden, lost in a universe of their own making, beyond the hedge, unbeknownst to them, Alba watched them. His dark silhouette was concealed from view, but like a giant bird perched on a branch, he followed their every movement and heard their whispered words.

When their arms had finally entwined and their lips had touched, he'd felt a pain grip his heart like a vise. Sofonisba had never gazed at him the way she looked at this stranger, nor would he have ever dared touch her so intimately. Yet here, in a dark garden, it only took a moment for her to fall under another man's spell. His eyes flashed red in fury. How dare the man!

He watched in agony as the stranger took Sofonisba's hand and drew her deeper into the heart of the garden maze. Now out of sight, his mind was in complete turmoil. *What are they doing? Is he undressing her completely? Is she running her hands through his hair? Will he touch her thighs and make her tremble with ecstasy?*

With a shudder, he admonished himself. How could he think such things about her? He struggled to regain control of his raging mind. She was not like other women, the other harlots at court who let strange men crawl into their beds to perform perverted acts!

It was too unbearable, but still his mind raced on. *Is she doing this to punish me?* Yes, she had been angry with him of late. He could feel her contempt growing daily... Was this some kind of game she played to torment him? Taunting him with another man.

"You fool!" he hissed, berating himself again. *She has no feelings for you! She has never been yours, nor should she ever be tainted by your hands.*

He stepped back into the shadows, the bile of self-hatred filling his stomach. His past deeds were too horrendous to contemplate, and with an extreme force, he shoved them back into the black pit of his soul.

He loved a woman he could never have and whom he feared to touch. But, still, he didn't wish to see her happy with another.

He truly was an evil man.

Chapter 23

Broken Hearts, Doubts, and Promises

Sofonisba glanced up from the canvas she was working on and looked out the window at the golden leaves that indicated fall was approaching. With a soft sigh, she turned her attention back to her latest self-portrait. As she studied her work, she barely recognized the woman who gazed back at her. This woman had satiny cheeks tinged a rosy pink and lush, full lips that tilted up in a knowing smile. But most striking of all was the woman's luminous brown eyes that gleamed as if she had a secret to share.

Through the years, Sofonisba had painted many portraits of herself. It had become a soothing pastime, and in each one, she conveyed a message that reflected the state of her mind. Sometimes she focused on her skills as an artist, expressing the belief she was as talented as any man—as evidenced in the double portrait she had painted of herself and Bernardino Campi. In others she emphasized the pride she felt for the education she had received—just one of the many gifts and legacies her father provided her.

But this new portrait—completed in her thirty-fifth year—was unlike any of the previous. Stylistically, she had come a long way from her youthful days in Cremona. It was also evident by the proud tilt of her head and squaring of her shoulders that she matured from the naive young woman who had worked with Michelangelo in Rome. The poised young lady who regarded her with a slight smile was worldly and could hold her own among the Spanish nobility.

Still, there was something more profound about this version of herself. And up until this fateful summer, Sofonisba never would have been able to paint it. For in the eyes of this woman was the look of someone in love. They reflected not only self-confidence but also the knowledge gained from experiencing a man's passionate kiss. And more than that... this woman who gazed back at her now knew the incredibly intimate touch that only a husband should bestow upon his wife.

Sofonisba sighed and set down her brush and thought of the man who had returned the glow to her cheeks and sparkle in her eyes. After the queen's ball, Orazio had chosen to remain the summer at the Spanish court, giving his crewmen a holiday. For several glorious summer months, they had taken the time to get to know one another, and each passing hour was a gift; as the days blended into nights, the pleasure they took in each other's company only increased.

When their ardent regard for one another began to raise eyebrows—as well as cause more downturned scowls from Alba—to stave off gossip, they'd escaped into the copse of woods at the back of the royal palace where they'd row out onto a small lake, where no one else could see them. Other times they had walked through the halls of the castle, holding hands. But hearing footsteps echoing off the marble floors, they quickly ducked into one of the many secret passageways that Sofonisba was privy to. Squeezed into their hidden nook, they'd smothered their laughter and continued kissing even when hearing Philip or Alba's voices on the other side of the wooden panel.

As the late days of summer had flowed together, alone in her painting studio, Sofonisba took the time to instruct Orazio how to draw. She had been surprised to see he had a natural draftsman's talent with a pen and ink. While she'd worked on his portrait, he'd drawn ships and exotic birds. Once he'd even attempted to sketch her likeness, and in her estimation, it was quite good. As she critiqued his drawing, he'd cradled her in his arms and whispered into her ear, he loved her.

During the balmy evenings, they would stroll the grounds and make their way into the center of the maze. As they lay on the soft grass, they looked up at the star-sprinkled sky, and Sofonisba told him about life in the court. She recounted for him all the silly anecdotes and people she lived with and the lunacy and troublesome antics of Don Carlos. Orazio often grew solemn when she told him about the troubling tales surrounding the prince and the rudeness she had endured. But, when Sofonisba saw a vein pulsing in Orazio's temple, she'd adeptly steered the conversation toward more light-hearted subjects.

How he had quickly regained his buoyant spirit and doubled over from hysterics at the story of the unfortunate Madame Margherita Charpentier—one of the French-born ladies-in-waiting—who had suffered miserably because of her vanity. To keep up with trends, she'd instructed her maid to tease up her mane so high and hold it in place with pig's lard. Unbeknownst to her, while she slept, little mice—lured by the smell—created a nest in her hair.

"Can you just imagine, the next day, a dozen ladies screaming in fright when Margherita's head began to tremble violently, and a tiny pink nose with whiskers poked out of her elaborate hairdo to say hello?"

Orazio had shaken his head in amusement. "Your accounts of court life are almost as amusing as what I encountered in Madagascar's jungles, where monkeys steal men's hats and scamper away into trees."

When she had plied him for more details, he had happily regaled her with stories about his numerous journeys to Africa and the scents and the sights that greeted him when he walked into the kasbahs. As he spoke, she was right there with him—his vivid language brought the faraway places to life, and she could almost smell the fragrant air and taste the exotic spices.

"But what of your sea adventures and the storms you encountered? Surely it couldn't have always been smooth sailing and funny moments with tropical birds who mimic your words and call out your name?"

"Oh, Sofi! I've had my fair share of tribulations on the water—storms that rocked my ship so fiercely that I thought we'd be tasty morsels in a shark's belly before the hurricane ended. Perhaps the most terrible thing of all were the Barbary corsairs we encountered along the coast of North Africa near Tripoli. They were dark and dangerous—their heads wrapped in turbans with beards down to their knees. They sailed out of Algeria and Tunisia—the Ottoman Empire's homeland—hoping to find ships to board, ravage, and then burn."

"Did you engage them in battle?"

"We most certainly did! We had no choice but to stand and fight."

"But how did you escape? I've heard reports they are quite savage. Last year Philip lost an entire fleet to their attack. They raided the ships and stole the cargo, and everyone on board was taken."

"It is true... they are a miserable, heartless lot who sneak up and scramble onto a ship, intent on slitting the captain's throat and pilfering the hold. They then gather all on board, including the women and children, to send back to Constantinople to work as concubines in brothels. The men they chain together and sell to slave markets to any who will buy them. Such unfortunate souls remain in captivity for years unless their relatives pay out a sizable ransom."

"So, tell me, how did you avoid such a dreadful fate?"

"That day, we met them head on in combat. Not one man on my crew is a coward. But that was a bloody battle—I lost some good sailors... but by sunset the barbarians were defeated. Although we had razor-sharp blades, I knew after that skirmish, if we were to survive on the seas, we needed a better weapon."

"What did you do?"

"I had heard of Da Vinci's cannon... It is a large wooden catapult that sits upon the ship's deck, and with it we can launch flaming barrels of oil at the corsairs' ships. Leonardo's cannon never worked... or he never took the time to tweak his design. But I figured out the mechanisms—"

"And you put it to the test and it worked?"

"Yes. Without it, I would never again sail into the Algerian seas."

"How many times have you used it?"

"Enough," he said. "Once, sailing the straits of Gibraltar, we encountered another crew of surly Turks, but because of the cannon it took but a few hours to send those black-hearted bastards to the bottom of the sea. By midnight, the sky was illuminated by blazing, sinking ships and the air filled with curdling cries of drowning men."

Orazio hesitated, and she knew he was envisioning the chaos of the attack. After a moment, he let out a sigh and said, "That was the night I first met Khidr Aruj. The boy came aboard with the pirates who attempted to capture my ship. But, instead of engaging my men during the battle on deck, he hid away in a coil of rope. I only learned of his existence after we sailed on the next day."

"If he was a spy and a pirate, why did you let him live?"

"At first, I had my doubts. When Khidr Aruj was dragged before me, I placed my blade on his throat and threatened to take his life right there and then. Bravely, he looked me squarely in the eye and said not a word. As I pushed the dagger in a little further, a trickle of blood ran down the boy's neck and he finally spoke."

"What did he say?"

"He begged me to finish the task, as death would be more welcome than the previous hell he had come from."

"And you believed him?"

"There was something in the boy's eyes. And then he began to tell me a strange tale. He said he was a scholar—that's all he ever wanted to be. From the moment his grandfather gave him the Koran to read, he only wanted to continue learning. Through books he said he could travel to distant lands. One day, though, on his way home from the market, Khidr Aruj caught the Sultan's attention and was taken against his will to live in the king's pleasure palace. However, after a few hours in captivity, he cleverly managed to poison the oranges intended for his new master."

"Poison! Wherever did he acquire that?"

"Before he was abducted, the boy was on an errand to acquire medicine for his mother who was ill. In his pocket, he still had the vial of belladonna. When used in small amounts, the drug is restorative and eases pain..."

"Yes, I know about that," said Sofonisba, "but it can be lethal in larger doses. So, did the Sultan die?"

"Unfortunately, the boy's plot was found out—a lackey who tasted the king's food precisely for this reason perished instead. When Khidr Aruj was identified as the culprit, they cut off one of his ears and threw him into the hull of a Turkish ship to work as a slave. Apparently, it was a miserable fate far crueler than death. When the pirates attacked my ship, he took a chance and attempted another escape."

"And because of his story, you let him live..."

"Yes. But still, for several days and weeks, I kept close scrutiny on the boy. In the end, I realized the truth about him."

"What is that?"

"Khidr Aruj is a poet—no more a barbaric corsair than I. Still, that doesn't mean the boy didn't grow into an excellent seaman. He's an agile sort. I trained him to the best of my ability. He handles a rope and a sail as well as he does a blade, and I trust him with my life."

Orazio had tucked a strand of curling hair behind her ear and said, "I am an excellent judge of character... just as I determined yours so long ago—I knew then as I know now I can trust you, Sofi, with my heart."

Whatever response she had been about to give was quickly smothered by the touch of his lips upon hers. He rolled her over, and she could feel the cool grass on her back. The world melted away, and they lost all interest in the Spanish court and Barbary corsairs.

Instead, they gave in to heated kisses and let their passion take them to new heights. Letting him push up her skirts, she granted him access to her warm center, allowing him to explore her freely with his gentle yet determined hands. He shimmied out of his britches, and in the privacy of their secret grotto, tucked deep inside the maze where no one would ever find them, they came together, moving slowly at first. As the joy of being so intimately united filled their senses, their hearts hammered until they were carried higher into a new realm of love and shimmering, pulsating sensations. Together they lay, joined in body and mind, and with hands intertwined they spoke in intimate whispers and sighs as lovers do, savoring the stolen moments.

Their mid-summer affair had been blissful, but as the autumn winds began to blow, their interlude was rudely disrupted when Orazio was summoned by the king. After hours spent sequestered behind closed doors with Alba, Orazio finally returned to her side, and with a solemn expression, he informed her Philip had an assignment for him and he was to leave as soon as he had prepared his ship and crew.

"What is this task you have been entrusted to carry out?" she'd asked.

"I sail to Africa to acquire spices for Philip and..."

As his voice trailed away, she'd looked at him in dismay. But, instead of divulging more, he remained quiet. His reticence worried her further. They'd shared so many intimate thoughts and plans, so it was strange he wasn't sharing with her all the details of this new venture.

When she pushed him further, Orazio had finally said, "Just know, for the moment, my services are needed elsewhere. I will miss you terribly. But Philip offers quite a large purse for my efforts, and I have too many debts not to miss the chance to profit by this opportunity."

Sofonisba opened her mouth to speak, then closed it abruptly as an inexplicable chill gripped her heart. "I fear it will be a long time before we see one another again. You think only of gold and obtaining more riches..."

"*Amore mio.* What are you saying? Where are these thoughts coming from? Do you not trust me? The gold that will fill my cargo hull will be rare spices—curries, saffron, and cinnamon—that dazzle the senses and keep Philip's palate and belly content. For this, he will pay a fortune."

When she'd given him a dubious look, he drew her nearer and said, "Truly, Sofi, that is the only gold that I'm commissioned to bring back to the Spanish court. I am no pirate! I am no spy! Is that what preoccupies your thoughts? Surely you know I'd trade a thousand of Porsena's coins to have you with me forever."

His words had appeased her a little. Still, Sofonisba was puzzled by this mission. Over the next few days, when she saw Orazio in the company of the king and Alba, she couldn't help but believe they were all plotting something more than just acquiring spices.

Sofonisba also wondered why Alba had suddenly taken such a particular interest in Orazio, inviting him into their war chamber and offering him the chance to work for the crown. She was astute at recognizing that her dashing sea captain did little to amuse the duke. Since Orazio's arrival, Alba had been gloomier by the hour and never said a kind word about him in her presence. And when she saw the two men together, it was evident by their tone and demeanor there was no love lost between them. She'd questioned Orazio about this, but once again, he'd remained mute.

Time that had seemed to stand still for a brief idyllic moment seemed to accelerate once Sofonisba learned of Orazio's departure date. As her fears continued to mount, the hours melted away until they faced their last evening together. It was a bittersweet moment when he came to her bedchamber, for despite her last-minute pleas, there was nothing she could do to change his mind and keep him by her side.

Instead, he had held her in his arms as they waited for the dawn to break, and he did his best to ease her troubled mind. "*Ehi*, Sofi! You mustn't look so glum. I won't be gone that long..." Brushing away a strand of hair, he'd added, "I will return in three weeks, my love—the time it takes for you to paint a new portrait."

She'd looked at him wanting to believe him, but still she could tell he held something back. When she said nothing, he whispered into her ear, "Sofi, don't be sad. I will always find my way back to you, *amore mio*. I love you now, and I will love you when you are a very old woman—"

"Ah!" she scoffed, interrupting him, venting her frustration. "You will love me when I am old and gray, and when my eyesight begins to fade?" She held up her thin, supple fingers and teased, "Will you still look fondly on me when I can no longer hold a brush in my wrinkled, scrawny hands?"

He only smiled at her churlishness, reached for her, and said, "I will cherish every part of you even if you are a hundred years old, my love! When I am a very old man, I will bring you lemon cakes and flowers on a fine silver tray..."

She sighed wistfully at the thought of growing old with him. "It is a lovely story you weave, Orazio. You know far too well how I love lemon cakes! But what if I die before you? I am, after all, older..."

"Not by that much," he said with a grin. "Only a year or two!"

"Five," she said, entwining her fingers in his.

"That's what makes you so fascinating. Don't you know I'm beguiled by older women? Let's see, Circe must be thousands of years older than you—"

She swatted him on the arm in mock offense. "Should I be worried? I mean about you being beguiled by another woman?"

"Not in the slightest. You are the only one for me—and it would be my fondest dream to live to be a hundred minus one day so I never have to live without you."

"But if I were to die before you," she had challenged him in a teasing tone, "what pretty words would you inscribe upon my tomb?"

She watched as Orazio rolled onto his back, crossed his arms behind his head, then said, "Hmmm. Let me think. What would I write?"

He glanced back at her and said, "I would make sure the world remembered how special you are. I'd write: *To Sofonisba, my wife... who is recorded among the illustrious women of the world, outstanding in portraying the images of man. Orazio Lomellino, in sorrow for the loss of his great love, dedicates this little tribute to such a great woman.*"

"Such pretty speeches you would make about your wife... Wife?" she'd exclaimed as his meaning sank in. Sitting up on her knees, she gazed down at him. Seeing her expression, Orazio suppressed the urge to laugh.

Then rising onto his knees to join her, he clasped her hands in his and said, "I've loved you from the beginning and will be with you to the end. In you, I have found the one who my soul desires. Sofonisba, *tesoro*, will you do me the extreme pleasure and honor of accepting me as your husband?"

Sofonisba nodded and a warm sense of belonging enveloped her. This man before her was a rare individual, and together they made sense.

When he saw a brilliant smile spread across her face, Orazio gathered her into his arms and together they lay back down upon the bed. He held her close, and they could feel their hearts beating rhythmically together.

"That night so long ago, when we first met, I wasn't expecting you."

"Nor I you," he replied.

"I didn't think we would find our way back to each other ever again."

"And yet... we did. So, believe me, Sofi when I say I will return. Although the sea beckons to me now, I will come back... for in your arms I've found a place to rest and remain forever."

Orazio had spoken such sweet words Sofonisba thought, as she looked at her recent self-portrait. She studied her image a moment longer, then with a heavy heart, she set down her brush and untied her smock. He was gone now, and a fall chill had seeped into her heart. Orazio had slipped away and out of her arms, and now the promises he had whispered into her ear as they lay entangled together seemed like unobtainable fantasies constructed of pretty phrases and lustful longings. In her lonely bed, as Sofonisba inspected the Etruscan coin, it seemed once again the only tangible proof he existed.

That was until the new moon's cycle passed, and with it came the knowledge she carried a babe inside her. With the stop of her monthly flow, she had living proof that Orazio was real and that he loved her—he was hers, and now—together—they had created a new life.

At first she had been overjoyed at the thought of carrying Orazio's child. When she placed a hand upon her waist—which was still flat as a washboard—she recalled with a smile, how it had been conceived. Her thoughts turned pensive, however, as she wondered when she could tell him in person the happy news. Now more than ever she missed him and longed to let him know he would be a father within the year.

Sofonisba told herself she could endure anything, knowing Orazio would return to marry her before anyone was the wiser. Her reputation would be significantly damaged, and she would leave the Spanish court in disgrace if he should fail to come back and make her his wife. Something Sofonisba couldn't endure—the end of her brilliant career. As she lay in bed, she could see her father's face filled with disapproval, and already she felt the first waves of shame.

But Orazio will return. Of course he will; he promised.

She had to hold onto that. But, as the days and weeks passed, when there was no word from him, and he didn't appear at court in the time he'd promised, her initial elation gave way to dread. A snarl of emotions engulfed her mind, and with each passing minute it became more difficult to untangle the questions and doubts that whirled around in her head.

Perhaps the call of the sea was too great. Orazio once told me it enchanted him like a siren's song. Did he heed Circe's whispers once again, leaving me to stand alone on the shore as he sailed away into the bosom of his only true love?

Or, maybe, she thought irrationally, *he did have a woman in every port and I have just been duped...*

With a shake of her head, she admonished herself. *Silly girl, have some faith—he has pledged himself only to you!*

Unable to remain inside the palace, restlessly she wandered the maze in the queen's garden. As she meandered into the labyrinth, her thoughts continued their circuitous course, just like the twisted shrubbery that lined the path.

What is the real reason Orazio came to the Spanish court? He claimed he came for me, but was it a coincidence and a convenient excuse to cover a far more dangerous game of espionage? Was he, in fact, a spy for the Spanish king or a pawn in Alba's strategies against the Protestant heretics?

She settled herself on the ground in the heart of the labyrinth. As she sank down, her skirts billowed around her, and she wondered what was said inside the king's chamber. *Did they promise to line Orazio's pockets with money if he returned with news from the Elizabethan court? It fit his nature... Orazio was always after an elusive pot of gold.*

Then another notion more chilling than the others occurred to her. *What if Orazio was a counter-informant? Did he, in fact, use words of love and flattery to acquire information for the English? And, like a silly fool, I played into his hand, allowing him to capture my heart and giving him access to my bed, where we shared many intimate secrets...*

Sofonisba put her hands to her temple and commanded herself, *Stop! How can I possibly question Orazio's integrity or his motives?*

She caressed her midriff and tried to draw courage from the child she carried. Sofonisba stood up, shook out her skirts, and hurried out of the maze. As she approached the terrace, she saw the queen walking with a small entourage.

When Elisabeth recognized her, she beckoned her forward with a broad smile. "Good afternoon, *cara*," she said in a breezy voice. Then, seeing her face, she commented, "My dear, you could use a little more makeup to cover those dark circles under your eyes... and a little more blush in those cheeks. You've been working far too hard in the studio lately."

When Sofonisba said nothing, Elisabeth narrowed her eyes and scrutinized her. Then, giving her an understanding nod, she turned to the others and bid them continue down the path without her. When they were alone, Elisabeth reached out a hand and stroked Sofonisba's cheek. "Ah, *tesoro*! I see you are suffering." Then, taking her hand, she exclaimed, "Your fingers are so cold—they are like ice! Are you not feeling well?"

"I... I'm fine, really. I just feel so alone since..."

"Ah... I should have guessed. You are missing your sea captain."

They walked a few steps, then Elisabeth said, "If you recall, I too know what it feels like to be confused by new love and not trust your feelings. When I arrived here, despite his sweet attentions, I feared the worst of my husband. Remember how I worried he'd taken a lover and that my marriage would be a hollow one?" She squeezed Sofonisba's hand compassionately. "But it was with your help that I was able to prove my husband was true of heart."

"It's not the same thing," Sofonisba whispered, looking down at the ground and suddenly feeling the urge to cry.

"Perhaps, but the path of true *amore* is difficult for all of us. We all have doubts and despair... but with time things become clear."

Instead of responding, Sofonisba continued staring at the gravel path. With a gentle touch, Elisabeth reached over and lifted her chin and looked directly into her eyes. "Now it is your turn to be strong and weather the storm. I know how much you miss Captain Lomellino, and you long for his return... But you must have patience and trust him too."

Sofonisba only shook her head sorrowfully. "You don't understand... He promised he'd return after three weeks... that we would marry. But now six weeks have passed and there is no news. And now that I am with—" She quickly closed her mouth, not wanting to reveal to Elisabeth her current circumstances.

Gently, Elisabeth said, "You need never worry about your future. If your captain should not return to you for some reason, my dearest friend, you will want for nothing. I will make sure you and your child are safe."

Subconsciously, Sofonisba placed a hand on the front of her gown and raised her startled eyes to meet Elisabeth's. "You know?"

"Of course!" Elisabeth said. "Remember, I have informants everywhere. Even the chambermaids prove to be useful from time to time."

"Yes, they are quite resourceful," said Sofonisba ruefully. "The one who collects my sheets told me if Orazio doesn't return, she has a remedy to make it go away... but I could never do that."

"Nor shall you!" Elisabeth responded adamantly. "And that is why I've made Philip promise me if anything should happen to Captain Lomellino, he will provide you with a dowry and a proper husband to keep the wagging tongues at court quiet. Your talents are too great to waste, and whatever the cost, you will be able to paint."

"You would arrange a marriage for me? Thank you, of course," said Sofonisba. "But I'm sure your plans for me will not be necessary. Orazio has promised he will return."

"Let us hope so, my dear. But in these times of trouble in foreign lands..."

When Sofonisba looked at her in trepidation, Elisabeth hastily said, "Oh my dear, perhaps I've said too much." Then, in a bright tone, she added, "Of course your sea captain will return. I've seen the way that man looks at you!" With an encouraging pat on the arm, she continued. "Just know... whatever the fates have in store for us all... I am here to protect you. These men may think they rule the world, but we women are the ones who show it how to go."

Chapter 24

Troubled Kings and Mad Men

Sofonisba went about her business, trying to stay occupied, keeping thoughts of Orazio at bay. But it seemed all her old haunts now held a special memory of their time together. Still, Elisabeth's words did much to appease her concerns, and she resolved to be patient, trusting things would work themselves out.

As the queen's pregnancy progressed, knowing Sofonisba carried a child in her womb too, Elisabeth invited her into her private chambers to discuss the intimate details of women in their delicate conditions. It had become their habit, while the courtiers of the palace rested during the afternoon hours, to retire to Elisabeth's chambers and eat sweet pies and sip apple wine and talk.

But one day, toward the end of October, when Sofonisba arrived at the royal couple's bedroom door and was about to knock, she became aware of a commotion on the other side. Startled to hear the voices of angry men, she let the hand she'd raised to rap on the door fall to her side. It took but a moment for her to recognize Don Carlos's voice and the other as that of his father. In a daze, she stood in the hall listening to the voices as they continued their furious tirade.

Sofonisba took a step backward and glanced furtively down the long corridor, hoping to see Elisabeth approaching. Only the queen could calm the two inside. But when Sofonisba saw the hallway was empty, and no soon-to-be-mother was waddling down the dark corridor, she turned to go but was stopped by another furious cry from inside.

"Hitting a defenseless woman and leaving her bleeding in your bed... again!" cried Philip. "Your actions are deplorable! Why can't you get a hold of yourself, boy—act like a decent, respectable man? Like..."

"Like who?" snarled Don Carlos. "Like Alba? I've heard the stories, how he treats women. He isn't the saint he pretends to be!"

"Don't drag Alba into this," Philip retorted. "I expect you to act like my son... heir to my throne."

"And what will you do that you haven't already done to me? Hmmm. Beat me? Lock me in a tower room, deprive me of bread and water? I'm not a boy of thirteen anymore."

Although Sofonisba knew it would be dangerous to be caught eavesdropping and listening to the two men so openly, she was too intrigued by the conversation and so she remained. It was her duty, she told herself, to keep Elisabeth informed of troubling activities. And from what she could tell from what she had already heard, this was genuinely disturbing.

So, instead of departing, she eased back into the shadows and stood partially disguised by an oversized Greek urn and an immense Flemish tapestry that hung on the wall. At such a vantage point, she could keep an eye on things and still make out what was being said inside. It wasn't a difficult task, as the men continued to berate one another.

"You act as if you are a spoiled child, still swaddled in linen. I hoped you could be tamed, but your wild and unruly nature continues to be driven by demons. Since the moment you took your first breath, they have controlled you."

"How you've viewed me with disgust—oh, the disdain that fills your eyes when I enter a room. I've never measured up to your high expectations."

"Don Carlos, you entered this world deformed, but I've overlooked that your spine was twisted, making you walk with a limp. From the day you were born, I embraced you as my son—heir to the throne. But now..."

"Yes, now?" sneered the prince.

"Your mind is more twisted than your miserable bones. Now you disgust me!"

Quiet descended and Sofonisba hesitantly moved a little closer to the door and strained her ears to hear better. After a moment, the silence was broken when Philip said in a terse tone, "Teasing and toying with the noble ladies of the court is one thing, but taking malicious pleasure... hurting them? This cannot go unpunished. They all look at you in perfect horror—even the artist views you with a wary eye."

When she heard herself referenced, Sofonisba's breath caught in her throat. She glanced around guiltily and slipped back against the wall into the shadows.

"That artist! What do I care about her... or any of them? They are all—"

"You had better care," Philip interrupted him. "These people are your subjects. If you can't act decently to them now, how will you carry out your responsibilities as king? It is becoming more apparent by the day you are utterly unfit to succeed to the throne of your ancestors. I see it. The ministers see it. It will be the ruin of Spain if you do!"

It is true, Sofonisba thought. She and the others believed Don Carlos was unfit to rule... and if such a thing came to pass, the country would suffer terribly at his hands.

Distracted again by Philip's voice, Sofonisba heard him say, "From the very beginning, you were a terror, even when you were first suckled. You inflicted such pain on the wet nurses with those razor-sharp teeth of yours, they had to be changed repeatedly. No right-minded woman would agree to perform the task. So I ordered them to wean you... It was that or find a goat to suckle you!"

"Such tender doting paternal sentiments..." jeered Don Carlos.

Ignoring him, Philip continued. "I've been cleaning up your messes since then... stables set afire, barn animals dismembered, running through the town shooting off guns, scaring the local villagers."

"Boys' pranks," hissed Don Carlos.

"And when you were seven?"

"Seven? Why bring up ancient history? I can't believe you still hold me accountable for that."

"Yes, when it involves hanging one of your attendants, I do!"

"He didn't hang in the end."

"No! Because I prevented it. But you raised such dread amongst your tutors demanding that the offender be punished. The only way to appease you was to hang the culprit in effigy from your window to fool you."

"And, as I recall, you boxed my ears soundly for that... until the blood ran down my face."

"Because you were a wicked, wicked boy who wouldn't listen to reason," Philip bellowed.

"But the whippings didn't stop then, did they, Father?" Don Carlos said snidely. "You took great pleasure in punishing me."

"I wouldn't have confined you to your room if you would have listened to reason. But you were always a belligerent boy... throwing tantrums, breaking dishes, torturing horses..."

"How I hate you!" cried Don Carlos. "I've wished you dead now for many years. You and your sycophants... and Alba! He is the vilest of them all. How they cater to your every whim! They should be listening to me! Me! I will be the next king after you are long gone and buried... The worms will make a fine meal on your flesh as I rule over this land."

"Enough!"

Not heeding the warning, Don Carlos griped, "All through my life, you have despised me! You ordered the servants to imprison me in my room. They weren't anything but glorified watchdogs. I've always resented you for that. You, my father, should have been my champion."

"It was for your own good, boy! You thought you were above everyone else. I wanted to cure you of your violent ways. But it is quite clear your mind continues to be clouded by insanity! Why, I can see the hysteria in your eyes right now! The foam is collecting in the vilest of ways at the corners of your mouth!"

"It is not my fault the germ of lunacy descends to me through all the branches of this family," cried Don Carlos. "It was you who was so infatuated with a slut..."

A slap rang out and Don Carlos let out a wail. Sofonisba could only imagine Philip's violent reaction to his son's words and the red stain of humiliation that flooded the prince's face. Through clenched teeth, she heard Philip say, "Never speak of your mother like that again."

"It was an ill-starred union. You caused this insanity in me, marrying Maria Manuella, your cousin, the Portuguese infanta."

"Perhaps you are right. Your mother was young and beautiful—but together we created a monster. And now God is punishing me for not controlling my passions."

Silence fell again and Sofonisba wondered what was transpiring inside the room. And then she heard Philip say in a weary tone, "I thought I could help you..."

"What? Help me how? By hiring those simpering *hidalgos* to teach me chivalry?"

"Those nobles are gentlemen, the finest Spain has to offer. They taught my father and me how to act like a king! Yet little good they did you! You reviled them, made them shrink in horror by merely suggesting you eat with a proper fork."

"They were all fools, braggarts, every one of them."

"I tried everything to help you... medicines, isolation, floggings... but nothing—nothing got through that thick skull of yours!"

"Yet here I am at twenty-three! And it seems you have given up on me at last. You have no more desire to make me king than making me a stable boy. I can see what you think of me! I've always known I'd never be good enough..."

"You will always be my son... but you will never rule Spain. I'll see to that. I'd select Alba over you any day. He I trust entirely."

"How can you say that when you've never let me prove my mettle? You've never given me any responsibility... You've never allowed me to lead men into battle."

"Why would I let you—an unstable, delusional fool—command an army? I'd cut off my own hand before I'd let you speak to a solitary soldier."

"I have every right to assume the throne; it is my destiny—not Alba's. You are the intolerable tyrant—a man who tortures his own son! You are a relic... I'm surprised you could even impregnate your wife!"

A loud crack split the air, and once again Don Carlos cried out in pain. "See... I prove my point."

Sofonisba heard a heavy, clumping foot dragged across the floor, and she knew the prince was drawing closer to the door. However, before he could turn the handle, she heard him say, "You will see, Father... I will be king. Nothing and no one will stop me. And if the queen gives you a son, I will not only hate you but also the child for the rest of its life. But perhaps she will never give birth... a careless step here, a gentle push there, it would be an easy thing to accomplish."

"You will not harm Elisabeth... or the child she bears," Philip said tightly.

It was menacingly quiet, and Sofonisba imagined the two men glaring at one another, seeing who could outlast the other... one man's face showing signs of stress and age, the other sickly and sallow. But the standoff between two wildly opposed men—one sane and one entirely mad—lasted only a moment. Brooking no more insolence, Philip said in a low growl, "Get out of my sight."

The only response he received was a wild ripple of mirth that burst from Don Carlos's mouth. It echoed around the room and into the hall. Then, as quickly as it began, the outburst subsided and he said, "I will replace you. You will be dead, and I will be the ruler of Spain." With a chortle, he added, "Long live Don Carlos—the mad king."

When the door to the chamber was wrenched open, Sofonisba pulled herself back against the wall. Don Carlos, in his fury, failed to see her there. Instead, the prince strode away in the opposite direction, but he did not go away quietly. With a flick of his hand, he began knocking over the busts of his ancestors that lined the hall on pedestals.

It was a symphony of terror, composed of raucous laughter and the shattering shards of marble—that all the king's men and all the king's horses would never be able to put together again.

Chapter 25

Rebellions and Regrets

*T*hat afternoon and well into the evening, tensions were high within the palace walls. It seemed the bad energy pulsed throughout the queen's salons, buzzed into the king's war room, and whirred down the corridors—past secret passageways and along garden paths. It was a prickly force, like the magnetic vibrations before a violent thunderstorm. It was so palpable that one could smell the air's disruption, and one could feel the hairs at the back of one's neck raised due to the static.

Alone in her studio, Sofonisba replayed the words of Don Carlos and Philip, recalling the horrific things that had been said. The prince was clearly out of control and not of sound mind. Without Orazio to steady her and make sense of the situation, she felt as if she were standing on a pitching deck, not quite sure who to believe or whom she could trust. The relationship between the prince and his father was more problematic than ever; with Alba, she was barely on speaking terms; and now she even wondered about Elisabeth—her one calm spot in the tempest. Did she know more than she was telling her about Orazio? Had her offer of assistance been an attempt to assuage a guilty conscience?

Just when it seemed nothing more could go wrong—or her worries could escalate any further—there was the sound of gunshots.

Shortly after midnight, Sofonisba awoke from a sound sleep. Hearing the sharp volley of rounds fired from a pistol, she bolted upright, climbed out of bed, and eased her way to the window where she had a view of the watchtower. Sofonisba squinted her eyes, trying to see into the darkness, but in the shifting shadows that flitted over the ramparts, she could determine nothing. Then, from across the rooftops came cries, and she could see the bobbing of torches; after that, all was quiet. Carefully, she closed the wooden shutters, wondering what had happened.

It was only the next day, mingling with the other ladies in Elisabeth's reception room, that she heard the whispers and murmurings. It seemed, after leaving the king's chambers in one of his absurd fits, Don Carlos had sat on the parapet, taking target practice. But, rather than shooting at inanimate objects, he decided to shoot at a guard instead. Luckily for the soldier, the bullet grazed his shoulder.

Elisabeth perched on her satin chair, shifted uncomfortably. With her hands, she caressed the ripe bulge that indicated the birth of her child was near. When the queen looked across the room and met Sofonisba's gaze, she shook her head distractedly. Sofonisba knew her friend could no longer gloss over the rancor that existed between the king and his son. When Sofonisba drew nearer, in hushed tones, Elisabeth whispered into her ear, "No good will come of this, and I fear for my child."

Despite the private words spoken between the queen and her lady-in-waiting, it seemed the entire court heard them, and a pall fell over the palace. But the domestic depression brought on by Don Carlos's most recent scandal was made even gloomier over the following days by the news that came to them from the Netherlands. Uprisings, discord, and riots were breaking out in the lowlands, causing turmoil and strife. It angered Philip to no end that Catholic dominance in the region was being put to the test once again. The question on everyone's lips was how to deal with the miscreant Protestants who questioned Spanish authority. The appalling reports of brutal attacks upon monks and priests had the king pacing his rooms at night and spending long hours with his ministers, the Duke of Alba being the most prominent influencer.

To rally the Spanish people and the noble *hildagas* into dipping into coffers to support the next military venture, the king enlisted the court painter's expertise to document his military council at work. The drawings would be turned into prints and circulated all over town—patriotic proof to remind his people their king, the defender of a Catholic God, was working tirelessly in their service.

To this end, Philip summoned Sofonisba to witness the final

military-strategic session. When she arrived, one of the king's ministers indicated she should sit in the back along a far wall, where she would have a better vantage point. As the men filed into the room and took their seats, Sofonisba began sketching each of their faces. *Perhaps,* she thought, *I'll turn these designs into a larger painting.*

When the Duke of Alba stood up and addressed the assembly, she looked up expectantly. She watched as he shuffled a few papers, cleared his throat, then said, "We must take immediate action. It is our God-given duty to put down the heretics and restore peace. They are toppling statues, destroying churches and monasteries. We must protect Catholic interests, squash the rebels, and keep England—which is strategically close to the insurgents—in its place. If we don't..."

He had barely begun his discourse when the sound of a fist pounding on the door echoed around the chamber. Without invitation the door flew open, and all eyes turned to see Don Carlos burst into the room.

At the sight of the prince, Philip said tersely, "Get out! Can't you see there is work to be done here?"

"I will take my seat with the others on your advisory committee. It is my right... my duty... as enfant. I only—"

"I said..." Philip said through gritted teeth, "you are not welcome here."

"Just hear me out," said Don Carlos in a pleading tone. "You believe me incapable of strategic maneuvers or thinking judiciously like a born leader. If I can't convince you any other way, let me show you. Let me be the one to take command of crushing these imposters and restoring order in the north. I swear I will make you proud. Give me the chance to prove myself."

Sofonisba, from her position at the back of the room, eyed the prince in amazement. It seemed the boy had forgotten the previous day's heated discussion as well as the threats and the hatred he had slung at his father. It amazed her to see such a mercurial reversal of moods. But, then again, it was true to Don Carlos's nature.

Tiredly, Philip said, "And why would I do that? As I told you before, you are incapable..." It seemed Philip was disgusted with himself for even attempting to reason with Don Carlos, and he shouted, "Enough! This is not something I will debate with you. Alba will travel to Brussels and restore the peace. He will make the bastards toe the line and remember which crown and sovereign they pay allegiance to."

"Alba!" The Prince turned sullen again and looked at the duke. "You choose Alba again over me?"

"Yes, Alba! It is upon my order that he carry out this operation. He is a seasoned veteran and will—"

"You've never given me a chance to prove my worth," cried Don Carlos, his face now white with rage. He turned to the other noblemen in the room and desperately beseeched, "You all must know I am the most miserable, unfortunate prince. I am treated like a slave and deprived of the smallest participation in state affairs. I have no authority or office confided to me, rendering me incapable of governing this—my future realm!"

Coldly, Philip addressed his son. "You are not worthy of the task of the office. You are—"

Ignoring his father, Don Carlos spun around and pointed a finger menacingly at Alba. In an unnaturally high-pitched whine, he shouted, "You shall not go to Flanders. It is my intent to lead the mission."

Alba slowly rose from his chair, placed his hands firmly on the table, and pierced him with his steely gaze. In measured words he said, "Hush, boy. I answer to no man but the king. Get yourself back to your room. Your nanny is waiting."

Don Carlos wrinkled his brow. "Don't talk to me as if I were a child. I am just as capable as you to command this mission."

Moving a step closer to Philip, Don Carlos swiftly removed a dagger from his boot. Then, brandishing it in the air, he grabbed Philip by the arm and pointed it at the king's throat.

Horrified, Sofonisba let out a small gasp. So absorbed by the prince's terrifying theatrics, her drawing completely forgotten, she watched as Don Carlos lifted the knife higher and drew it across the king's left cheek.

Below his eye, he nicked him, causing blood to flow down his face.

The prince glanced wildly around and saw Sofonisba observing him. "Such wide eyes you have, artist!" he said with a sneer. "You best capture this in your precious drawings." He turned back to the others and added, "By my father's life, Alba shall not go! I will kill the king and then I will kill you all!"

Before he could say another word, Alba rounded the table and lunged at the younger man. Despite his age, he had the advantage. His limbs, although stiff, moved with more speed than the prince's twisted legs ever could. With minimal effort, he grappled for the blade and tightly gripped Don Carlos's wrist. Unable to hang on to the dagger, he let it slip from his fingers. It clattered onto the wood floor, skittered, and slid out of reach, where it was secured by one of the other ministers.

Now that the prince had been disarmed, Alba stepped back, letting him go.

Mortified to have been so easily bested, Don Carlos stood before them panting, trying to calm his breathing. "So you assume my rightful place, Duke, and lead my father's men into battle?" He spat at Alba's feet, then said in a menacing tone, "Go then! Carry out this important assignment my father has tasked you with. Leave this court and all of us in it!"

With a sly look, he glanced back at Sofonisba, then swiveled around and said to Alba, "Have no fear, Duke... for I will make sure to keep a watchful eye over your precious artist while you are gone."

Not waiting for a response, Don Carlos shuffled out of the room and disappeared. A deafening silence fell over the counselors. The king was the first to break the spell. He nodded to the soldier at the door and said, "Go quickly. Keep your eye on the Enfant Terrible. I will deal with him later."

Then, turning back to the pressing matter at hand, he focused his attention on the map of the Netherlands. The others followed suit, many of them by now accustomed to the prince's outbursts.

But one man gazed at the open door and then back at Sofonisba. Don Carlos's boastful speech put more dread in his heart than the blade pointed at the king's neck. What cruel intent did the Enfant Terrible have in mind, and what foul play might befall the artist at the madman's hands when he was gone? Without Alba's protection, Sofonisba would be at the mercy of a prince who hated him as much as he did his father, and now by default he hated her too.

When Philip called his name, Alba reluctantly turned back to the others and they continued plotting.

Don Carlos, too, did not sit idly by, and he also resumed his conspiring. Later that night, slipping past the guards, he sat in the shadows of the highest tower. With rage burning in his heart, he followed Alba's progress as the duke crossed the central courtyard on the way to his chambers.

Raising a firing arm, the prince took careful aim then slowly pulled back the trigger and took the shot. This time, instead of a sharp explosion, the gun admitted only a small click. Don Carlos let out a chortle of glee and rested his head against the tower's cold wall.

The day was coming, and soon he would be rid of them all.

Chapter 26

The Tournament

Sofonisba's faithfully illustrated prints of the men who sat on the king's council served their purpose of fanning the Spaniards' loyalty. Depicted with crosses displayed upon their breasts accompanied by determined expressions, the men seemed united delegates of God, sworn to their sovereign, and ready to fight for Catholic domination.

With the consolidation of the local nobility assured, Philip next decided to bolster and impassion his subjects by hosting a tournament in which men could test their prowess with a lance. While mounted on a fine steed, and dressed in a full suit of armor, riders would take turns running the courses and sparring.

Since the troops set to depart within the week, it was decided that the joust would take place on the Feast Day of Saint Teresa of Ávila. Invitations were quickly dispatched to all the noble houses to send their most able sons. To demonstrate that the king showed no favoritism, he instructed Alba to open the lists posted in via della Corsia, encouraging the participation of commoners.

The subsequent days were employed in a flurry of activities in preparation for the sparring. Magnificent stands were constructed from which hung banners of all the most influential families' colors. A joust was enough to stir competitive fervor in participants and spectators alike. Still, the excitement was pitched even higher when a day before the tournament, Philip declared he, too, would participate, boasting to those around him he would be happy to break a lance with any cavalier who wanted to spar with him.

When the feast day of Teresa arrived, the court and township assembled to witness the men's athleticism on horseback. Dressed in their finest—the women in silk gowns and men in embroidered coats—they waved their standards ardently, cheering for the favored knights and stomping their feet when their adversaries rode onto the field.

From the royal box, Elisabeth's entourage sat high above the crowd, under a canopy of blue cypress silk emblazoned with her august consort's armorial devices. In attendance were the lords and ladies. Sofonisba sat to her right, and there was an empty seat allotted to Alba to her immediate left. Behind the queen sat the king's guards.

All around the stands, the colorful banners bearing the insignia of the crown billowed in the breeze. When a fanfare of horns blared triumphant notes, it stirred the crowd to stand up and clap. At the sound, even the horses in their corrals lifted up on hind legs, as if dancing in anticipation of what was soon to come.

As they waited for the first riders to take their run, Sofonisba watched Elisabeth fluttering her fan. It was apparent she was nervous by how she craned her neck, following the activity below her. Despite her ripe figure, she'd confided in Sofonisba she didn't want to miss the event. She had also told Sofonisba she feared for Philip. Given his age, she believed he was not as hearty as the others; nonetheless, there had been nothing she could say or do to dissuade him. She knew he rode to please her and demonstrate what a handsome figure he cut atop his favorite steed... as well as display his prowess with a lance before all the Spanish grandees.

When Alba finally arrived and took his seat next to the queen, Sofonisba glanced at the duke in consternation. Several more weeks had passed, and still there was no word from Orazio. She longed to question Alba about the nature of his mission. Sofonisba looked at the duke's firmly clenched jaw and couldn't rid herself of the suspicion that he and Philip were complicit in Orazio's disappearance. It was so frustrating to be left in the dark by the very people she thought she could trust.

At the final blasting of the trumpets, Sofonisba focused her attention on the field and saw Philip enter the track dressed in full battle regalia. A roar emanated from the crowd as he galloped down the raised dirt track. Then, stopping in front of the royal box, the king took off his helmet and bowed his head to his queen. When he waved to his subjects, they bellowed out a wild roar in response, chanting, "Elisabeth! Philip! Protectors of the realm!" By the palpable excitement and the jubilant faces all around, it seemed—to Sofonisba—the royals had achieved what they had set out to accomplish.

Still, some didn't join in the unbridled fervor. Since Philip had voiced his desire to ride, not only had Elisabeth been against it but also two of his closest advisors—Alba and Diego Montrado, his personal physician. The three had done their best to convince him to forego the dangerous pastime, but Philip—who excelled in sports and believed himself an excellent horseman—merely laughed at their worries.

Even now, from her lofty position, Sofonisba could see Montrado talking to the king, giving him dark looks and shaking his head. Philip merely scoffed and waved the doctor away. Then, holding the reins firmly in his hands, he directed his horse to the staging point and motioned to the field marshal to arm him for the encounter. Federico Zapatero did as he was obeyed and stepped up to hand the king his lance.

Philip rode forward into the arena, took his mark, and saluted the man mounted on a magnificent steed on the opposite side. A hush fell over the crowd, but when the field marshal let down his scepter, it burst into cries as the first round began and the two mounted men rushed toward one another. With mighty force, the two lances collided, and with a loud crack, they shivered and fell to pieces on the ground. Although neither of the men was unseated, the match was considered a tie and scratched.

The crowd roared its approval, and as page boys ran onto the track to collect the splintered pieces of wood, the king rode back to the start and prepared himself for his next opponent, the Duke of de Guise.

Once again, at the field marshal's signal, the two men launched into a fierce gallop. But de Guise, who was more a dandy than a soldier, was no match for Philip. As their lances met, Philip had the advantage and knocked the man so forcefully that he could not maintain his position in the saddle. The weight of his heavy armor dragged him down, and he tumbled backward onto the ground.

As de Guise fell, the assemblage let out a groan, but when Philip rode past the stands, victorious, they broke into ecstatic cheers once again.

The dueling continued for another two hours, with the king taking turns with the others. But, by the late afternoon, both Sofonisba and Elisabeth could tell the king was growing tired. Ready for him to dismount, Elisabeth instructed a page boy to give her husband a note, imploring him to refrain from further activity.

After one more run, Philip conceded to his queen, and seeing the lists were empty, he raised his hand to motion to Zapatero that he too was done for the day. Before he could remove his helmet or the field marshal could take possession of Philip's lance, a final participant rode onto the track.

The new opponent's face was covered with a steel mask with a large plume, and he wore a dark cloak which covered his entire body. He was seated on a splendid white horse that bore no insignia, and without a distinguishing coat of arms, it was impossible to know which noble house he represented, or if he were a commoner. As a murmur rippled through the crowd, anticipation for the last joust was heightened.

Philip, too, curious to know who his mysterious opponent might be, chuckled delightedly to face a new adversary. Instead of retiring or giving up his lance, Philip turned his horse, ready to ride again.

As the jouster in black took his position, his horse fretfully side-stepped in place. Impatiently the man snapped his reins, commanding the horse to obey, then called out in a muffled voice, "Beware, sire! Hold firmly to your mount as I am determined to unhorse you."

Unfazed, Philip grinned, settled his visor into place, and grasped his lance more firmly.

Sofonisba could see Zapatero and the royal doctor step up to Philip's side again, imploring the king to step down. Still, Philip wouldn't listen. It seemed no one, not Alba, nor Elisabeth, nor his ministers could do anything to stop him. He looked up at the stands and called out to his wife, "My lovely queen, it is for your love, and in your honor, I am going to run this final course."

The spectators clapped appreciatively, and without another word Philip patted the side of his horse, then turned it around. With the lance firmly in his hand, Philip faced the other man.

When the field marshal lowered his scepter one last time, the jousters raced at great speed to encounter the other. It took but a few seconds for them to clash, and as had happened earlier in the day, upon the first blow their wooden lances shivered and split apart.

The joust was over—the last encounter ending in a tie. To the spectators, it seemed a dull conclusion to an otherwise exciting tournament. Neither man had been unseated, but to their dismay—because of the last blow—Philip leaned unsteadily in his saddle.

As was tradition, the king flung aside his broken lance, raised his visor, and waited for his opponent to do the same. However, the other cavalier kept his face covered and didn't throw his broken lance to the ground. And, just as Philip attempted to pull himself back up, his opponent took aim and pointed the needle-sharp splinter at the king. In a show of great speed, he rushed down the track, and as he passed by, he thrust the long fragment through Philip's open helmet.

With an anguished cry, the king fell backward, but with his feet caught in the stirrups he was dragged down the track several yards before the frightened animal came to a stop. The field marshal rushed to the scene and grabbed the horse's reins as others gathered about trying to disentangle the king. When freed of the leather straps, the attendants laid Philip on the ground and removed his helmet. As they did, a thick pool of blood gushed from the wound, and the king lolled his head back and fainted.

The crowd roared in dismay, and a scene of terror and confusion ensued. The queen, her face pale, tilted her head to see better and watched as her husband's lifeless body was carried from the field. With her composure draining, she cried out to the king's guardsmen, "Arrest the man who did this! Find out his identity. He shall be hanged."

Although her voice barely carried over the din, the soldiers nearest her followed her orders. Overcome with worry, Elisabeth sank back down in her chair and gripped Sofonisba's hand until her knuckles turned white. "My poor Philip! I must go to him at once."

"The king has the best physicians," reassured Sofonisba. "They will..."

Before she could finish, Elisabeth slumped in her chair and lost consciousness.

Frantically, Sofonisba looked around for Alba to enlist his services to assist the queen back to the palace. All around them was pandemonium, and the duke was nowhere to be seen. Sofonisba put a hand to her forehead to avoid the glare of the late afternoon sun.

Slowly, she let her gaze drift over the crowd and finally to the jousting field. It was then that she saw him—the man who had assaulted the king. Sitting on his horse at the far end of the track, he turned to the crowd and, with a great show of bravado, took off his helmet.

Before them sat Don Carlos.

With a confident gesture, he cheerily saluted them. Then, digging in his heels, he turned the horse toward the distant horizon and galloped away.

The man who had hoped to be king had committed treason. In one desperate act, he condemned himself to hell... and to swing from a beam in the prison gallows.

Chapter 27

A Death, A Farewell, A Wedding,

*A*fter a massive search led by Alba, the duke returned later that night with the magnificent steed that had been Don Carlos's horse and what remained of the Enfant Terrible. Alba reported directly to the other ministers, giving them an account of the search he had led to find the man responsible for attacking the king.

It didn't take long for the news to spread throughout the palace and become common knowledge from the lowliest servant to the loftiest of nobles. Soon everyone knew that Alba, along with a party of ten men, had tracked the prince well into the night. But it was the duke who finally found the madman riding along a steep ravine. Before the prince could be apprehended, however, Don Carlos's horse reared up; unable to maintain his balance, he had been thrown and subsequently hit his head on an outcropping of rocks. While Alba did his best to revive him, the prince died in his arms.

Upon examination by Diego Montrado of the bloody and mutilated skull, it was determined Don Carlos had indeed sustained such terrible wounds and there was nothing to be done to revive him.

That was the story Alba told them all and what Montrado confirmed—but who could really know for sure if it had been a fall upon the rocky ground or a well-placed blow to the head that killed him in the end? It appeared no one really wanted to know the truth, the doctor least of all, so they let the matter die along with the prince.

There should have been more tears, but in reality it was welcome news to learn the reckless child who'd tried to kill the king was no longer a threat. Still, with respect to the house of the Holy Roman Empire, Alba instructed the guards to place Don Carlos's body in the palace chapel.

Resting in State, the troubled, problematic man whose brain had never been quite right spent his final hours above ground, perhaps finding the first solace he had ever known in his short life.

The prince was soon joined in death by the stallion he escaped upon. After Alba wrangled it and brought it back to the royal stables, it later expired—despite the groomsmen's best efforts—from extreme exhaustion.

The Enfant Terrible may have killed the horse, but he hadn't managed to accomplish his main objective; the king, after a week, still lived—but barely.

After being carried to his chambers, Philip lay pallid and insensible, his fate hanging in the balance. By the directions of Montrado, the doors of the king's private apartments were closed and no one was admitted, not even Elisabeth. Realizing the injuries were beyond his ken, the doctor called in six of Madrid's most skillful surgeons to assist him. While collaborating for hours, they tried to extract the needle-like splinters that remained lodged around his left eye and forehead, which they believed had pierced his brain.

The doctors worked to the best of their abilities but they still lacked the proper expertise and halted their procedures. To help them understand better how to treat Philip, Alba gave the order to decapitate several derelicts on death row in the king's dungeon. It was hoped that after an anatomical inspection of the prisoner's skulls, the surgeons would be able to administer the surgical relief needed to save Philip.

It appeared the murdering of prisoners indeed saved the king. On the sixth day, armed with new surgical knowledge, the doctors successfully extracted the fragments with no cortical cerebrum damage. Still, there was nothing to be done for his eye, and Philip lost sight on his left side and would be obliged to wear a patch from then on.

After the operation, the king lashed around in his bed for days, suffering from pain, elevated temperatures, and delirium. But, when the fever finally subsided, he gradually recovered his senses, and when he regained the ability to talk, the first name he uttered was Elisabeth's.

But she was not able to answer his call. Distraught by the injuries sustained by her husband, and overwhelmed by sorrow of Don Carlos's actions and death, Elisabeth was overcome by a strange tingling numbness that crept up her arm and then gripped her heart. Alarmed, she called for Sofonisba, who assisted her to her chambers, where she rested fitfully.

The news of Philip's return to the land of the living brought color back to the queen's cheeks. But later that same evening, while being fed the clear broth of a chicken, a severe pain gripped her abdomen and she began retching and vomiting.

As the hours passed, the nausea and spasms continued, and blood from her womb seeped onto the sheets. It seemed the angel of death now hovered over Elisabeth. The midwives did their best to keep the child inside, but the little one couldn't be stopped and defied them all by slipping into the world on her own schedule.

Sofonisba, who hadn't left Elisabeth's side, witnessed the birth of the little infanta. At first, there was silence in the room, but after a moment— to the relief of all—the little girl, small and sallow, let out a tiny mew and began to breathe. The queen peeked at the babe in wonder and whispered, "Such a terrible world you have entered, my princess."

Hearing the infant's kittenish cries, Mademoiselle de Cassincourt, the royal wet nurse, whisked the baby away. Soon after that, Elisabeth began to lose contact with those around her, and the elation of bringing forth new life subsided. Instead, she lay languidly on her bed and a great despondency overcame her. Weeping into her pillow, she murmured over and over, "Please forgive me... Philip... I've failed you... I know you wished for a son... I'm so sorry."

Elisabeth continued to moan forlornly, calling out to Sofonisba. "Where is she? I must speak to Sofonisba..."

As Elisabeth's tortured ramblings continued, Sofonisba took her limp hand and gently caressed it. And when the queen moaned, Sofonisba reached over with a cool cloth to wipe the perspiration from her brow. Not sure if Elisabeth could hear her, Sofonisba continued speaking soothing words of comfort, hoping to see the light rekindled in her friend's eye.

Shortly around three o'clock, it seemed her words reached the befuddled mind of the invalid. Slowly rising through the mists of pain that engulfed her, Elisabeth turned her head toward Sofonisba and murmured, "I am not long for this world. I can feel it."

"Hush," responded Sofonisba, soothing her brow again.

Through parched and blistered lips, not heeding her words, Elisabeth whispered, "I am so sorry, Sofonisba. Please forgive me. He is gone... He won't be coming back..."

Sofonisba squeezed her hand. "What are you saying?"

"You must know the affection I have for you has always been great and sincere. Please forgive me... Remember, you will be taken care of. I want to make things right... never forget that... but your sea captain..."

"Orazio... what has happened to Orazio? What are you saying? What do you know?"

Elisabeth was gripped by a spasm of coughing; the exertion of speaking had proven too much. Carefully, Sofonisba lifted her head and offered her a little water from a silver cup.

"Orazio, he loved you so..."

Elisabeth's words hung in the dim candlelit room that smelled of approaching death. Sofonisba leaned closer to hear her words but it was no use. Once again the queen drifted into a profound slumber. The artist looked at her friend who lay motionless on the bed. Her breathing was labored, and her nightgown clung moistly to her puffy and misshapen body.

It didn't seem fair. This woman, much younger than she, now faced her last minuet with death that lurked in the shadows. Sofonisba scanned Elisabeth's ethereal face, willing her to awaken and tell her the secret that troubled her so.

But the merry, coquettish twinkle in Elisabeth's eyes never returned. Instead, they remained blank and unseeing. And as the sun broke through the window, Elisabeth, in the waning of her twenty-third year, escaped earthly bonds and rose to join her lost children in heaven.

When the bells at the court started to toll, ushering in the fateful news, it was a dismal sound. Rising to greet a bleak new dawn, the people wept to realize the French princess whom they had grown to love and who had brought peace was gone. The graceful and lovely Elisabeth of Valois was no more.

Despite Philip's immense grief, he couldn't stop and mourn. The affairs of the country needed immediate tending. When he received word of more heinous acts in the Netherlands, from his bed he instructed Alba to leave at once with the Spanish forces. "I will not allow these acts of lawlessness to continue. Do whatever is necessary to crush those bastards. Let them know the Spanish sovereign is their master and they are to abide by the Catholic faith."

On the eve of his departure, Alba approached Sofonisba. Noting the sorrow in her eyes, he said, "Although I will be gone for several weeks, you will be safe here now that Don Carlos is dead. The prince will never threaten you again, and although Elisabeth is no longer with us, Philip will provide for you."

"The queen spoke to me before she died of matters that pertained to Orazio Lomellino," Sofonisba said slowly. "Before you leave, you must tell me what you know of this affair. I know you have something to do with his disappearance..."

Alba gave her a wary look. "There is nothing to tell."

Unconvinced, Sofonisba pushed him further. "On her deathbed, Elisabeth was beside herself with remorse... Surely you are aware of what the king asked him to do?"

The duke shrugged. "Lomellino is a sea merchant... The king sent him to the African coast to bring back rare spices... that is all. Trust me."

Alba's story corroborated what Orazio had told her, but still she had some doubts. "But why then was Elisabeth so upset? At the very end, she was so insistent... Something doesn't seem right."

"I didn't want to alarm you..."

"Yes... What is it?"

"We have had no word of Lomellino in weeks... The current belief is he met his demise at the hands of the corsairs that frequent that region."

She gripped her stomach in shock. "But surely—"

Alba shook his head. "This is the news we wanted to spare you..."

Sofonisba gazed at him dully. The duke was still speaking, but she barely heard him. It seemed the world had just spun out of control, and Sofonisba's head was filled with a loud ringing. She focused her attention and only managed to catch him say, "I must depart, but I will return. And when I do... we will be united."

So saddened by grief, Sofonisba let his words flow over her. And later that morning, still in a state of shock, she watched as the duke and his garrison of men rode out of the palace gates. It seemed she had left her body and watched herself from afar as the other nobles cheered and waved colorful banners, encouraging the soldiers on to victory.

Distractedly, Sofonisba elbowed her way through the assembly, needing to be alone, her thoughts focused on Orazio. Sorrowfully, a tear slid down her face as she thought of the man she loved and the child they had created together. Her mind reeled at the possibility that he was now dead.

And then, in a rush, the words Alba had spoken earlier came back to her: *The prince will never threaten you again... When I return, we will be united.*

Was the duke intimating he had personally eliminated the threat of Don Carlos to protect her... and now that Orazio was gone he wished to marry her?

In astonishment, she shook her head. *I owe Alba so much, but I certainly don't love him... and, indeed, that doesn't mean he should kill a man who threatened me... a man who was the king's son.*

Now, with Elisabeth gone and Orazio lost and presumed dead, she was at a loss for what to do. She felt totally alone in the world. In her condition, she also realized her days as court painter were coming to an end. If she couldn't continue painting, how would she earn a living and provide for her child? Perhaps it was finally time to return to her family. But it made her feel ashamed to leave the court in disgrace.

She was sure of only one thing: *I have to be gone from the Spanish court by the time Alba returns.*

Just when she reached her wit's end and had started a letter to her father, Sofonisba received a summons from King Philip, saying there were matters to discuss. Not sure what he would say to her now, fully expecting a dismissal, the artist approached his chambers with a heavy heart. When Sofonisba knocked on his door and a servant invited her into the king's private sanctum, the first thing that struck her was his ravaged appearance and the black patch he now wore to cover his damaged eye. The death of his mad son and his precious wife, and his recent illness, had taken their toll. Still, he rose to greet her and managed a wan smile. Forgoing protocol, he drew her into his arms.

After a moment, he whispered, "Elisabeth loved you so... Come, sit with me. I have something to tell you." Philip eased himself into his chair and indicated she make herself comfortable opposite him. "I won't deny that you make me think of my dear Elisabeth when I see your face. The two of you were so close, and you made her so happy with your painting instructions."

"Elisabeth was quite accomplished," admitted Sofonisba kindly. "She had a talent for portraiture."

"Well, she had a little ability, I suppose. The fact is, she was kept quite entertained by you. Painting, dancing, pretty gowns, and sonnets... making pictures... Those were the things that made my queen happy." He was quiet, then added, "I'm glad you were with her to the last. But now that Elisabeth is no longer with us, I believe it is time for us to make other arrangements for you."

Sofonisba folded her hands in her lap and nodded.

"As you know, Elisabeth entrusted me to take care of you. She made me promise if anything happened to her you would be provided for. The queen wanted you to live an independent life so that you could continue your profession. For Elisabeth, my beloved wife, and to show you this court's royal appreciation, I have arranged for you to receive a pension of one hundred ducats a month to give you the freedom to continue painting and tutoring students. There will also be plenty to support your family in Cremona."

Although Elisabeth had intimated earlier to Sofonisba that this would be the case, she hadn't really believed it. This news came as a welcome surprise, but nothing prepared her for what the king said next.

"In addition to your salary, I'm prepared to provide you a dowry of twelve thousand *scudi*—"

"But Your Majesty," exclaimed Sofonisba, "a dowry is only intended for a woman who is to be married."

"Yes," said Philip. "I have arranged that for you too."

"I am to marry?" she said, shocked.

Sofonisba held her breath, fearing he would next say Alba's name. Instead, he said, "You will marry Fabrizio Moncada Pignatelli, son of the prince of Paternò the Viceroy of Sicily. You will make a home and a life for yourself there with your new husband."

All Sofonisba could do was shake her head in disbelief. "Fabrizio Pignatelli? But I've never met him..."

"Pignatelli is a loyal friend to the crown. He is here now, having traveled from the south of Italy to pay his respects to the queen."

"But who is he?" she inquired, hiding the turmoil that roiled inside her. "Why would he want to marry me?"

"Fabrizio met you several years ago here at court. He was quite taken with you and your paintings. Sadly, he lost his wife a few months ago and seeks a young bride with a substantial dowry... and someone to keep his daughter Cinzia company."

Ah, thought Sofonisba, *it is the king's ransom he really is after and a mother to his child.*

"He assures me he will be quite supportive of your career and wishes you to continue. You will live in his palazzo by the sea."

Gently he added, "He is a good man. You will have a happy life."

As his words sank in, suddenly a handsome man with curling hair appeared before her. How could she relinquish the dreams they had made together and settle for another? But her situation was dire... Orazio was gone... Alba had said he was dead...

Sofonisba considered Philip solemnly, thinking about what he was offering. All she had ever wanted was to be an independent artist, and now Philip's plan seemed most advantageous—she would continue to paint and would have her own money and income. This Fabrizio, whoever he was, sounded like a good and decent person—someone who already valued and respected her talents. There was also her child to think of. Now it would have a father and be raised with dignity. That reassurance made Philip's proposal palatable, and slowly she nodded, accepting his terms.

A few days later, as Sofonisba stood at an altar in the palace chapel, she looked at her future husband. He was not such a terrible fellow, despite being a little plump and having a sparse head of hair. His gray beard, she also noted, disguised a weak chin—but she reminded herself he had a pleasant laugh and a delightful sense of humor.

Perhaps it was not such a bad thing to stand in calm serenity beside a man whose physical appearance did little to inspire feelings of love. It was better, she told herself, to stand on solid ground than to be swept out to sea on a tide of passionate feelings that would only pull her down into their dark depths to drown her completely.

Oh, Orazio, my love, Sofonisba thought one last time before she relinquished the Anguissola name and took that of her husband—Pignatelli.

As the wedding was performed in a small chapel in the palace in Madrid, presided over by King Philip, Sofonisba had no way of knowing in a military tent, near a distant village just outside of Brussels, the Duke of Alba ripped open a parchment bearing the king's seal.

Having successfully laid waste to the rebellion, he hoped he was being summoned home. The stability in the region had been guaranteed after forcefully killing the heretics.

After calm was restored to the area, he placed Margaret of Parma, the king's sister, to preside over civil jurisdiction. But when the local nobility reacted violently to these measures, they openly rebelled again. In light of this, the duke was ordered by Philip to take an even stronger stance. He instructed Alba to establish a Council of Troubles to prosecute those responsible for the riots.

To put dread into the hearts of the northerners who dared defy the Spanish king's authority again, Alba slaughtered the rebels—some even in their beds. Soon the streets were lined with heads on spikes and bodies dangled from bridges. It didn't take long for Alba to be called the ruthless butcher who presided over a Court of Blood.

Now weary and ashamed of the acts of vengeance he committed once again for the crown, the duke scanned the king's letter. He swore under his breath when he read he was to remain and ensure Philip's sister Margaret was safe in her new position. Alba sighed in disgust, realizing it would be several more weeks before returning home to Madrid.

The duke was just about to fold up the letter but stopped when he saw the postscript. In disbelief, he read of Sofonisba's recent marriage to Fabrizio Moncada Pignatelli who lived in Sicily. Immediately his temper flared, and Alba slammed his fist upon the table. As he did, a glass of red wine spilled its contents over a military map of the lowlands.

In menacing words, he vowed to kill the Sicilian who had just come between them.

As the candles flickered in the Spanish chapel and Sofonisba's new husband slipped the wedding band onto her finger, the artist also had no way of knowing that a handsome sea captain had docked his ship in Barcelona and was now galloping across the Spanish plains to claim her as his bride.

Catania, Sicily—1568

I love you without knowing how, or when,
or from where. I love you simply, without
problems or pride: I love you in this way
because I do not know any other
way of loving but this...

—P. Neruda

Chapter 28

In the Shadow of Etna

Sofonisba stood on a prominent piece of land that rose high above the sea and felt the soft wind caress her cheek. There the air smelled of sweet ripe figs, fresh grass, and the tangy scent of oranges. She raised her face to the bright sun and basked in its warmth. She liked to take her morning walks along the cliff before the heat became too intolerable. Gazing at the harbor, she saw the ships resting below her, their white masts contrasting starkly with the deep azure sky.

Knowing her propensity for walking in the morning, Fabrizio had instructed his servants to pave a path to the farthest point of the bluff with crushed seashells and finely ground lava stone. There he had them place a marble bench for her to admire the sea in its various phases.

It was a preferred spot, where she liked to pass serene hours watching the vessels move in and out of port. She wondered where they were headed. Were they off to find new trade routes, travel to India or China? Would they sail into port with their hulls filled with spices and exotic wines? Or were they pirate ships destined to sail the Barbary Coast, off to capture innocent women's hearts and abscond with chests of gold from kings?

Sofonisba smiled wistfully. Once she had dreamt of sailing away, discovering foreign lands, and realizing her destiny of being an independent woman painting on her own terms. She longed to dazzle the world with her portraits and be the toast of kings and queens. Hadn't it also been a more recent fantasy to marry a man who admired and respected her and encouraged her career?

It had all come true. So why wasn't she happy?

She sighed and looked back at the sea. Yes, everything she had ever asked for had been neatly presented to her on a silver platter. Yet...

Lightly, she touched her midriff and then twisted the gold ring around her finger. Turning away from the white-capped waves, she gazed at the volcano that rose up before her. This was the land of Homer's Cyclops, and here could be found the caves of the sea nymph Calypso. And on such a clear day, the dark bulk of Etna was clearly delineated. She detected a wisp of white smoke from the top, as if the monster Typhon, whom Zeus trapped inside, let out an occasional puff on his pipe.

Philip had been right—Fabrizio was a good man. She could have a happy life if she let herself. Given her new status as a respectable married woman, she could go and come as she pleased. Here in her new island home—the Pignatelli villa outside the town of Catania—her days were her own. She could paint, be mistress of her own schedule, and no longer needed to stand for hours adhering to court protocol in shoes that pinched her feet. Instead, not obligated to wear layers of petticoats and heavy brocades, she could dress as she pleased, pulling on instead loose gowns to accommodate her changing figure.

Of course she had brought trunkloads of expensive attire with her— Philip, kind man that he was, hadn't let her leave without completing her wedding trousseau. But it was a relief to discover Sicilians moved at a far more relaxed pace. She only needed to put on a farthingale on the rare occasion she called upon other Sicilian nobility or attended an occasional evening affair.

And although now she could pull her hair from its tight pins and let the strands flow gently in the early morning breeze, still there were things she missed. She pined for her family—her sisters, all married now—and Amilcare, who was getting on in years. The one person she didn't miss as much as the others was Asdrubale, who had recently taken over managing the Anguissola's fortunes and her stipend from Philip in Spain. At first it seemed a logical step, as Sofonisba wanted to provide for her father. But it hadn't taken long before her younger brother put on airs and began doling out funds in a miserly manner, keeping a large portion for himself.

Sofonisba shook her head and marveled, *To think I am the one who changed the little brat's swaddling clothes, yet now I am the one who takes orders from that irritating little pest!* At times she longed for the days when she could scare him by merely wiggling her fingers and growling.

In addition to her family, she mourned Elisabeth—she missed her friend's vivacious nature, dancing steps, witty commentaries, *and* the intrigues at court. Sofonisba had lived amongst the royals for so long, and now in the shadow of Etna, life was a bit *too* tranquil. Sicily seemed a long, long way from everyone—and everything.

But this was better. Much better, she reminded herself again. Here her life was falling into place. Yet... Suddenly Orazio's face flashed before her. She shook her head to clear his image. Even though Alba intimated her sea captain had perished on the high seas, part of her refused to believe it. He was far too clever, and with Khidr Aruj at his side, surely they would have survived.

What mad adventure was he on, then? she wondered. *Surely I'd know deep inside if Orazio was actually dead. Perhaps, even now, he was chartering a course back...*

Abruptly she reprimanded herself. It made no sense to continue in this vein of romantic yearnings. Even if Orazio were alive, there was little possibility he would ever find her again here in this remote place. Where the fates had placed her, not even the savviest sea captain—or pirate—could find her. Given the leap she had made from Madrid to Catania—she might as well have flown to the moon or Venus and made a home amongst the stars.

Furthermore, she was married, and—even if by magic he should appear, how could she face him? She hadn't waited for him; instead, out of self-preservation, she had married another. How would she ever explain that to him?

No, they could never be together, and although she carried Orazio's child, she had convinced Fabrizio the babe was his. Although she was now five months along, it had never occurred to her new husband to question this happy news when she'd first told him shortly after their arrival in Sicily. It had pained her to no end when she'd seen Fabrizio's elated face and she'd regretted lying to him, for he was a kind man. Still, despite her remorse, she believed it necessary to protect her, Orazio's child, and the Anguissola fortunes.

Letting the sea breeze whip away her longings and desires, Sofonisba faced into the wind and once again accepted her new reality. Catania was her home now. It was a sleepy little town built on the slopes of a volcano, and once upon a time it had been a strategic point in the Mediterranean. Set in the middle of favorable trade routes—where east meets west—everyone at one time wanted a piece of this land. But over the years, although many people came and went, eventually they abandoned it; once a charming girl, full of life and sensual appeal, she was now an aging dowager, quickly fading from everyone's memory.

It seemed the only indication the island might still be alive was the occasional trembling from the volcano that rumbled from hidden depths. At first, Sofonisba had been wary of the earth moving precariously under her feet. But, since her arrival, she'd become more accustomed to the occasional tremors. Fabrizio had readily dismissed her jitters that the volcano would erupt and spew down upon them fiery flames as had happened recently in Naples with Vesuvius's explosion.

"But, when I lived in Rome several years ago, it was all the talk... how the volcano blew out ash and smoke that covered the nearby city for days." Fabrizio had chuckled and patted her hand reassuringly. "Have no fear, mia cara, our sleeping giant is just that—a cranky old brooder. Unlike his more active Vesuvian cousin, he's too tired to really let loose his rage."

Sofonisba hadn't been entirely convinced but appreciated Fabrizio's attempts to reassure her. He was proving to be reliable, and despite being thirty-two years older than she, he was a sweet man, if not a little dull. Still, she would take tedium over cruelty. Right from the start, her new "groom" approached their marriage bed with respect and performed his husbandly duties briefly and perfunctorily. Afterward, he chastely kissed her on the forehead before retiring to his own room, preferring to sleep alone in the adjoining chamber.

In Spain, he had been more ardent, but since returning to Sicily, he was less capable of rising to the occasion and frequently apologized for his lackluster performance. "You are delightful, my dear, but I am an old man, my back aches, and this body just doesn't respond like it once did in my youth. We will attempt this again soon."

The next time, however, proved to be just as dismal, and over the weeks—to save face—he stopped knocking on their connecting doors. Sofonisba didn't mind when they drifted into a casual state of coexistence. It wasn't Fabrizio's fault entirely. Although he didn't inspire a heady state of romance or incite the sexual desire she once experienced, she did very little on her part to encourage his nighttime passions.

Sofonisba took a deep breath of fresh morning air. Moving on down the path, her footsteps crunched along the trail, kicking up loose bits of pumice. When the call of a sea bird caught her attention, she placed a hand to her eyes to shield them from the bright light and followed its path. This might not be where she envisioned ending her days and whom she would be spending them with; still, she marveled at the island's unparalleled beauty.

This land had once been home to her Carthaginian ancestors. After defeating the Phoenicians, one of the first inhabitants of the island, they expanded the early primitive settlements, creating magnificent mythical cities. Over time, Carthage—overextending itself as mighty nations often do—had crumbled and fallen, as had the Etruscan and Roman civilizations, until finally over two hundred years ago the Kingdom of the Two Sicilies became the dominant force that ruled the southern territories. Naples went to the English kings and Sicily went to the Spaniards.

But neither King Philip nor his father—Charles the Holy Roman Emperor—took an active interest in this island. With no substantial support from the Spanish crown, Sicily was quickly becoming a place for declining nobility to live out their days, managing a suffocating and antiquated feudal system. It didn't help matters that the Spaniards hadn't cultivated innovation. Instead, they introduced to Sicily the Inquisition that continued to muzzle any thought of modernity. And now the local peasants were beginning to rebel.

Despite the grumblings of late by the servants and peasants who worked the land and wished to be treated better, Fabrizio thought of himself as a benevolent manner lord—in control and still commanding their undying respect. Like the other princes and viceroys that populated the island, he was utterly oblivious to the plight of the poor. He left most details to his estate manager and was unaware of his overseer's grifting or the man's cruel mistreatment of the plantation's worker. Instead, Fabrizio ignorantly flaunted his dwindling wealth in front of his servants, thinking he was doing his part to help them by attending church, paying alms, and giving to local charities.

Aside from his daughter, Cinzia—whom he was quite fond of—Fabrizio's great passions were gambling, a habit that over the years had grown progressively worse, and watching over the plantation's orange and lemon groves. He tended the Pignatelli crops with great care, enjoying his status as a gentleman farmer; he was at his happiest puttering about the villa, overseeing repairs, and mingling with the tenants and more impoverished peasants, discussing the weather and grafting fruit trees.

The first time Sofonisba had tasted his oranges, she rolled her eyes in ecstasy. Proudly, Fabrizio watched her, telling her the secret of such sweetness was due to the care and love he provided his plants. He also told her that it had been the Arabs who brought the plants to the islands. At first the fruit was bitter and hard, but once planted in the fertile volcanic soil and blessed by the Sicilian sun and the gods above, the oranges became more succulent and turned the color of blood red. The lemons were equally tasty and grew in abundance all over the island; so yellow in tone, the slopes and valleys around Catania were named *la Conca d'Oro*—hills of golden seashells.

Every morning, Fabrizio loved to traverse those slopes, checking in on his prized plantings. Often, he returned to the villa soaked in sweat, his face red from exertion.

"Oh, Papa!" exclaimed Cinzia a few days after their arrival home, "you should take better care of yourself. This heat will be the death of you." With a swift accusatory glance at Sofonisba, she'd said, "My father is not a young man. You should be attending to his needs."

"Relax, Cinzia," Fabrizio said in a reproachful tone. "I can take care of myself."

"But..."

"I know you are used to fussing over me, organizing everything to perfection. But now there is Sofonisba, the lady of the villa who will help you. You can relax. I know how trying it has been to care for this monstrosity of a house. You have a new mother to care for you, too, and help shoulder the estate's responsibilities."

Cinzia, a thin, gaunt woman, sniffed. "Mother, indeed! I had only one mamma, and now she is dead. Died of malaria eight months ago. And, now, if you don't take care of yourself, you will be dead too of heat exhaustion."

When King Philip first mentioned Fabrizio's daughter to Sofonisba, she had imagined the girl would be relatively young and in need of a mother. She was astonished to discover Cinzia Pignatelli was older than she. Sofonisba was further dismayed when Fabrizio had told her, "Cinzia is a stoic woman and she wasn't happy with my decision to remarry. She thought it was too soon." He took Sofonisba's hands and pressed them between his and assured her, "Give her time and she will come to accept you."

Heartened by his words, Sofonisba was open to the possibility that she and Fabrizio's daughter would become friends. So, with high expectations, she stepped from the coach that had carried them up from the port to the Pignatelli villa. Rapidly she assessed her new daughter, expecting to find someone who resembled Fabrizio, quick-witted with effusive charm. But Cinzia, her silver tinted hair pulled sharply back from her face—without ornamentation—looked every bit the dour old matron and every one of her forty-five years. Despite the elegance of her high cheekbones, they did nothing to compensate for her prominent nose.

Sofonisba smiled at her politely, ready to embrace the woman, but Cinzia only regarded her warily, greeting her with a curt nod of her head before stepping over to instruct the groomsmen to unpack the trunks. Sofonisba felt the sting of the woman's perfunctory appraisal and when Cinzia opened her mouth to speak, she was further taken aback by her deep throaty voice that issued sharp demands to the servant. By her harsh words and stilted manners, nothing at all like the generous and warm manners of Fabrizio, she could only assume the woman took after her dearly departed mother.

During the passage from Spain, Fabrizio had told her Cinzia's mother, Rosetta Morelli Trebecca, had been the daughter of a prince from the Court of Naples. Rosetta, although a God-fearing woman, raised her daughter with a firm hand, rarely doling out compliments. Cinzia, while she respected her mother, clearly doted on her father.

Fabrizio had confided in her, "We share a special bond. Because of her mother's admonitions to better herself and her appearance, I often felt sorry for Cinzia and took it upon myself to spoil her just a little to compensate for my wife's strict ways. The past year was quite difficult, but Cinzia was most valuable tending her mother when she was ill... as well as me. With her mother bedridden for so long... at times it was as if we were an old married couple."

"But what of Cinzia?" Sofonisba had inquired. "Surely she should have had a family of her own by now. Did she ever marry? Does she have aspirations of her own?"

"Oh, she was engaged to be wed some time ago... to Count Rebonati's son, Enzio, but it ended badly."

"What happened?"

"It was all a bit dramatic—and tragic. The morning of the wedding, the young man jilted Cinzia at the altar."

"How devastating! What caused Enzio to change his mind?"

"In the end, he ran off with another girl. It was as simple as that."

"And who was this woman?"

Sighing, he said, "She was Cinzia's closest and dearest friend—

Letizia Clemintine della Sosperanza. And when Cinzia found out her friend carried Enzio's child—and had known for some time, further duping her—it was the final straw. Cinzia was never quite the same after that. She ranted and raved for days, locking herself in her room, crying, saying she'd been betrayed by her two closest friends."

"And since then there has been no one else?"

"Oh, believe me, I tried to find her a husband. But here in Catania... well, there are just so many families to choose from. With declining fortunes, young men venture to the mainland. They go to Naples or Rome to find brides with larger dowries. And now... Cinzia is past the age of courtship."

He shook his head in despair. "No, I'm afraid—despite my best efforts—I was never successful in finding my daughter a proper husband. Since the *incident*, she claims she has no use for a man—nor will she trust another woman. It seems long ago, the poor dear gave up the idea of becoming someone's wife. But we are settled in our ways now... and she seems quite content to stay here with me."

As the sun rose higher in the morning sky, Sofonisba continued walking to the end of the ocean path. When she reached the edge of the promontory, she looked down at the boats in the harbor that seemed like little toy boats. She raised her gaze to the far horizon and sighed. So much of the world left to explore... She closed her eyes and remembered the words Orazio had spoken to her the day they met: *I never watch a ship sailing out of a harbor and down a channel, or look up at a gull soaring over a sandbar, without wishing I was on board. It is my fondest desire to fly as they do into the heart of the storm.*

Shaking her head to clear her thoughts, she gazed back down at the pounding surf that rolled onto the beach at the bottom of the cliff and wondered again about Cinzia—perhaps she too wanted to fly away and experience things unknown. Sofonisba couldn't help but think about living on this isolated island without love or companionship—other than that of her parents—and not being able to realize her own dreams. Over time, it would curdle anyone's disposition. She pondered Fabrizio's words, coming to the conclusion the woman really needed a female companion and friend. Perhaps she could fill that role, as she had done with Elisabeth. Heaven knew, she too, was lonely and ready to try.

But Sofonisba knew she would have to move cautiously. She'd only been at the villa a short while, but she'd seen the wary looks Cinzia gave her when Fabrizio's back was turned and heard the aggrieved exhale of breath and the gruff words she muttered under her breath when something wasn't to her liking.

Like the sleeping volcano who raised its head and grumbled, let out a bit of steam, and then lay dormant, Sofonisba believed Cinzia comported herself in such a manner—sighing and complaining, then retreating back into a passive acceptance of the situation. And now that she was here, Sofonisba couldn't help but worry that the molten lava in the volcano's heart had been disturbed and was now churning below the surface.

As she continued walking along the cliff path, returning to the villa, she thought, *If I am to win the affections of Fabrizio's daughter, I will have to tread lightly so as not to cause a full-blown eruption.*

Chapter 29

The Desires of Men

When Sofonisba reached the solarium, where her new husband nurtured his most prized plantings in large ceramic vases, Fabrizio was there to greet her. As had become their habit, she raised her cheek to receive his kiss. Then, stepping away, Sofonisba took off her hat and tossed it onto a nearby chair. She glanced around the spacious room filled with potted plants and breathed in the scent of oranges and salt air. To one side of the room, facing a large pane of glass, was a brightly colored mosaic table. She saw, as usual, the young maid, Maria Rosaria, had set it for breakfast. Inhaling the tantalizing scents, she smiled at the bountiful feast of Sicilian wines, fluffy biscuits, and thick, steaming porridges laid out before her. But no meal was ever complete without a large bowl of ripe oranges placed in the center.

"I see you've been out early, perusing your usual haunts," Fabrizio said in a pleasant tone.

She eyed the basket of oranges he held in his hands, some with the twigs and leaves still attached and replied, "As have you."

"I've been back for quite a while, though," said Fabrizio. "When you didn't return at the usual hour, I started to worry... You haven't exhausted yourself, have you? You must think of the child... I have just the thing to refresh you."

He dug into the basket, picked out an orange, and peeled it for her. "Here, taste this one! Tell me what you think. It will do you and the babe good."

Sofonisba was admittedly thirsty and tired and accepted the fruit gratefully. As she bit into the warm, succulent pulp, the sticky juices ran down her chin.

Fabrizio peeled an orange for himself and popped it into his mouth. Wiping his chin with the back of his hand, he said, "These come from trees on the south slope."

"They are delectable. Already I feel revived."

"We must keep you strong and healthy, my dear."

He reached out a hand and caressed the expanding bump around her middle. "How is the little one today? He seems to be growing fast. It must be because of the sun and the fruit here in Sicily. You know for years it has been my greatest desire to become a father again."

Instantly, Sofonisba felt a twinge of guilt. But when she looked over Fabrizio's shoulder and saw Cinzia standing on the solarium threshold, watching them disapprovingly, she felt even more culpable. A few weeks after their return home, they had shared with her the news of Sofonisba's impending state of motherhood. Despite Cinzia's polite acceptance that she would soon have a sibling, Sofonisba could tell it had been a difficult pill to swallow. She often saw a displeased expression on her face when Fabrizio caressed her affectionately.

But now, by the grim expression on her face, Sofonisba knew something else had upset her. "What has happened?" Sofonisba asked in a concerned tone. "Are you all right?"

Fabrizio looked up too, and chuckled, "Come on, daughter! Out with it. By the look on your face, I'd think you had just been attacked by a flustered hen."

Cinzia glanced from her father's hand, which still caressed Sofonisba's midriff, to gaze at their faces. "Well, if you must know, it is the maid..."

"Maria Rosaria?" asked Sofonisba, suddenly concerned.

"Yes," replied Cinzia a little too sharply. "That's the one. That good for nothing housemaid! She broke another vase. I think we will have to let her go."

"Let her go!" exclaimed Sofonisba. "But she is so young... her family is quite poor and she needs this position."

Wiping her hands over the morning apron she wore, Cinzia said, "I don't care if the girl has to walk the streets to earn her bread. She must go. She is far too clumsy! I am in charge of the house and I have decided that..." Cinzia stopped when she heard her father's slight cough. She turned toward him and asked, "What have you to say? Have I not always been a good judge of character?"

"Yes, Cinzia, but now we have Sofonisba, and I value her ideas and would like to hear what her opinion is on the matter."

"But..."

"Sofonisba has a say in how things are run here now too, and that is final. If she believes this girl—this Maria Rosaria—should remain, then the matter is settled."

"But Papa! Haven't I always done a good job? Sofonisba..." she said, drawing out the name, almost like a taunt, "she is so new, she won't even know where to begin."

"She did a remarkable job with the menu the other evening when the Manfreddis came for dinner. Sofonisba brings charm and sophistication to our table. She is like a breath of fresh air in this mausoleum of a house. I think she should handle that task from now on."

"You've always loved this house and how it has been run! I've kept it just as Mother did," exclaimed Cinzia. "I've always been in charge of social engagements and menus..."

"You try my patience, Cinzia." Then, with a dismissive air, he waved her away. "You must learn to share the household responsibilities—goodness, there is enough for the both of you. Now, be a good daughter and take this basket to the cook. Don't forget the crate of lemons I left on the steps. You can make us mamma's famous *limonata* and then join us on the terrace."

Fabrizio turned his attention back to Sofonisba and didn't see the annoyance on his daughter's face or how she narrowed her eyes at her father's new wife. But Sofonisba did. Like shots fired across the bow of a ship, she knew Cinzia had just issued a warning. And should her new "mother" not steer away, there would be rocky times and trouble ahead.

Without another word, Cinzia picked up the basket of oranges and spun about on her heels and re-entered the house. Oblivious to his daughter's moods, Fabrizio smiled at Sofonisba like a besotted lover. Taking her hand, he led her to the mosaic table upon which lay several letters and a small leather box.

"What's all this?" she asked.

"A ship arrived this morning with packets of mail from the mainland. The courier brought it to me this morning. In it were three letters addressed to you."

"And what is in the box?"

"That is a special surprise for you!"

He reached for the leather container stamped with a gold foil fleur-de-lis and held it out. "I thought you would like this. It is just a small token of my appreciation. Now that you are my wife, I wanted you to have it."

Sofonisba eyed Fabrizio curiously. Taking the box from his extended hand, she undid the little gold catch and opened the lid. Inside, nestled upon an emerald green cloth, was a ruby pendant set in gold filigree.

"It's beautiful," murmured Sofonisba. "Stunning, actually."

"I thought you'd like it," Fabrizio said, beaming. He picked up the pendant out of its nest, stepped behind her, and fastened the heavy gold chain at the back of her neck.

He turned her around in his arms and kissed her. As his warm fleshy lips met hers, she felt his prickly beard upon her face, and she winced just a little at its abrasive texture. But, assembling her face in a pleasant expression, she said, "Fabrizio, you are the sweetest man. I—"

"Have you given her mother's necklace?" came an indignant cry from the door.

Sofonisba turned to see Cinzia had returned. In her hands she held a silver tray, and on it were crystal glasses and a pitcher filled with the juice of the lemons Fabrizio had collected earlier.

"Take it off! What are you thinking? It's mine now."

"Cinzia!" commanded Fabrizio. "Stop this at once."

"But she can't wear it... Mother promised it to me."

"Rosetta is dead now, daughter. She left you many other beautiful things. This was my mother's and her mother's before her. It has been in my family for ages."

"Precisely my point! She has just been a part of your life for a few weeks... Now you go and give a precious thing to someone you barely know."

"Cinzia, my dear," Sofonisba hastened to say, "of course this should be yours." Lifting her fingers, she began to unfasten the catch, but Fabrizio's commanding voice stopped her.

"You will not give it back!"

He turned to Cinzia again. "Behave yourself, daughter. What has gotten into you? You are embarrassing me. We are family now, and I expect you to accept this new state of affairs. It is my desire to give the necklace to my new bride."

"Your bride! She is ten years younger than me! Do you realize how that makes me feel? You didn't even ask my consent!"

"Your consent!"

"Yes! We always decide things together. Even when Mother was alive, it was you and me... You never questioned my abilities and suddenly, since she arrived, you treat me differently."

Fabrizio sighed and softened his tone. "You knew why I went to Spain. I told you I went to speak to Philip and find a wife..."

"You sought a silken purse... someone to pay off debt and keep this estate afloat."

Fabrizio glanced uncomfortably at Sofonisba and then back at his daughter. "Cinzia, *tesoro*, you must accept my good fortune. Sofonisba brings us many gifts, her dowry... her painting... her education. You would do best to learn from her. She can teach you—"

Ignoring him, Cinzia cried, "Haven't I been enough? We've always been good company for one another."

"You will always be my daughter... nothing has changed between us. But men get lonely and need companionship..."

Cinzia glanced over at Sofonisba and opened her mouth to say something, but seeing the warning look on her father's face immediately shut it. The words she couldn't say out loud, however, were clearly expressed by her eyes.

With a nervous chuckle, Fabrizio cajoled, "Come, come, my sweet daughter... Let me give you a hug and show you how much I care for you."

Obstinate at first, Cinzia stubbornly refused to budge. But when he opened his arms, she relented. Slipping into his embrace, she murmured, "I'm sorry."

"Don't apologize to me," he said. "Apologize to my wife... your new mother."

Almost as if she had forgotten that Sofonisba was still in the room, Cinzia lifted her face and said contritely, "Excuse my outburst... It's just..."

"Really, there is no need to apologize to me," Sofonisba said quickly, embarrassed for the other woman. But, if truth be told, Cinzia's attitude toward her was becoming increasingly annoying. Cinzia was acting like a spoiled brat, and personally Sofonisba found it appalling, especially for a woman so advanced in years.

Fabrizio gave Sofonisba a meaningful look that communicated she need not worry and all would turn out all right. He then turned to Cinzia and said, "Come, let's you and I take a walk. We will leave Sofonisba to read her letters."

"All right, Father," Cinzia said at last. She looked at Sofonisba and said, "I'm sorry if I offended you. It is just all so new..." After pouring a glass of lemonade into one of the crystal goblets, she offered it to Sofonisba. "Here. Drink this. It is my special recipe—I've added just the right amount of sugar to make the drink sweet without ruining the taste of my father's lemons."

Fabrizio beamed. "Perhaps you can leave a pitcher for her in her studio. She will be working there this afternoon."

"It would be my pleasure," said Cinzia with a tight smile.

After they left, Sofonisba took a sip and grimaced slightly. There was little sugar in the blend, and her face puckered at the first taste, but she still managed to swallow the golden liquid. Like the woman who prepared it, it was a bit tart and a little too sour. But it was hot, and she was thirsty, so she drank the entire glass and filled another. The sourness was an acquired taste, she decided, rubbing her forehead. If it wouldn't offend the woman's sensibilities to tamper with mother's recipe, she'd ask Cinzia to add a little more sugar the next time.

Then, turning her attention to the three envelopes sitting on the table, she picked up the one on top and turned it over. Immediately she recognized the handwriting of Asdrubale. She hadn't seen her brother in years, but now that he controlled her fortunes, she regularly corresponded with him.

In a previous letter, Elena had told her their baby brother had turned into a chubby young aristocrat. Her sister also intimated that Asdrubale was in love with a young woman he had met in Milan. Sofonisba smiled at that, and despite her best attempts to think of Asdrubale all grown up, she could only envision his baby face imposed on the body of a man dressed in toddler's clothing. Breaking open the Anguissola seal, Sofonisba quickly scanned the contents. She imagined he was writing to tell her the news of his upcoming nuptials. After the first introductory paragraph, she quickly learned the real reason he had written to her: Amilcare was dead.

Asdrubale wrote in flowing cursive handwriting that Amilcare had taken ill with pneumonia. The fits of coughing and fever came on quickly and had taken him just as swiftly. There hadn't been time to contact her sooner; for this, he was genuinely sorry. They buried Amilcare in the family grave near his beloved wife, near the hill where he liked to believe the Carthaginian ancestors fought near Cremona.

And now, dearest sister, this, of course, doesn't change a thing regarding your finances. I desire to continue overseeing the monies you receive from the crown. You will kindly direct all financial and legal matters to me, and I will disperse your inheritance as I see fit. Rest assured, as I have done in the past, I will make sure it is secure. Give my best to your husband. Fondly, Asdrubale.

Sofonisba lifted her eyes from the letter and gazed out the window. Her dear father was dead. She could hardly believe it. Amilcare had been the first who truly believed in her—the one who first recognized her talent. He'd made sure she received a good education and taught her the classics. It was Amilcare who gave her a paintbrush and told her to make pictures when she was only six. Together they ventured far from home on an extraordinary journey that took her from Cremona, Rome, Milan, and to Madrid. If not for those first shaky steps with her father by her side, she wouldn't be the woman she was today.

She sighed softly, folded her brother's letter, placed it back on the table, and picked up the next. She imagined this one would be from Elena. But when she saw her name written in a tight black script, her heart skipped a beat. This signature, too, she knew far too well... The letter she held in her hands had been penned by the Duke of Alba.

Gingerly she broke the red seal bearing the coat of arms of his noble house and unfolded a single page of yellow parchment and read:

Most honorable Madame, I write to inform you that I returned to Spain from the lowlands after completing a successful mission. We encountered much opposition, but in the end we secured peace in the region. Upon my return, while I brought happy news to King Philip, I was profoundly surprised to learn you had married Fabrizio Moncada Pignatelli, son of the Prince of Paternò, the Viceroy of Sicily.

The wars in the north were successful, and now our sovereign has granted me leave to rest and restore my spirits. It is my sincerest wish, dear lady, to see you again. And thus, I have traveled to Sicily to renew our happy rapport and bid you well and meet your husband. To this end, I request that you visit me in my apartments in the Spanish Consulate in Via Marguda, near the Duomo of Catania. Please let me know at your earliest convenience a favorable date.

Your servant, forever, Fernando Álvarez de Toledo and Pimentel, 3rd Duke of Alba

When Sofonisba finished reading the letter, her hands trembled just a little. The Duke of Alba was there in Sicily... It hardly seemed possible. What was she to think of this strange turn of events? Mystified, Sofonisba could only wonder at the man's intentions. When they parted company, he intimated he wished for a closer union, but now she was married... Why was he here and what could he possibly want to accomplish?

In turmoil, she set the letter down and picked up the last one. Examining it, she saw her name—*Sofonisba*—written in bold, confident strokes. This time, however, she didn't recognize the author by his penmanship. She turned the letter over, enjoying the silky quality of the paper. It was rare—like nothing she had ever seen before.

Curiously she studied the gold sealing wax that fastened the letter and saw an image had been pressed into the seal. Holding it up to the light, she instantly recognized the face of an Etruscan king. Encircling his profile, she read the words: *Rex Porsena*.

"No," she whispered, "It can't be."

Careful not to destroy the seal, she pried the paper loose and unfolded the parchment. This letter, unlike the others, contained no finely penned words. Instead, as Sofonisba pressed the page flat, she saw a drawing of a ship. It was a grand vessel with tall masts that pitched forward through rough waves. A lone man stood on the deck, his feet planted firmly as he gazed up at the sky sprinkled with stars.

Just as a writer's penmanship gave away his identity, so did the artist's design—even if he was an amateur. Still, if she had any doubts, she smiled to see inscribed upon the ship's bow the name: *Sofonisba—my heart's only desire.*

With great care, she folded the drawing and slipped it into her bodice, close to her heart. Forgetting Cinzia, the duke, and even her husband, a warm sensation washed over her.

Orazio had returned.

Chapter 30

The Duke Speaks

*A*fter pondering the news she had received from the four diverse men in her life, Sofonisba came to four different decisions.

First, she would give back the necklace Fabrizio had given her as it rightfully belonged to Cinzia. Sofonisba would not deprive the woman of a family heirloom, even if it was Fabrizio's greatest wish that his wife should have it. The complications incurred from Cinzia's wrath simply weren't worth it.

Then, drafting a message to Asdrubale later that morning, Sofonisba relayed her heartfelt sorrow over their father's death. But, turning the page, she wrote in strong language under no uncertain terms did she approve of his continuing to handle her money. Now that Amilcare was gone and no longer needed her funds, she didn't want her brother helping himself freely to what was rightfully hers. She would be hiring lawyers to review the matter and expected to hear from them within the month.

After sealing her letter with her artist's insignia, Sofonisba picked up the duke's letter and re-read it several more times. She sighed. What could she do but accept his summons? It would be the last time she would ever see him—she owed him one final meeting.

Sofonisba picked up her pen and dipped it in ink, then wrote in determined strokes, telling him she would visit in two days' time at two o'clock, accompanied by her husband.

She rang the bell on her desk, summoning her maid, and resolutely handed the letters to Maria Rosaria, asking her to give them to the groomsman to dispatch.

Finally, she pulled out the last letter she had stowed away in her bodice and held it to her cheek. It was warm from her own body heat, and she detected the fragrance of exotic spices.

This was the hardest decision because the only choice to be made was to ignore what her heart begged her to do. She couldn't run from Fabrizio's house like a lovestruck fool into Orazio's arms. As she had resolved before, she was a married woman and could no longer entertain thoughts of him. Instead, she folded the parchment and placed it in the box where she kept his coin and the small Etruscan bronze sailor and shut the lid firmly.

On Thursday, at the appointed hour, in the company of Fabrizio and Cinzia, Sofonisba set out in the Pignatelli coach. Their destination was the Spanish consulate in Via Marguda—the current address of Alba. Upon their arrival, the three were ushered into the grand foyer. They didn't have to wait long, as minutes later the duke descended from the upper apartments to greet them.

"It is a pleasure to see you again, Signorina Anguissola." Then, with a slight bow of his head, he corrected himself. "Excuse my blunder... Signora Pignatelli." He turned to Fabrizio and extended his hand. "Messer, it is with great honor I welcome you into my home here in Sicily." Then, glancing over at Cinzia, he acknowledged her presence with a courteous raise of his noble brow. "And who might this be?"

Sofonisba was amazed by his cordial manners. He was usually so taciturn—a man of few words. "This is my husband's daughter by his first wife, Cinzia Pignatelli."

Fabrizio's daughter lifted the lace scarf wrapped around her head and let it fall to her shoulders, then extended her hand to the duke. Leaning over, Alba kissed it lightly. "It is a pleasure, signorina, to meet such a charming lady."

At the touch of his lips upon her skin, Cinzia blushed. Sofonisba noticed her reaction, imagining it had been quite a while since a man, other than her father, had shown her such attention. She watched as the woman's eyes trailed after Alba when he turned back to Fabrizio.

"Marriage agrees with you also, messer. You are positively radiant! You are a fortunate man to have married Sofonisba. She will make as fine a wife as she is a painter."

He slapped him good-naturedly on the back. "How was the trip from Spain?"

As the men discussed the sea voyage and the current affairs at the Spanish embassy and foreign policy abroad, Sofonisba marveled again at the duke's transformation. He made polite inquiries as if he actually cared about what they had to say, engaging them all in conversation and bestowing effusive compliments.

When there was a pause in the men's conversation, Sofonisba spoke up. "It is indeed like old times to see you again, duke... and looking so fit. Nary a scratch upon you. I heard rumors the campaign in the north was"—she paused and then diplomatically added—"rather difficult."

"I won't bore you with the details, dear lady. War is neither pleasant nor something to be discussed in the company of ladies. But the matter was dealt with quickly... over practically before it began. Fortunately, I was able to cut short my mission and return to Spain earlier than expected. Imagine my surprise to learn you had so recently departed... and that you had acquired a husband."

"Yes, things happened rather quickly after you left," Sofonisba said. "It is hard to believe all that transpired since I last saw you. Imagine *my* surprise to receive your letter! And to learn you had traveled so far to see me."

"There were a few matters to discuss," he replied quickly. He glanced at Fabrizio and added, "Philip sent me to ensure his wife's dearest friend had arrived and all was in good order."

"How are things at the court?" Sofonisba asked with concern. "Is the king well? Is there a problem?"

Alba turned toward her and met her gaze directly. "Things progress as well as can be expected. King Philip suffers greatly from melancholy and depression over the loss of his queen... and his son. His physical wounds have healed... but I fear his eye still bothers him."

"And what of the infanta, little Isabella?"

"She is growing stronger by the day. The child is the king's only consolation. She has her mother's blithe spirit." He smiled. "Do you recall the betrothal band, the diamond ring I placed on Elisabeth's finger during her marriage by proxy in Notre Dame?"

When she nodded, he said, "Philip keeps it safe for his daughter and intends to present it to Isabel when she turns fourteen. He hopes she will wear it in memory of her mother..."

Once again, Sofonisba was touched by this tender side of the duke. He seemed so relaxed—far from the cold, brooding disposition he had often displayed in Milan or at the court in Spain.

Stepping forward, Cinzia interrupted their friendly repartee. "Duke Alba, we have brought you a gift."

"A gift, you say? How amusing, almost as delightful as you, signorina."

"Sir... you are generous with your compliments, and you haven't even seen what we have brought." Cinzia signaled to a servant who was standing behind her to move forward. "My father cultivates lemons and oranges on the lands surrounding our villa. I've selected some of the ripest and juiciest for you to enjoy."

Out of the assortment of citrus fruit, she picked one and held it up for his inspection. "One day, you must come and see us at the villa and I will make you my famous *limonata*."

The duke bowed graciously. "A tempting offer, signorina."

He took the lemon from her hand, held it to his nose, and inhaled deeply. "Such a lovely gift, fair Cinzia. Of course, I accept." Addressing Sofonisba's husband, he added, "So, Fabrizio... you are a gentleman farmer?"

"Yes, it would seem so," supplied the other man proudly. "I must confess it is a pleasant hobby. But here in Sicily, it is an easy task to grow such delicious specimens. The soil is rich from the volcano. Etna is the real reason for each successful harvest. I've been experimenting with grafting new varietals and—"

Interrupting him, Alba said, "Perhaps you'd be interested in investigating the gardens around the palace. We have quite an orchard..."

Without waiting for an answer, he motioned to the footman standing by the door. "Renzo, would you be so kind as to escort Fabrizio and Signorina Pignatelli to the terrace and show them around?" He shrugged his shoulders apologetically. "With your permission, there are a few things I'd like to discuss with your wife that pertain to the late queen."

When Fabrizio lifted an eyebrow, the duke hurried on to say, "I'm sure you will oblige me and have no objection if I have a private conversation regarding Elisabeth's will and a few bequests... and a portrait the king would like commissioned of his late wife. It won't take long. While you are strolling about the grounds, you could also offer some counsel to the master gardener. I'm sure he'd be most appreciative."

"Of course, Alba. Of course," replied Fabrizio immediately.

Sofonisba looked at her husband in some amusement. *Poor Fabrizio.* She could tell he was flustered by Alba. Moreover, she knew he certainly didn't want to incur the Spanish king's displeasure or interfere with her dowry.

When the servant approached and gestured with his arm toward the gardens, Fabrizio acknowledged him politely. Then, to the Alba, he said, "I'm totally at your disposal, messer, and I'd be happy to speak with your man."

Alba smiled at him and then bowed his head slightly at Cinzia. "Why don't you accompany your father, signorina. I think you will find the grounds quite lovely." Then, seeing one of his military attendants standing at the door, he excused himself for a moment and walked over to see what the man required.

Cinzia's eyes followed his movements with interest, and it seemed to Sofonisba she wasn't willing or eager to part with the duke's company so soon after their first introduction.

"Come, daughter," urged Fabrizio, "let's leave these two alone to discuss their business matters.

Realizing her part had been played out and she was no longer the focus of the duke's attention, Cinzia took her father's arm possessively and walked with him to the door that led out to the sunny terrace. As she passed by Sofonisba, she raised an eyebrow, and as they drew away, she heard her whisper into Fabrizio's ear, "Aren't you concerned, Father? Did you see how the duke looked at her... and did you see how she flirted with him right in front of you? Who knows what happens behind closed doors at the Spanish court... Oh, I've heard the rumors..."

As their voices died out, Sofonisba shook her head, wondering what other thoughts the woman was harboring. Perhaps Cinzia had noticed her lush and rounded figure—far more advanced in pregnancy than she should be. Maybe she had guessed Sofonisba's secret. Did she suspect she carried a child conceived by another man?

Horrified, she suddenly thought, *Does she think it is Alba's?*

The duke dismissed his aid, then carefully closed the door, enclosing them in privacy. He turned his full attention upon Sofonisba and smiled at her, unaware of the father-daughter exchange. Pleasantly he asked, "Can I get you something? You must be parched from the drive to town."

"No, thank you," Sofonisba said, unnerved by his effusive demeanor and more than a little anxious to know what was on his mind. "Has something happened that I should know about? What news do you have for me from Spain?"

He regarded her for a long moment. "You must know the reason I have come to Sicily."

When she didn't answer, he continued. "When I returned from the Netherlands, I had hoped to find you still at the Spanish court. Instead, my world was turned upside down the night I received word from Philip of your marriage."

Astonished, Sofonisba held her tongue, fearful of what he might say next.

Taking her silence as encouragement, he continued. "Surely you realize, dear lady, how I admire and respect you. My life... has not been easy. It has been fraught with strife... war... deeds that no man ever should have to commit."

Alba paused and drew in a breath. "I'm a sinful man, but these things were all done in God's name. To only him must I be accountable for. But I feel now I must confess them to you..."

"Oh, no! You have nothing to confess to me, messer. Nothing at all!"

"But I feel compelled to."

"I am not your confessor. Any secrets you wish to reveal to me should remain between you, God, the devil, and the dead."

Alba took a step toward her, and as he did, she moved back.

"I can't contain my feelings any longer. I am in love with you."

With the utterance of those words, a deadly silence fell upon them.

He studied her face, and Sofonisba realized that he was searching for signs that deep inside she harbored affection for him. But if truth be told, the only thing she felt when she looked at him was doubt and dread.

As if coming to the same conclusion, Sofonisba watched as a shadow of despair crossed his face. He should have known from the moment he set sail from Spain to find her, this supplication to win her heart would fail. She almost felt sorry for him.

When she remained silent, Alba cleared his throat and tried again. "Perhaps I wasn't clear... Don't you see I need you? I may not be worthy of you, but I need you to ease my suffering and—"

"Stop!" Sofonisba said, taking another step back before he could reach for her hand. "I am married. By the king's order, I am the wife of Fabrizio Moncada Pignatelli."

"Any order the king has made can also be rescinded. He can denounce this marriage as easily as he approved it. We can sail back to Spain—just you and me. We can be..."

"What? Married? No!" exclaimed Sofonisba, more forcefully than she intended. "Fabrizio is my husband in God's eyes. We are united by God, not by a king. Until death do us part... no man can put asunder. No man, no king, can break the holy bonds of marriage. That would be sacrilege."

By his haunted expression, Sofonisba could see this was not going at all as Alba had planned. She imagined he had repeated over and over the phrases he'd hoped would win her over. But, despite using cordial manners and carefully chosen words, she was spurning him before he had even finished proposing his plan.

Still, she was resolved to speak her mind at last. "You have sins that weigh heavily upon you. You suffer greatly from the things in your past. That sad, melancholy expression has crossed your face before, and I can only imagine what you keep deep inside of you."

She took a step closer to him and said, "I believe you do care for me—you've been so generous... But don't let me add another sin to your burden by breaking a religious sacrament. You are a God-fearing man. Surely, one day you would hate me for it."

"I could never hate you, Sofonisba. You are good and pure... all the things I am not." Alba walked to the window and stared at the garden beyond. Then he turned around and said tightly, "But I do hate the man you are bound to now. He is the only thing standing between us. But trust me. As I got rid of the sea captain by sending him away on a bloody fool's mission to England, I can do away with Fabrizio... It won't take much imagination."

"Sea captain?" Her head shot up. "Orazio? What do you know? What have you learned?" Suddenly her face drained of color. "Fool's mission... What do you mean?" she cried. "Where did you send him?"

When he said nothing, in a sharper voice she added, "What right had you all—"

"We are waging war with England... Lomellino knew the risks."

"I came to you... You told me he'd been sent to Africa... You lied to my face! Then you told me he died, presumably at the hands of the corsairs... but in reality you sent him to be slaughtered by the English queen... What kind of man does that?" She looked wildly around. "We were to be married... I carry Orazio's child!"

Alba gazed at her in shock. "What? How could you..."

At the sound of steps re-entering the salon through the terrace door, they both turned around. Sofonisba blanched when she saw her husband's jovial face.

Next to him was Cinzia, who observed them with suspicious eyes. "Is everything all right?" she asked. "Have we interrupted something unpleasant..."

"Of course not," responded Sofonisba a little too brightly. "We were just speaking of old times... and old friends." Sofonisba cleared her throat, then glanced at her husband. "Fabrizio, you are looking a little tired and overheated from your exertions in the garden. Are you ready to return home and rest?"

Oblivious to the tension in the room, Fabrizio said, "I'm fine, my dear, but if you are ready to say your goodbyes to the duke, I'm ready to make my salutations as well." He made a courteous bow before the duke. "It was delightful to make your acquaintance again. Your gardens are lovely, but your orange trees could use a little more pruning. I gave your man specific instructions. In the meantime, enjoy the fruits we have given to you."

He offered his arm to his wife, which she took gratefully.

Sofonisba nodded at the duke, and in a cool but polite tone, she said, "It was enlightening to see you again, Duke. May God have mercy on your soul. I hope you have a safe trip back to Spain. Please give King Philip my regards upon your safe return."

Chapter 31

The Moon and Venus

*O*utside the Spanish Embassy, as the trio waited for their carriage to be brought around, across the way Sofonisba saw the cathedral dedicated to Sant'Agata looming high into the sky. At this time of day, the piazza was bustling with people. Some took respite near the large marble fountain in the center, others in the shade of the porticos that connected the buildings. There were women selling their wares on the street and tradesmen carrying barrels and wooden boxes into the nearby shops.

Sofonisba scanned the scene, her instincts on high alert; she knew Orazio was here somewhere. Then, out of the corner of her eye, she saw a tall man with long dark hair step into the piazza and her heart beat a little faster. But when the gentleman turned in her direction, she was immediately crestfallen. It wasn't him.

"Is everything all right, my dear?" inquired Fabrizio. "You seem a little anxious... and you look a little faint."

"I'm fine," she said reassuringly.

"Social visits can be a bit draining, but it's pleasant to renew acquaintances," he said. "The duke is a charming man. Not at all as I remembered him."

"Yes, to me he appears changed, too. But I can't say I knew him all that well... or what he was ever thinking, really. He is a private man." She glanced back at the piazza again, scanning it anxiously for a familiar face. But, this time, her attention was arrested by the sight of Cinzia standing a few steps away, regarding her curiously.

"You spent many years together with Alba at the Spanish court, did you not? Come now! Surely you know him better than you let on. How ever did you two meet in the first place?"

"The duke is King Philip's most trusted advisor," Sofonisba replied carefully. "We first met in my hometown of Cremona. I was fortunate that he admired my skills, took me under his wing, and introduced me to the Spanish court."

"Very fortunate, indeed," agreed Cinzia. She turned to Fabrizio, and with a raised eyebrow asked, "Father, what do you think of a man who admires a woman's skills so ardently that he..."

Her words trailed off when she saw Fabrizio wasn't listening. Instead, he waved to a friend who stood on the opposite side of the square, outside their favorite tavern. When a boy passed by pulling a cart filled with wine bottles destined for the same locale, Sofonisba smiled in amusement.

To avoid Cinzia's probing questions, she tapped Fabrizio lightly on the sleeve and said, "Does my husband desire something to drink?"

"You are beginning to know me well, Sofonisba... You seem to anticipate my desires before I say them out loud," he said with a chuckle.

"Oh, I'd recognize that thirsty gleam in any man's eye," she replied brightly, pleased to have distracted him so readily.

By the way Cinzia narrowed her eyes, Sofonisba was embarrassed to think perhaps Fabrizio's daughter had misconstrued her words. Did the woman think she referred not to his drinking habits but rather those in the bedroom?

To dispel the woman's misguided imaginings and smooth things over with her, Sofonisba quickly said, "Cinzia knows your likes and dislikes too when it comes to a glass of ale." Then, patting Fabrizio on his sleeve, she hastily said to him, "Well, then... you go and have a tankard. Cinzia and I will return to the villa and send the groomsman back to you in an hour. Will that be long enough?"

"Make it two," he said good-naturedly. "I might want to sample more than one draft."

When the open-air coach pulled up, Fabrizio kissed his wife on the cheek, gave Cinzia a quick peck on the forehead, and briskly crossed the square, whistling an airy tune. Sofonisba watched him depart, plagued by guilt for the lies she'd told Fabrizio and worried about Cinzia's conclusions. But now, to add to her concerns, she was troubled by her recent encounter with Alba and his admission he had been the one to send Orazio away. She could barely keep the rage at bay. The cocktail of emotions was exhausting her.

When she heard the whinny of the Pignatelli's horse, she looked over her shoulder in relief at the open-air carriage, more than ready for it to transport her home. Although it sat low to the ground, it still required a bit of finesse for a lady with long, flowing skirts to enter the vehicle. When Sofonisba placed a foot on the first rung, the young driver extended a hand to help her. Despite his assistance, the lace of her undergarments caught on the second metal step, but before it could tear, Cinzia leaned down to unhook it.

"Careful," she scolded. "You don't want to rip your expensive petticoat paid with money from a Spanish king."

Sofonisba suddenly had a flashback to her younger days in Cremona and the squabble that had once occurred over a petticoat between her two younger sisters. Something softened in her, and she looked at Cinzia with more fondness. Perhaps, like Minerva, Cinzia was all vinegar and spice but—like her sister who quickly succumbed to jealousy—she too had a kind heart and meant well. After all, she was clearly devoted to the health and happiness of her father. She only wanted to protect him.

Wanting desperately to have this woman as her ally, with more warmth and new understanding, Sofonisba slid over to make room for the other woman in the carriage. "Thank you, Cinzia," she said, patting the seat next to her. "Come, join me. I'd like to talk and get to know you better."

Cinzia hesitated ever so slightly. "I'd like that..." Then with a shake of her head, she said quickly, "I can't. I just remembered I have an errand to run here in town. You go on. I'll come home with my father." With a small snort, she added, "I want to make sure he doesn't stay and imbibe a third glass of ale."

Cinzia contemplated her for a moment then gave her a wan smile and said, "I wish to apologize again... well... thank you for giving me back my mother's necklace." As she spoke, she began unwinding the long, flowing lace scarf from around her head and held it up for Sofonisba to inspect. "This was my mother's scarf. Isn't it beautiful? It was made by the sisters at the convent of Sant'Agata."

"It is exquisite," Sofonisba agreed, admiring the lace and beadwork.

"Take it," she urged. "It will protect you from the winds blowing up from the ocean."

Sofonisba hesitated a beat; then, realizing it as a conciliatory gesture, she accepted Cinzia's gift and wrapped it loosely around her head. It took only a moment, however, before the breeze blew it off again and the long flowing ends fluttered playfully in the air like an out of control kite.

"Here, let me help you secure it better," said Cinzia. Winding it around Sofonisba's head, she then tied a firm knot securely at her neck, letting the longs ends flutter freely. "Before you go, would you like something sweet?" Without waiting for an answer, Cinzia opened her purse and withdrew a small parchment envelope filled with soft candies. She popped one into her mouth and then extended the pouch to Sofonisba.

"What is this?" she asked as she drew one out and took a bite of the soft morsel, enjoying the burst of toasty brown sugar and cinnamon.

"It is a caramel. I made them the other day from my grandmother's recipe. I used to love them as a child. I'd sneak them from her silver candy dish and run off to the stables where I'd eat them up, but never without sharing a few with the horses... They loved them too."

Cinzia moved to the front of the carriage, and with a crooning tone she spoke softly to the horse. Then she pulled out a second envelope tied with string, undid it, and offered the entire contents to the horse. When the last candy was consumed, the animal nudged her hand. She turned to Sofonisba and said, "See? He wants another. He is a bit of a glutton."

After petting the horse on his velvet nose, she took a step back and said, "Well, you and the horse enjoy the drive... See you at home."

The coachman saluted her with a tilt of his hat, then he whistled and the horse lurched forward. Sofonisba settled into her seat and thoughtfully chewed the soft caramel. Cinzia was temperamental like Minerva—scary at times with her angry outbursts—but once she'd stamped her foot, she eventually calmed down and listened to reason. Maybe Fabrizio was correct in his assumption that Cinzia just needed time to get used to having another female at the villa.

Sofonisba turned around to give her a friendly wave, but saw Cinzia had just disappeared into a small shop over which was a sign that advertised: *Apothecary: Crystals, Botanicals, and Curiosities.*

Tiredly, she laid her head against the seat and, feeling the warmth of the sun on her face, Sofonisba stopped thinking about Cinzia and turned her attention instead to the ocean's view as the carriage turned onto the shoreline road. When they neared the top of the crest, the winds picked up and the fluttering scarf rose and fell, dancing gaily on the salty breeze. Sofonisba closed her eyes, letting the even clip-clopping of the horse's hooves lull her into a lazy sleep.

After progressing idyllically on for several more miles, the mare's gait became choppy, causing Sofonisba's head to bounce uncomfortably against the wall of the vehicle. She sat up and saw they were approaching the villa along the road that circumvented the sea wall. They hadn't much farther to go, but still the horse shook its head from side to side in agitation.

The driver called out over his shoulder, "Hang on tight... the mare is panicking. There might be an animal... or worse, someone hiding in the—"

Before he could finish his sentence, he pulled hard on the reins to avoid a deep rut in the road. Sofonisba could see the driver was battling the beast as best he could to avoid veering into a drainage ditch or being pulled too close to the cliff wall.

They proceeded a few more choppy paces until, suddenly, the horse reared up. The carriage tilted at a vicarious angle and Sofonisba was flung against the cab's wall. The wind caught her scarf, making it flap erratically. When the horse touched down and moved forward, the wayward scarf became entangled in the spokes. As the wheels of the carriage accelerated, rotating faster and faster, with each revolution the scarf wound tighter around the axle.

As the lace was pulled tighter against her neck, Sofonisba was wrenched forcefully downward, and the knot Cinzia had tied at her neck began to choke her. Desperately, she clawed at the tightening noose, calling for help, but the fabric cut into her vocal cords, making it impossible to scream. When the horse lifted up again, waving its hooves in the air, the tension finally ripped the fabric in two. When the carriage bolted forward again, Sofonisba was thrown back; losing her balance, she was pitched out of the open box.

Fortunately, her voluminous skirts and yards and yards of crinolines and petticoats she had dressed in to meet the duke cushioned her fall. She landed unceremoniously in a heap near the ditch. When she looked up, she saw the carriage disappearing down the road. Still trying to gain control of the stallion, the driver hadn't noticed she was no longer traveling with him.

In a dazed state, Sofonisba lay for a moment listening to the shrill sounds of insects. Then, in a panic, she placed her hands on her waist. The child, she thought wildly. *Are you all right, my precious babe?*

After a moment, Sofonisba's breathing returned to normal and she relaxed, realizing nothing was amiss. She hadn't fallen that far and wasn't hurt; only her pride had been bruised.

Sofonisba was about to push herself up but paused when she heard the pounding of approaching hoofs. She panicked, knowing the remote country roads surrounding the villa were often frequented by bands of outlaws who raised havoc by harassing the local gentry. That was what the coachman had alluded to earlier when the horse first became agitated.

Since her arrival, Fabrizio's lands had not been immune to the wrath of disgruntled tenants. Only a month before, one of their herds of goats had suffered mutilation, and a field had been burned. She was also aware some of the marauders sought out the unscrupulous tax bailiffs, capturing and torturing them, leaving them to dangle from trees. These same vicious villains also considered their landlords' wives and daughters fair game and ravished and brutalized them.

Sofonisba didn't want to fall prey to another act of aggression. Fearful of being trampled, with all her might she struggled to roll out of the way to hide in the drainage channel. However, her efforts were hampered by the cumbersome skirts that still entangled and imprisoned her, and the rider's advancement was too quick. She barely had time to scream for help before the man jumped from his galloping horse and was upon her. When he knelt over and touched her, instinctively she began kicking her legs, trying to scratch his face.

But the man quickly subdued her by pinning her arms behind her back. With her flailing limbs contained, the man leaned down to kiss her. But it was not the brutal kiss of a thug; there was something tender and passionate about the lips that moved over hers. In astonishment, she pushed the man away, and as she did she looked up into Orazio's face.

"Are you all right?" he asked worriedly. "I was following you and saw you fall from that blasted contraption."

He pulled up her skirts and examined her legs. "It appears you haven't suffered severe injury."

"You were following me? For how long?"

"Since you left the piazza."

She gave him a look of disbelief and he laughed and kissed her again. "*Amore mio.* You gave me such a fright!"

"I gave *you* a fright," she said, pushing him away. "The fall nearly scared the life out of me, but hearing you arriving at such a frightful rush put me in my grave for sure."

She sat up, pulled down her skirts, and brushed back her hair, which had come undone. As the winds picked up again, it blew around her face, across her eyes, and into her mouth. She tucked the long strands behind her ears, looked at Orazio, and said, "You came back."

"I told you I would."

He leaned down to kiss her again, but this time she turned her head.

"It is too late," she whispered.

He sighed and placed his forehead on hers. For one brief moment, as Sofonisba breathed in his scent, she let herself believe she was a free woman. She reached up a hand and caressed his curling hair, remembering the feel of him. Once it might have been possible; it had been her greatest desire to spend her life with this man. But then reality crashed back down.

"Yes, it is too late for us," she said with great regret.

"Sofi... it can never be too late for us."

How she yearned to hear those words spoken to her by this man.

"You received my letter?"

"Yes, it was a beautiful drawing. You were an able student."

For a moment she remembered sitting in the palace garden, giving him his first drawing lesson. It hadn't been all that successful as he had interrupted her repeatedly with kisses.

"*Ehi,* Sofi. Look at me now. I told you a long time ago—the moon and Venus, they follow their own paths, but they are destined to meet again and again."

"Yes, but only for a brief time," she reminded him. "That is our destiny too." She disentangled herself from his embrace and attempted to stand. "Here, help me up. I need to get home. The groomsman by now will be wondering where I am."

Obligingly, Orazio stood and pulled her up next to him. She shook out her skirts and started walking in the direction of the villa. If she hurried, she could be there in a quarter of an hour.

"Sofonisba, wait!"

"There is nothing more to discuss, Orazio. You must know by now... I am a married woman. I'm so very sorry... I was a fool to listen to—" Without another word, she faced forward. Resolutely, she put one step in front of the other, trying to put distance between them. If she didn't, she feared what she might do. Orazio, her beloved Orazio, had returned—and he still wanted a future with her.

"Sofi! Wait! *Tesoro...*"

She glanced over her shoulder and saw him grabbing the reins of his horse. Then, with long strides, he caught up to her.

"We can't be together—surely you know that. You must take your horse, ride back to your ship, and sail away from here. I am not the woman I once was—the one you left in Spain. I have my work, responsibilities—I have a husband! What am I supposed to do now that you are here? Runaway with you?"

"Yes!"

This time she stopped and faced him, her mouth agape.

"I've come this far to find you, and I won't let you slip away again."

Tiredly, she said, "I've told you it is too late."

He reached out to her but she stepped away.

"This is not the place for you to be," he said. "Look around you. There is nothing here for you. This island is remote and secluded. You have gifts to share with the world! You were taught by Michelangelo! You painted for a queen. You were born for notoriety. You will die from boredom here..."

"Stop!" She tried to curb her racing emotions. It infuriated her that men wanted to control her every move. Her brother administered her money; the duke had separated them with his twisted idea of love... and now Fabrizio would forever keep them apart. "I need no one! Not you or anybody!"

She sighed, seeing his pained expression. "I told you once, a long time ago, I never wished to marry! All I ever wanted to do was paint. And now here I am chained to Fabrizio, who is twice my age..." With her hands on her hips, she said, "And now here you are—the only man I really *do* love—proclaiming I should abandon my reputation for—"

"So you do love me, a little," he said with a tilt of his head.

"Of course I love you, Orazio!" she cried. "From the first day we met, you entered my heart and there you have stayed. You are the only one I will ever love. When I saw your letter, I was so overjoyed. And yet..."

"There can be nothing more to say. It is simple. I love you, and you love me..."

She shook her head. "You are as blind as he! As I told Alba this afternoon, I am a married woman! Both of you are delusional."

"Alba is here in Sicilia?"

"Yes," she said bitterly. "He is the reason you and I are not together. He was the one who sent you away..."

Her voice trailed off when Orazio's face darkened, and he interjected, "So, it was Alba's intention all along to send me into the English Channel to be apprehended. I took risks when I accepted their offer and money, but I never expected that it would be the duke who would ultimately betray me—and because of him, I lost you."

He shook his head, and more to himself then to her, he said, "Now it all makes sense. As soon as we approached the English coast, it felt like we were sailing into a trap. My guess is it was Alba who planted information that the Spaniards were attempting a plot on the English queen's life because the English descended upon us in droves. We sailed for several weeks, dodging their armada until they caught us and accused me of being an assassin. Then I spent long, tedious days in a stinking, dank English prison waiting to swing from the gallows. There wasn't a trial..."

"You were captured and almost hung?" Sofonisba blanched. "Oh, Orazio! I didn't know. So, you *are* a spy after all!"

"As you were an informant for Elisabeth!" His words hung in the air as he waited for her to challenge him, but under his intense scrutiny, she looked away.

"Do you deny it?"

She said nothing at first, but when he looked at her with one brow raised, she finally shrugged her shoulders, let out an exasperated sigh, and said, "I told you back in Spain, I only gathered silly observations and reported back to the queen... Nothing more than idle court gossip."

He rolled his eyes heavenward and drew in a long calming breath. "Yes, I always knew that. But when Alba came to me wanting to engage my crew and my vessel, he led me to believe, where you were concerned, a more sinister plot was afoot. He told me Don Carlos had given him substantial evidence that would condemn you for treason for passing false information to the crown. He said if I were to perform this one special mission for Philip—that of making a foray into English waters to pick up one of his couriers—the duke would see to it that you wouldn't be implicated. He—"

"He lied! Alba would never listen to Don Carlos nor act on his allegations. There was no love lost between those two... Besides, you of all people knew how crazy Don Carlos was! I told you countless stories of his bizarre antics. So, how could you have believed Alba's concocted story or that he'd take the word of the prince as accurate?"

"I know that now... but at the time, although I believed you'd never been involved in something so dangerous, I still feared for you. The Spanish court is a viper's nest, and I was prepared to do anything to keep you out of trouble and away from Don Carlos and the lot of them. Before I could do that, I needed more money, and Alba was compelling in his arguments. Despite his fondness for you, he made sure I knew his loyalties lay with Philip. He also told me he was aware of our relationship—had even overheard us in the gardens. He suggested if I didn't agree to help the crown, he'd expose us, implying your reputation at court would be ruined."

She shuddered at the thought of Alba lurking in the shadows, observing them. "So he blackmailed you?" Sofonisba shook her head in disbelief. "After you went away and there was no word, I thought you had abandoned me... then Alba told me that he and Philip believed you'd been killed by the corsairs along the African coast. It corroborated the story you'd told me..."

"Of course he would be quick to tell you that I was dead," said Orazio. "I suppose it served his ultimate purpose."

"So, you didn't sail to Africa to acquire spices as you told me—"

"I told you that fib because I didn't want to alarm you."

She scoffed. "So instead of being beheaded by corsairs, you sailed in the opposite direction—into waters just as dangerous—where you were apprehended—"

"Yes, as we sailed along the coast near Falmouth, we were boarded. The English purloined the goods in the hull, then dragged me off the ship and threw me into the waterfront maritime prison to await hanging."

"And your ship and crew? What happened to them?"

"They seized the ship and towed it into the harbor where they kept the crew aboard, but under house arrest."

"But how did you escape?"

"It was Khidr Aruj who organized the raid. In the dead of night, he set off the cannon aboard the ship. It didn't take long before the buildings and prison along the shore were ablaze. As the walls caved in, I found my way out and down to the docks. It was a welcome sight to behold *The Sofonisba* with her sails out. I wasted no time and dove into the water and swam to the ship. Once aboard, we set course for Spain."

"And I was not there when you returned."

"They told me you married Fabrizio Pignatelli."

"It wasn't by choice," Sofonisba said. "The queen ordered it. She told Philip if anything should happen to her, I was to be protected. Elisabeth knew what Alba had done... She tried to tell me at the very end. Philip was only carrying out her dying wish." She was quiet, then added, "It was such a confusing time."

Orazio listened pensively as she recounted the climatic events that occurred after his departure—the death of Don Carlos, the queen, and the infanta's birth.

"You were gone, and I had no word from you. I had no way of knowing if I'd ever see you again. I was filled with so many doubts. There was my future to think of, my painting career... and—"

Interrupting her, he said incredulously, "But surely you knew I'd return."

She shook her head. "Alba told me you were dead. Anyway, when no word came, how could I know you weren't truly a pirate or a spy or..."

"Or what?" he retorted.

"Or that the sea called to you again, and instead of returning to me, you had heeded Circe's call."

"Oh, Sofonisba! Don't you know by now you are the only siren in my life, and it is you and only you who I now hear calling my name."

When she said nothing, he gazed out over the horizon and said harshly, "I'm done with them all! Never again! I thought the heavy purse that Spanish bastard offered me would be enough to begin our new life together. In the beginning, Porsena's gold brought us together, and in the end it was the Devil's gold that separated us."

Sofonisba eyed him suspiciously. "Porsena's gold? You found it the night we met?"

Now it was his turn to say nothing.

"And you used stolen Etruscan bronzes and gold coins to purchase your ship?"

"Who did it really belong to?"

"Not to you!" she said. "You could have..."

"I only found a small part of it. If you had found a small treasure, a trinket would you have given it back... and if so, to whom?"

"I certainly..." She fumbled to a stop, remembering the small bronze ship she had found in the dust and pocketed. Shaking her head, she thought, *It's not the same thing.*

"After weeks of scouring the hills around Chiusi, I found such a small amount for all my troubles. So, in answer to your question, no, I didn't purchase my ship solely on the pilfered gold of Porsena. I used the gold I won that night at the gaming tables."

"Money you won by cheating!" she exclaimed.

"If you are keeping score, go ahead and add it to my list of sins; for now, I'm paying three-fold for all my crimes—gambling, stealing, and spying." Reaching for her hand, he said, "I know I've made my mistakes... but the biggest one was leaving you in Spain."

When she kept her eyes averted, he turned her face gently to his with his strong brown fingers and urged, "Life is filled with false steps and new beginnings. Surely you know that. But now it is our time... Come away with me. We can set sail tonight."

She studied him for a moment, part of her yearning to forgive him everything, walk into his arms, and never look back. But another part said she was a fool to do so.

She took a step back and said firmly, "I can't. You must board your ship and leave me here. Perhaps we have all been cursed by disturbing the fortunes of a sleeping king. And now the fates have had their say. Our timing is wrong... It was a beautiful, brief reunion, but now we must part again."

"I will not lose you. I'd move heaven and earth to change things... disrupt the alignment of the stars to have you with me forever. I'd even kill a man..."

"Stop." She reached up and placed her hand over his mouth. "Don't say such things. This is out of our hands."

"Sofonisba, you can't mean this. You know I'd choose you a thousand times..."

"Why?" she asked.

He shook his head in disbelief. "Because you, Sofonisba Anguissola, you are worth every ounce of effort I have put forth to conquer your heart. We are fated by the stars to be together."

"Orazio," she said, "that was a beautiful dream we had in Madrid. But now things are so different. They are..."

"They are what? Tell me. Together we can figure this out."

"They are just too complicated."

"What could be too complicated... What obstacle can't we overcome?"

"I am married now."

When he only shook his head as if it were an infinitesimal problem, she skimmed her hands over her expanding waist and said a little desperately, "I'm with child... *your* child!"

A flash of joy crossed his face but was extinguished by her next words.

"Fabrizio believes the babe is his... and that is how it must remain. The king has provided me with a dowry. I am free to paint... and our baby will be provided for."

Sorrowfully, she touched his stunned face with her slim fingers, then kissed him one last time. Without another word, she turned and hurried down the path, returning to her husband's villa, all the while breathing in the scent of regret and blood-red oranges.

Chapter 32

Passion Fruit

Sofonisba stood by the window in her chamber and gazed out into the night. All was calm, and there was a breeze that blew in from the sea. Even from her room, she could hear the faint crashing of waves, and in the distance she could see the tall mast and white sails of *The Sofonisba* gently rocking in the port far below.

She thought of her ship captain and wondered if he too paced in the dark, thinking of her. Sofonisba had told him to depart the day they met on the road but now, three days later, he remained—and a small part of her was glad to see his ship was still there. Somehow it comforted her.

When she heard a soft knock on her bedroom door, she sighed, quickly lit a candle, and invited Fabrizio to enter.

"There you are, my dear! I hope I'm not disturbing you," Fabrizio said with an appreciative smile. "By the light of the candle, dressed in your nightgown with your hair down around your shoulders, you look like an angel, *mia cara.*"

He moved into the room and stood by her side. Lifting a hand, he gently caressed her midriff. "How is the child tonight? How are you feeling?"

"I'm fine, just a bit tired," she said. "Exhausted, really."

Fabrizio glanced around the room. On a table under the window, he noticed a large bowl of oranges. Next to it lay a letter written in a bold hand.

"What's this?" he asked, picking up the note.

"Oh... a gift from the duke. Oranges from his garden."

"As if we didn't have enough already!" He chuckled. "When did it arrive? Should I be jealous?"

Sofonisba shook her head. "Of course not! The basket was delivered to Cinzia by one of his servants. As you can see in the note, he thanks you for your advice the other day. He writes that he will be returning to Spain at the end of the week."

"Too bad for Cinzia," he said with a gleam in his eye. "She was quite taken with the duke and hoped he'd stay a while longer. Long enough, at least, to secure a dance with him at the Countess Merlini's affair next Saturday."

"In my experience, the duke doesn't dance," said Sofonisba.

"Come," said Fabrizio. "Would you care to dance with me now?"

Reaching for her hand, he drew her to the bed and lifted her up onto the soft mattress. Sofonisba lay back, gazed at the ceiling, and drifted to another time and place. She tried not to shudder as her husband fumbled with her nightdress and raised himself on top of her. As had happened before, the minutes passed slowly as Fabrizio caressed her breasts and rubbed her thighs. But, after several false attempts to become fully aroused, her husband rolled from her with a sigh.

"It has nothing to do with you, my love. You are enough to awaken any man's desire. The will is there, but I fear I've had one too many glasses of port this evening."

"No matter," she murmured. "The meal was heavy, and in this heat..." It was becoming a tedious task to play the adoring wife, especially when she thought of another.

Rising from the bed, Fabrizio gently stroked her cheek and said in chagrin, "I'll take my leave now."

He moved to the door but stopped, noticing the basket of fruit on the table once more. "I may have disappointed you tonight, but how about a sweet morsel?"

Fabrizio picked up a plump orange and began peeling it. Then, holding it up, he said, "Would you like a bite?"

She shook her head. The last thing she wanted tonight was another reminder of Alba. To her, the basket contained tainted fruit.

"Really? Not even one little section?"

"No," she insisted. "You eat it."

"As you wish," said Fabrizio, popping the whole thing into his mouth. The pleasure on his face was evident as he chewed and swallowed. "It is a little bitter," he finally said. "But not intolerable."

"You are a harsh critic, sir," she said, raising an eyebrow.

"I'm a most discerning man, Signora Pignatelli." Then, with a wink, he added, "And... I know how to pick the sweetest fruit."

With a sigh, he added, "Ah... *tesoro*... I know tonight was a disaster, but I want you to know I am quite content with our marriage. You are a dear and patient wife. And Cinzia... well, these past few weeks have been difficult. But I sense she is warming to you. Just today, she told me how much she admires you and your paintings. And now that the child is on the way, how could she not grow to love you?"

Sofonisba shook her head, knowing he was greatly exaggerating Cinzia's affections for her.

Scanning her dubious face, Fabrizio added sympathetically, "Cinzia will come around eventually. You will see." He gave her a fond smile. "Are you sure you wouldn't like a piece of fruit, *mia cara*?"

"Yes, quite sure. In fact, take the whole basket," Sofonisba encouraged.

"I believe I will," said Fabrizio. "It is rather hot out tonight, and this will keep me refreshed."

She lay back in bed against the soft cushions as he crossed the room. Before he opened the door, Fabrizio glanced back and smiled fondly at his wife. "Sweet dreams and sleep well, mia cara *pittrice*."

And that was the last time Sofonisba saw her husband alive.

Chapter 33

Seeds of Suspicion

*F*abrizio was found dead the next day, lying twisted in his sheets. His nightshirt was wrapped around his contorted body as if he had put up a good fight and battled fiercely with the grim reaper who came to take him away. His hair stuck out bizarrely, and there was an expression of disbelief in his eyes. From his mouth, dribbled orange saliva and a crusty foam had collected around his lips.

It was Cinzia who'd discovered him. In the morning, she went to open the blinds and make up his sheets. Considering her father's habit of rising early to walk the plantation to inspect the orange groves and the goats, she expected the room to be empty. What she hadn't anticipated was to see her beloved father in rigor mortis.

Her screams aroused the household, and Sofonisba, who was working in her studios, dropped her brush. As paint splattered on the floor, she quickly turned and followed Cinzia's cries. She arrived at Fabrizio's door, shouldered through the maids and the footmen gathered there, and moved to her husband's side. There she stared down in horror at her husband's wide, staring eyes.

She watched as Fabrizio's manservant stepped forward and gently closed his lids. In disbelief, Sofonisba pulled Cinzia away and wrapped her in her arms. Cinzia, beside herself with grief, allowed herself to be comforted. Then, as if remembering whom she clung too, Cinzia stepped abruptly away, and with venom in her voice, she accused, "You did this!"

"What do you mean? I had nothing—"

"His heart. It was never strong. You did this with your wanton ways and desires to be pleasured. He overexerted himself—and now he is dead!" Without waiting for an answer, the tears coursing down her face,

Cinzia retreated to her room.

Regaining her composure, Sofonisba looked at the gaping faces of the servants. "Call the physician," she ordered. "My husband must be examined."

Dottore Attinori arrived an hour later. After examining the body and noting the yellow foam that pooled onto Fabrizio's pillow, he grimly said, "Signora, your husband has been poisoned."

"Poisoned?"

The doctor looked around the room, and when he saw the basket of oranges, now half gone, he picked one up and examined it. Carefully, he pulled back the rind, passed it under his nose, and flinched at the aroma.

He held the fruit out to her and said, "Look here, the fruit has been injected with belladonna. See this slit... just under the skin?" He picked up another orange and then another. Shaking his head, he said, "They all have been tampered with."

"But how is that possible?" she asked.

"It's not so hard to find nightshade in these parts. Blended in small amounts and with the proper intentions, it can be a remedy. But if not..."

"But who would want to harm Fabrizio?" she demanded. "Who hated him so much they wanted him dead? He is... was... a kind man."

The doctor patted her sleeve in sympathy. "I'm sorry, signora. There was a case like this a few months ago. The Viceroy of Tracania met a similar demise eating tainted meat prepared by his housekeeper. There is much rancor among the peasants, and they are retaliating..."

When Sofonisba let out a distraught sigh, he gently advised, "I don't mean to upset... You should get some rest, signora. Go now. I'll attend to the body."

Sofonisba spent the day in a stupor. By nightfall, when Cinzia hadn't come out of her room, growing concerned, Sofonisba instructed the servants to leave a tray of food at her door. Before turning in for the night, she knocked on Cinzia's door, but on the other side of the panel it was ominously quiet. During the following days, she often passed by and attempted to console Cinzia, but the woman responded in a harsh voice, telling her to go away.

With no one to lean on, Sofonisba wandered the cliff path, trying to make sense of Fabrizio's death. Her husband was dead practically before their marriage had started. She hugged her arms tightly around her body and shivered despite the heat of the late afternoon sun. Absently, she noticed the long shadow she cast over the waving sea grass and wondered who had killed him.

Did a disgruntled hooligan creep into the villa and plant the tainted oranges? Was Fabrizio a victim of the decaying Sicilian feudal system that caused this violent retaliation? Still, this act of poisoning fruit seemed more calculated and strangely personal.

Sofonisba looked out over the sea, and her eye caught sight of a ship in the harbor. She inhaled sharply, and her breath caught in her throat. In a flash, Orazio's words came back to her: "I'd move heaven and earth to change things... I'd even kill a man..."

"No!" she said. "Orazio would never..."

A cloud crossed the sun, and a shadow passed over her heart as she recalled a story he had told her about Khidr Aruj, who used tainted fruit to free himself of an unwanted master.

From his friend, had Orazio learned this trick and had he used it on Fabrizio? Or, perhaps it had been Khidr Aruj, out of his loyalty and sense of duty to his captain, who committed the crime. After all, the Turk swore his allegiance to him.

Sofonisba, mesmerized by the churning sea, watched as the white-capped waves rolled up and onto the shore. Despite these troublesome thoughts, she wasn't ready to condemn Orazio or Khidr Aruj for this crime—at least, not yet.

If not, Orazio, then who? she wondered.

In her mind's eye, she saw Fabrizio's face smiling as he held up the basket of oranges for her inspection. When she had told him they had been a gift from Alba, she recalled him saying: "Should I be jealous?"

Sofonisba's thoughts careened in her head. The duke admitted his love for her but she had rebuked him. She vividly saw the hatred in his eyes. In horror, his words came back to haunt her: "I don't hate you... but I hate the man you are bound to now."

Was Alba the one who had murdered her husband? Or were his bitter words merely those of a man who suffered unrequited love? But Alba was a formidable strategist who eliminated all obstacles in his path not only on the battlefield but also in private life. After all, hadn't he admitted to removing Orazio from her life? And when Don Carlos's body had been recovered, she had been suspicious that Alba had played a more active part in his demise, believing he was protecting her from the prince's ire.

Then Sofonisba remembered a snippet of servant gossip. Hadn't Bibiana once told her the duke's wife had taken her own life after imbibing too much belladonna? It seemed an uncanny coincidence.

Sofonisba wasn't sure which of the players in this dreadful situation wanted Fabrizio dead the most. And then, a new thought struck her. *Perhaps it wasn't a man at all.*

Suddenly the face of Cinzia appeared before her. Ever since her arrival, Fabrizio's daughter had treated her with suspicion and malice. How many times had she seen that hostile expression on her face? Sofonisba had married her father, and now that Cinzia believed she carried his child, had it served to fuel the woman's resentment?

And then there was the bizarre incident that involved the carriage. At the time, Sofonisba believed Cinzia's gesture of offering her the lacy scarf a friendly one, but perhaps it had been a ploy to throw her off guard, to mask a more devious intent. In retrospect, the woman's actions now seemed rather strange... and then she remembered Cinzia feeding the horse a treat before she set off for the villa... and shortly after that, the stallion's violent reaction.

Maybe it wasn't a coincidence but something premeditated... and didn't Cinzia also say that day she wouldn't return home because she had an errand at the apothecary to attend to? Was it a cure she had purchased... or was it something more lethal?

As this idea took root, Sofonisba thought, *Perhaps the tainted fruit really wasn't intended for Fabrizio. Perhaps it was meant for me.*

Chapter 34

The Unbearable Heat

Sofonisba wiped her brow and then wearily put down her brush. She had just a little more to do to complete the portrait of Fabrizio she'd begun shortly after his death, but her progress these days was slow. She lifted her face to feel the sluggish suggestion of air pass into the studio through the open window. Her lids were heavy, and her limbs felt like lead; even her hair seemed to ache. To soothe her parched throat, she picked up an earthenware cup and took a sip of *limonata*.

Tendrils of moist hair clung to her neck. To find further relief, she lifted her mass of dark hair and fanned herself with Asdrubale's most recent letter. As her lids sagged shut, she heard a fly begin to buzz around her head. Idly, she swatted it away with her hand.

It was the heat, she told herself—the damned Sicilian heat of summer that made her so lethargic. She had been warned by her maid, Maria Rosaria, that the day would come when it would be upon them. And now the blazing August sun was doing its best to punish them all. It seemed they moved through the very fires of hell.

"You just aren't used to this kind of weather, milady," Maria Rosaria had said as she set out her mistress's noon meal. "Being a northerner, I'm not surprised our southern climes are difficult to adjust to."

"I've spent many years in Spain..."

"Yes, but here it is different. We are closer to the volcano, and the fires that burn in the center of the Earth. This is the gods' playground, and they like to torture us mere mortals," she said.

Sofonisba dabbed at her neck with a lace handkerchief and studied the painting again. Fabrizio had been a gentle man and she thought it was the least she could do to pay a final tribute to a man whose life had been cut short, perhaps on account of her.

As she gazed dully at the image of her dead husband on the easel before her, Sofonisba thought about his funeral. Fittingly, Fabrizio had been laid to rest in the family crypt on the west hill in Mount Etna's shadow. It was a serene spot with a sea view. His tomb was surrounded by the orange trees he was so fond of. The service had been conducted by Don Antonio, and friends of the family—other prestigious nobles—had dutifully paid their respects. In addition to showing an outpouring of love, each had also demonstrated a healthy amount of concern, fearing Fabrizio's death was a precursor for more violence against the landed nobility.

With no other explanation at hand, and riddled with doubt and suspicions of her own, Sofonisba had not contradicted them.

But still, some lay the blame at her feet. They were suspicious of her being a foreigner from the north—an artist turned charlatan nonetheless. Given the brevity of her marriage and the small amount of money she was due to inherit, rumors quickly spread that Fabrizio's new bride had poisoned him. In the close-knit, gentrified society, it didn't take long for her neighbors to look at her askance.

Sofonisba had been all too aware of the gossip, yet she'd stood amongst them assuming her part as the tragic young widow. When the priest had concluded the ceremony in the family's chapel, cut short by the heat, she'd followed along with the others trailing behind the cart that carried Fabrizio's body to the Pignatelli crypt.

As the priest intoned words about death and salvation over her husband's coffin, she'd let her mind wander and thought instead about her father and mother whose funerals she had never attended. She'd gazed unseeingly at the crosses and small mausoleums that decked the hillside filled with her husband's relatives' remains. It had seemed ironic, to be mourning a man she didn't love but hadn't been allowed home to mourn her own beloved parents. A tear had rolled down her cheek, and she'd taken a calm, steadying breath. As she did, she'd inhaled the scent of fresh dirt, wild sage, and always, always the scent of oranges.

Today, however, as Sofonisba picked up a rag and began cleaning her brush, she inhaled the aroma of fresh oil paint and turpentine. Momentarily she was revived and brought back to her senses. Still, her limbs felt so heavy, and she was so weary. She had thought that returning to her studio the day after the funeral would bring her solace and revive her, but now she was too tired to continue work on Fabrizio's painting. So, instead, she let her eyes flutter shut, and images of those who had attended floated behind her closed lids.

Cinzia had been there, of course. Shrouded in black with her face covered by a thick lace veil, she'd been a menacing presence. Throughout the entire day, she'd perfectly played out the role of the distraught and bereaved daughter, wronged by her evil step-mother. Cinzia had even gone so far as to distance herself far away from Sofonisba, casting scathing looks at Fabrizio's widow. Her performance had not gone unnoticed by the public and had only served to fuel the gossips.

Despite her harsh ways, Sofonisba couldn't help but feel sorry for the woman. She knew Cinzia's grief was real, and it pained Sofonisba that since they'd found Fabrizio's dead body they hadn't talked or comforted one another. It was only through the servants they communicated the necessary information to keep the house running smoothly. Once again, Sofonisba sighed tiredly. She knew she needed to rally her strength and reach out to Cinzia to let her know that she wanted no part of Fabrizio's fortune and that after the mourning period she'd take her leave of the Pignatelli household.

Sofonisba walked to the window and gazed out in the direction of the sea. Yesterday had been an exhausting day due to Cinzia's antics and also by the presence of Alba. She hadn't expected him to make an appearance at the funeral, and it was only toward the end of the ceremony she had noticed him. Just as the priest had begun to intone his final prayer, she'd looked around at the small crowd gathered in front of the small mausoleum, and out of the corner of her eye, she'd caught sight of his drab black coat and shiny black boots. She hadn't deigned to look him in the face or acknowledge him directly. Infact she'd thought it hypocritical that he should stand among the others, paying his respects as if he genuinely admired the man.

Still, she'd marveled at the duke's tenacity. When he'd learned the news of Fabrizio, he'd postponed his plans to return to Spain. Then, with her husband barely cold, he had come to her and had tried to plead his case again. However, whatever guilt he felt or feelings of love he wished to express, once again, she wanted no part of him. Feeling faint and unwell, she'd begged him to leave, calling for Maria Rosaria to see the duke out.

The only person she had acknowledged yesterday had been Orazio. So unlike Alba's dismal attire, it had been Khidr Aruj's colorful garb that had attracted her attention, alerting her to the fact that Orazio was standing next to him. Behind her black veil and fan, she had smiled at them both, feeling a sense of relief. Just knowing Orazio and his friend were present and standing a respectful distance away reassured her and gave her the confidence to endure the rest of the sad proceedings.

In the immediate days following Fabrizio's death, Orazio, like the duke, had been persistent in his attempts to contact her. At first, as she had done with Alba, she had kept her distance, not allowing Orazio to speak his mind or come too close to her.

Orazio hurt by her cool reception, had pleaded, "Tell me what I can do, *amore mio*. Tell me what you need."

"Don't," she'd admonished.

Not understanding he'd taken a step toward her and said, "Sofi, now Fabrizio is gone, God rest his soul, we can be together..."

She'd only turned away from him, murmuring, "It is too soon... Besides, I'm so confused..."

"Confused by what?"

Warily she eyed him.

"What is it?" he'd demanded grabbing her arm shaking her. "Surely you can't think me capable of..."

With a heavy heart, she'd observed the play of horror and rage on his face, and her shoulders had sagged. In a flat tone, she'd said, "But that day on the road... you said you would move heaven and earth to change things—that you'd kill a man..."

Orazio had only looked at her in disbelief. "It was just a manner of speech... something said impulsively."

"It seems a strange coincidence that Fabrizio died from eating poisoned oranges. Didn't you once tell me Khidr Aruj..."

"Stop!" said Orazio. Never in a thousand days would I kill an innocent man like Fabrizio."

Sofonisba had wanted to believe him. *Is it possible? Did he, indeed, disrupt the alignment of the stars to bring them together?*

Even as she'd thought this, she'd tiredly told herself it didn't matter. If Orazio had a hand in this crime, she loved and forgave him—he was the father of her child. If she examined her heart, she knew she would go to great lengths to keep him safe—even lie to protect him. Just as Orazio had risked his life and endured a jail cell for her, she would do the same for him.

Does this make me a wicked woman? she'd asked herself.

She searched Orazio's face, looking for signs of the truth, and under her intense scrutiny, he hadn't shirked or turned away. Instead, he'd met her gaze directly, and finally, she saw what she'd needed to see.

Yes, she had thought, relieved, *I am ready to trust him again.*

As the accusations left her, she had let Orazio pull her into his embrace. There she'd rested against his strong shoulder and felt she had come into a safe harbor. Free of doubt, they'd began to plan their future in whispered words—where they would go and what they would call the babe.

"This child will be strong and talented, like its mother," Orazio had said.

"With a spirit of adventure, like its father," Sofonisba had added. "If she is a girl, we shall call her Elisabeth..."

"And if a boy?"

Smiling, in unison, they'd pronounced the name: Porsena.

It seemed only fitting, the wise and benevolent king who brought them together that magical night so long ago should continue to bring them good fortune.

For propriety's sake, Sofonisba had told Orazio to keep a safe distance, and after a respectful period of mourning, they would marry. To this end, Sofonisba had immediately wrote a letter to Asdrubale to tell him of her husband's death and her plans to wed Orazio.

She'd expected a favorable reply but instead had received the letter she now used to angrily fan her face. Plopping into a chair, Sofonisba fumed at her brother's audacity. Although by now she knew the contents by heart, Sofonisba unfolded it and bitterly read his letter again.

If you think for one moment, sister, that I will approve of your marrying Orazio Lomellino, you are much mistaken. I will not squander the Anguissola fortune on a ner'er-do-well sea captain. I've done some investigating. The man spent time in an English prison! He is a convict and a criminal. I'm sure you think you are in love with the man... but he will only bring you pain and misery. No, you must return to Cremona. I will arrange a suitable marriage for you once you are home.

Sofonisba's eyelids drooped once more as she swatted away the annoying fly. Her body felt swollen, and the heaviness was too much to bear. She needed to think... but couldn't form a logical thought. She needed to speak with Orazio.

Where is he? she thought angrily. *Why isn't he here with me... Where has he gone?*

She wiped her forehead and sat listlessly, looking up at the ceiling. *It is this damned unbearable heat of Sicilia that is making me feel so lightheaded, confused, and irritable.*

Parched and seeking relief, blearily Sofonisba reached for the earthenware jug and poured out another dose of *limonata* into her cup and drank down the sour, tepid contents.

Chapter 35

The Night of Sant'Agata

"*W*ill you attend the festivities in town tonight, signora?" asked Maria Rosaria, helping her mistress to dress.

Listlessly, Sofonisba raised her arms and allowed her maid to pull her dress down over her torso and plump out her skirts over the stiff crinolines.

"I intended to," Sofonisba said with a yawn, looking longingly at the bed. It was so inviting, even though it was only six o'clock in the evening. She wanted to lie upon the fresh, crisp sheets and give in to sleep. The achiness she had felt for days seemed to have invaded her every pore—her legs were stiff and her arms were too heavy to bear.

She laid a hand to her midriff, and when she did, a frown crossed her face. How it had thrilled her to feel the first quickening sensations of her unborn child. But, recently, she hadn't felt any little punches or kicks, indicating life was growing inside her. The lack of movement was beginning to concern her.

When Sofonisba let out a little sigh of distress, Maria Rosaria said, "Don't worry, milady... the wee one is just sleeping... Come, let me brush out your hair. Then I will fix it up high on your head, in a style that will keep you cool."

Sofonisba obeyed her and sat down in front of her mirror and let her maid comb out her long hair. She watched as Maria Rosaria wound it around her head, creating the effect of a crown. When she finished, Sofonisba rummaged around her jewelry box and pulled out a medallion fastened to a chain. It was Orazio's gold Etruscan coin she had made into a necklace. "Here," she prompted Maria Rosaria, "help me with this. My fingers are too swollen to work the clasp."

The maid took the chain and draped it around Sofonisba's neck and secured it. Then she placed her hands lightly on her mistress's shoulders. "You are beautiful, signora... especially with your hair done up so." Maria Rosaria handed her a mirror and asked, "What do you think?"

Sofonisba took the glass and examined herself, then leaned forward and began pinching her cheeks. "You've done a good job, Maria Rosaria. You've made me look... almost passable."

"You are just a little pale. It is to be understandable. The mourning period can be draining... and when one is with a child, it is only normal."

Hearing a knock on the door, they looked at one another knowingly. The only person it could possibly be was Cinzia. Maria Rosaria rapidly tidied up the dressing table, then moved to answer the door. When she opened it, both women saw Fabrizio's daughter dressed in black, holding a tray with a pitcher, glasses, and a small vase containing a few purple bougainvillea sprigs.

The maid departed and Cinzia moved into the room. "I bring you some refreshment..."

Sofonisba smiled at the kind gesture, marveling at Cinzia's recently changed demeanor. It had been a surprise when Cinzia broke her frigid silence a few days after Fabrizio's funeral and had made the first move toward reconciliation. It seemed, during a long night of sorrow and anguish, her beloved departed parents had visited her, and in as dream, her elders had encouraged her to show more compassion to Fabrizio's widow.

To Sofonisba, it seemed a little strange; still, she was happy for the divine intervention—once again, it was typical of Fabrizio to have the last say. In light of the Cinzia's tearful apologies, which seemed to ring true, the doubts Sofonisba had once entertained concerning her odd conduct or plots she might have been hatching began to evaporate. In retrospect, she reasoned that it was grief that drove Cinzia's actions and unkind words. Certainly, the woman wasn't capable of harming a person. Furthermore, Sofonisba didn't think she had neither creativity nor the imagination for such elaborate machinations.

During their heart-felt talk, Sofonisba had confessed the child she carried was not Fabrizio's. Cinzia had regarded her thoughtfully but seemed to accept this revelation gracefully. And when Sofonisba told Cinzia she intended to leave Sicily soon, it appeared the woman's chilly demeanor toward her warmed another few degrees. Biding her time until Sofonisba left, and as if to apologize for her previous unpleasant behavior, Cinzia began to show Sofonisba small kindnesses, bringing her refreshments and small gifts like the bougainvillea bouquet on the tray before her.

"Thank you," said Sofonisba. "The flowers are beautiful."

"They are from the trellis right below your window. My father planted them for my dear mamma."

Cinzia poured out a glass of *limonata* and came to stand behind Sofonisba. As they peered into the mirror, Cinzia said, "My! How pale you look tonight!"

"It's nothing really," said Sofonisba tiredly. "I'm just—"

"Here drink this," she urged handing her the glass. "It will make you feel better.

Gratefully, Sofonisba accepted it and took a small sip, then hesitated. In her condition, things just weren't tasting quite the same. She had come to enjoy Cinzia's *limonata*, but lately it seemed more bitter than ever. Shakily, she set the glass down. However, Cinzia picked it up again and exclaimed, "Go on, finish all of it. It will do you good."

Sofonisba did as she was bid and then looked over at Cinzia and saw her satisfied smile. "Now what you need is a breath of fresh air! I've arranged for the hansom to take us into town. You don't want to miss the festival. You will be revived by the music and—"

"Oh, I thought I could earlier... but now... my head is so dizzy and..."

"Nonsense! The drive will be so delightful, and it is sure to restore you... and along the cliff road, there is a beautiful view. Tonight there should be a marvelous sunset."

Without waiting for an answer, Cinzia helped Sofonisba out of her chair. She conducted her down the stairs, out the door, and into the waiting carriage.

Perhaps Cinzia was right, thought Sofonisba, settling back and feeling the refreshing breeze on her face. With her head lolling back on the cushion, she gazed up at the inky blue night sky, watching the last traces of the sun's rays descend into the ocean. Blinking to bring things into focus, she saw the moon cresting over Etna's western slope.

Her vision blurred, and she was disoriented by the dark clouds that scuttled past the mountainside. She heard the crashing of waves from the sea, and it seemed nature's forces were conspiring together, ebbing and flowing in a frantic dance growing louder and louder.

She must have drifted to sleep but was awakened by Cinzia, who gently nudged her arm. Opening her eyes, Sofonisba saw they were now in the center of town. She could hear loud guitar music and was mesmerized by the weirdly flickering torches that lined the streets. There were halos around everything, making the scene ethereal.

The vehicle continued rolling down the smooth stone streets, entering a more crowded part of town. Sofonisba tried to focus her vision but could only vaguely make out the mass of people milling about. Squinting, she saw some were dancing to the frenzied beat and others were singing. As they entered the piazza, the noise became louder—people shouting, horns blaring, horses braying. All around her was a kaleidoscope of colors, flowers, and fireworks—and looming large, passing by her, was a flotilla of men carrying the statue of Sant'Agata. As she watched, it seemed the saint grew in size until it towered above her.

It was all too much. The images blurred together in an unintelligible smear, and there was a terrible buzzing sound in her ears. Suddenly, Sofonisba felt her face grow hot and she gripped her stomach. "Stop the carriage!"

Looking wildly at Cinzia, she wailed, "I'm going to be sick. Oh, not here! What am I to do?"

Cinzia called out to the driver to take them to the church steps just a few yards away. As the conveyance slowed and came to a stop, Sofonisba grasped onto Cinzia's arm for comfort, but her face seemed so far away and her words were indistinguishable.

Dizzily, Sofonisba put a hand to her head. "We must go back."

"You just need to take a deep breath," Cinzia said gently. Pulling out a flask from her purse, she offered it to Sofonisba. "Here, take a sip... It will calm your nerves."

Eagerly Sofonisba took the small silver container and raised it to her parched lips. Her tongue felt thick as if it were wrapped in cotton. As the warm liquid filled her mouth and glided down her throat, she felt a little better. But, after she swallowed, she detected a familiar bitter taste.

Suddenly a tremendous boom reverberated through the air, followed by a flash of light. Hearing the explosion, the startled horses began to clip-clop in restless agitation.

Sofonisba felt beads of perspiration drip down her brow and handed back the flask. "What was that?" Before Cinzia could reply, Sofonisba doubled over again, gripped by another terrible spasm.

"Here, let me help you down," said Cinzia. Then giving orders to the driver, she instructed, "Pull the carriage forward and wait for us around the corner."

Sofonisba allowed the woman to take her arm and assist her from the gig. Still dizzy, Sofonisba stood for a moment on the firm marble stone outside the church, trying to maintain her equilibrium. Hesitantly she took a step forward, but as she did, her legs buckled and she stumbled. It felt as if she were stepping into oozing mud. At first, she thought it was the queasiness that made her unstable, but then she saw Cinzia also struggling to keep her balance.

From across the piazza, people began to scream. "*Oh, Dio! Un terremoto!* It's an earthquake! Etna has erupted!"

Like a ship in choppy water, the earth fluctuated, and people in the piazza huddled together in a frightened, tangled mob.

"Come!" cried Cinzia. "Don't be afraid. It won't last long. It is nothing I haven't felt before. You will be more comfortable inside the church. It is cooler in there..."

"But isn't it dangerous to go inside? Shouldn't we stay in the piazza?"

"You will be safe, trust me. All this will be over in a minute..."

Cinzia guided Sofonisba into the church, where she helped her lie down on one of the pews. But in a prone position, Sofonisba's head began to throb again, and her belly twisted in pain. The smoke from the flickering candles and the heady scent of incense filled her nostrils and made her stomach roil. Sitting up suddenly, she leaned over the bench and vomited onto the floor.

Sofonisba wiped a hand across her mouth, then whispered, "I'm so sorry."

But, instead of a comforting response, the kind woman she had come to know over the past few days—the one who gave her flowers—vanished and the old Cinzia emerged and responded. "You are disgusting, you miserable woman! Disgracing yourself inside this sanctified space... just as you disgraced yourself by marrying my father, knowing you carried a bastard son."

Cinzia clamped Sofonisba's face with her free hand, and with the other, she pressed the silver container to her lips. "I knew all along you were no good for him. After you arrived, I feared you might bear his child and did my best to prevent it..."

"What? What did you do?"

"I know my medicines. I learned from my mother..." She laughed harshly. "Then, when the duke arrived, I believed otherwise. That a child already grew in your womb. You might have fooled my father, but I can't be so easily duped. And then you went and confessed to me. How I hated you... But still, I smiled knowing, in the end, you would get what you deserve."

Once again, Cinzia pressed the flask to Sofonisba's mouth, but this time she was unsuccessful. Not deterred, Cinzia grunted. "Stop fighting me. What's done is done... and now it must be finished."

"What have you done?" whimpered Sofonisba.

When another wave of nausea rolled over her, she gripped her stomach. "What have you given me? How could you harm an unborn child? What kind of monster are you?"

"This is all your fault," Cinzia said. "You brought this upon yourself.

First, you lied to my father—then you murdered him!"

"I didn't kill your father."

"You might as well have," Cinzia said bitterly. "He wasn't supposed to eat those oranges... They were meant for you! Now he is dead..."

Another new tidal wave hit Sofonisba, but this time it wasn't a spasm of nausea but a seismic undulation that caused the church's floor to oscillate. The rumbling vibrations came again and again. And with each new onslaught, the wooden statues in their niches rocked back and forth and finally toppled over. In the high altar, the rows of candelabras rolled crazily from side to side until they finally upended and fell with a crash to the floor.

To Sofonisba, it seemed a hundred candles were glowing all around her. Desperately, she pushed them away to keep them from igniting her skirts. She heard Cinzia cry out, and saw her lose her balance and pitch sideways. In a fog, Sofonisba listened to the silver flask clatter and skitter toward her. With tremendous effort, she reached for it and tucked it into the pocket of her skirt.

Cinzia righted herself and stood above Sofonisba, scanning the floor, searching for the container she had dropped. But when another rolling wave struck, bending the stone floor like malleable clay—causing the stained-glass windows to shatter and rain down colorful shards around them—she screamed and ran toward the door.

Sofonisba tried to stand up but her body was too heavy. Staying low to the ground, she began crawling. But when another spasm rocked the ground, she heard a mighty ripping sound, and a beam fell from the ceiling and hit the ground with a tremendous crash. It barely missed crushing her, but still it pinned her skirts in place. Unable to move, she softly mewed, "Cinzia, for God's sake, where are you? Please help me..."

But there was no response.

Had Cinzia fallen too and been knocked out? Or had she made her escape, leaving her to perish in the crumbling church?

She attempted to muster her strength and move forward over the debris and glass-strewn floor. But it was useless; the heavy beam entrapped her completely. Too tired to inch her way any farther, Sofonisba rested her cheek on the stone pavement. From behind closed lids, she saw a blue light. It felt so cool... so very cool, just resting there. It was almost peaceful now that the floor had stopped moving. Perhaps it was better just to lie there and wait for help.

But suddenly the color changed to orange, and she felt a rising heat consume her. It was so hot... so very hot now. She inhaled the stench of acrid smoke and started to cough. Opening one eye, she tried to locate Cinzia but instead saw the statue of Sant'Agata was ablaze, and next to her, as if he cried sorrowful tears, a waxen figure of Christ began to melt.

As the smoke engulfed her senses, she slipped into a misty void. All at once, she felt lighter than air, and she was walking along the cliff wall overlooking the sea. Strangely, although she was propelled forward, her feet didn't touch the ground. Following the path that Fabrizio had built, she found herself at the farthest rocky point. As she fingered the ruby pendant her husband had given her, she looked out over the ocean and saw a ship, its sails untethered and blowing in the wind. With all her heart, Sofonisba longed to be aboard the vessel.

She heard her name, paused, and glanced back. She recognized that voice... It was Orazio's, she thought dreamily. How I've missed him. But then she realized she was terribly angry with him.

Why am I so angry with Orazio? she wondered. As hard as she tried, her muddled mind refused to give her the answer. She forced herself to think. Then it came to her. Orazio promised me he would return... then he lost his way... but now he is here again! He has come back as he said he would. This time we will be together... Finally, the timing is right.

Sofonisba opened her mouth and urged him to hurry, but the words wouldn't come. Frustrated, she tried again, silently screaming his name. Then, feeling a touch on her arm, she sighed contentedly as he pulled her into his arms. Yes! It is him. He has found me.

Her eyes fluttered open, but instead of Orazio's face, she saw the hulking form of a man in a black cloak like an overbearing crow. She cringed in horror and moaned, trying to back away. But the figure kept advancing. She slipped and fell into a swirling dark mist that threatened to consume her.

To her horror, the giant black bird dissolved, and in its place she saw Don Carlos looming over her, holding a gun. When she heard the sharp report of a revolver, she winced and convulsed and felt the pain of the bullet piercing her stomach.

Moaning, she stumbled and fell onto the cold stone floor. Above her, the statue of Christ shed more hot waxy tears upon her. And then there was another explosion, and all around her were dazzling gold sparks. She laughed delightedly as the glimmers of light turned into gold coins— coins of an Etruscan king—that cascaded from the heavens.

She turned her face upward as the ceiling of the church dissolved, replaced by a canopy of stars that glimmered around her. And glowing ever so brightly was the moon that eclipsed her senses, calling her nearer. She let herself be carried upward on a riptide into the heavens, not minding the slightest she was leaving this earth. She felt buoyant and light—like a gossamer veil that floated on the air.

But becoming aware of a cool breeze upon her face, she hesitated. Suddenly her body felt heavy, as if she were weighted by a necklace made of lead beads. She hovered for a moment in indecision. She was just about to touch the heavens but something called her back. After a moment, she reluctantly let go of a small child's hand and bid him farewell. As he continued his upward journey, she slowly descended back to Earth.

As she floated swiftly downward, it was funny, but she didn't fear the fall. She knew she was protected and cradled in a warm and secure embrace. A fresh sea breeze fanned her face, and with great effort she forced her eyes open. This time she was rewarded. Above her, his face covered with grime and soot, was Orazio. Smiling at her, he appeared an avenging angel with the flames of the burning cathedral forming a halo around his head.

"Sofonisba. I'm here, just as I promised."

"I've been waiting for you. I knew you'd come," Sofonisba whispered.

She let her head fall onto his shoulder and sank back into a deep, dark sleep.

Chapter 36

Setting Sail

*A*s she gradually came back to her senses, Sofonisba felt a gentle rocking motion. She lay on her back and gave into the rhythmic swaying. She tried to lift her arms, but they still felt heavy and leaden. For an instant, she wished to be floating again—rising effortlessly, free of the world's weary burdens. She longed to be traveling toward heaven, to see and touch the face of her mother and father... and all the angels in heaven.

But, once again, something called her back. She strained her ears and heard a man's voice begin to sing:

> *Like the gently rocking waves*
> *your arms are a perfect place*
> *to which I'd return and stay forever.*
> *Restore, restore my heart again*
> *with your fair and lovely eyes.*

In her sleep, she stirred. It was a familiar voice singing of love and devotion. Drifting back toward the sound, she opened her lips and implored, "Don't leave me."

"Never again for the rest of my days."

She relaxed into the song and drifted in a misty realm of blue... but sensing the warm sun on her eyelids, she knew it was time to return again. Feeling a hand caress her brow, she blinked with great effort and once again saw Orazio smiling down at her.

Sofonisba let her gaze roam around the room, confused by the surroundings. "Where am I?"

"You are right where you are meant to be, Sofi."

"And where is that?" she whispered.

"In the captain's quarters, *amore mio*. We are on *The Sofonisba* and have set sail for the mainland."

"So I've been kidnapped by a pirate?" she said in a teasing tone. "Will you next be making me walk the plank with my eyes blindfolded as sharks swim about in the sea below me?"

He looked into her eyes and said, "Hearing your quips does my heart good. You know you are far too precious a cargo to be tossed overboard." He brushed a kiss over her forehead and he whispered, "Besides, you and only you possess the key to my heart."

As he continued to caress her cheek, she let out a small sigh. "It is welcome news I have surpassed Circe and have conquered your heart once and for all... for I've made a rather momentous decision."

"Ah, yes," he said. "What have you decided, my love?"

She turned her cheek into his palm and said, "I go willingly with you, my wicked captain. I believe I'd like to spend a lifetime with you as every day together will be a new adventure."

"This is quite a decision! I couldn't be happier... For a minute there, I thought you wanted to return to shore," Orazio said. "But let me assure you, this time I'd never have agreed to let you go." He leaned down and kissed her gently on the lips. "For me, you are the beginning of everything. We will make a life together. I'll even give up the sea..."

"Hush," she said, raising a finger to his lips. "Just as you'd never ask me to give up painting, I will never ask you to give up sailing." She smiled at him. "Now, lift me up, captain, so that I might see your magnificent ocean. I need to see the horizon so we may start dreaming again."

"All right," he said. "Your wish is my command."

Gently he scooped her into his arms—blankets and all—and carried her to the bay window. To make her more comfortable, he propped a pillow behind her head. Then, after he settled beside her, they looked out over the water. Together they listened to the gently lapping waves and observed the silvery-white moon disappear into the morning mists. After a few more minutes, the sun appeared and began to arc into the sky, creating a shimmering gold path that led straight to the sea's edge.

"Where are we headed?" she finally asked.

"We are bound for Genova."

"Genova! How wonderful. I've never been there before." She nestled closer against him, feeling his strong arms around her. "Tell me what happened last night. Things are still a bit blurry. The last thing I recall, I was with Cinzia and..." She rubbed her temple. "I felt so strange... and then the ground began to shake and we were in a church... and there was fire..."

"There was an earthquake... Etna erupted."

"Of course, that is why the ground swayed beneath our feet..." She tried to sit up, but he gently pushed her back down into the pillow. "Relax, Sofi. You are safe now."

Suddenly she gripped her stomach and turned to him, her eyes enormous. "The babe!"

When he said nothing, she rolled away and lay back against the cushion, knowing instinctively she had lost it.

"*Ehi*... careful. Don't move too quickly. The doctor gave you an antidote for the poison. He says you will be a little groggy for a few days." Tenderly, he tucked back a lock of hair. "I'm so sorry, my love. The ship's doctor examined you, but it was too late to save the wee one. He did what he could, but the mixture you were given was too strong."

"What...?" she whispered as a tear slid down her cheek.

He held up a silver flask. "I found this in your pocket. It is filled with tainted water... Cinzia made you drink this, yes?"

Slowly Sofonisba nodded. "Just when I started to trust her again... but she was lying to me all along, wasn't she? All the kind gestures... the scarf, the flowers... the candies and *limonatas*..."

Orazio shook his head sadly. "According to the ship's doctor, it seems by introducing small amounts of the nightshade into your food and drink, she thought it would go undetected and you would eventually succumb to a mysterious malaise..."

Sofonisba recalled Cinzia's words and said, "She admitted to me last night it was by her own hand she killed her father. The fruit Fabrizio ate was intended for me."

Orazio caressed her brow. "Yes, it is such a tragedy. One orange would have made you or anyone else nauseous—but eating too many, well, it was simply too much for old Fabrizio to handle. It was Alba who told me this. He..."

"Alba? What has Alba to do with any of this?"

Orazio took a deep breath. "That you are here with me now has much to do with Alba. We spoke..."

She shook her head in confusion. "Why would Alba speak with you? He despises you! He is the one who sent you away...."

"Whatever he did in the past, the man cares deeply for you. He thought only of your protection. After the funeral, for whatever reasons, Alba's suspicions were aroused. He discovered Cinzia had bought a good amount of *belladonna*, and other medicinal herbs as well, needed to rid a woman of a child. The chemist said she also purchased arsenic to render a man impotent. If you were not with child, she wanted to make sure Fabrizio wouldn't father one in the future. That combined with the poisoned fruit... well..."

Sofonisba sighed. It seemed Cinzia's interference in all their lives had taken a heavy toll. Oh, sweet Fabrizio and his fumbling attempts to sire a child. It hadn't been old age or for want of trying—but from an elixir his loving daughter had poured into his wine.

"Poor Cinzia," Sofonisba whispered. "What a great corrosion of the heart to be so jealous of another. I pity her. But last night... where was she taking me?"

"It's all a bit unclear. There were rumors fanned by Cinzia that you were responsible for Fabrizio's death. Perhaps, after feeding you the last bit of nightshade, she intended to leave you in the church to die... making it look like you committed suicide out of remorse for murdering Fabrizio. Or perhaps, on the way home, she intended for you to have another carriage accident..."

Sofonisba shook her head. As her thoughts drifted from Cinzia to the duke and finally to her lost child, she placed a hand upon her midriff.

Watching her, Orazio said, "*Ehi... amore*, there will be others."

She was quiet. As sure as she had known she'd lost their babe, with equal certainty, Sofonisba knew she would never bear another. Not looking at him, she murmured, "And if I can't have any more children..."

"Shhh," he said, kissing her on the lips." I will always love you. No matter what."

Sofonisba, comforted by his words, entwined her fingers with his and then asked, "But last night... how did you know where to find me?"

"After speaking with Alba, I rode out to the villa, but you weren't there. Maria Rosaria told me you and Cinzia had gone into town to see the festival. Wasting no time, I returned to the city, hoping to encounter you along the road. But there was no sign of the Pignatelli carriage. I arrived in town just after Etna's tremors began and was delayed by the confusion. With all the pandemonium in the piazza, it took a while before I noticed the vehicle with Fabrizio's coat of arms parked around the corner of the church.

Just as I made my way up the steps, the wooden supports of the church gave way. I knew the entire structure was compromised. But what destroyed it ultimately was the fire caused by the overturned candles. The dry wood caught and blew up into a raging inferno. Inside the nave, I could see a shadowy figure of a woman in the dim light. As the flames reached higher, she was illuminated, and I saw it was Cinzia. I called out to her but she ignored my pleas and slipped down the side aisle. At that moment, I didn't care if she perished in the fire. I let her go... My thoughts were only of you. Thank God I found you there on the floor. I got you out in time... but still I feared for you—you were so limp and lifeless."

"And the duke? What has happened to him?"

He shook his head. "I know not where he has gone. But, before I left him last evening, he asked me to give you a message."

Cautiously she waited for him to continue.

"He said for me to take care of you. He said all he ever wanted was for you to be loved and protected. He wishes that you remember him fondly and think of him with humility."

Sofonisba closed her eyes. To the very end, although she had rejected him, Alba had protected her. How hard it must have been to set aside his differences and approach Orazio. But the duke lived his life with such honor, and she was not surprised.

Who can say why one heart chooses another... and why love is not reciprocated. It was a mystery for the ages, one that harked back to Carthage's ancient days and a princess named Sophonisba.

Chapter 37

How the Mighty Fall

*I*n a final letter to Sofonisba that he composed around midnight, Alba poured out his heart and bid a final farewell to the only woman he had ever loved. He had vowed to protect her but in the end failed her completely. Due to selfish motives, Alba had exposed her to a mad king's son, then blackmailed and tricked her sea captain, condemning him to rot in an English prison. His actions had forced her to marry an elderly viscount to live on this god-forsaken island. And now his ultimate failure—she had fallen prey and had nearly been killed by a vengeful woman.

He sighed heavily. It was shortly after Fabrizio's funeral that he finally realized the error of his ways. It had come as a shock to see Orazio standing in the grove of trees a short distance from the other mourners. He hadn't expected to ever see the sea captain again. Covertly, he watched the man observing Sofonisba and saw how she looked back at him. As in Spain, their stolen glances and the palpable affection they felt for one another pierced him to the core, further fueling his jealousy. Not to be bested by the younger man and not convinced the viscount had died at the hands of a disgruntled tenant or servant, he laid the blame entirely at Orazio's feet.

Before the funeral, he'd tried several times to speak to Sofonisba, wanting another chance to plead his case. At first she refused, but when he persisted, she'd agreed to one last meeting. When he entered her painting salon in the Pignatelli villa, he was shocked by the pallor of her skin. But what alarmed him the most were her eyes. Those magnificent eyes that usually sparkled with such clarity had been sunken, dull, and lifeless.

Sofonisba had greeted him listlessly, and after a few moments of banal conversation, before he could even broach the subject that was so dear to his heart, she abruptly excused herself, saying she didn't feel well. She'd called for Maria Rosaria and instructed the girl to show the duke the door.

Alba went, but unwillingly. With a heavy heart, troubled by Sofonisba's appearance, he couldn't help but worry she suffered from something much more than the fatigue of pregnancy and the sorrow of mourning. Before the duke stepped into his carriage, he'd looked back one last time, hoping to see a sign of his protégé. Instead, he saw Fabrizio's daughter staring back at him with great disdain.

In that instant, a suspicion was planted in his mind. Returning to town, Alba began making inquiries among the local tradesman and friends of the Pignatelli family. He soon learned of Cinzia's flagrant dislike of Sofonisba and the rumors and insinuations she was spreading regarding Fabrizio's new fortune-seeking young wife. He also learned of some unorthodox purchases Cinzia had made in town at the local apothecary. An astute man, it hadn't taken Alba long to piece things together and discover who was actually responsible for Fabrizio's death... and who was now threatening the life of Sofonisba.

As the chilling truth about Cinzia's intent crystalized, a new terror gripped the duke's heart—it was because of him, once again, Sofonisba was put into harm's way. He hadn't kept her safe, far from it.

Years ago, Alba had believed if only he could win Sofonisba's love and affection, she would be the one to liberate him of his sins. It had been an entirely selfish pursuit on his part. After tallying his crimes and misdeeds, he knew his soul was too black to expect a woman to absolve him. That was too heavy a burden for anyone, and one only God could shoulder.

He realized with astonishing clarity, to protect her and ensure her future happiness, it was time to step out of the way, right the wrongs he had committed, and reunite the couple he had forced apart. The once-proud general, who rode out of every skirmish a conquering hero, was now laid humble. With honor, he recognized Lomellino as the better soldier and the winner of this battle. The game had finally played out, and Alba had been check-mated. Rather than sacrifice his queen, the only thing left to do was let her go and let the other chess pieces fall away. Sofonisba's place was with her sea captain... and now they had a child to think of.

Of all the things he had recently learned, that was the thing that had finally opened his eyes. With extreme humility, Alba laid aside the loathing and rage he felt for Lomellino and called him to the Spanish Embassy. It had been just last night—on the evening of the festival of Sant'Agata. As the festival participants prepared to celebrate their patron saint, the duke told the younger man everything.

Then concluding in an authoritative voice, Alba said, "You must go now... remove her from the villa and set sail back to the mainland. Take her away from this miserable island..." He shook his head in sorrow. "I tried my best to give her a life of fame and fortune... to keep her safe. It is no longer my place—she is lost to me now. If only..."

Lomellino listened to the duke, the anger visible on his face. "She was never yours to lose, Alba. She never loved you. Why regret what cannot be?" Orazio clenched his jaw. "You, sir, fancied yourself her protector and benefactor... You may have granted her access to the right society but you didn't create her. She is a vibrant woman who thinks for herself. It is through her own hard work and determination she is recognized and succeeds."

Filled with humility and shame, Alba accepted the truth in Orazio's words. Once again, he thought, *How wrong I've been... such a stupid, wretched fool.*

With great fatigue, he concluded his letter and folded it in two. Then, dripping hot wax over the surface, he stamped and sealed it with his ring that bore the emblem of his family's crest. With the matter forever concluded, Alba, with great remorse in his heart, picked up his violin and played one last sweet, melancholy serenade.

After a quarter of an hour, he laid the instrument gently upon the table and ventured into the murky dawn. He knew exactly where he was going and what needed to be done. It was the last thing he did for her, although she had never asked it of him.

And now, as the last evening star faded away, he wandered the sea cliff near the Pignatelli estate. Standing at the farthest point, he faced the ocean, mesmerized by the hues that changed from deep midnight blue to sapphire. The sun had just begun to tinge the morning sky fiery orange, and seagulls were swooping through the air, calling to their mates, creating quite a clamor.

He looked down and saw his boots were dusted with the ash of gray pumice rock. Absently he tried to brush it off to see them gleam again. Fixated on the ground, he admired the tenacious plants at his feet that clung to the rock wall, despite being buffeted by the strong winds.

But he was tired of clinging to life. So very tired. Feeling the relentless sweep of the wind pushing him further, Alba took a step closer to the edge. From his lofty position, the boulders below, seemed like pebbles on the beach. In a trance, he watched the white-capped waves crash into the rocks, causing great plumes of ocean spray to spew into the air. The relentless motion was hypnotic, as if a sea maiden beckoned him into her lair—promising a kiss and a warm embrace.

With the villa at his back, it seemed his entire existence lay behind him. As the light grew brighter, he gazed relentlessly forward and could just make out a ship sailing toward the horizon to that thin band that separated the sky from the cresting waves. Mesmerized by the sight, he realized it was time. If he really loved her, he had to let her go.

Alba laughed suddenly at the irony. In truth, how could he love someone if there was no love inside of him to give? Many years ago, that had died—sucked out of his breast the first time he held a gun to a man's head and killed him in cold blood or condemned a woman to be beheaded for believing in a Protestant religion. How could he live with himself for murdering innocent children, all in the name of God and the Spanish king?

And now, in the end, she who he had hoped would be his salvation was his damnation. He loved her beyond reason, and this had driven him to commit one last heinous act.

In his mind's eye, he saw the scene play out. As the sun rose higher in the sky, he knew Cinzia would soon be waking. She would stretch her arms and yawn, thinking she had won and outsmarted them all. Soon she would reach for the pitcher of water that stood on the nightstand. She would fill a glass and drink it down. Only then, standing in front of the mirror brushing out her hair, would she see the vial of poison sitting next to a sprig of blood-red bougainvillea on the dresser. As the toxin made her throat constrict, she would never know it had been he, the Duke of Alba, who settled the final score.

Killing Cinzia had been a terrible act of vengeance... but it wasn't his last. He had one more life to take. Just as it was Sofonisba's nature to create, it was his to murder and destroy.

Alba gazed at the swirling sea below then lifted his eyes to the horizon and saw a ship disappear over the skyline. She was gone... but she was safe. The duke took comfort in that, and now there was no turning back.

He took another step forward and then another... until finally he stepped into the vast open void. For one glorious moment, as the sun's rays burst over the horizon, touching his face and nearly blinding him, he was caressed by the divine and he was free.

And then he felt the downward plummet.

Down, down, down into the depths of hell he fell.

Genova—1624

*You are never too old to set another goal
or dream a new dream.*

—*C.S. Lewis*

Chapter 38

Passing the Brush

*W*hen Sofonisba finished her story, she sat quietly in her red leather chair with the brass hardware, her hands folded in her lap. Only the ticking of the clock and the whispered sigh of a log falling into the grate could be heard. Although the curtains remained open, the sun had set, and as Cecilia hadn't entered to light the lamps, the room was illuminated only by the fire's dying embers. Van Dyke, who had been holding his breath, let it out in a soft whistle—the drawing he had made forgotten on his lap. On his face was a bemused look that reminded Sofonisba of the expression a time traveler might wear after being transported into another age and then abruptly brought back to the present.

But, for one incredible moment longer, it seemed to Sofonisba the room was filled not with the presence of a ninety-two-year-old woman but rather the radiant spirit of the girl she had once been. She no longer wore a plain black velvet dress with a crisp white ruff. Instead, she was dressed in a deep blue gown, trimmed in gold and lace. She did not wear a lace scarf on her head—instead, her hair was done up in a thick crown of braids. Woven through the locks were blue silk flowers and seed pearls. Her skin was fresh and dewy, and her eyes were large and luminous.

When she cleared her throat, Anthony blinked and looked at her. She pointed to the portrait over his shoulder and said, "You are right, Anthony. No matter how old I am... that girl and her stories—she will always be inside of me. Oh, her hair may be a bit more lustrous, her figure more supple and desirable... and her jowls don't sag like mine... but still I believe we share a rather fine nose—a reminder of my Carthaginian ancestors."

Anthony chuckled. "Time has been kind to you, Signora Sofonisba. To me, you are a vision... Your eyes still sparkle with youthful wit, wisdom, and you still possess a keen sense of imagination—that is the ultimate sign of beauty."

She acknowledged the compliment with a tilt of her head, then said in a pleased voice, "Didn't I tell you I could weave a fine tale?"

"Aye, that you did, madame. I believe that instead of handling a paintbrush all these years, you should have used a pen. Your stories rival those of Shakespeare! They leave me breathless. But I am most impressed with how your passion for your work carried you so far."

"Yes, that is a great part of it," she admitted. Leaning forward, she added, "Anyone can draw! It is a trainable skill. But a true artist captures the spark of the divine and translates it to the canvas. He sees beyond the ordinary and captures the extraordinary."

With a soft sigh she added, "I always wanted to paint the perfect portrait. I wanted to dazzle the world with my talent and have people ooh and ahh over my work. That is what drove me all those years. I dreamt of sailing away, discovering a foreign land, and living life on my own terms. I wanted to learn from the masters and paint for dukes, kings, and queens! I wanted fame and fortune."

"And you did that," Van Dyke exclaimed.

"Perhaps," she agreed. "But as I look back over my life, do you know what stands out the most?"

Van Dyke shook his head, curious to know what she would say next.

"It isn't painting the perfect painting. It doesn't exist! Oh, you can come close... many painters have tried. But everyone has a different perspective and a different way of seeing things. Take, for instance, Raphael who painted marvelous Madonnas, and Michelangelo who painted... well, he painted the Sistine Chapel! They were two vastly different men and expressed themselves in diverse ways. And yet each of them painted perfect pictures."

Van Dyke sat back in his chair, rolling his pen around in his hands, and silently encouraged her to continue.

"In the end, it doesn't matter if you dazzle foreign courts with your work. It is very nice, I guarantee you that. But the important thing is to please yourself, young man. And if you keep advancing and growing, it will show in your work. The key is to never stop learning!"

She chuckled. "You see, Anthony, in the end... it is a life well-lived that really matters. Now at the end of my life, what a thrill to see the colorful tapestry I have created! To acknowledge all the highs and the lows... to see the many lives I've lived and revel in the memories... That, my friend, is the most perfect picture of all."

She clapped her hands together. "Enough wisdom from an ancient old fool. Now... at the beginning of the hour, I tasked you with finding the lie in my story. Have you detected it?"

He grinned. "This is very challenging, indeed! I know you studied with the master Michelangelo. Vasari writes of you in his book. Very complimentary things, I might add."

She nodded, her pleasure evident. "That is definitely true!"

"Now... I do wonder about your sea captain? It all sounds quite romantic but..."

He paused when he heard a soft rap on the door. When it swung open, an old man walked into the room, carrying a tray with a vase of flowers and another plate of lemon cakes.

Sofonisba looked over at him and indicated their guest, saying, "*Caro*, I'd like you to meet Messer Van Dyke, the painter I've been telling you about."

To Anthony, she said, "This is my husband, Orazio Lomellino."

The young man stood up and acknowledged the older gentleman politely. "It is an honor, signore. So, you are the pirate that stole this lady's heart? She tells me you were a spy and were imprisoned—"

"Has my girl been filling your head with stories?" Orazio interrupted.

"Do you deny it?"

Orazio's eyes twinkled. "No, I don't deny it. For those very reasons, Asdrubale, my wife's brother, refused to consent to our marriage. He claimed I was a criminal and not worthy of his sister."

Sofonisba let out a little snort. "But in the end, we took things into our own hands, didn't we, *amore mio*? When he found me again in Sicily, this sea captain of mine, he picked me up, carried me to his ship, and off we sailed."

"And once our feet touched the mainland again, we married regardless of her brother!" concluded Orazio.

Van Dyke shook his head. "So if that is true... where in God's name is the fabrication in all of this?"

Orazio gave his wife a questioning look and asked, "What games are you playing this day, my love?"

"I've only told him a nice long story about my life. All of it true... except for one thing," Sofonisba said.

"She's filled my head with tales of murder by poison, a mad prince... a capricious Spanish queen. Let's see what else...?"

"Don't forget about the earthquake or the duke's violin..." said Sofonisba.

"Or that you were named for a Carthaginian princess..." supplied Orazio.

"And what about the night we danced at Elisabeth's ball in Madrid... or Porsena's gold, and the Turks who bordered your ship and Khidr Aruj who—" said Sofonisba.

"Rescued me from an English prison," supplied Orazio. "Or the time you got your scarf wrapped around the spokes of a carriage..."

"And how you came thundering down upon me on your horse to save me."

Anthony watched the two bantering back and forth with growing amusement. When Sofonisba turned to look at him, she laughed at the expression on his face. "What you must think of us, Anthony!"

"How I enjoy listening to you two and how you finish each other's sentences," he replied. "It is evident you are both still madly in love. I need no trick of light to see you as you both must have been—a handsome couple, strong and straight—full of determination ready to meet life head-on and on their own terms. It seems, like fine wine, you have gotten better with age."

He sat back in his chair, regarding them both. Then, shaking his head, he said in an awed tone, "Moreover, I'm beginning to realize all the tales I've heard this afternoon—they were all true!" He shook his head. "What a life you have lived, Signora Anguissola... a marvelous secret life! It all seems so fantastic. I'd have said you made it all up! Tell me please, dear lady, where have you duped me?"

Sofonisba looked at him askance. "My dear boy, I should think it obvious! Do you really believe we discovered the Etruscan king's fortune?" She looked at him with wide, innocent eyes and added, "Do you think it possible that Orazio was the one to solve the secret of Porsena's labyrinth and found a royal tomb filled with pots of gold?"

"Well, I..." Anthony stammered. "How else could your husband purchase his sailing vessel?"

"Remember, he was a bit of a gambler back in the day."

"*Ehi*! I'm still quite adept at cards," claimed Orazio in an injured tone.

Anthony looked from one to the other, then noting the grin on Sofonisba's face, he said in warm admiration, "You, my dear lady, have confounded me... from your accounting, it all seems plausible."

Setting down the plate of fragrant cakes, Orazio raised an eyebrow. "If I dare ask, what is all this nonsense about Etruscan treasure, pray tell?"

Sofonisba smiled obliquely at her husband. "Oh, I might have intimated the night we met you carried with you a large bag filled with Etruscan coins."

The old man looked at Anthony and shook his head. "Dear boy... clearly, this is the lie you should have spotted right from the start."

When the clock on the mantel began to chime the hour, Anthony glanced up in dismay. "Forgive me, it is time for me to depart. I've enjoyed your company immensely. In one afternoon, I have learned more from you about life, the ways of men, painting, and creativity—than I have learned in my entire life. You have given me many gifts this afternoon."

He held up the portrait of her he had drawn and added, "This I will turn into a painting. It will be a reminder to the world what a wonderful woman you are and what an extraordinary life you have lived."

"It is a remarkable likeness," Sofonisba replied earnestly.

Gesturing to the other portraits in the room, she added sprightly,

"Almost as good as the ones painted by this female artist!"

Stiffly, Sofonisba rose and shook out her skirts. Tucking a lock of hair that escaped her cap, she added, "You, dear Anthony, you have filled my afternoon with pleasure." With a smile, she added, "Remember to be proud of your accomplishments. Keep drawing everything you see and notice all the possibilities. Just as Michelangelo offered encouragement and passed his brush to me, I wish to pass mine on to you! In time you, too, will pass your wisdom on to another."

Van Dyke nodded thoughtfully then replaced his drawing tools into his satchel. When all was stowed away, he picked up the cloak lying over the back of his chair then turned and bowed reverently to his hostess. Seeing such formality, Sofonisba shook her head and said, "Oh, poppycock, give us a kiss." With slow but sure steps, she moved to his side and when he bent down she turned her cheek so he could kiss it.

Then, with her arm on his, she escorted him to the door. On the threshold, she stopped and gently patted his sleeve. When he gave her a questioning look, she said in a confidential tone, "Before you leave, I believe I have one more secret to share with you."

She reached into her pocket and withdrew a small object. After polishing it on her sleeve, she gave a little laugh, then tossed it into the air. Deftly Anthony caught it. When he opened his hand, there resting in his palm was a gold coin with a king's profile. Etched into the disk around his head were the words—*Rex Porsena*.

When he gave her a questioning look, she said, "Keep it! I have no need for it now. Perhaps a touch of Porsena's magic will bring you the good luck it has brought me... as well as true love."

In astonishment, Anthony looked at her. "But... you said Porsena's gold was the lie..."

She winked at him. "Perhaps the lie in my tale is that there was no lie at all."

Before he could say another word, with a silvery laugh she bid him adieu and gently closed the door. Slowly she turned around and saw Orazio looking at her quizzically.

"It was just a little fun I was having with the boy," she exclaimed in mock defense.

"I've lived with you, *mia cara*, for over fifty-three years, and I am well acquainted with your wit and tricks! I love you now as I did the first night we met."

Stepping to her side, he pulled her into his arms. Once again, Sofonisba warmed to the touch of his lips on hers. When she looked back into his eyes, she said playfully, "Yes, we've been married forever and a day—longer than the sea is deep. I'd have lived my days happily alone, but then I fell in love with a thief and a pirate. It was a lucky thing for you that I allowed you to catch and kidnap me."

Orazio matched her teasing tone and said, "Thief? It is you, Sofonisba, who abducted my heart so many years ago. And if my memory serves me well... you were very content to sail away with me."

"Very content, indeed," Sofonisba said. "It certainly is no secret that I'd roam the ocean a hundred times over with you at my side." She drew back slightly and eyed him thoughtfully. "Husband, I think it is high time we returned to the sea. What say you?"

Orazio chuckled. "My dear old darling, we are but two rusty old vessels resting in a safe harbor..."

"But that's not what ships are built for! Like me, you long for adventure. I also know, despite your love for me, Circe still calls to you. You can't deny the two of us—our voices are far too strong! Besides, the sea shall keep us young."

"You never were one to rest upon your laurels. I see that familiar, lovely, inquisitive look in your eyes. All right, this sea captain will sail with his artist to the ends of the earth." Wrapping his arms around her, he whispered into her ear, "So tell me, love, where shall we go?"

"Oh, it doesn't matter," she replied. "Life is full of surprises. As long as we have air, the sea, and each other—with our hearts wide open—there will always be a new portrait to paint."

"Or story to tell..." Orazio added.

"And always, always a precious moment to capture with wide eyes," said Sofonisba, delighted by the thought of a new adventure.

Historical Notes

After Sir Anthony's visit to Sofonisba Anguissola in Genova in 1624, the Flemish painter returned to his studio to finish his portrait of Sofonisba. To friends, he confirmed that at ninety-two Sofonisba Anguissola, known for her mental aptitude, still had a sharp mind despite her advancing years. As he sketched her likeness, they talked about art and the principles of art, and later he said their conversation taught him more about painting and human nature than any other episode in his life.

Although the story is creatively imagined, and a few dates have been altered to fit the fictional timeline, most events pertaining to Sofonisba happened. She was a highly educated noblewoman, the eldest daughter of Amilcare and Bianca Anguissola, descended from a Carthaginian princess. She was the eldest of seven children, six of whom were girls. (For fictional purposes, the siblings have been reduced to five.) Amilcare, recognizing his daughter's artistic abilities, promoted her career as a painter. Through his connections, Sofonisba met and received instruction from Michelangelo, who praised her skills to Giorgio Vasari—the first art historian—who included her in his reprinting of *The Lives of the Artists* in 1568.

Sofonisba achieved international acclaim when the Duke of Alba, her most significant patron, introduced her to Philip II and Elisabeth Valois of Spain. Sofonisba became the royal painter, and amid court intrigue gave Elisabeth painting lessons. She also served as a lady-in-waiting and close confidant to Elisabeth, who was the daughter of Caterina de' Medici. It is reported that both Sofonisba and Elisabeth liked to dance and did so very well.

All the bizarre incidents that pertain to Don Carlos and his mental instability are accurate and are recorded in the queen's diaries. The threats against the king and the Duke of Alba by Don Carlos transpired—it is reported the prince made known to others at court his desire to murder his father, and he tried to stab and kill Alba in public in broad daylight with a knife hidden in his boot. Eventually, Philip imprisoned him for treason. He died in confinement. Some say, to be rid of him, it was Philip who poisoned his son. But Don Carlos, known for his hunger strikes during his numerous imprisonments, could have died of malnutrition by his own hands at the age of twenty-three.

The mishap with the lance during the joust also happened—not to Philip but rather to Elisabeth's father, the King of France, during the celebration of her marriage before departing for Spain. The French king died from his injuries, having been stabbed by a splinter through the eye that pierced his brain.

The incident with the scarf wrapping around the wheel happened to Elisabeth of Valois and not Sofonisba. Interestingly enough, a similar thing happened to Isabella Duncan, an American dancer in 1927. Her silk scarf draped around her neck became entangled around the open-spoked wheels and rear axle, pulling her from the open car and breaking her neck.

Elisabeth of Valois died of a miscarriage on October 3, 1568. She was the same age as Don Carlos and they perished the same year. Sofonisba was almost forty when Philip arranged her marriage to Fabrizio Pignatelli, the Sicilian nobleman. Philip provided her with a dowry and a generous pension that allowed her to continue painting and to support her family following her father's death.

After their marriage, Fabrizio died a few years later under mysterious circumstances. It was during a voyage to the mainland where Sofonisba met and fell in love with Orazio Lomellino, a sea merchant. Against her brother Asdrubale's wishes, they married on December 24, 1584. They lived their remaining years together but they had no children.

Etna is currently an active volcano but the eruption of 1669 was its most destructive since 122 BC, producing lava flows that destroyed villages on the southern flank before reaching the city walls of Catania, where it filled the harbor of the city. A small portion of lava destroyed buildings on the western edge before stopping at the rear of the Benedictine monastery. In 1693, the Cathedral in Catania suffered a catastrophic earthquake that left the church in ruins. It was subsequently rebuilt in the Baroque style.

Fernando Alvarez de Toledo, 3rd Duke of Alba, did ride into battle at six years of age. He was King Philip the II's majordomo mayor and trusted administrator until he died. He was a fearsome general, achieving notoriety as a brutal governor of the Spanish Netherlands after establishing the Court of Blood to prosecute those responsible for the riots in the Netherlands. For the most part, his personal history and military achievements are true, except that he didn't jump off a cliff in Sicily. That is the fabrication, dear readers.

Shortly after meeting with Van Dyke in 1624, Sofonisba and her husband Orazio Lomellino left their home in Genova and traveled back to Sicilia. She was ninety-two years young and he was eighty-seven. In 1625, Sofonisba painted her last self-portrait. She died later that same year in the Sicilian town of Palermo.

True to his word, Orazio inscribed on her gravestone the words of love he expressed to her in her youth: *To Sofonisba, my wife... who is recorded among the illustrious women of the world, outstanding in portraying the images of man... Orazio Lomellino, in sorrow for the loss of his great love, dedicates this little tribute to such a great woman.*

Acknowledgements

Heartfelt thanks to the sixteenth-century woman who inspired this story, Sofonisba Anguissola.

Edith Pray: My mother who always encouraged me in all my pursuits and made me believe there was nothing I couldn't do. She continues to be a role model and fount of inspiration. She will always be with me in spirit.

My Family Circle: My three sons, my daughter, and my husband. Thanks for supporting me, putting up with my late-night writing hours, and encouraging me to live my great big Italian dream.

Kate Braithwaite: Developmental editor.

Lia Fairchild: Editor and proof reader.

Amber Richberger: Editor and proof reader.

Tara Cribley: E-Pub Formatter.

First Readers: Dianne Hales, Barbara Reeves, Kathryn Occhipinti, Martha Bakerjian.

Heartfelt thanks to: Laura Ghezzi and Laura Folli, my Italian muses who encourage and inspire me with their creativity. Thank you for all your support, for organizing book events in the town of Arezzo, and helping spread the word about my books in the U.S. and in Italy.

Special thanks to: Kara Schleunes for her support and encouragement. She always knows the right thing to say to make me laugh and bring me joy.

Thanks to: Martha Walker Freer, author of Elisabeth de Valois, Queen of Spain, and the Court of Philip II. The book is comprised of numerous unpublished sources in the archives of France, Italy, and Spain. (2015)

Thanks to: Fiorentina Costuming and Natalia Zinkevych for giving me permission to use a photograph of her model wearing a recreation of Eleonora Toledo's 16-century ball gown. The image inspired the original cover illustration that I create of Sofonisba.

Thanks to: All the readers who have responded favorably to my novels and who have shown their enthusiasm for my body of work by taking the time to write reviews and share my books in their social media platforms. Your comments are like gold and I appreciate your feedback.

Melissa Muldoon is the author of four novels set in Italy: *Dreaming Sophia, Waking Isabella, Eternally Artemisia,* and *The Secret Life of Sofonisba Anguissola.* All four books tell the stories of women and their journeys of self-discovery to find love, uncover hidden truths, and follow their destinies to shape a better future for themselves.

Melissa is also the author of the *Studentessa Matta* website, where she promotes the study of Italian language and culture through her dual-language blog written in Italian and English (studentessamatta.com). *Studentessa Matta* means the "crazy linguist" and has grown to include a podcast, *Tutti Matti per l'Italiano* and the *Studentessa Matta,* YouTube channel, Facebook page and Instagram feed. Melissa also created *Matta* Italian Language Immersion Programs, which she co-leads with Italian schools in Italy to learn Italian in Italy. Through her website, she also offers the opportunities to live and study in Italy through Homestay programs.

Melissa has a B.A. in fine arts, art history, and European history from Knox College, a liberal arts college in Galesburg, Illinois, as well as a master's degree in art history from the University of Illinois at Champaign-Urbana. She has also studied painting and art history in Florence. She is an artist, designer, and illustrated the cover art for all four of her books. Melissa is the managing director of Matta Press

As a student, Melissa lived in Florence with an Italian family. She studied art history and painting and took beginner Italian classes. When she returned home, she threw away her Italian dictionary, assuming she'd never need it again, but after launching a successful design career and starting a family, she realized something was missing in her life. That "thing" was the connection she had made with Italy and the friends who live there. Living in Florence was indeed a life-changing event. Wanting to reconnect with Italy, she decided to start learning the language again from scratch. As if indeed possessed by an Italian muse, she bought a new Italian dictionary and began her journey to fluency—a path that has led her back to Italy many times and enriched her life in countless ways. Now, many dictionaries and grammar books later, she dedicates her time to promoting Italian language studies, further travels in Italy, and sharing her stories and insights about Italy with others.

Melissa designed and illustrated the cover art for *The Secret Life of Sofonisba Anguissola, Eternally Artemisia, Waking Isabella,* and *Dreaming Sophia.* She also curates the *Art of Loving Italy* Art blog site and Pinterest site where you will find companion pictures for all four books. Visit MelissaMuldoon.com for more information about immersion trips to learn the language with Melissa in Italy, as well as the Studentessa Matta blog for practice and tips to learn the Italian language.

MelissaMuldoon.com
ArtLovingItaly.com
Pinterest.com/ArtofLovingItaly
StudentessaMatta.com

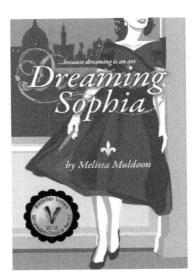

Dreaming Sophia

Because dreaming is an art.

**Winner of the 2018 Reader Views Best Adult
Classic Fiction Novel Award—*First Place***

Dreaming Sophia is a magical look into Italy and art history as seen through the eyes of a young American artist. Sophia is the daughter of a beautiful free-spirited artist who studied in Italy in the 1960s during a time when the Mud Angels saved Florence. She is brought up in the Sonoma Valley in California, in a home full of love, laughter, art, and Italian dreams. When tragedy strikes, she finds herself alone in the world with only her Italian muses for company. Through dream-like encounters she meets Renaissance artists, Medici princes, sixteenth-century duchesses, Risorgimento generals, and Cinecitta movie stars, each giving her advice and a gift to help her put her life back together. *Dreaming Sophia* is the story of a young woman's love for Italy and how she turns her fantasies into reality as she follows her muses back to Florence.

Sheri Hoyte for Blog Critics: Author Melissa Muldoon presents spellbinding artistic expression in her delightful story, Dreaming Sophia. Not your typical Italian romantic adventure, Dreaming Sophia is a wonderful multifaceted story that pushes through several genres, with layers and layers of exquisite entertainment. The development of her characters is flawless and effortless, as is her ability to draw readers into her world.

Dianne Hales, author of La Bella Lingua: In Dreaming Sophia, Melissa Muldoon weaves many strands of Italian culture into a delightful blend of fantasy, romance, art, and history. With an artist's keen eye and deft touch, she brings to life the titans of Italian culture in a touching tale of a young woman reeling from loss who discovers that Italy is the answer. The many Italophiles who share her belief will revel in the adventures of this kindred spirit.

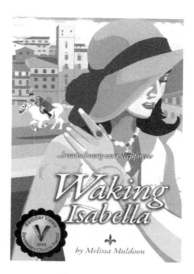

Waking Isabella

Because beauty can't sleep forever

**Winner of the 2019 Reader Views Best Adult
Classic Fiction Novel Award—*Second Place***

Waking Isabella is a story about uncovering hidden beauty that, over time, has been lost, erased, or suppressed. It also weaves together several love stories as well as a few mysteries. Nora, an assistant researcher, is a catalyst for resolving the puzzle of a painting that has been missing for decades. Set in Arezzo, a small Tuscan town, the plot unfolds against the backdrop of the city's antique trade and the fanfare and pageantry of its medieval jousting festival. While filming a documentary about Isabella de' Medici— the Renaissance princess who was murdered by her husband—Nora connects with the lives of two remarkable women from the past. Unraveling the stories of Isabella, the daughter of a fifteenth-century Tuscan duke, and Margherita, a young girl trying to survive the war in Nazi-occupied Italy, Nora questions the choices that have shaped her own life up to this point. As she does, hidden beauty is awakened deep inside of her, and she discovers the keys to her creativity and happiness. It is a story of love and deceit, forgeries and masterpieces—all held together by the allure and intrigue of a beautiful Tuscan ghost.

Torre de Babel: Through wildly imaginative eyes, scenes from the past come alive with emotion and turmoil. I loved those. The novel is fluid and easy to read, yet it still manages to convey beauty and heart.

Olio Review: Waking Isabella is a story of passion, love, grief and redemption that is built upon the stories of the characters we meet - their pasts, their secrets, their insecurities and their passions. Kudos to the author on a well-crafted story.

Books & Tea: Waking Isabella by Melissa Muldoon is an absolutely beautiful book with rich and lush description. I was swept along Nora's journey to discover more about Isabella. A little paranormal, a pinch of love and a spoonful of intrigue. A perfect blend to keep you reading until the last page.

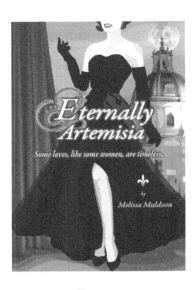

Eternally Artemisia

Some loves, like some women are timeless.

They say some loves travel through time and are fated to meet over and over again. For Maddie, an art therapist, who wrestles with the "peculiar feeling" she has lived previous lives and is being called to Italy by voices that have left imprints on her soul, this idea is intriguing. Despite her best efforts, however, proof of this has always eluded her. That is, until one illuminating summer in Italy when Maddie's previous existences start to bleed through into her current reality. When she is introduced to the Crociani family—a noble clan with ties to the seventeenth-century Medici court that boasts of ancestors with colorful pasts—she finally meets the loves of her life. One is a romantic love, and another is a special kind of passion that only women share, strong amongst those who have suffered greatly yet have triumphed despite it. As Maddie's relationship develops with Artemisia Gentileschi—an artist who in a time when it was unheard of to denounce a man for the crime of rape, did just that—Maddie discovers a kindred spirit and a role model, and just what women are capable of when united together. In a journey that arcs back to biblical days and moves forward in time, Maddie encounters artists, dukes, designers, and movie stars as well as baser and ignoble men. With Artemisia never far from her side, she proves that when we dare to take control of our lives and find the "thing" we are most passionate about, we are limitless and can touch the stars.

Dianne Hales, author of La Bella Lingua: A true Renaissance woman, Melissa Muldoon weaves her passions for art and Italy into a stirring saga that sweeps across centuries. As her time-traveling heroine Maddie reconnects with kindred souls, we meet Artemisia Gentileschi, the 17th–century artist who overcame rape and ignominy to gain respect and acclaim. Historic figures such as Galileo and Mussolini also come to life in this intricately plotted novel, but the women who defy all constraints to take control of their destinies are the ones who prove to be eternally fascinating.

Made in the USA
Coppell, TX
21 September 2022

83498262R00193